Touched

By AJ Aalto

www.AJAalto.com

Cover design by Robert Goldie

ISBN	Soft Cover:	978-1-77084-145-1
	Hard Cover:	978-1-77084-146-8

Published by: FIRSTCHOICE BOOKS
#2, 460 Tennyson Place
VICTORIA
V8Z 6S8
Phone: (250) 383-6353
Fax: (250) 383-2247
e-mail: mail@firstchoicebooks.ca
www.firstchoicebooks.ca

Printed in Canada

This book is dedicated to my mother, Lynda,
for always calling me a writer, even when the words wouldn't come,
and to my father Marc, the best damn storyteller I know.

Acknowledgements

This book would not have been possible without the support of some amazing people, whom I am blessed to know and honoured to mention here. A huge thanks to Berenice "Machinery" Jones—editor, inspiration, mad genius and treasured friend, always ready with a red pen and a cup of Earl Grey—and to Jason-Jones, for not being afraid to apply a judicious layer of Painful Truth when and where it's needed, and for being the most entertaining person I know. Life's so much fun when the Joneses are around.

I owe an enormous debt to my Thursday Morning Beta Reader and personal assistant, Heather Goldie, whose laughter is the best ego boost a writer could hope for, and whose honest criticism I can count on at every step of the journey. What would I do without you, miss H? I offer a warm thanks to Rob Goldie, my photographer and graphic artist, who knows all about techy contraptions. When I was lost and needed someone, he snorted and said "Hey dummy, I can do that." I dig that guy.

To my kids, Jenny and Derek, I want to say thanks for understanding when mom's distracted, thanks for cooperating when I need just a bit more quiet time, thanks for being wildly sweet and totally amazing, and filling my life with giggles. To Daxon and Sara Flynn, thanks for reading and giving me feedback and encouragement, and to my delightfully nutty sister, Robin Landry, for always "getting me" even when I tilt way past weird.

But most importantly, I want to thank my absurdly patient husband, who has supported my broke ass while I pursued this dream, and fully expects to continue supporting my broke ass until book equals profits, no matter how long that takes. For the overtime he works, for the artistic tantrums he benevolently ignores, for the thousands of cups of tea he has lovingly tiptoed into my office, for the many "lets go for a bike ride, kids, and let mummy work", I owe him more than these few lines can express. Probably I should buy him a sports car. Probably I should give him a kidney. Probably I should save half this Twix bar for him. Not *gonna*, but I *should*. He'll understand. He always does.

I love you, Jason.

C1

I didn't have enough eyes for this job, counting the two in my skull and the thirteen eyes of newt in a jar of alcohol on the corner of my housemate's antique ebony desk; when you track killers the way I had, vision and clarity take on layers like you wouldn't believe. I say "had" because I had retired from my position as consulting forensic psychic for the FBI six weeks ago, after my first and only case.

My name's Marnie Baranuik, and most of the time I'm OK with being a one-fail wonder. The case had gone wrong in every possible way, and blame the psychic is a convenient fallback position. While I'm the first to admit my failings, proudly in some cases, I like to think it wasn't entirely my fault.

My reasons for retiring at the tender age of 27 haven't gone anywhere: they're the choking miasma of other people's sins, and they're out there, waiting to show me their worst, strangers forever rubbing me with their prickly, often-horrifying inner selves. Sadly, the reasons for my breakdown haven't gone anywhere either. This morning, two of them sat across from me in my home office, a forty-five minute drive outside the city of Ten Springs, Colorado. One of them was politely ignoring the goggling newt eyeballs and drinking my espresso. The other was glaring at me expectantly while the relentless tick of hail pelting the window filled an increasingly awkward silence.

To borrow a cliché, Supervisory Special Agent Gary Chapel—the Polite One—was the silver lining on the black cloud that was his subordinate, Special Agent Mark Batten. Long-jawed with a receding hairline of short sandy curls, Chapel wore beige in varying shades that complimented both his hazel eyes and the tortoise shell frames of his glasses. He'd always been patient with me, unobtrusive and gentle, his all-forgiving gaze and agreeable nature veiling a past in behavioural science studying the most abhorrent criminal minds in the nation's prison system. How anyone could be so pleasant, knowing what Chapel knew, was beyond me. They didn't make chairs to fit his lanky frame; he sat tall in my office chair as comfortably as possible, reminding me of a Great Dane secure in his alpha-status, quietly confident. There was no fight in his eyes: there was no need.

From the way Agent Batten gripped his espresso cup, dwarfing it in the palm of his left hand to keep his dominant hand free, I could easily imagine his former life as a vampire hunter. He was all hard lines, an immovable wall, 90 percent inanimate object but carrying the underlying threat of action along the tension of his forearms, and shady from black military buzz cut, to cinnamon tan, to delphinium-blue eyes framed strikingly by dark, thick lashes. Those eyes were by far his best feature; it sure as hell wasn't his personality. His black-on-black wardrobe made a lousy attempt to disguise the brain-melting body that lurked beneath waiting to fry the self-control of innocent women. He peered at me over the rims of Oakley sunglasses with a gaze I'd classify as both cunning and wary. Unlike his boss, there was plenty of fight in "Kill-Notch" Batten, a lifeguard with a hangover presiding over an airless pool of disapproval and suspicion. Without any outward effort, Batten managed to dial my mood from uncomfortable to downright hostile.

Which man I'd less like to meet in a dark alley, I couldn't say, nor was I sure that day wouldn't come, considering what my housemate was; for a moment, despite our acquaintance, I felt intimidated. I took a bracing sip of espresso and pictured Batten prancing out in the snow wearing nothing but a sport sock, trilling Tiptoe Through the Tulips in Tiny Tim falsetto. *Better.* In fact, I had to work not to smirk. Judging by the further narrowing of Batten's glare, my twitching lips nudged him off balance. *Much better.*

Chapel leaned forward, elbows on knees, palms out. The familiarity of the gesture struck a warning bell: Chapel and his body language tricks, trying to put me at ease. If memory served, he'd use only our first names, consistently. I was about to be handled with all the determination of a Hollywood dermatologist on a starlet's rash.

"Marnie, Mark and I have already ruled out werewolf," Chapel said.

"No bite marks?" I blurted like a dummy, kneejerk. *Ugh. Point: Chapel.*

"Plenty," Batten replied. "Space between's too small. No broken bones. No tearing. Tidy."

I hadn't expected Batten's grim tone and economy of speech to slug my chest the way it did; he never elaborated, and he rarely softened his tone. I focused on Chapel, keeping my face dispassionate.

"Then you're right: it's not a lycanthrope. Could be a young revenant, un-Bonded and solo, not running with clutch mentality, though not completely feral or you'd find tearing." I struggled with the stirring of temper and loins, bickering Siamese twins, linked in flesh and blood at hip level. "Agent Chapel, you do understand the word "retired" and all it implies?"

Batten made a throaty noise. I refused to look at him. Childish, me?

"Mark and I understand you're on a break, Marnie." Chapel nodded like an FBI bobble head. Behold! The world's most agreeable man. His voice warmed a degree. "You need some time."

Only a few decades or so. "Gold-Drake & Cross represents 25 other federally-licensed psychics you can consult," I reminded him. "All of them outrank me in Talent, goodwill and general friendliness."

"Now, you know the first part's not possible," Chapel said.

I didn't miss the implication, and smiled for the first time. *Point, Chapel*: an attempt to disagree with the last two would have been blatantly ridiculous and would have ended this conversation, and he knew it.

"There are more powerful psychics," Batten hedged. "But how many have a doctorate in preternatural biology and more than a passing understanding of the dark arts?"

As far as I knew, I was the only one, but admitting that wasn't going to make them go away. I played with my cup and shrugged at Chapel, expression neutral. "You'd have to ask my old boss at GD & C."

"And how many have a media nickname?" Batten drew a rolled-up newspaper from his back, where it must have been crammed in his pocket. For a second I thought he was going to swat me on the nose like a misbehaving puppy; he waved it in my face, then dropped it on the desk. "Must be famous for a reason?"

I felt my face go carefully blank; as far as I knew I didn't have a nickname. Certainly, I didn't want one. I could only imagine. "If you hit a wall, there's some hardcore unlicensed Talent in Denver."

"Freaks and lunatics," Batten translated.

I sucked wind through my teeth; it was getting harder to ignore him. Was that sweat on my upper lip? It had to be a kajillion degrees in my office. Chapel must have noted my discomfort; he smiled to disarm, an excellent smile for a lawman: quick, genuine, safe. It was hard not to smile back at him, and while a part of me unintentionally loosened, I kept my guard up. Having worked with him in close quarters once before, it hadn't taken me long to note all his tricks; this one wasn't going to work as well as he thought, not this time.

"Marnie, we're not here to lure you back into something you're not comfortable with. We're not here to haul you back into the field. Mark and I were just hoping, since we were in the area, you'd do a quick consult for us, look at some pictures, give us your first impress—"

"Doesn't work that way."

He corrected himself immediately. "I didn't mean psychic impressions. I know you need an object to touch."

"Or a victim to feel-up," Batten said, like I was guilty of something questionable.

Yes, I'm dual-Talented. GD&C used to promote me from their third-floor retrocognition department in forensic psychometry, otherwise known as token-object reading; this is my main Talent, a touch psychic. In-house lingo pegged me as a Groper, but we Gropers didn't like our slang to leave the office, for obvious reasons. Neither did the Feelers, the empaths who felt both the real-time emotions of the living and strong emotional residues left behind. The fact that I wielded both empathy and psychometry had given GD &C the opportunity to boast of a rare dual-Talented employee in their ranks, touched by the Blue Sense not once but twice, earning me the title Groper-Feeler; anyone who called me that to my face landed just below Batten's permanent spot on my shit list.

"Marnie, I only meant," Chapel was saying, "Using your experience with preternatural biology, just have a look at some pictures and tell us what you think we're dealing with."

(Only. Just. Just have a look...) "Just at a bit of gore to start off my day," I drawled. "In case the hail storm and oppressive cloud cover weren't depressing enough?"

Neither man called me on it. I should have known they weren't here on a social call from the moment I eyeballed them through the peephole: the way they stood there on my porch, looking nowhere in particular with that habit cops develop, their gazes devouring every detail, missing nothing. Right then and there, I should have listened to my impulse to scrunch down and pretend I wasn't home, though honestly at the time that urge had been based on my desperate need for a makeover, or at least a sweep of lip-gloss.

Another murder. Another grisly set of photos in full unfortunate colour. At least they didn't want me on a crime scene, still I was amazed at their nerve. Specifically, Batten's nerve. What part of "I quit" did they not get? What part of "go hop up your own ass" did *he* not get?

"Tell me, Agent Chapel, was the secluded cabin not a big enough hint?" I asked. "No offense, but you FBI guys should be way better at grasping clues."

Again, I was on the receiving end of not one but two stony silences. I'd have classified them as chilly, my housemate is moody and I had survived true chilly silences. These didn't even remotely compare. I pressed my back into my chair and turned my attention at last to Batten's face.

Even blank-faced, as he was now, those freshwater blue eyes were alive, bright, calculating. Shrewd. My stomach twisted into a quivering ball. I'd never been able to read his emotions with either of my psychic Talents. Not because he was in any way adept at hiding them; Batten was as mundane as a man could get. I wanted to read him too badly, that was the problem. The harder I tried, the more it was like trying to pick a wet watermelon seed off a Formica table: think you've got it, then it squirts away. To get an easy free-flow of psi, I had to relax to the point where I almost didn't care. I was never that relaxed in Batten's presence. I doubted I ever could be.

I hadn't seen him since Buffalo. Brains had come to check on me in the hospital, but Brawn hadn't. I'd hoped that by some bizarre happenstance Batten had lost his magnetism, or that some clever, savage creature had taken him down a notch, wrested his ego, humbled him. I saw it wasn't true. He was as cocky as ever and a few degrees hotter. Considering I looked like I'd just been released from a typhoid clinic, I thought it highly unfair.

I watched Batten's jaw ripple as he clenched and unclenched his teeth. I gave him credit for not looking away; he met my glare and must have read the fury stirring there, but he took it like a man.

"Agent Batten can ask me to look at the file," I said coolly. "He can say pretty please, and follow up with tulips and a pack of Double-Stuf Oreos."

Batten's answer was the quirk of one dusky eyebrow. He took a deep breath and let it out slowly and noisily without speaking. Nor did he look away. Maybe this was his way of apologizing. Maybe it was all I was going to get. It sucked, frankly. I'd have loved to see him hang his head in shame for what he'd done. Even when I fantasized that moment, though, it felt wrong; Kill-Notch wasn't the apologetic type.

My warring body parts continued to bicker. I wanted to taste him again. I also wanted to whap him in the face with a ball-peen hammer. Probably I couldn't do both. Shouldn't do either, really. Memories of his abs pressing hard against my soft naked belly intruded, sending heat prickling down my thighs.

Kill-Notch wasn't going to say please any more than I was going to win the Miss Congeniality award at the annual GD&C ball, and the tulips were a long shot. I could get a please out of Chapel, maybe cookies too, but it wouldn't be the same.

"I'm not on vacation," I told Chapel. "I know that's how GD&C spun it." I eyeballed Batten's newspaper, sluggishly unrolling on the desk. *(How many have a nickname?)* "For what it's worth, I didn't leave because of the Prost case or how it ended. I knew working a serial of a preternatural sort would land me in the spotlight. Bad press wasn't a shocker, neither was the injury."

Batten grumbled, "Who'd have thought a vamp would be packing?"

"I'm not taking time off to nurse old gunshot wounds. I'm not suffering from post traumatic stress or whatever you guys are calling it now. I'd just like to be done." That sounded too much like asking permission, so I rallied the troops and tried again: "Quitting is not a whim. I'm done."

"The team trying to find Kristin Davis' head will be disappointed to hear that," Batten said.

I rocked forward. "Kristin Davis the actress?"

"No, Kristin Davis the twelve year old girl from Denver." He mimed opening the file like a dickhead.

Point: Batten. I had the almost irresistible urge to crack my jar of newt eyes over his head. My scruples jabbed me. "Gimme the damn file."

C2

The manila folder Chapel drew out of his laptop case was slim. Edges of photo paper peeked out of this folder like black mold on the lid of Tupperware long forgotten behind the pickles in the back of the fridge. A complicated file number was written in blue ink, in Chapel's recognizable blocky handwriting: **PCU18744**. I reached out one leather-gloved hand and tapped the folder. Leather gloves (I have them in all colours imaginable) are a Groper's best friend, a necessity for any touch-psychic of merit. One never knows where horrible images are lurking, ready to jump out an assault a sensitive brain.

Out of habit, I took a No. 2 pencil from my frog-shaped ceramic jar to make notes in the margins of an abandoned Sudoku puzzle, but also to make Batten wait. When someone says "jump", Marnie Baranuik is more liable to kick them in the yambag than ask how high. I doodled a googly-eyed caricature of him with Xs for eyes and a protruding tongue. I added a ukulele and some tulips. Knowing I couldn't draw the sport sock without cracking up drained an ounce of throbbing heat out of my temples.

Standing vigil as a doorstop in one corner of the office was a weighted stuffed teddy-frog, and another stuffed frog with a shocked expression rested in a chair in the corner. My espresso cup was decorated with Monet's water lilies, across which some internet artist had added fanciful cartoon frogs. Two of the three of us in the room knew I had a tiny poison dart frog tattooed between my shoulder blades. Some people collect teapots. I'm froggy-obsessed.

Summoning my nerve, I flipped to the first photo. It was dated and time-stamped early this morning and it was worse than I thought it would be; they always are. Instantly I regretted my big greasy breakfast.

A headless body in the early stages of blossoming into a woman lay naked and fragile, too pale against the dirty grey asphalt. Conscious of today's pelting hail, I imagined laying nude and prone in that hard grit and ice-strewn alleyway between an overflowing dumpster and a brown brick wall filthily stained with who knows what. Kristin Davis' remains were surrounded by countless standard-issue boots in mid-shuffle. There are always too many witnesses to a bad end. You'd think the cold weather would hinder some of the curious; it doesn't, especially if the case has even the faintest whiff of the preternatural. I found my shoulders aching and realized I'd pulled them up to keep my neck warm, even though the woodstove was blasting and the cabin was toasty.

The next picture in the series was a close-up of small matching pairs of puncture wounds on the pale, tender inside of the right thigh. I clenched my fist and the leather creaked. I wished I wasn't wearing the crimson gloves. They felt gory.

"We thought vampire," Batten said.

"The '90s called, Kill-Notch, they want their politically incorrect terminology back. No one uses the V-word anymore," I murmured, not wanting to bring the next picture closer for inspection and doing it anyway. "That being said, I see why you'd suspect a revenant. No livor mortis, not enough blood left in her body to pool. But here's the problem with your theory: I'm not seeing necrosis, no early signs of crypt plague. When *yersinia sanguinaria* strikes, the early signs pop within minutes: black marks across the side of the neck," *When the body has a neck*, my cruel brain piped up, "And under the armpits, anywhere the lymph nodes are." I brushed my fingertips over the picture to show them. "Has toxicology screened the tissue around the wounds for V-telomerase and ms-lipotropin?"

"They will. If this is the primary crime scene, he drained her before he took her head off, as there's very little blood at the scene," Chapel said, his pen moving without benefit of his full attention. Neat trick. "Why did he want the head?"

"Trophy?" Batten suggested.

I shook my head no, hoping he was wrong. "Anything's possible. What I know about aberrant revenant psychology could fill a change purse."

"Find that hard to believe," Batten replied; his attitude made me want to put him in a head lock, so I eye-rolled my focus back to Chapel.

"If you came here to ask me what a revenant needs a girl's head for, Agent Chapel, you wasted the drive. I don't know."

"We're not profiling a human being." Batten edged forward in his chair. "The why doesn't matter. The laws are clear on vampire crimes."

"Revenant," I corrected stubbornly.

"We find it, we stake it."

"There's no we," I made a gloved fist on the desk. "You find him, you stake him. Butchering men was never part of my job description."

His knuckles whitened on the corner of my desk. "They're not men."

Chapel cleared his throat; the noise was soft and polite, yet succeeded in withering Batten and I like two schoolyard scrappers caught by a teacher. I wilted back into my chair. Batten went to the window to finger apart the wood slats of the blinds and peer out across the front yard, where their black SUV in the driveway practically screamed federal law enforcement. Hail continued to strike the glass in front of his unreadable face.

"We don't believe it's the primary scene," Chapel continued, "Draining someone isn't a silent crime and takes time. This alley is in a high traffic spot in lower downtown Denver. She would have called out for help."

"Not necessarily," I told him. "If the revenant was over a century dead, he may have been able to override her attempts to scream with mind control. Some develop it, some don't."

"Has yours?" Batten said without turning around.

My already taut shoulders tightened a notch, the desire to spin-kick the holy shit out of him quelled only by the fact that I can't kick without falling on my ass. Also: there was the probability that Kill-Notch would grab my foot en route to his face and snap it in half.

"It's conceivable that she sat there in silence while he drained her," I said.

"Maybe you can't help us," Batten conceded, returning to claim space up against my desk as he got in my face. "But is there any way I can pry your stubborn ass out of this little log mausoleum here to try?"

Shit. *Don't look at his zipper don't look at his zipper ...*

Amazingly, my eyes obeyed and met his with a cool steadiness I didn't feel; I was fine until I realized memories of our enthusiastic sex were written all over his face, subtle but unmistakable, a hot glint in his eye meant only for me. My self-control jerked off-balance like a high heel on a patch of ice. Mental clutzery, my specialty. I was forced to swallow hard, broadcasting the direction of my thoughts. One corner of his lips twitched into a knowing curve. He returned to his chair, leaning back, knees open in invitation. *Point: Batten.*

I forced my eyes on the last picture; grossing myself out helped. This photo captured the slight headless body plus a set of women's long legs. Instant recognition sucker-punched me: Michael Kors wedges, opaque nylons on shapely calves, silver ankle bracelet with dangly charms. Silver bells. I knew the clappers tinkled with every step she took.

I slapped the folder closed and shot it back across the desk in Batten's direction. It spilled onto the floor in a great fan of photographic gore.

"You don't need me." I heard my voice tremor and forced it out evenly. "Time for you to go."

Chapel scrambled to gather up his pictures. "Is there something …"

"Sorry, Gary," I clipped. "You have to leave. Now."

Batten stood. "Marnie—"

"*Get out,"* I shouted, bolting up. My chair clattered to the floor. If I was pyrokinetic, Mark Batten would be a pile of ash in a second. He opened his mouth, and there wasn't any way I could hear him say my name again without bursting into tears. "Are you fucking deaf? *Get the hell out of my house*."

"Too right," a crisp British voice agreed from the office doorway. "I should think that will not be an issue, now that I am here."

The knot in my gut dissolved instantly. The sound of Harry's smart London accent was an injection of refinement and gravitas, like switching on the BBC news or summoning one's English butler. My housemate lounged in the threshold, effortlessly more vibrant than either of the humans. He was only five foot seven, short for a man, but the unnamable otherness that marked him as immortal made him loom, and his whip-slim build masked infernal strength. Any room Harry entered soon became ten degrees cooler; he carried it with him like an immutable cloak, the chill that seeped in around my ankles.

Harry was a revenant who refused to dress it down. His nobility predated his turning. I suspected his egotism and fastidiousness did too. Today he looked like Fred Astaire might have, sartorially speaking, if Fred had been undead while tapping Putting on the Ritz: black coat tails and dove grey ascot, white spats on immaculate black Oxfords. Garnet cufflinks were like fat droplets of old blood on French cuffs that covered a fresh tattoo on his pale wrist. Except for the three tiny platinum loop piercings in his left eyebrow, and the thin white iPod ear bud cord snaking down into his shirt collar, he looked like the perfect aristocrat. The top hat was missing; I was sure it would be resting on his end of the kitchen table.

"Gentlemen, it would appear that you have worn out what short-lived welcome my DaySitter had afforded you," he observed. "I must insist on escorting you to the door. Might I recommend you not return without an invitation?"

It was not a question. Batten's square jaw worked on clenching and unclenching again. If he wasn't careful, he was going to gnaw a hole in his cheek. His eyes were impenetrable dark matter, nailing me across the vast expanse of Harry's desk. It satisfied me to know Harry could sidle up silent and unheard behind the infamous vampire hunter: Kill-Notch was only human, after all.

"Got a license for that thing?" Batten said low. He knew perfectly well that Harry was legal.

"Why?" I leaned across the desk, splaying my fingers like I was planning on doing push-ups. "Did you bring rowan wood into my house?"

"Kit's in the trunk of the car," he assured me.

I felt my lip curl. "And what makes you think you'd make it as far as the fucking car?"

"Ducky," Harry reprimanded me softly, then addressed the hunter. "I salute your optimism, Mr. Batten."

"Agent," Batten corrected.

"Hmm, yes." Harry sounded unconvinced. "Your darling imitation of testicular fortitude notwithstanding, I have offered to escort you out. T'is conceivable you have grown muscles betwixt your ears and consequently may be excused for not hearing. To be sure, I should not have expected to repeat myself for an attentive gentleman such as Agent Gary Chapel. How do you do, Agent Chapel?"

"Good morning, Lord Dreppenstedt," Chapel said over his shoulder, as he subtly checked his watch. "I hadn't anticipated you to be ... around, at this time of day." He stood, swiftly collected his things, zipped his heavy coat right to the neck almost protectively. "I'm sorry you had to see any of this, Marnie."

"She's seen worse." Batten's eyes flicked meaningfully at Harry and settled on his chin, avoiding direct eye contact. "Nice tux."

Harry performed the shallowest of bows. When he straightened, the feather grey of his irises had fled, leaving a thin warning ring of high-gloss chrome. I lifted my cup to my lips to hide my smile and let my Cold Company have his moment; how he did enjoy his subtle dramatics.

Harry's unearthly glance flicked at me in question, seeking permission; through our Bond I felt the stirring push of anticipation. I gave the barest shake of my head: *don't you dare.*

Chapel paused at the door, lingering close to the revenant: ballsy or trusting? Gary Unflappable Chapel. "Marnie, I have to ask you both where you were on Tuesday night?"

"Don't even." I set my cup down hard. "You know my Harry doesn't do shit like this."

"May I phone you, pick your brain about this case?" Chapel pressed.

"You have another psychic working it." My stomach coiled-up like a snake spitting hot acid. "So there's really no need."

I strode out from behind my desk, backing them into the hallway. I like to think it was me who was intimidating them, not Harry.

"Don't ever doubt you're needed, Baranuik," Batten said gruffly. "Happy Shark week."

Shark Week? I scowled my confusion, speechless until he was out the front door, jogging to the SUV with his leather jacket pulled over his head to shield from the hail storm. *Baranuik,* like I was one of the team. One of the guys. My gloved hands were shaking as I balled them into fists.

"Go to hell, Mark," I said, too late. Chapel was barely in the car, his door ajar, when Batten slammed into reverse. I watched them lurch out, the spinning tires spitting frozen gravel in the drive.

Thunder rolled overhead. Thunder in December. Hail mixed with cold sleet instead of thigh-high snow. Was nothing as it should be? At nearly nine in the morning, it still looked like midnight outside, the sky blanketed with dark wool and misery. Naked branches shivered and clawed at the edges of the property, clicking together, making woeful music with the wind that moaned against my little cabin. Kristin Davis would be at the morgue now, waiting in a drawer for her turn to endure the indignities of an autopsy.

My Cold Company moved behind me, raising all the little hairs on the back of my neck, not an unpleasant experience and very familiar. Discomfort washed through me; I knew it was as much Harry's as it was mine.

"I thought you quit so you would not have to see that man again," he said.

It wasn't until I noticed the box of Kleenex in his hands that I started to cry.

C3

Even chin-deep in bubbles, with aromatherapy candles and a much-too-early cocktail, it's difficult to relax in the bath when a 435 year old vampire is sitting cross-legged on the closed lid of the toilet, staring at you. *Revenant,* I thought-corrected fiercely, pissed that Batten had stuck the v-word in my head.

"So they have replaced you already, and with such meager substitution," Harry said, inching forward as though it was fascinating gossip I'd collected on someone else.

I did my admittedly bad Al Pacino, clenching a sudsy fist. "Just when I think I'm out, they pull me back in."

"Thrown you in a mopple, has it?"

As I soaped, I felt his preternatural probing wash over me, licking through our Bond to taste my emotions; it was like being probed in the brain by rubber-fingered aliens. He didn't have to do it that way. Harry could be exceptionally subtle. Apparently Harry wasn't in the mood for subtle. The FBI agents in his home had him flustered like a murder of crows disturbed from their roadside pecking.

"I'm fine. In fact, I'm relieved." It was pointless to lie to Harry of all people, but fuck it, it sounded good. "Now that Batten's officially recruited his little airhead, he's got no reason to pester me."

"Yet they were here, and one is forced to wonder why," Harry said with a hint of a smile. "It is increasingly evident that without you the police, most notably your agents of the preternatural crimes unit, have the devil by the nose."

I said dryly, "They're not *my* agents."

"You must concede that you have made an impression with the hunter." Now there was a full-fledged twinkle in his eyes. "He moved Shark Week up several months to celebrate it with you."

He showed me the newspaper headline again: Marnie Baranuik, the Great White Shark of psychic investigations, lets child serial killer slip through her jaws.

I hate sharks. Sharks eat people. I, on the other hand, do not. I have no plans to start, either. So how the hell am I remotely shark-like? And why was it *my* fault the killer escaped? I wasn't the only person on that team. I motioned for Harry to throw the paper in the trash; he tucked it behind his back.

I narrowed my eyes. "Batten's only coming around to get close enough to stake the cheeky dead guy I share my life with."

Harry nodded once in genial concurrence. "Are you quite sure it was Danika Sherlock in the photograph?"

I sank deeper in the shelter of hot water, not wanting to think about those ankles: claimed ankles, spoken-for ankles, betrothed ankles. That silver bracelet might as well have been a sparkling engagement ring with a lady killer diamond, the way it twisted like a jagged piece of ice shoved under my heart and jerked around in my vitals.

"My gut would recognize those ankles anywhere."

Harry frowned as though my sentence hadn't made sense. It made his eyebrow rings twitch, the platinum reflecting candlelight. "The bigger issue is: how can they employ this over-switched nizzle-toppin without rousing controversy?"

"Nizzle-toppin," I repeated, as though just making sure I heard him right. I felt my lips tug into a reluctant smile. "At least she's not downright phony."

"Oh, but she is, if we are speaking of boobs," Harry offered. I loved how he said con-*trov*-ersy, and how his "issue" was said with soft, snake-y Ss, but it never failed to strike me as bizarre when words like "boobs" popped out of his mouth in his posh Queen's English. He'd slipped off his jacket, but the ascot remained, and the mother of pearl buttons running the front of his crisp white shirt were sheer perfection. He'd rolled up his sleeves to the elbow; now I could see my name in calligraphy tattooed on his left wrist.

"Though it grieves me to say so," he continued, "Agent Chapel appears to be recruiting a fine tribe of malefactors; scullions and kitchen knaves, blackguards and fools, your codding bully-rook of a hunter, now this rigmutton rumpstall. And whilst your nemesis, she of the bejeweled ankle, certainly possesses a resplendent flair for staring attire, something which you obstinately refuse to adopt ..."

He paused to give me space to retort, lifting his eyebrows as though expecting an explanation. I blinked long and hard at him; I was sure there must be an insult buried in all that antiquated rigmarole, aimed at me.

When I couldn't find it, I said, "I'm a *what?*"

Harry closed his eyes for a moment as if he could draw patience from the ether. "For certain, her clairvoyant abilities have been steadily decreasing for the better part of seven years."

"That's hardly her fault, since George got dusted."

As soon as I said it, I wished I hadn't. My gaze dropped from Harry's; he looked like I'd sorrow-slapped him into another decade. *Yeah, that's what he needs: paint him a picture of three hunters staking Sherlock's companion while he lay prone in his casket. Hey, while you're at it, why don't you remind him about that spectacular day that Ville Aaman revealed during one of his precognition seminars that all psychics in the entire spectrum of Talent were in fact DaySitters for revenants, a great old shitpile of memories to stir, right Big Mouth? Or how about when Aaman's companion, Reginald Davidoff Renault, stepped forward to offer his body up for scientific testing against the screaming protest of his kind, and also ended up as a pile of dust? Party time!*

As though reading my mind, Harry offered me a smile that didn't go anywhere near touching his eyes; history weighed heavy in the corners of his mouth. "Are you so simple as to believe that these assassinations did not occur before the notorious Finn and his dreadfully honest companion exposed my kind?"

"What I believe, Harry, is that without George, Danika Sherlock has lost her flippin' mind," I said. Seven years post-Bond, like a tire leaking around a nail, Danika Sherlock's residual Talent was hissing flat; without her revenant, the solo DaySitter had no way of gassing up the proverbial psychic tank. In the next few years she'd be no more psychic than your average 1-900 daily tarot reader *(only $4.99 a minute! First minute free!)* "Last I heard, she was working on a reality show about her day-to-day life. That ought to be about as intellectually stimulating as a Teletubbies marathon."

"I suppose you'd have me accept that you would get on just fine without me?"

"Of course, I'd be fine. I'd have Tinky Winky and Po," I teased, but chasing off the unease wasn't that easy. I couldn't imagine ...I glanced up at Harry while he meticulously filed a thumbnail, blowing daintily on the edge. No, I couldn't, didn't want to imagine being in Danika's place; I had reasons not to like her, but no one should have to lose a part of themselves like that.

"You should have collectively denied Mr. Aaman's claim," Harry said without energy, an old argument spoken by every Bonded revenant who craved a return to anonymity. One by one, other psychics had reluctantly followed Aaman's example and admitted the truth about the source of their powers—that we were guardians who merely borrowed and directed power that belonged to a revenant we secretly protected, nourished and nurtured. After Renault's proof of his true nature, what choice did we have?

Now any psychic who denied having a revenant in their care was either fake, or good at hiding the casket. Harry was right, of course: admitting it had put us all at risk. The laws in both Canada and the United States had no provisions to protect the undead, though they were pretty swift about spelling out that any crimes committed by revenants were punishable by death. Vampire hunters, once considered eccentric weirdoes chasing shadows, were the new superheroes. A few of the prolific vampire hunters, like the inexhaustible Mark "105 Kills" Batten, were eventually hired by the FBI.

Instead of wasting my breath—to the one person in the world who understood my feelings better than I did, no less—I said, "That's my favourite shirt, Harry."

His head came up and he touched his chest, fingertips languorously grazing the buttons. "I know."

"I'd be a smoking ruin without you."

"So kind of you to say, my dulcet doe."

"A gibbering lunatic, slobbering and raving, trapped in a state of permanent psychosis," I expounded.

His eyes became heavy-lidded; he released through the Bond a dollop of appeasement. "Not a terribly drastic change, then."

I sank deeper into the claw foot tub, turned the water on with my toes to heat the water back to near-scalding. "Boy, you're awfully sassy, considering I have a vampire hunter on speed dial."

My thoughts strayed back to Sherlock and her lying, cheating hard-bodied fiancé and her TV show and her drooping Talent. I may have only worked one case with the FBI, but I'd been training with GD&C since I inherited Harry when I was 17, working mostly on missing persons cases gone cold. Because of the media attention on psychics and their work since 2001, I had always tried to be careful not to say anything catty about Danika, unless it was to Harry; my Cold Company always shouldered my troubles with unflagging loyalty and compassionate dedication.

"When was the last time you had a pedicure, love?" he said with displeasure. "Your nail polish looks as though it has been chewed off by rats."

"I was just thinking nice things about you, but I take 'em all back."

"Or a manicure?" he continued. "You know, sometimes the gloves come off in mixed company. For example, in the bath. I say, that is a decidedly unladylike finger gesture."

"Shouldn't you be in your casket?"

He motioned meaningfully at the dark frosted window, where hail had turned to a noisy winter snowstorm. Clouds had blacked-out the sun; until the burden of the hidden sun's reign became too taxing on him, he'd stay with me.

After tidying and folding my mess of tossed-aside clothes, he opened the linen closet and removed a dark burgundy box, from which he drew his G. B. Kent & Sons hairbrush. A "Military Oval," he'd once told me, the disappointed inflection in his voice indicating I should have recognized what it was. His last DaySitter, my grandma Vi, would have known. Grooming his short-clipped hair by touch, he kept his back to the empty mirror. He'd been blond in life, his hair thinning in front . While his hair had darkened to sandy, death hadn't changed his hairline. He wasn't about to lose any more hair, but it wasn't going to grow back, either. Hence, Harry's enduring fondness of hats.

He sensed me inspecting him and paused in his grooming, meeting my gaze steadily until he was satisfied that I was pleased with what I saw. I showed him an adoring smile.

"Why did you open the door this morning?" he asked.

"What else am I'm gonna do, leavc them on the porch in a hail storm?" I mulled that over. "Why *didn't* I leave them out in the hail storm?"

"One can only assume that you wanted Agent Batten inside." He gave me a long, questioning look. "If he had come alone, would you have let him in?"

"Did it occur to you that maybe it was Gary Chapel I wanted to chat with?"

"Don't be absurd," he said gravely. "Are you holding Agent Batten to blame for the attack in Buffalo?"

He wanted to hear me say it; Harry didn't need to ask me that or anything else. Thanks to our Bond he knew exactly how I felt. Frankly, I was no longer sure if the weight of his mind pressing down on mine hadn't evolved over the years into something stronger, something worse; that an empathic revenant could eventually tinker with your emotions, as he crossed from old to truly ancient, could dabble with the puzzle of your heart, was an horrific prospect. If that was the case with Harry, he wasn't dumb enough to admit it to me.

I motioned for him to pass the nail brush. "He couldn't have predicted the shooting. No one expected a rev to be armed."

"Revenants choosing firearms over fangs and superhuman strength. What is this world coming to?" Harry agreed.

"That rev—" At Harry's displeased *tsk,* I remembered my manners. "Jeremiah Prost was over a century dead and his mind control was excellent. It took less than 10 seconds: Batten was his, I was his."

"May I remind you?" He paused in his hair brushing. "I hate to, but may I?"

"Yes, I know. Fourth Canon."

"Fourth Canon," Harry said as though he hadn't heard me. "Safeguard oneself chiefly against the dead, for the mind of a DaySitter is far more vulnerable to the call of the grave than is the mind of a mundane."

"I got it." I scrubbed with the nail brush more vigorously than was necessary. "Something to do with open channels in my mind … not sure how I could fix that."

"By avoiding revenants altogether, I should say, unless your advocate was backing you up," he said, meaning himself. "T'would not be a difficult task. My kind is hardly roaming ten-deep in the streets. There are, at most, four dozen immortals left in America. You should only come upon one if you meant to, as was the case with Mr. Prost." He plucked an imaginary piece of lint off the front of his shirt. "Alas, I fear you do not always learn from your mistakes."

My mistakes? It had been Harry's decision not to come with me from Portland to Buffalo on my first official FBI case. If he had …Harry cocked his head at me curiously and I scratched the critical thought.

Sinking up to my chin, blowing the bubbles away from my lips, I remembered with perfect clarity everything about the encounter with Prost: the slip-splash as cabs cruised the glittering, rain-soaked streets; the smells of the bakery on the corner, sewer gas from the manholes, but mostly the snap of singed sweets, that distinct scent of revenant magic that should have sparked a warning in my mind; the buzz ramping up through my veins like a cold thrill when I saw Jeremiah's form emerge into the pale circle of the streetlight; the frosty brush of the rogue revenant raising my hackles as he brazenly walked past us despite Batten's barked orders and drawn gun. As he defied us, the whole alley frothed in his wake, rolling up off the cement like the mist from Niagara Falls. Savage was his hunger, unrelenting, breathtaking, coursing through my veins, blocking out coherent thought until all that was left were base urges, primal needs.

Not in pursuit of justice, no, but rushing toward his company, delirious in my desire to present myself in submission before him, I had taken three sprinting steps after Prost when he spun *(he'd won, dear God, he'd already won, with the first step)* grinning around an enormous pair of fully extended fangs, and drew from a shoulder holster no one expected him to be wearing. He fired a .22 three times before I knew what was happening, hitting me once in the shoulder and spinning me backwards off my feet. The second bullet took me high in the back, missing my spine by a hair. The third bullet sang down the alley, jerking Batten out of the revenant's mind control. There'd been a jumble of activity, Batten calling for backup, giving a brief chase with his kit clanging open and stakes scattering in the grit, before he'd thrown himself to his knees beside me; Jeremiah had melted into the distance, and I, heels digging asphalt, bled into the rotting sludge behind a dumpster for a good five minutes before the ambulance got there.

Harry's grip hit the countertop and something cracked. He said thickly, "Please, stop that."

"Sorry." I brushed the bitterness aside. "Like I said, the gun made no sense. Then again, Prost was being arrested by the FBI for killing…" *Don't say the number*, "Children. He was obviously capable of abnormal behavior. I should have known to expect anything."

Harry nodded. "Mr. Prost was hungry, yet he chose to execute you instead of draining you."

"It was just me and Batten in that alley." And we might have seen the homicidal revenant lurking in the shadows if Mark and I hadn't been fighting like a couple of stray cats in heat. Harry didn't need to hear that part. "If Jeremiah wanted to feed, he could have taken his time, sat me down across his lap, ripped my heart out of my ribcage and chowed down. But I wasn't his preference."

"Love by the dram," Harry said quietly, almost to himself. "Poor little bobbins."

"As it was, only the sound of the gunshot snapped Batten out of the spell or whatever."

Harry smiled indulgently. "Or whatever."

"Spell, Mojo, juju, the Blue Sense, psi …magic is all the same no matter what you call it." Sometimes the word "whatever" encompassed everything best, but Harry didn't share my opinion; Harry was a stickler.

"So you do not blame Agent Batten?" he probed, putting away his oval hairbrush and returning it to its spot on the shelf. He took a bottle of vitamins out of the medicine cabinet and shook two into his palm.

"Not for that."

"Just for instigating the intercourse." Harry passed me a pumice stone and two small white pills, barely worth taking. I dry-swallowed, then sighed at him.

"No," I said rolling my eyes at "intercourse". "I blame him for instigating the sex even though he was engaged, for neglecting to mention that he was already engaged before the sex, for being a total jerkwad after the sex. And for not coming to see me in the hospital." *And for being unforgettable.*

"And for having the appalling taste to propose to Danika Sherlock?" Harry unfolded a towel and fluffed it while I pulled the plug.

"That's his problem, not mine."

"Yes, I imagine it probably is." He wasn't buying it. He wrapped the towel around me while I pointed at my chest.

"Seriously, if he wants to screw Plain Jane and then marry Bimbo Barbie ..." I didn't know how to finish that. It was pointless to pretend it hadn't hurt. Finding out the facts had sent me reeling, but to be fair, Batten hadn't promised me anything. He just hadn't told me the whole truth.

"Is that what I should have tattooed on my wrist, then? Plain Jane?" Harry studied me, head cocked. "Perhaps if you cut your hair, a bit of fringe, some layering."

I grabbed a handful of ash blond hair protectively. Damp trails of it curled around my fist and I wagged it at him. "It took me a whole year to grow it this long."

"Queen Anne's dead." Harry's version of *duh*.

"And what do you mean, "if you cut your hair"?" I demanded. "What's wrong with my hair?"

"You always wear it in a ponytail. I have often thought it rather dull."

"This from a man who hasn't changed his hairstyle since 1720."

"Insolent bird!" Harry laughed, delighted, his smile revealing a row of straight white teeth without the slightest hint of fang; while Harry was closer to plain than handsome, his mouth looked soft and scandalously kissable, though I'd given up hopes of ever finding out. "You cannot possibly know that!"

"You're forgetting James Latham painted a lovely portrait of you that year," I happily reminded him. "It hangs above our mantle in the living room."

"What manner of maniac builds a mantle above that modern monstrosity of a wood stove, I ask you? Despite affording us with the purest good fortune of having a place to put our candelabra, it is completely inappropriate to the space."

"Changing the subject!" I accused. "You look exactly the same as you always have, Lord Dreppenstedt, except for the lace cravats and tricorne hats. Whatever happened to that stuff, anyway?"

Harry flicked me in the butt with a hand towel. "I keep them in storage, of course. I plan to look dashing at your funeral."

C4

You might think that a dead guy would be immune to a Colorado winter's cruel temperatures. That being undead might render one's body impervious to discomfort. *So* not true. I couldn't speak for all revenants, but Harry claimed to be prone to chill, professed that he could not bear the wind that whipped off the lake at Shaw's Fist. I suppose it was plausible; his body temperature measured a mere 68 degrees at most, after a solid feed made him comfortable. He slept with an electric blanket tucked under the goose down duvet in his casket, and some evenings his feet were so cold we soaked them in a pot of hot water. Twice a year he received shipments of angora and wool blend socks from Iceland. If he caught chill, not only would he gripe and moan for hours (complete with chattering teeth of drama king proportions), but he'd burrow his frigid toes under my legs for warmth while we sat watching evening TV, or steal my coffee to warm his hands. That being said, shoveling snow almost always fell to me.

This morning's hail had turned to a hard, spitty not-quite-snow that was entirely unlike the fat magical flakes of a holiday postcard, and it pelted me while I tried not to think about Kristin Davis. I focused on the miserable weather, forcing my brain away from thoughts of missing heads and Y-incisions. The temperature was dropping fast, but the moisture in the air was high. It was like December was having a psychotic break, and I was a ward-weary nurse wishing I had extra Thorazine on hand. Despite my puffy pink parka, I could feel the damp cold down to the bone that made me want to curl in on myself and hide. Wind snuck into the neckline and licked my collarbone in the most irritating way. My breath made a humid steam that drifted back into my face, which was also pretty annoying.

All right, maybe everything was annoying me today. I was jumpy from lots of caffeine and Chapel's terrible crime scene photos. I was miserable from seeing Sherlock's ankles, flustered from seeing Batten all unapologetic and business-as-usual, like nothing had happened between us. Maybe it was nothing to him. Maybe if I stopped calling him Mark in my head and started thinking of him as Jerkface it would make the transition from accidental lover to ex-associate easier. Maybe a nice Thorazine fog would help me, too.

On the bright side, being irritated was preferable to being sad and horrified; when in doubt, choose rage, that's my motto. I pushed my knit hat back up onto my forehead so I could see, and chiseled at the indefinable coating on the steps: part snow, crusted with ice, scary-slick on top. I'd left my hair down just to prove to Harry that I didn't always wear it in a boring-yet-practical ponytail. He hadn't seemed too impressed. Of course, at the time he'd been highly distracted listening to Black Eyed Peas on his iPod and rapping: *"What you gon' do with all that junk? All that junk inside your trunk?"*. My hair issues didn't compete with his lively hip-grinding in the kitchen. The thought of him outlined in the shadows of the closed wood blinds by the sink, rocking out in his tuxedo pants and singing about his "lady lumps" just made me smile. I had, no doubt, the goofiest vamp this side of the Atlantic. *Revenant, dammit!* Screw Batten and his stubborn slang; now he had me doing it. *Lord and Lady, if Harry hears me say the v-word, my ass is meatloaf.*

Wherever my tangled locks hung out of my cap, they were coated with hoary frost-hard tips, and when the wind blew the wrong way, they whipped across my face, poking my eyes and tickling my sweaty brow. My nostrils started to burn and I wondered if I was going to get chapped red, and wouldn't that be oh-so-attractive if Jerkface returned, smelling like a blend of watered-down Brut cologne (which Harry found absolutely hilarious) and body-warmed leather …

I stopped my fantasizing abruptly with a self-loathing scowl and went back to shoveling.

Why had I ever thought that working with the FBI would be fun? There had never been a single fun thing about it. Just a grim, never-ending line of wee bloodless bodies smelling of open abdominal cavities and, depending on freshness, putrecine and cadaverine, two scents I wish I wasn't familiar with.

The sun peeked above briefly, winking out when the heavy clouds trundled on stage left. Lovely of me to be thinking of rotting corpses when a perfectly healthy dead guy had finally wandered off to his bedroom in the basement. I felt his weariness, that slow progression of my Bonded partner as he approached his daily reprieve.

The cell phone in my back pocket matched the one tucked under the satin pillow in his casket. Only three people had my number: Harry, SSA Chapel, and Jerkface. When it started trilling Taco's version of "Putting on the Ritz" I didn't have to wonder who changed my ringtone.

"Yes, Lord Fancy Pants?"

"Are you going out?"

I'd planned on curling up on the couch to cheer myself up with the newest Janet Evanovich mystery and some Oreos, and I was going to chomp about 20 of them *(like a Great White Shark, maybe?)* but when your companion has needs …"What do you want, Harry?"

"May I issue a warning, ducky? I hate to, but may I?"

"Must you?" I replied.

"I must," he continued, clearly missing the testy tone of my voice. "For I suspect you'd fancy a wee drive into town, where you would no doubt get on Agent Batten's wick. To be sure, that can only end in disaster."

"On Batten's wick" sure sounded like a coy euphemism to me. Leaning against the snow shovel, I peered up at the gloomy skies, wondered if the sun was direct enough through those clouds to dust my smart-assed housemate.

"I used to own a crucifix," I mused. "Solid silver, blessed by a Roman Catholic archbishop. Wonder where it got to?"

"They probably revoked it from your heathen arse when you went witchy." I could picture him wiggling his fingers mysteriously the way he did.

"Rest in peace, Harry."

"T-minus five, my pet." He sucked wind before he hung up on me and I knew he was finishing up a menthol cigarette in his casket again. Embers in an enclosed wooden box with a highly flammable revenant? Shaking my head, I filled in the *four, three, two, one* ... I clutched the shovel handle in anticipation, but it didn't help much.

The loss of Harry as he settled to rest was always like having my entrails jerked out, leaving a yawning chasm in my lower belly. I heard someone moan and knew it was me. It took a few deep breaths Lamaze-style through pursed lips before the immediate effects faded, and then I was okay. Not great, but okay.

I scanned the yard, paying close attention to any hint of new movement in the pale white expanse spread before me; the wind flicked crystal ice from the trees, evergreen boughs brushed side to side, my eyes were kept busy as I went back to shoveling. With my Cold Company technically dead for a few hours, I was on deck. There was a .45 Beretta mini Cougar, a powerful little hand-cannon suited for my diminutive grip size, tucked in an innerpants holster at the small of my back. Even still, being in charge is never a good place for me; it's no secret I tend to spaz under pressure.

An expected dark shape passed overhead casting a shadow that skimmed the glittering landscape and settled in a nearby tree. I craned up, narrowing my eyes against the gritty snow pelting down; this was no ordinary bird.

They called them *debitum naturae*, from the Latin, debt of nature: the debt vulture. Every revenant had one, a specific bird who shadowed his steps, forever waiting, forever watching through the centuries, confused by the walking carrion that would not lie down to be eaten. Its cry was a haunting shrill of eternal frustration. The debt vulture was immortal, God's answer to the demonic promise of eternal life, a subtle living reminder of the way the food chain should work. Fixed to Harry's personal mark, it would follow him everywhere, and appeared from hiding soon after Harry went to casket, as though it sensed Harry's death on the air the same way I did.

The debt vulture (whom we named Ajax) could hardly eat Harry when he was locked in his casket, safely indoors. I was more worried about the things the vulture often attracted, unnatural things that used debt vultures to track their favorite snack. Carrion beetles were the most common, but not the regular sort: *necrophila noveboracensis* were brain-eating, crypt-plague-spreading beetles that found a juicy orifice and shot up through flesh, organ and cartilage to get to their prize. Called zombie beetles by laymen, they didn't care whether their meal was alive, dead or undead; they'd eat just about anything if they got hungry enough. They travelled in swarms called draughts, as many as a thousand bugs per, meaty little morsels with wings for short bursts of flight and meat-shredding pincers for burrowing.

Why anything would think a dead man might be tasty was beyond me, but it's my job to make sure nothing got a nibble. It had taken about two weeks after our move from Portland for Ajax to locate Harry here in Colorado. Any time now, the beetles would show. They didn't just give me the willies; they made me want to run away like the Stooges, complete with whooping cries and flailing limbs.

I was subjected to Taco again, muffled within my pocket. It could only be the FBI. Probably, I'd been wretched enough to scare off Agent Chapel for the day. That meant Jerkface was on my phone. Something instinctual intoned, *don't answer*. Dread curled through my belly to combat the floundering, helpless arousal there. Wishing I could resist the urge to hear his voice again, even if it was just to fight with him, I breathed out two misty trails from my nostrils, hating myself, before answering:

"Cram it, fucksock, I'm busy."

"Oh! Oh, my." It was a woman's voice, soft and lilting in an accent I couldn't define. "Miss Baranuik?"

My brain scrambled for recognition and came up with nil. "Uh, possibly?"

"This is Danika Sherlock."

C5

"I got your number from Special Agent Mark Batten," Danika purred in my ear, "Of the FBI? Quantico? Virginia?"

Like I'd never heard of such an agency. Or such a person. When my jaw snapped shut I bit my tongue; my eyes instantly watered.

"I'm sorry to call your unlisted number. I know how much we in the industry depend on our privacy and I totally understand that you're retired and I shouldn't even be calling, except that I really need your help." She tripped over her tongue long enough to catch a breath. "Like, really-*really* need your help."

"Like, totally really-really?" I couldn't help it. It just slipped out. I pinched my lips together to squelch a giggle. Marnie Baranuik *(the Great White Shark, uber-serious)* most certainly did not giggle. Ever. My only excuse was the cocktail Harry had served me in the bath. My stomach squeezed down around tumbling butterflies spitting fire into a churning void; I didn't know whether to laugh or throw up, and prayed I wouldn't do either.

"Miss Baranuik," she said softly, the hurt in her cute Midwestern voice vibrating down the line. "Are you making fun of me? Because I assure you, I am in some seriously fucked-up trouble. God, why else would I be calling *you* unless I absolutely had nowhere else to fucking turn?"

I was gob smacked; I didn't know which surprised me more, the profanity spoken in that dainty, babydoll voice, or the way she implied she'd rather be talking to Lucifer Himself than me. Had Mark ... no, he wouldn't have told her about what happened in Buffalo. But he wouldn't have to, would he? She's clairvoyant. Did she know? If she did, she wouldn't be asking me for help, would she? *Well, shit.* My brain reeled and the snow shovel, forgotten, clattered from my hands to the frozen ground.

I looked around as though the answers to my problems were to be found in the ice clinging to the Aspens. Ajax the vulture watched me intently, bald head cocked, dusted ruff stirring in the snow fall.

"Let me just get inside, you've caught me at a bad time. Hold on."

I threw my parka off in the door, kicked off my squeaking Keds and nearly ran to my espresso machine, skidding in cold, damp sock feet. I had a feeling more caffeine was needed, big time. Not tossing the phone in the sink in a jealous, chickening-out fit was the bravest thing I'd done in a while.

Since I didn't hang up on her, she took that as an invitation to blather, and her words ran together the way they will when someone's out of their mind with worry. I pulled three shots into a regular-sized mug hand-painted with a cartoon frog tap dancing on a log, doctored it super-sweet, and tried to make sense of what she was saying.

"Hold on," I repeated. "Say that last part again?"

"I'm positive a DaySitter and an elder revenant are responsible for the murder of Kristin Davis."

Elder revenant. What Batten and the hunter lot would call an ancient vampire. I took a bag of Oreos out of the pantry and tossed them on my sister's old turquoise Formica kitchen table. Harry had bought me "reduced fat" Oreos again. Probably he had a death wish.

"How do you figure?" I asked.

"Do you know what I do, miss Baranuik?"

"You're Top Floor, a second degree clairvoyant in the forensic retrocognition department." I politely avoided the subject of her companion or lack thereof. It would have been shamefully rude, like doing the Charleston on your mother-in-law's grave. "You're capable of perceiving objects or people at a distance. Second degree means you've completed training in DEV, distant event viewing; you get visions about events that have recently occurred by applying focus to psi. It's still inadmissible in court. GD & C are working on a way to properly test and regulate DEV so the results can be used as evidence in a criminal court case."

"Just now, I was able to see Kristin's murder. I saw a revenant taking her head off with a big saw, with jagged teeth, like lumberjacks use? It was messy, so much blood. I saw Kristin in the alley ..."

She was making it too personal by using the victim's name, an amateur mistake; I felt sorry for her. But a couple of things struck me as off. Firstly, there wasn't any blood in the pictures Chapel had shown me. There were bite marks, indicating that Davis had been probably drained completely. So if the head was taken afterward, it wouldn't have been messy, blood-wise. Maybe Danika's definition of messy was different than mine. Secondly, because it was such a busy area of LoDo, Chapel didn't believe the alley was the primary crime scene, just a dump site. Even if quietly done, draining someone of 5-6 quarts of blood does take time, even from the fattest arteries. Thirdly, I didn't think any revenant would have to use a *saw,* or any other cutting implement for that matter. Even the new undead have immortal strength, can tear a limb clean off just by twisting it. Since it only takes 2 pounds of pressure to break a human neck if you know how to do it, the saw was overkill.

"And then?" I prompted

"He took it so he could have her eyes."

I sat, hard. "Her eyes?" My already queasy stomach did an uncomfortable flip-roll. "Eyeballs have very little blood in them. They're made of mostly vitreous fluid, water mainly. A revenant would have no use for—"

"Miss Baranuik," she interrupted. I heard her breathing shakily. "He took them for his DaySitter. In the vision, I saw them, both of them. The psychic was aware of me. I don't have a clue who they might be, I have faces but no names to go with them. Miss Baranuik …"

"If we're going to talk dirty like this, you might as well call me Marnie," I tried to joke. It fell flat on both ends of the phone.

"He recognized me from television. He knows exactly who I am. It's no secret where I am. His revenant was …" Her words failed her, and I thought I heard her retch a little. More than her words, that made my eyes creep wide. "So terribly old. I felt him moving around their room, over the miles I could feel the burden of centuries of pent-up rage in him."

Rage? What we were dealing with, another mental-case? She couldn't mean Jeremiah Prost. As far as I knew he was UnBonded and not much more than a century old.

"They'll come for me. And when they do …" She let out a sound of panic, a cross between a sob and a whinny. "Oh, miss Baranuik, I'm royally fucked."

I wanted to hate her guts, I really did. I wanted to hang up. She made me feel like an insignificant little bug, outshone me in every way. And she had the guy I lusted for. But worry trumped jealousy and I couldn't feel anything but her distress amplifying mine. She was right …she was royally fucked. Letting someone you dislike die when you could have helped is not exactly cool. I like to think when it comes down to it and things get dead serious, I always do the capital-R Right thing.

"Why does he want human eyes?"

"How the hell should I know?" she shouted.

I was tempted to quip "cuz you're psychic?" but she was already losing it so I pinched it back. *Point: Marnie.* "You're safe until dark," I reminded her. "And if you've paid for a bed and laid in it once, he can't come into your hotel room uninvited."

"It's not the revenant I'm worried about, it's the Talent he's given his DaySitter; he's a ninth caliber telekinetic."

"Ninth?" He wouldn't even have to come into her room to kill her, he could just thought-toss a Mack truck through the front window. We talked degrees of psychic strength, but when you got into kinetics

(pyrokinesis, hydrokinesis, sanguinetics) you spoke in rising calibers like you did with weapons. I'd never heard of a ninth caliber anything. There was a fifth degree precognitive once in Belgium, but he went crazy in his early twenties and had to be locked up. Revenants had no such power limits, as far as I knew, but the human mind could only wield so much psi before it fried.

"What are we going to do?" she demanded, hyper. "Please hurry, miss Baranuik, I need you. I don't want to die tonight."

Wonka wha--was I going somewhere? I swallowed my too-hot espresso, choked on the burn. I didn't know how much protection I could offer, with my itty bitty gun (that I'd never actually fired at anyone) and my psychic Talents. I could tell her how the rogue DaySitter *felt* just before he killed us, though I failed to see how that would improve the situation. If I Groped him, I could tell her *how* he planned to slaughter us. That didn't sound particularly helpful either.

Besides, a ninth degree telekinetic wouldn't even be arrest-able. How would you get him into handcuffs? How could you get him into the squad car without him throwing it on its side? He'd turn bullets mid-air and tear craters in asphalt. My brain tripped along this fantasy a bit while I thought of some way to get out of helping her. What would he need eyeballs for? Why get the revenant to steal them when a telekinetic of that magnitude could just thought-pluck them right out of your living head? That image made my tongue stutter into action.

"OK. We'll figure this out. There's got to be something that can be done. Where's Mar—Agent Batten?" *Christ on a Cheez Nip, Marnie, he's just a coworker. Ex-coworker. Last name basis!*

"We're staying at a little motel called the Ten Springs Motor Inn, just off—"

"I know where it is. Tell him to bring you here immediately, you'll be far safer at my place."

"He's not here."

"Why the hell not? Didn't you tell him?"

There was a long beat of silence, during which the nape of my neck crawled unpleasantly. This was not a good sign; why *wouldn't* someone call in Big Guns Batten and the monster killing guts of his kit? He was a gigantic jerkwad, but he was still the first person I'd call if the bad guys were on my ass, and she was his fiancée …something felt wrong.

I said tentatively, "Look, I'm retired. I really shouldn't get involved in a federal case." *Especially since I told them to go take a flying leap only an hour ago.* "You need to contact the PCU immediately."

"You're just going to let me die?" she squawked.

"Of course not. Call Chapel, he'll bring you to me—"

"Bad cell phone reception, can't reach him."

Grimacing, I slipped off my left glove and wrapped it around the receiver of the phone; it rarely worked unless the other person was really keyed-up, pouring out emotions in a palpable fashion, but it was easy this time: *distrust, suspicion, fury, disgust, fear.* Mostly *fear.* I was about to tell her I was on my way to pick her up when she snarled, literally snarled, and the feral sound of it stole my voice.

"You need to get here," she ground out. "Now. I don't want cops. I don't want Mundanes. I want *you.*" Gone was the shaky voice. She didn't wait a beat for me to accept or refuse. "If I don't see your scrawny, bleached ass within the hour, I'm going to call assistant director Geoff Johnston at Quantico and tell him you screwed a PCU agent on the job. You'll never work for the FBI again."

Bleached ass? I boggled at the phone, holding it away from my face as if gawking down the line at her. *Who bleaches their ass? What does that even mean?*

Laughing incredulously, I spluttered, "I'm retired. Why would I give a rat's left tit what anyone thinks of me?"

"You've got 30 minutes," she shouted. "Or I make you sorry you ever entered the circuit!"

"I'm already sorry I ever worked the circuit!" I shouted back. "Look lady, I was fully prepared to drive out and help you, but I don't respond well to ultimatums. Tell Director Johnston I say howdy-doo!"

Her tone became frosty, enunciating each word clearly. "I'll tell Johnston that Special Agent Mark Batten compromised the Jeremiah Prost investigation and let a child killer escape because he was too busy fucking your brains out, and that SSA Gary Chapel knew and covered it up. Because of you, they'll both lose their jobs."

Silence dropped like a bomb in my kitchen, and I reeled back in the chair. *Point: Sherlock, that bitch.* Again I had to hold the phone away from my head, this time so I wouldn't take her head off. All my objections died in my mouth; my jaw worked around a hundred of them, but my pinched lips were a fortress of reluctant compliance. There was no way I could let my inability to keep my knees together get Chapel and Batten fired.

"It'll take me about 50 min to drive in," I growled, not believing what I was hearing myself say. "Do you have clary sage?"

"What for?"

"I'll bring the sage," I told her, going to the pantry to pull down my big yellow Tupperware box. Not all psychics practice green magic of an herb-and-gemstone sort. Most did, simply because once you witnessed magic in one form, you believed, and belief is a potent ingredient. "Go take a bath, saltwater if you can find salt, and as cold as you can stand. That should slow down the vibration of your psi signature. If they're using that to track you, he might miss you on a first pass. Stay chilly. I'll be there as soon as I can."

"And then?" she asked.

I was supposed to have an answer. I didn't. I had a glimmer of several rotten ideas that no doubt would get us both killed, I had sage and I had my mini gun. I was hoping when I got there, Batten would be back. I could turn the problem over to the law and just forget this whole shit day had ever happened. The lovebirds (ex-lovebirds?) could catch a flight out of Colorado to a safe house wherever, and I could wake my Cold Company for his nighttime feed and an old black and white movie with popcorn before bed.

"Then we end it," I promised her with far more bravery than I felt. "We figure our shit out, and deal with the rogue together. Like adults. Like professionals. I'm sure we can work it out."

"Yes," she said, dreadful relief flooding through the phone. Her *disgust* had been replaced by *hope*. "You and me. We end it. Together."

I hung up by chucking the phone clear across the room, where it smashed and the battery pack went spinning across the floor. I slipped my glove back on angrily. As if Batten were standing in front of me, I muttered, "I knew your dick was going to come back and bite me in the ass."

C6

When I was 17, I had inherited the care and feeding of Lord Guy "Harry" Harrick Dreppenstedt on the recommendation of my grandma Vi's last will and testament. Sharing his psychic Talents wasn't a conscious decision on Harry's part, not a gift or an honour bestowed on his caregiver. It was more like living in the same house as a chain-smoker: one day you realize that, never mind your clothes or your hair, even your flesh is embedded with their stink.

Being as my power was his, that he effortlessly feels my intensions through our Bond, you'd think Harry never has to ask me anything, never mind stupid questions like: "just where is it you think you are going?", which is what his text message read. I could practically hear the disdain.

I hurtled down the ice-slicked Interstate in my old reliable Buick Century, the bumpy ride barely felt by the mammoth car, hugging curves and charging uphill and plunging in and out of dim mountain pass tunnels. The sun was full-strength now at winter's distance, brilliant without warmth, glinting off crumbled frost shards and salt patches. The car's heat was cranked. Fat heavy clouds warned that the sunny moment was fleeting; I'd be needing my headlights and wipers soon. Daft Punk was thudding my car's old speakers. I didn't have the time or attention to take one hand off the wheel and thumb-in a reply; Half-Asleep Harry could just figure it out for himself. I didn't know what had roused him early from his rest—I'd been too far away to feel him wake—but I did know he wouldn't be overjoyed about me riding to Danika's rescue, regardless of the reason. I was not in the mood to hear bleated objections in his lofty Londoner's tongue.

For half the ride, my thoughts revolved around Batten. OK, more like 90 percent. Should I call him, tell him about the rogue DaySitter and the blackmail? He was the capital-L Law. He was the big tough FBI dude, the PCU's preternatural crimes expert (if there was such a thing), Mr. Guns Ablazin' with the bullet proof vest stamped with big white letters and a liscence to kill misbehaving monsters, 105 kill-notch tattoos on his left pectoral to prove it.

I'd never had bad reception in the area, not even out at the lake at Shaw's Fist, but I hadn't felt a lie from within Sherlock's transmitted goulash of disgust and desperation. Had Chapel turned off his phone? I thought FBI dudes shouldn't be allowed to do that. Had Batten had more pressing matters this morning? What could be more important than a crazy-scary telekinetic after your fiancée? Certainly not coming to my cabin to flap pictures of dead people at me, mock me with stupid nicknames and take pot shots at my living arrangements. That, we both could have skipped.

I should call him. Could I bring myself to say her name to him? Had Batten told his fiancée about us, even if there was really no "us"? Confession, full disclosure? Or had she found out on her own? Had she confronted him? It niggled at my conscience when I should have been paying more attention to navigating sharp turns; I fishtailed once and nearly went off on the runaway truck ramp, had to crank the wheel and yelp a quick prayer. When the Buick was back under control and I had called myself all the synonyms for moron I could scrounge up, I went back to obsessing. The Buick sailed into a murky mountain tunnel. The overhead lights strobed across the long hood rhythmically.

When I showed up and Danika opened the motel door, I'd be facing a woman who knew I'd boffed her man behind her back, a woman who didn't sound too pleased about it. To be fair, when I was with him in Cheektowaga, up against that bathroom door breathless with lust, thinking I might just be the luckiest/stupidest woman on Earth, I didn't have any idea he was engaged. He gave me no reason to believe so. I like to think it would have stopped me.

I could tell her that. It would be my only defense. But stuff like hindsight didn't mean much when a man swapped bodily fluids with more than one woman. I mean, it wasn't like I was planning to fuck him again, right? *(Don't ever doubt that you're needed, Baranuik.)* With a sick heart, I managed the last sharp turn near the gas bar and barreled downhill into town in my civilian tank.

Ten Springs, Colorado, population 540, was forty five minutes northwest of Denver, nestled between two small mountain lakes, Shaw's Fist and Cleaver's Rest, named after two of the three founding families. The town was entered from the north by a one-way bridge that had no official name but which locals called Lambert's Crossing, named after the third.

Ten Springs is the kind of place where proprietors ran shops like "Bobbi-Sue's Classi Hair" right next to the head-scratching combination of "Indian Gourmet and Saloon" featuring "town-famous Tikka Masala". In front of the Salon and the Saloon was a scuffed budgie-yellow emergency phone that was a direct line to the Lambert County sheriff's office, presumably in case of a butchered haircut or hot curry attack. It was sort of redundant; the sheriff's office was across the street and you could stand at the phone waving at the bored dispatcher through the plate glass window.

The town had the distinction of boasting the best breakfast-only cafe in the state, Claire's Early Bird. Claire's was open at midnight and through the moonlit hours for truckers passing through on US-36, and closed at 1:30 pm. I'd never understood why Claire kept undead hours when she was human, and hadn't yet summoned the courage to ask anyone.

I was the last customer of the day to grab a couple of coffees and a cherry Danish to settle my growling tummy. Claire herself was there, a serious woman of wiry hair and indeterminate age, manning the cash register while her waitress finished spritz-cleaning the tables. Claire was a rare gem; she knew who I was and what I was, and didn't give a crap. I appreciated that. In a tiny speck of a town where it was an unwritten law that people know their neighbours' business, Claire held the opinion that we were all on an even playing field. As such, I deserved the same flat crocodilian stare she gave everyone, no more, no less.

I took my coffee black, and left Danika's black because I didn't know how she took it. Claire packed me some creamer and sugar packets and off I went, cramming the Danish in my cheek and sucking clean my fingers. Harry would have a conniption fit if he saw it: *gasp,* me without my serviette.

As I cruised the only street through Ten Springs, I wondered why Batten and Sherlock (and I assumed Chapel) had come to stay here of all places, when Denver had better hotels closer to the crime scene. I knew they were still together, I'd seen her ankles in those pictures, dammit. Maybe they chose Ten Springs because they had to come see me? How did Danika feel about that? Why did they come to me at all? They had her, a clairvoyant, a Witness; even with her ability to focus psi fading-out, a Witness still trumped a Groper like me any day. Danika really was better than me in every way. Lovely thought.

And then I thought of the only compromise that made sense for me. I dialed Chapel's cell and waited for his pleasant, business-casual reply.

"Gary, it's Marnie. I've got an issue, here. Your psychic is in trouble." I explained what Danika had seen, and how she needed me, but left out the blackmail part and any mention of Batten. "I'm pulling up to your motel now."

"We're half way to Denver," Chapel replied, said something hurried that I didn't catch to someone off the phone, and I heard Battens' gruff, unintelligible reply. Then he came back with: "We'll be at the hotel ASAP. Hang tight, Marnie."

I signed off, feeling a thousand times better. *Hooray, the knights in Kevlar armour are on their way.* Now, to shuffle my feet through the inevitable me-Danika-Batten moment in the same room, but only briefly, because once they arrived, I could probably scram. I'm no super hero. I don't have kickass fighting skills. Like I told Danika, I'm just a Groper-Feeler.

Wait, did he say hotel or motel? Probably it meant nothing. The Ten Springs Motor Inn came into view, eight rooms in a long L-shape, each room shaded from behind by stands of Blue Spruce and Bosnian Pine. An Aspen with ghostly branches, leaves lost two months ago, scratched at the weathered shingles with grey talons, a hibernating monster looming over the dark lot. She'd said room 4, and by the looks of the parking lot, it was the only one occupied. Obscene fluorescent lights gleamed in the office, under the sign that said ***v can y.*** I mentally filled one missing letter and thought the resulting "v-candy" sounded vaguely pornographic.

Then, because my brain hates me, I wondered how many times Mark and Danika had made love in room four. Did he turn on the charm for her, award her those rare Mark Batten smiles that carved unexpected, deep-secret laugh lines in the corners of his eyes that hit you below the belt? The ones he shared one night with everyone on his team but me? Did he buy her flowers? Did he know what her favorites were? My favorites were tulips, followed closely by peonies, the rose's voluptuous cousin; I was pretty sure he didn't know that, and probably he didn't care.

I never got flowers from Batten. I got frantic, panting animal sex (*baby, oh baby, don't stop, oh fuck yes*) followed by a jaw-clenched silence, as though it had been all my fault, even though he (*soon baby, oh God*) was the one who had ... I grit my teeth. If only I could safely jam a fork up behind my eye and dig around until all my memories of Buffalo and Kill-Notch were destroyed.

Wearily, I took off my knit cap and whipped it into the back seat. I tightened my ponytail. Yep, back to basics. I was sick of spitting out stray hairs and didn't care what I looked like. When you're putting yourself between a telekinetic and a person whose life you don't honestly want to save, looks no longer matter; the coroner isn't going to stall your Y-incision to rate your style.

I paused for a moment to take notes, something I am admittedly obsessive about. In the glove box, next to my gun, under a pair of chocolate brown leather gloves, was a pale aquamarine Moleskine notebook and half a dozen No. 2 pencils. I had switched from pens because Batten once told me (on one of our boring Prost stake-outs) you could use a sharp No. 2 pencil as a weapon in a pinch, if you jammed it up into someone's soft under-jaw area. He had a word for that, but I didn't remember it. My word for it was owies.

I took note of the psychic impressions I'd gotten from Sherlock over the phone: *distrust, suspicion, fury, disgust, fear.* I jotted them down with my makeshift weapon, indicating time date and circumstance, then threw the notebook and pencil on the dash.

It was amazing how effortlessly the empathic impressions came from Danika; even from the parking space I could feel her anxiety thrumming through the frigid air. I'd love to say it was because I was badass (*the Great White Shark bites off more than she can chew*), but the truth was I didn't care about her feelings. I wasn't sure I cared about her life either, but then why was I here? Oh yeah. If saving her life wasn't the capital-R Right thing to do, saving Batten's and Chapel's careers was. One day, my stupid morals are going to get me killed.

Balancing the cardboard tray of coffees, I hip-bumped the door closed on the Buick, pondered locking it. If the rogue DaySitter showed up in broad daylight with his revenant companion huddled in his trunk, they weren't going to steal my shitty car and go for a joyride, were they? I almost hoped they would. The Buick's brakes were touchy. Maybe they'd careen off a cliff.

My cell phone again encouraged me to put on the Ritz from the back pocket of my jeans. I turned it to vibrate so I could ignore Harry. He should have been resting anyways.

I knocked on the door to room four and waited, letting her see I was alone and I'd come bearing hot coffee. I shouldn't have another; this would be my fourth? Fifth! It was barely 1:45. Caffeine poisoning anyone? Waiting gave me cramps, and the anxiety of not knowing if I was about to have a yelling-shouting-screaming match about Jerkface and his meandering dick made me wish I'd used the bathroom at Claire's; I was pretty sure one hefty scowl out of Sherlock and I'd pee my pants. Wonder woman, I am not.

Finally she opened the door, and if the back draft of wind from that action didn't blow her strawberry tresses in a perfect whirl from her shoulders …it was a honeyed Hollywood moment. I felt like we were being filmed. Consummate TV star, she was made-up perfectly but underdressed; black track pants showed under a brown terrycloth bathrobe. No jewelry. Her eyes were red. Had she been crying? Blackmailing a rival wouldn't make *me* weepy, just saying. Her hand shook midair as she motioned for me to come in.

"Coffee, gosh that smells good," she said. Relief radiated off her in waves. She was glad I was here. Jittery. The Blue Sense prickled back to life in response, sending an uncomfortable zing of electricity up my spine. I suddenly wanted my Moleskine and No. 2 to capture it.

She stepped back to let me in, gave a sob-hiccup-hysterical giggle. "Look, I'm sorry. I've been such a bitch. I've been out of my mind. You don't know how much I wanted you to come."

But I *did* know; usually my empathic powers worked better on remnants of emotions, traces left by the recently dead, but the room was so filled with emotion that it choked me. It felt like she'd been waiting for this a lot longer than an hour, like the culmination of something huge. I told myself: panic amplifies emotions. I wouldn't be familiar with that; the dead don't panic.

Again it struck me as odd that no one was here for her—*too* odd, in fact. If anyone was in mortal danger, Batten would be there, especially the love of his life. Even if they'd had had a knock-down drag-out break-up fight. Of course he'd be here. What was I thinking? If he knew, he'd slay dragons to be here. Kill-Notch Batten was a dyed-in-the-wool uberdouche, but he was damn good at his job.

She shut the door behind me with a solid click. The motel room was pristine; no smell of Mark's weak cologne lingering under old third-hand smoke, no shirt slung across the bed or folded on the dresser; I felt nothing of him here, or her, for that matter. The bed hadn't been touched.

No jewelry. No engagement ring.

The hairs on the back of my neck pricked up.

C7

Something cold and sharp sank into my back. The coffee tray tilted and went spilling from my hand, lashing cheap beige Berber carpeting with a bloodbath of hot caffeine. I opened my mouth to demand *what the fuck?*; what came out was a terrified mewl. I was on my knees before I knew what was happening. I gave over to instinct, rolled onto my back to face her just in time to see her rush me, her beautiful face screwed into a tight grimace of hatred. She had a knife.

I threw my gloved hands up, palms out in front of my neck, angling my body away from her. She slashed through calf skin, slicing into the meat of my hand. *The gun, need the gun.* I tried to whip to the side, hit the rusted bed frame. *The gun.* Her arm was coming down again. All I could see was the tart-bright blade edge arching through grimy motel air. I blocked with crossed forearms, she snarled her frustration. Kicking out to keep her at a distance, I shoved my hand under me for the gun; she closed in fast, ignoring my efforts, pinning my right hand under my weight, straddling my hips. The knife came up again, and my gun hand floundered, empty. *Where is it whereisitwhereisit!* Instead, I grabbed the sea salt baggy from my pocket, gouged into it with all my fingers in one big squeeze, and flung it at her eyes.

She shrieked, swiping her face with the back of her hand. I bucked to throw her off, but her thighs were unyielding. Taking a chance, I aimed a left-handed punch at her throat, but it glanced, and that's when the knife shot through my guard; it hit me in the gut and sank in deep.

I grunted, felt hot bile sting the back of my throat. *Bitchratfuck!* The next few seconds were a blur of rage and steel, tears and the thin roping splatter of blood. Then everything went black.

When I opened my eyes it could have been minutes later or hours; I had no concept. Shaking uncontrollably, I inched my fingers around my hip for the Beretta. It wasn't there. I rolled just my eyeballs around. It wasn't anywhere. *Oh God,* I remembered, *it's in the car.*

The motel room had been redecorated by a frenzied tantrum. *Motel. Not hotel.* I thought with sinking dread. *Chapel said hotel. He meant Denver.* The flat-screen lay disemboweled, ripped right off its bolted stand. A disheveled, hollow-eyed version of Danika sat splay-legged on the floor by the door beside an overturned table, staring at what she'd done to me. She didn't look particularly upset about it. The knife was held loosely. I could have kicked it out of her hand but I was in no condition to fight off a second wave if she got going again. *Chapel's not coming. Batten's not coming. No one knows I'm here.*

No gun, no weapon, bleeding out fast, I had few options; I crammed my bleeding hand into my jacket pocket and pinched the sachet there. Without making too much noise or obvious motion, I rubbed my right glove off against the carpet and spilled the sachet one-handed under the shadow of the bed frame. I dug my fingernail into the plastic baggy of clary sage. My right hand was bloody and the sage stuck to my fingertip, using it to draw a hurried pentagram under the bed, dipping back into the powdered herb to carefully trace it a second time.

She noticed that my eyes were open.

"The first time I saw you," she said dully, "Was in the hospital. Buffalo." She was staring at the knife; I could feel that her adrenalin had fled, leaving her numb. "I figured since you were Mark's coworker, and you were injured, I should come to New York to make sure you were ok. I brought you yellow roses. Do you remember? Yellow roses. For friendship."

I couldn't have forgotten that day if I tried. She'd walked in looking like the embodiment of Venus, all curves and feminine fluttering, and told me in a voice butter-soft and shortbread-sweet that she was going to be Batten's wife in June, and that she hoped I was feeling better in time to come to their engagement party. In that moment, I could honestly say I'd never felt worse. Prost's .22s hadn't hurt nearly as much.

"The minute I walked in the hospital room, I knew he'd been on you," she told me, her accent mysteriously gone flat. "It wasn't in your face. You were a great little actress. Did you know about me? I didn't get any impression about that. I just knew you'd had him. And more than once. I guess once wasn't enough for you."

Blood rattled in the back of my throat and I coughed, letting my head slump to the side. If this was going to work, she had to stay distracted. There was no way I'd fool a clairvoyant if she felt the magic beforehand.

"I could practically see his hands on you. Exploring your hips. Grabbing your tits. Pulling through your hair while he fucked you. He always did like petite athletic blondes. That's his *type*." She spat it like it tasted rotten. "Are you a natural blonde, Marnie?"

I am, but no way was I stupid enough to answer her. With no superfluous movement, I tapped out a paper sliver of ghostly winter birch bark, silently acknowledged the appearance of death on it. The pouch held a tiny bit of ground blessed thistle and angelica root that I clumsily fingered out, while nudging a polished shard of tumbled black onyx, murky as the embrace of the grave, into the north position on the pentagram. Danika's breathing was becoming ragged, phlegm-thick with emotion. The light outside had faded again, and the room was dim. With the weather uncertain, I couldn't guess the time. She didn't turn on a light, just sat on the floor in the shadows.

"What did he see when he was down there? Do you shave it?" she went on, low and husky like she was running out of batteries. "I know where he's been, Marnie. Mark loves going down. Doesn't he? Yeah. Mark Batten could eat a peach for an hour."

Dizzy, frantic that she might have hit an artery, wondering how much blood I'd lost while unconscious, how much I was still losing and how fast, the last thing I wanted to think about was oral sex.

"I could have seen the act," she enunciated crisply, and I felt another blast of her homicidal disgust. "Could have seen it all, but I couldn't face it. Being there at the foot of your hospital bed, seeing you stare up at me with those big blue doe-eyes, I had to actually block it out."

A warm pool of blood had settled in my cheek and I let it drool out down the side of my face. I had no time for making a proper circle or polite invitations. The need to protect myself was ringing alarm bells in my ears. I stared blankly at the underside of the bed frame and began in my head,

Dread Aradia, Mother mine/mistress of the night divine/Thy servant's blood adorn Thy shrine/and thus I charge our darkest sign.

A rush of goosebumps spread across my scalp as the magic in me stirred, a lumbering giant throwing off the dust of months of hibernation, a heathen's adamant call under a desolate sky pricked with distant stars.

"Don't you die yet, Marnie," she warned me, and I knew my colour was fading as I willed each sign of life to dial down. My left foot was twitching, but I seemed to have no motor control below my hips to stop it. Had she hit my spine?

"The last time my power blessed me with a vision and that's what I have to remember? To cling to? Watching him screw some scrawny little whore?" She pressed her palms into her forehead, scrubbing as though she could scour her brain clean of the image. "I've been faking it since then. I'm a great little actress too, Marnie. The truth is it's gone, except for flickers I can't control. I'm psi-blind. Caused by the shock of your betrayal."

My betrayal? Not his, mine. Well then, it was unanimous: all my fault. It's super that everyone could agree on that. Hopefully my scarlet letter would arrive in the mail in time for my funeral.

She had something new in her hand. I didn't know where it came from but it glinted in my peripheral. Oh God. Scissors.

Hear my summons, mighty Crone/cold and darkness dost Thou own/Rule the night, command the sky/cold and dark upon me lie ...

"Don't you die on me yet, bitch!" she shrieked, moving forward on all fours too fast. I forced myself not to flinch and pressed my bleeding palm down to cover the sage pentagram on the carpet; the blood hit the center of the spell's sacred circle, mixed with the sea salt still clinging to my palm and flared hot like a blast of sour frost, tart and blistering and terribly vigorous.

All too readily, death magic answered my call.

She grabbed my chin and pulled it to face her, held the scissors above her head as though she planned to drive them down into my skull.

"A misunderstanding! Danielle, please—" I whispered.

"That's not my name!" she frothed, and instead punched me hard with her clenched scissor-hand in the face again and again until she tired of it. The silver streak of the scissors flashed at me up close, lashed across my vision, held in her knuckles. Terror stole my voice. My head swam and my sight blurred. She left me staring under the TV stand, where tangled snaking cords connected to a dust-coated power bar. The urge to draw on that power instead of the cold touch of death, to use the electricity there to zap Danika Sherlock with a world-class heart attack, tugged me fiercely, fleetingly; I knew the consequences of using witchcraft to do harm. Thrice-fold it came back. But if I was already dying, would it really matter?

Then I thought of Harry, and his lectures about the soul and redemption. Of purity, and salvation. *Oh, Harry,* my mind cried out, wishing now I'd answered his last call.

Danika took a fistful of my hair in her hand and I heard the *snick* of the scissors. The sawing motion of my hair being shorn away pulled my head back and forth. Handful by handful she threw it aside, dropped it in sprinkling, tickling piles across my face, and on the blood-soaked carpet.

My fingertips brushed the onyx and I focused on slowing my breath again. Tears welled in my eyes, leaked across my face in thin rivulets. I just let them fall.

I wanted Mark. No, strike that. I wanted my Harry. He was too far away for me to feel him, so I knew he probably couldn't feel me either. It was for the best; he'd been wide awake for grandma Vi's death. I didn't want him to experience the gut-wrenching on-off switch of mine.

Hail Aradia, to thee I bend/Grant thy touch, my life to end/ Death's embrace dost Thou command/ Unlock the gates, take me in Hand./Breath to cease and pulse to flee/An' it harm none, so mote it be!

My heart stuttered to a sudden stand-still. It was far from pleasant. The sinking weight of the Lady's dark and grudging gift was not much better. My body fought death immediately; frantically my diaphragm jerked and spasmed, trying to pull air and the pain from the stab wounds diminished, only to be replaced with something far worse: desperate contraction in my chest, the cramp of need in heart and lungs. My tongue crawled against the back of my teeth. I kept my jaw clamped tight. I was drowning, drowning, my airways burned.

I could hear Danika panting, rattling thick with phlegm, as she straddled me again, and I felt her stare. My dry eyes longed to blink through a mat of shorn hair strands.

"Not so pretty now," she said softly, sliding her fingers to my throat. They were slick; she had cut herself while stabbing me to death. Poor baby.

Despite my lack of pulse and breath, she'd know I wasn't really dead if she got one of her so-called "flickers" about what I was attempting one-handed under the bed. I wondered if my pupils were actually dilated like a real corpse as I stared unblinking. I knew I was still losing blood; I could hear it squelch in the carpet's padding under Danika's knees. She palpated my throat. A retching gag escaped her.

She rolled off me to all fours to vomit forcefully against the side of the bed, splattering my jeans with sour bile. When I retold this story to everyone I knew, I was definitely going to leave out that nasty detail. Add vomit to the stench of old cigarettes in the carpet, spilled coffee, and the coppery tang of blood, you had the horrible pot-pourri of her revenge. She stood, wavering uncertainly on her feet, turning her back on me.

She coughed, spitting to clear her mouth. "Getting late. Be on my way ..." she breathed, whipping off the robe and depositing it in a swish of terry on the floor. She peeled off the yoga pants to reveal weatherproof rubberized pants, the kind worn by hardcore all-weather fishermen. They were wet with my blood but would wipe off easily. "You had what's mine. Now I'll have what's yours. That's the promise."

And my brain shrieked, *Harry!*

C8

Funny things occur to you when you're dying. Bleeding out for the second time in three months, I thought deliriously, *I could have used that damned No. 2 pencil.* And: *Soft palate impalement. That's what Batten called it.* And: *I think Batten waters down his cologne. How can I prove it?* And then: *I'm going to die, here. I don't want the reek of vomit to be the last thing I smell.*

When I was sure she'd gone, I broke the sage pentagram with a trembling hand, accidentally flicking the onyx deep under the bed. The shuddering breath that followed was sweet, but the sharp pain of the stab wounds returned with my life; I'd never imagined anything could hurt more than gunshot wounds. Stab wounds gaped, flesh mouths silently screaming scarlet; every slight breath I hitched-in made it so much worse. Unfamiliar noises scratched and scrambled along the back of my throat, injured animal noises, sounds of plain, mindless desperation.

My cell phone was smeared with blood that had poured down my back to soak the rump of my jeans, and rolling over to free it from the sticky denim was torture. Sounds were starting to filter back: cars on the street, a motorcycle rumbling by. She'd left the door half open. Frigid winter air spilled in. Could I get up enough voice to shout for help? Would anyone hear? The front desk guy? A passerby? *Out here? Not likely.*

There was so much residual rage in the room I could taste it on the back of my tongue; I gagged, which tugged savagely in what must have been the worst stab wound, in my belly. I huddled around my pain, hissing through my teeth.

I should have dialed 911 first, but my heart contracted frantically for my Cold Company, hammered with an un-ignorable drumming, fists on taut skins, a violent thundering pushing hot urgency through my veins; I knew this was the Bond's doing, the near-severing of our mystical tether firing off unrelenting pressure to reach him: my partner, my advocate, my champion, nothing else mattered. Swallowing back panic, I thumbed-in his number.

One ring. No answer.

Two rings. *Harry, please!*

Three rings and it went to his civilized, articulate message. I sniveled something indecipherable and tried again. No answer. No answer. If he was prone now in his casket ... *Oh, Harry, get out get out!*

I spit out a blood-choked sob and dialed 911. Dispatch had barely said a syllable when I was gasping at her repeatedly, "she stabbed me, she stabbed me." Part of my brain told me to smarten up, stop being a victim, calm down and tell her how to find me. But it was too incredible. What I wanted to shout was: *That snot-gobbling fuckpuddle Danika Sherlock stabbed me* but what came out was a bawling: "Please, please send help!" My innards quivered nonstop. My vision started to blur. That's never good. The operator was asking me something. I didn't understand any of it. "Ten Springs Motor Inn ..." My clammy hand reached for and found the knife she'd used. I rubbed my other glove off against my hip, and gripped the knife in my left hand, hard.

A blast of imagery slammed my head back into the copper-soaked carpet. I wrenched my eyes shut, as if that could protect a Groper from what she was seeing: that crazy nutjob had watched my cabin, had been inside, *inside!* Plotting it out, she had been told explicitly, repeatedly like a drill, how to break the DaySitter Bond through death or refusal to feed, mine or his. Sherlock had been waiting for her chance to strike like an injured king cobra in the shade of a Jeep. This day had been earmarked. On a calendar. In smudgy blue ink. For some reason, that struck me as insult atop injury.

If she thought she could just waltz up to Harry and say: "Marnie's dead, so you're with me now" she was streaming headlong toward a bad death. What a low opinion of me she must have, to think my companion would be so easily lured away. Harry would put her through a wall, repeatedly, and when the authorities found out, they'd swear out a warrant to have him staked. Kill-Notch Batten would eagerly volunteer for the job. This was the end of everything. If I lived, I wouldn't want to.

The door swung open to the dusky outside and I froze, holding the phone half-leaning upright against one elbow. The jig was up. She'd put the blade across my jugular this time. I clutched the knife so tightly that my knuckles flared with pain, laying my thumb along the hilt like Harry had shown me long ago. I waved it at the figure in swift, warning arcs.

The legs that straddled the threshold were wide, sturdy and undeniably masculine. And dressed, I noted deliriously, for a winter night's ride. A double-breasted chesterfield overcoat I recognized flapped around his thighs, above salt-flecked biker boots that were otherwise perfectly polished. Only one man I knew was that persnickety. A cry of relief leaked from my throat.

Harry moved swiftly across the room in his dizzying blink-step, pale lips curled back in a silent snarl. He kicked the ruined TV out of his way; it tumbled through the air casting shards of glass and metal in a shower. Sweeping down beside the bed on one knee, whispering in furious French as he always did when angry, his tongue worked the words like a spell, his mouth caressing the sounds with a voice slightly sibilant around a hint of fang. The scent of blood in the air had him trembling badly. The old ones may play poker-face better than any human, but in times of bloodshed or in the face of arterial spray, even they inevitably lost their cool and had to work hard at controlling near-ejaculatory enthusiasm.

"Who's a brave soldier, then?" he said as he assessed and surveyed the damage with quick hands that scanned and catalogued too fast to follow, unzipping my jacket, clutching my shirt front to yank it out of his way. With a sharp jerk he shred its remains up the front.

"This ..." Apparently there was no word for it in any of his languages. He diagnosed the wounds rapidly with bleak ash-grey eyes that had seen centuries of triage and casualty, much of the latter caused by him. "Right, then. Do not fight me, love, there is no other way."

His hand snaked behind my head and pulled my face into his left elbow. I hadn't seen him break his skin there, but a small wound was pressed to my lips. Dizzily, I closed my eyes and calculated the odds that he knew better than me what was best. Something leaky-sweet passed my lips and hit my tongue, heady like thinned molasses but strangely tingling, alien and funky like a tomato gone bad. I didn't want to swallow as it trickled to the back of my throat; I gagged and turned my head.

Harry growled impatiently; the hand on the back of my head tightened, fingertips digging into my scalp as he forced my face back to his elbow.

"Time for trust, Dearheart."

"Don't rush me, I'm enjoying the foreplay," I groaned.

When I gagged a second time, he said, "You are out of options, now, DaySitter. You have lost too much."

I'm going to die in the vomit-stink room. I opened my mouth around the wound and sucked, hastily swallowing. Unfortunate images flashed in my mind's eye: a waterlogged grave, a dripping crypt, an age-slicked corpse in a swamp. Once the cool, runny fluid of Harry's veins cleared my taste buds, something deeper inside me rolled over with savage energy, swirled its cold fist around in my gut like it was stirring a slushy. I felt Harry's fingertips dabbing at my wounds, and that same ancient, unnatural energy ravaged my skin, tingled icy-hot like Vick's

Vapo-Rub. I thought deliriously, revenant blood would be great for chest congestion due to cold and flu.

Harry was watching me with a medic's attention. Satisfied, he shoved my gloves in his pocket and collected me carefully, lifted me as though I weighed nothing; considering he could bench press a two ton dumpster, my hundred and twenty pounds wasn't a huge struggle. He gathered me into his chest to shelter me from the cold, hurrying from the room before I could wail an objection; the clouds were good and deep above us, solid asylum, and the wind had picked up to howling intensity, screaming through the Aspens.

(Don't you die yet, Marnie—don't you die on me yet, bitch!)

Harry's candy persimmon-red Kawasaki Vulcan lay on its side, hastily-discarded next to room 4. He slid me into the back seat of the Buick awkwardly. I backpedaled on my hands across the faded plush tan fabric. Despite the pain ripping into various parts of my body, I'd never been happier. My Cold Company was here, and as close to alive as he'd ever be. As a big plus, I was now feeling pain right down to my toes. I wasn't paralyzed. Yippee!

"Lay still, perfectly still. Are you hearing me? Place your hands here," he advised, moving my hands to my burbling belly wound. "This is the one that yet requires attention."

"She wants you," I told him, my breath-fog making his face a momentary blur. My teeth started chattering. "She's after you."

He hovered inches above my face, shrugging out of his coat. He hadn't been able to calm down enough to retract his fangs yet; in his urgency, he'd nicked his bottom lip. A translucent droplet bloomed there like a pale blue drop of alien oil and my mouth watered in response. Turning my face, I buried my nose in the bench seat.

"Calm down," he said sternly. "Stop moving."

"Harry, you're in danger." I looked at him again, avoided his mouth this time.

"Yes, it is our very good fortune she is not *your* adversary, isn't it? Did you have a terribly nice visit?" Anger furrowed his brow. He hesitated, possibly considering stains, before tucking his coat around me. It smelled lightly of his 4711 cologne under embedded cigarette smoke, and the peculiar scent that marked the immortal, the burnt sugar tang of revenant power.

He whipped into the driver's seat and slammed the door. "Here's hoping blood can be removed from tweed. Hospital?"

I hesitated. "Can't you heal this much damage?"

He craned around in the front seat. "Not without turning you."

It didn't occur to me at the time that this might be a rare, once-only offer. What I was thinking was: *Surgery at the hospital with lots of drugs, or drinking sour blue vein-grease for three days before becoming eternally nocturnal? Decisions, decisions.* "North Suburban's closest. Thornton. Grant Street."

He shoved the Buick into gear and gunned it, firing the heat on full blast. We lurched backward, peeled out of the motel parking, swerving to avoid oncoming traffic.

I gripped the bench seat with one hand while holding my wound with the other. Under my palm, something pulsed, lively-exposed, slippery and wet, hotter than my bare skin. I tried not to think about what it could be.

Harry lived fast, if what he did could be called living. He had a never-ending string of speeding tickets, his sporting tastes ran to skydiving at midnight, bungee and base jumping in the inky dark, and when he night-skied he went black diamond every time. No joining me on the bunny hill with my miner's flashlight strapped around my head. I guess when you're already dead, you're sort of fearless. If my bones knit minutes after a bad break, I might fly down those hills too, head bent into the wind.

I sometimes wondered if he'd been a speed demon while alive, if Guy Harrick, Esquire had been as free-wheeling, if the breathing Lord Guy Harrick, Viscount Baldgate had been hard-living before he'd encountered the elder revenant, Wilhelm Dreppenstedt, who would become his master. If I pried, invariably Harry answered with a sly wink, which was really no answer at all.

We passed a wailing ambulance. I wondered if not staying had been a mistake. Then a brown Lambert County cop car hurtled past, siren screaming, lights flaring in the dark, and I knew: they'd have blamed Harry for the trouble. Lamaze-breathing though pursed lips, I could taste blood on the back on my tongue like a bad penny. Was it mine, or his? Was my body rejecting the essence of UnDeath that burned like a bowl of bad chili in my gut? I didn't want to swallow, but didn't want to spit blood in the back seat of my Buick either. Nauseous and dizzy, I could have been spitting up on an EMS guy. Harry took a wet corner at an insane speed and the car planed.

"Harry!" I cried.

"Such a fuss you make," he said over the noise of the heater. "Keep pressure on the abdominal wound."

"Are you hurrying for me, or to distance yourself from the scene of the crime?" I shouted.

"Right, that was offside!" He glanced over his shoulder with an injured scowl.

"I'll be nicer when I'm not bleeding from the front and back in agony from every jolt!" I said, acerbic through clenched teeth.

"Keep calm and carry on," he sang.

"How did you know I was in trouble?" I asked, mostly to keep my mind off the pain. "Or where I was? I thought you were resting."

"I woke from a distasteful dream before I could sink to full rest. I found you missing, and you didn't answer my texts. You may, on an average day, ignore one or two out of sheer stubbornness, but eventually you surrender to me. Unless, that is, you are up to something nefarious."

He said it as though I had some habit of disreputable activities. Before I could open my mouth to retort, he said: "After my third attempt I traced your GPS and hoped that this fortuitous cloud cover would hold."

I laughed despite the agony ripping through my midsection. I had no idea how to trace someone's GPS, but it didn't surprise me that he did. Most immortals his age were technophobes, change was not in their vocabulary; while Harry's fashion sense might be stuck in the roaring 1920s (change enough for a 435 yr old man) he bought each new gizmo. Thank the Dark Lady above that Harry was a techno-geek.

I was tired, unbelievably tired; it was going to be okay, now that Harry had me. I wanted to descend into the blessed, liquid-black trench of sleep and wallow there, breathless and without the burden of thought, for a solid year.

"Don't!" Harry's voice was a whip-crack. "Stay with me."

"Necromimesis," I slurred. "Really takes it outta ya."

"Insanity," he chided. I wasn't sure if he meant my talk or my spell. "You do realize that your pseudo-death has severed your half of the Bond?"

"So dizzy ..." (*Don't you die yet, Marnie...)*

"I asked you to remain awake, DaySitter." The authority in his husky command prickled my scalp, needling as it crawled down my spine. It was no longer Harry and me chatting; his voice dialed down to *obey your master* as his physical possession of my body pushed, claimed and curled like the slow spiraling pull of an icy whirlpool gripping low in my belly.

Deceptively calm, he repeated: "I asked you to remain awake and you shall. Awake and alert. You were going to tell me what happened, from the beginning?"

The voice was so polite, so pleasant, his English accent gone perfectly crisp as it always did when he was upset: Harry at his most dangerous, dripping honey from his tongue while he lulled you into submission. There was no high quite like being the focus of a revenant's audiomancy.

"Danika Sherlock phoned me," I reported. "She said she knew who had killed Chapel's vic, and she was in danger. I was going to protect her, even before she blackmailed me. I should have known it was a trick. Ninth caliber, my ass." I smirked, my head spinning. "Hey, you know who has a ninth caliber ass? Mark fuckin' Batten, that's who."

Harry huffed impatiently. "Twaddle," he muttered. "Do be serious. You didn't sense that Ms. Sherlock meant you harm?"

"I sensed she was upset, but I had to go: she was going to expose Mark."

Harry muttered, "He seems perfectly capable of getting his own tackle out for all and sundry."

"Besides, fighting made-up heebie-jeebies is a 2-woman job. I should be great at it, since I'm a shark. Maybe I gobble up crime. With my Great White teeth." I gnashed them to demonstrate. "*Chomp, chomp, chomp!*"

"This is getting us nowhere, I see."

"I should have called him, and not that other him." My pulse beat like a drum under my palm in that slippery-hot wound. "But we were scared together, like a big chicken stew."

"Other him? Odd's splutter, do try to make some sense, woman."

"Anyone would be upset about a ninth caliber telekinetic," I said defensively, closing my eyes so the roof of the car would stop spinning.

"*Who* is a ninth caliber telekinetic?"

"No one, not nobody for real." I tried to sit up but it hurt like hell. "No people."

Harry sucked his teeth. "Lord and Lady, your grammar is absolutely appalling."

(Please hurry, miss Baranuik, I need you.) "Don't I always do the right thing, Harry? I mean, to make up for doing all the wrong things?"

"I do believe you are going into shock."

"I can't let him get fired. It's what he loves best. It would kill him. He'd never forgive me."

He lifted his face, scenting the air in the car. "Peripheral perfusion. What's this about getting sacked?"

"She kept stabbing me over and over and over and--" My voice disappeared in a breathy, tremulous whimper. Tears stung my eyes. "I felt my pain and her pain every time she touched me. Hurt so much."

(You and me. We finish it. Together.)

"I know." He was anxiously lighting a cigarette with his monogrammed onyx lighter. "I thought ..."

He'd been close enough to sense the result of the spell. "About that." What else to say? "I'm sorry, Harry. I stuck my neck out, and this happened. I don't learn. I'll never leave the house again."

"What made you think it was wise to fanny about with a bloody necromimesis spell?" He sounded angry, but I couldn't feel him empathically. It was as if some higher power had hit the pause button on my Talent. Where usually my Cold Company's emotions shadowed mine like a 1940s pulp fiction private dick in trench coat and fedora, now my feelings stood alone under the streetlight, exposed and vulnerable. Harry was right: my half of our Bond was hinky.

"I was sure it would work." I tried to focus my vision on the back of the seat but my eyes wanted to cross and waver. "The chances of it failing ..."

"Oh yes," he sputtered. "Absolutely tiddly. Do you know how much power is required to call down the appearance of death, without calling death itself? How you managed not to cock it up is beyond me."

"Maybe you underestimate me, Harry."

He sucked the cig and flicked the butt out the window. "I hardly think so. You should not have retreated in such a drastic manner. Shooting her would have been self defense, love."

"I forgot to bring in my gun," I said, but realized that was his point. It wasn't my habit to whip the damn thing out at the first sign of danger. I never owned a gun before the Jeremiah fiasco. I don't like guns. Well, to be fair, I liked the gun Harry bought me more than others, because it was called a "mouse gun" and I thought that sounded cute. The Beretta Cougar mini normally lived in my bedside table drawer, which I had begun to call "the mouse house", beside a nylon innerpants holster and Mr. Buzz, my purple vibrator.

"I left my card and Agent Chapel's together on the floor beside that impressive pool of blood you spilled in the motel room." He swallowed hard, suppressing a shudder.

"Easy there, big fella."

"Hush, you," he chided, embarrassed. "The police will call Agent Chapel, who will know I was there. He will put it together. Not to worry."

No worries? What would Chapel think happened in that room? That Harry ate Mark's fiancée, probably. And that I helped him. And that maybe we had Kristin Davis, age twelve, as an appetizer.

"I shouldn't be involved," I moaned. "I'm retired."

Harry barked a curt laugh, and I did too, mine ending in a surprised squeak as pain ripped through my middle, squeezing tears from my eyes.

"Guess it's a bit late for that, now." I tried to bring the tough Marnie back, but she'd officially left the building. "Can we pretty please not mention the blackmail or the gun-fail to Batten?"

"We can do whatever you like," Harry said, eyes on the road. It was full dark as we approached Thornton. The headlights tunneled through dusk, slicing the fallen twilight. "Just stay with me, my only love. Stay with me."

I stared up at the fabric lining the roof of the Buick, tracked each long streak of light as the car passed under streetlights and the neon of bars and the glow of tacky fluorescents from store windows. When we veered to a sharp stop in front of the hospital at an angle, artificial light flooded the interior of the car. Harry vaulted out. Nothing I could do but lay there, bleeding and waiting. Seconds later a gurney clattered to the side of the car and Harry held the rear passenger side door open for the attendants. He spoke in confidential tones to them. They probably didn't have enough attention on him to recognize the preternatural strength radiating off of him, marking him distinctly as immortal.

But I felt it, as he wrapped a cool hand around mine, jogging beside the gurney as it crashed into the ER. I felt it.

C9

The sheriff of Lambert County had once been a Denver detective working homicide, and it showed in the shrewd tilt of his gaze. He moved like a blank-faced panther across the hospital room, sinuous and agile, oddly predatory for one of the good guys. If I hadn't checked his pupils for a primal hint of flash I'd have thought him a lycanthrope in human form, but he was one hundred percent man; werekin can't hide the gleam of lycanthropy.

The cop had perfect posture, loose at the joints, a confident bearing that warned other males his body was well-tuned, a trained weapon he knew how to use. I assumed he did a lot of martial arts in whatever spare time a small town sheriff might be afforded. He was young for his office, 35 at most, a true red-head, pale skinned with a smattering of freckles, narrow chin on a boy-next-door face, with swampy green eyes that were an interesting blend of sympathetic and skeptical: *skeptithetic*. If he smiled, I suspected he'd be handsome, though I was pretty sure I wasn't on his Smile-At list just yet. Probably, he thought I was a troublemaker. Maybe he was right. I sipped ice water through a bendy straw and watched him pull up a stool beside the cranked-up hospital bed.

"Marnie Baranuik," he began, rolling one shoulder. A shoulder holster creaked under the whisper of his heavy nylon jacket. The zipper was open in case he had to shoot me. *Verrrry* comforting. "I'm Sheriff Hood. Do you know why I'm here?"

"I'm assuming someone called you about my stabbing," I said between sips. "Did you happen to see two miserable-looking FBI agents out in the hallway? One nerdy beanpole with classic male pattern baldness, the other with big shoulders and a real jerk face?"

He looked at me thoughtfully for a beat before shaking his head.

"No, ma'am, I didn't. And yes, I'm here about the incident at the Ten Springs Motor Inn."

"Incident?" I asked, hearing blame.

"Rodney, the night clerk at the Inn, told me it was a homicide. Bit of a miscommunication." A brief apologetic smile flickered across his mouth. I was right: *Hubba hubba ooh-lala.* "I've since learned that you have a pulse."

He scooted the rubber-footed stool closer and propped his boots on the low rungs, letting his knees fall slightly apart. One of those knees started bouncing. He sucked on something minty, which clicked against the inside of his teeth, and I thought, *nicotine fit.* I've seen my share of them. The left cuff of his pants didn't sit exactly right: ankle holster for a back up gun. I've seen my share of those, too.

"You work for Gold-Drake & Cross out of Portland," he began. "How come you're living in my corner of Colorado?"

"I quit. I didn't want to work with a bunch of weirdoes who actually believe in the supernatural." *Who, plain ole Mundane Me?* I tried my winning-est smile. "I'm just a regular gal."

Hood gave me his cop face, shuttered. The knee-bouncing stilled. "In 2006, you wrote your dissertation on the comparison of black plague and crypt plague in Venice, 1630-1631, the rise of *Yersinia sanguinaria* at the lazarettos, and true and false accusations of vampirism. In 2008 you did a series of training seminars for the FBI and various state law enforcement agencies on preternatural crime prevention and revenant mental health crisis management." His lips did hinted at a smile again. "Revenant?"

My shoulders crept up a notch. "It's the term they prefer."

"You mean vampires," he clarified. "What sort of doctorate do you hold, exactly?"

I gave my best scowl. "Don't profile me, sheriff. It's rude, and I'm sure your mother raised you better."

"She did," he said pleasantly, like he had all the time in the world to play games with me. I certainly wasn't going anywhere, connected to tubes and beeping machinery, and unable to stand up on my own.

"I know damn well what I wrote my dissertation on. How much of my life did you research?"

"Got a hefty file. Looks like I'm in for a night of heavy reading. How about you save me some time, tell me what's not in there?"

"You're not going to write anything down?" I asked. "For your incident report?"

"You haven't really told me anything yet." The smile reappeared and I was rewarded this time with a hint of straight white teeth. My brain melted like butter left on a hot stovetop.

"Well, I will. I intend to. Tell you, I mean. Every thing of the truth." *What the hell am I even talking about?* "You're going to want this on paper."

"Maybe so," he mused, scratching the back of his neck. "Since you're about to tell me "every thing of the truth"."

He fished around for a notebook in his pocket that looked like it had never been used, clicked a brand new pen. Not a lot of serious crime in Lambert County.

I shifted in the pillows propping me slightly upright, and tried not to think of staples clawing flesh together and sutures keeping skin in a taut line. Post-surgery painkillers kept the pain at a safe distance, but I could almost hear it pacing like an impatient Attila the Hun considering the distant walls of Constantinople.

"One huge waste of your time, coming right up," I warned him, taking a deep cleansing breath. "My name is Marnie-*Jean* because my mother likes hyphenated names and the old cologne Jean Nate. I enjoy setting fires in a woodstove. Conversely, I'm afraid of BBQ grills; I'm sure the propane tank is going to explode and take my face right off. I'm also afraid of home invasions, clowns, Santa Claus, and the tooth fairy. I mean, what does she use those teeth for, anyway? It's disturbing, when you think about it."

Hood made no notes. I guess I hadn't said anything good yet. When I launched into the layman's explanation of my psychic Talents, and my former position at GD&C, Hood's pen moved but his eyes never left my face. Neat trick. He searched my eyes, his own face revealing nothing, then surprised me with a thoughtful question.

"If you know stuff just by touching things, doesn't that get a little ... busy in your head?"

Relief—validation perhaps—flooded me; for a second I thought I might embarrass myself by welling-up. I showed him my bare hands. "Usually I wear leather gloves all day, inside and out, to block influxes of information."

"We didn't find any gloves at the scene." So he'd been to the scene, check. I wondered if Harry's motorcycle was in evidence also. Boy, would he be ticked.

"Maybe she took them?" *Like she took my hair. And very nearly my life.* "I took them off. They were on the floor beside the bed last I saw." Or did Harry take them? I had a vague feeling he might have, but it all seemed foggy.

"Can't you "tell" where they are?" He wiggled his fingers mysteriously.

I shrugged. "I might be able to link to and trace my own possessions. I've never tried it. What I can't do is pull visions out of thin air. That's a clairvoyant. I have to touch something, or feel someone's changes in emotions. I *can* tell when I'm being lied to, 99 percent of the time. She fooled me. No, that's not entirely true: I knew she was pissed off. I misread the depth of her hatred, and I believed she had information, and that she was truly in trouble. Being fooled by a successful liar bothers me like I can't even describe. No one should be able to fool me."

Hood's lips twitched. "Ever thought of becoming a cop?"

"Criminals give me the wobbly-knees." I shook my head. "I do like the law. The law is one of the few things that makes me feel stable. Boundaries are good when the rest of you feels ready to fly apart."

Hood gave another unexpectedly understanding nod, and I tried to probe at his aura and see if he was faking the sympathy. I couldn't feel him. Lord and Lady, what the hell had I done to myself? Meanwhile he was watching expectantly, pen poised.

"Thanks to my partner, I've developed a strong sense of smell. I bet you didn't know that tulips have what revenants call an underscent. It's mild, kind of citrusy. I also like over-cooked roast beef, sun-warmed Key limes and Canadians."

"Canadians in general, or just the way they smell?"

"Canadians smell fantastic," I deadpanned. Hood half-smiled; I don't think he wanted to like me but I was winning him over. "I drink more espresso than is healthy and will undoubtedly die, de Balzac-like, of caffeine poisoning. I cannot say no to a cookie. Sometimes when I'm alone I sing old Monty Python songs in the bath. And at the moment, I have titanium staples where my belly button used to be." I shook my head. "But you don't need to know any of this. You don't need to know about my irregular periods or my crush on Wil Wheaton. So why don't you tell me what you're looking for?"

"You were injured in Buffalo on your first official FBI case." He watched me without blinking. "Gun shot wounds. The reports said you were shot by a vampire serial killer named Jeremiah Prost while you were working as a "preternatural forensic consultant" for the PCU. How did he escape?"

"Everyone's got theories on my failure. Why ask me?"

"Maybe I like the sound of your voice. Besides, I didn't say it was your failure; you were one of many on that team, correct?"

My shoulders fell. I told him a concise version of what happened, in Buffalo and at the Ten Springs Motor Inn, including the FBI but leaving out the sex and the vomit. Then I added the vomit, because I was pretty sure he'd seen that at the scene. I left Batten's name out of it, and implied that Danika was resentful of me but left it at professional jealousy. I hoped he bought it.

He didn't appear to buy a single word of it.

"Let's see if I wrote this down correctly," Hood said. The smile was gone and I didn't like his tone anymore, but I guess that was fair; probably he didn't like my story much. "You're a witch. And a psychic."

"Specifically, an ex-forensic psychometrist with secondary clairempathy who used to work for Gold-Drake & Cross. Third Floor, retrocognition."

He clarified: "And you live with a vampire."

"A revenant. There's no such thing as a human psychic who *isn't* DaySitting an immortal. The source of the Blue Sense is the revenant. You wield psi through the revenant. That's the only way it works. Where have you been living?"

"In my own quiet corner of this great state," he replied, and I picked up the undertone: *where there are no monsters.* I got a brief flash of understanding; Hood had left Denver for some small town serenity, and he wasn't too impressed that I was slamming it from wall to wall. "So this, uh, revenant buddy of yours, he's 400 years old?"

"Approximately. You don't ask an immortal how old he is. It's bad form, and could get you backhanded through a wall."

He exhaled slowly through his nostrils, and I thought *ginger dragon.* I bet he wished he'd sent a deputy to answer this call. "At 1:30 you were called by another psychic named Danika Sherlock." He tapped his pen. "As in Sherlock Holmes?"

"I didn't pick the crazy twat's name." I sighed. "And coming from a man named Robin Hood, I should think you'd understand: sometimes bad names just fucking happen."

A flinch around his eyes told me that even if I was wrong, his parents had done him no favors; he'd heard it ten thousand times. "I didn't tell you my first name," he said. "And Rob's short for Robert."

I offered him my open hand, as though for a handshake. He hesitated only for a second before laying his own huge paw in my small one. The skin between our palms crawled instantaneously as the spark of psi awoke to my command.

"Which is a partial lie," I announced flatly. "Your name *was* Robin. Your father had a closeted homoerotic crush on Errol Flynn, though it was no secret to your immediate family. It made you feel squinky, so you legally changed your name to Robert in 1997. April." I smiled at him. "A Tuesday. It was raining. And while I just made you feel violated right down to your toenails, you will successfully not show it on your face."

A thoroughbred version of spooked excitement thundered through him. I broke contact, laid my hands in my lap, and continued, "Look, I'm the stab-*ee* here, not the stabber. Why are you giving me a hard time?"

"I'm not trying to give you a hard time, Mrs.—"

"Miss." *Why make that correction?*

"You arrived at the Ten Springs Motor Inn at," he consulted his notes, unnecessarily, possibly to humour me. "Approximately 2 pm. At which point she invited you into unit four and stabbed you in the back, causing you to drop your coffee."

"And now she owes me two bucks."

"You were both helping the FBI work on a murder case in Lower Downtown? Why are the FBI involved?"

"It's a suspected preternatural crime, and the PCU was called in from Quantico. I only looked at a few pictures. She was assisting SSA Gary Chapel and Special Agent Mark Batten, who may or may not show up here any minute."

I didn't know whether they would or not. Last time I'd been injured, Chapel came every other day until my release; Batten hadn't shown. Considering this time, it was his fiancée who stabbed me, and she was pissed because of his cock's activities, I thought the least he could do is put in a few minutes at my bedside. Did Hallmark make a "sorry my Love Muffin stabbed you repeatedly until she thought you were dead" card? On second thought, maybe I didn't want to see him.

I realized that Sheriff Hood was reading the whole story as it crossed my face.

"Ok, fine! I nailed her man, OK?" I threw my hands up. "I'm a disgrace to society! Are you writing this down, word for word? Bowlegged slut can't keep her knees together. Go ahead. Write it!"

He leaned back slightly, letting surprise flood his face. Big shoulders shook under taupe nylon; I realized he was trying not to laugh. He didn't write a word. He just bounced his knee some more and gave me space to ramble.

"So she found out, and decided I was the worst person on Earth. I get that, I do. Hate my guts, fine, but don't stab them."

He waited, face gone cop-blank again.

"In my defense, I had no idea that Agent Jerkface was engaged," I pointed out. "He never bothered to tell me, and I can't read him psychically. So how is that my fault?"

"Agent Jerkface is ..."

"Ah, fuck," I straw-stirred the ice in angry circles in my big plastic cup. "Agent Batten. I know it's wrong. We worked together. Briefly. We don't even like each other. I'm not his type. *Hel-lo!* Do I look like a Barbie doll?" I sulked, stabbed at the ice chips with my bendy straw. He was staring curiously at my forehead. I wondered what the hell he was looking at. "I don't even know why it happened. We were under a lot of stress, and he didn't like needing to use my Talents and I didn't like his attitude—which, by the way, is as close to asshole as you can get without actually being a sphincter—and we were stuck in a car on stake-outs for hours, then stuck in a cramped motel room in bloody Cheektowaga for days, overtired, keyed up, always fighting …" I drifted off helplessly.

I looked up to see if he got what I meant. The keen glint in his eyes said he knew exactly how it must have happened; he nodded almost imperceptibly.

"So anyways, about room four: I faked dead with a mimicry spell called necromimesis. When psychobeast left, I called 911. Harry showed first, and drove me to the hospital. We should have stayed, but I was afraid of the cops getting the wrong idea about the revenant and the blood if I passed out unable to explain. Besides, Harry drives much faster than an ambulance."

"Go back to the faking dead part?"

"Bit of witchcraft involved. I'm not really sure how I pulled it off. Necromimesis is sort of out of my league."

He looked at me doubtfully. "Could you do it right now, show me?"

"No," I said truthfully. "I couldn't. I don't have any of the stuff …"

Hood took a clear plastic evidence baggy out of his inside jacket pocket, dangling it. In it was my onyx. "This yours, then?"

"Yes. Still, even with that, the bark and herbs are just symbolic objects for focus. The kind of energy output required for that level of spell is only drummed up by someone like me during periods of extreme stress. Energy, focus, belief, will, those are the real ingredients. This level of magic leaves a taint on your aura. I wouldn't attempt it again, it's not exactly clean."

Hardly a proud moment for a white witch, but death wasn't all black. It was the very definition of middle ground, the grey area, limbo, death being neither good nor evil. I'd only interrupted my own life, and I didn't think one emergency spell was crossing over to "official dabbling".

There was a soft knock at the door and we both turned our attention to Agent Chapel's long-jawed Great Dane face peering in.

"Pardon me, sheriff. We'll just wait in the hall until you're done."

We? My waffling heart flowed from boiling to frigid, flailed about like it was attempting a drunken River Dance under my ribcage, and then flushed back to hot, unable to decide between avid and avoidant. Probably my heart had finally lost its frigging mind. I no longer wanted to see Mark Batten walk through that door. There was a distinct chance that I was going to get blamed for this whole mess. It wasn't my fault, but since when did that matter?

"I'm about finished here." Hood stood, pushing the stool away with the back of his thick legs.

When Chapel disappeared, Hood scratched at the back of his neck with the end of his pen, his eyes playing down the length of the sheet over my legs. I picked up subtle flickers of his curiosity. It was wildly inappropriate, but he didn't seem aware he was doing it so I let it go.

He said, "Have you ever taken any self-defense classes?"

"No, but I should," I acknowledged. "Why do you ask?"

"Top of mind when I see an attack like this. Everyone should have at least some idea of how to fend an attacker off. I'm sort of biased," he said, nodding. "I teach police defensive tactics."

"Hence the hot bod," came out of my mouth before I even knew I was going to say it. Horrified, I stuck my straw in my mouth and pretended great interest in my ice water so I didn't have to meet his eyes.

He was quiet for a moment, assessing. "So when you played dead on the floor, you're saying you somehow slowed your heartbeat and held your breath? Autogenic training, some Zen thing?"

"That's not at all what I said," I looked up into his perfectly human eyes. We stared each other down for a minute, the witch and the skeptic.

"Just clarifying," he said amiably. The smile made another appearance, at which point I could have sworn I melted and slid into a puddle of mush beside the bed; it lingered lightly on his lips, like he wasn't sure whether to call a shrink for me, or himself. He made to leave.

"And ..." His boots scuffed the floor as he stopped suddenly. "When you called your revenant, did you do it with ..." He made a wand-motion in the air that he must have seen Mickey Mouse make in the Sorcerer's Apprentice. "Mystical abilities?"

"No," I said sourly. "I called his cell phone."

"Right. Blackberry?"

"iPhone," I sighed.

He nodded as though this made perfect sense, stroked his chin. "I'd like to speak to this Lord Dreppenstedt. Have him come into my little station in Ten Springs and make a statement? Or I could drop by your place?"

"Number 1, on Shaw's Fist. It's the last cabin in the row, or the first, if you're one of those annoying glass-half-full types. It would be better to come after dark."

"After dark," he repeated. "Because your buddy's a real live vampire, right?"

"Revenant," I reminded. "And I wouldn't call him *live,* exactly."

Hood paused in the doorway, tucking his notebook away inside his jacket. "Are you actually bowlegged?"

"No, but it sounded good at the time," I said miserably, sinking back into my pillows.

"Well, for what it's worth," he started, and then apparently thought better of it. He had that charming redhead habit of turning helplessly pink when he was embarrassed and a blush crept up his throat. He smiled it away, full-beam this time; it was dizzying how gorgeous it made him. "I'll check back with you if I have any further questions."

I found my voice by some miracle. "You do that, sheriff."

C10

There were so many things I should have seen looking back, proving once and for all that, as I suspected, I am an idiot. The phone call itself, for instance: of course neither Fed would have given out my private unlisted number. I hadn't yet figured out how she had it: could a failing clairvoyant ferret out phone numbers, or did she have friends in low places?

That nonsense about no cell reception, what a crock. I'd gotten Harry's text message no problem. She certainly had no trouble calling my cell phone at Shaw's Fist. I managed to get Chapel on the line with no issues. That should have been a red flag. *Stupid, Marnie, verrrrry stupid.*

Her story about the elder revenant, feeling him moving in his room, another clue that should have tipped me off, if I'd been thinking of anything other than Hardass Batten: Sherlock was a clairvoyant, a Witness, not a Feeler. Besides, even empaths didn't feel things over long distances. She could see things, no doubt, if she'd still had her power. Which she didn't, except for "tiny flickers" …

The eyeballs. I'd been mucking about with that damn jar, a baker's dozen of perfect, tiny newt eyeballs on and off all day. She'd plucked that scene out of my office, hadn't she, with her "flickers"? That's why she'd used the story about an eyeball-collecting DaySitter. Stealing eyeballs didn't sound too far-fetched to someone who had a whole jar of them.

Harry had gone home to check the cabin. Chapel and the sheriff were already there. There was a warrant out for Danika Sherlock's arrest, attempted murder. There were two bored plain clothes cops from the Boulder PD outside the door to the ward, and Batten had now settled into a sturdy plastic chair in the corner of my room, looking like he planned to stay there all night.

I took a deep breath. "So the wedding should be nice. June's popular for weddings. I've always thought I'd pick April Fool's Day. Seems like that kind of monkey business would be cosmic good luck."

He stared at me, his face unreadable. "What wedding are we talking about?"

I sucked my teeth. "Yours, jackass."

"My wedding," he clarified.

"Yeah, and hey, thanks for telling me you had a fiancée before we got naked. If I'd found out afterwards that might have been real awkward for me." I grit my molars together.

"I'm not getting married."

"Well, I guess not now, considering she's a nutbag. So when are you going to break it off with Sherlock? After sentencing?" I reached for my ice water and the movement yanked a staple in my stomach. I pressed my other hand to the wound, refusing to wince aloud. He must have seen something on my face regardless.

"You all right?"

"If you so much as reach a hand out to help me," I warned, "I'll beat you like rented mule."

He steepled his fingers in silent consideration of my attitude, did his watching-crazy-person-until-he-was-sure-it-was-safe thing. Sadly, it was a look I was used to getting.

"Why would think I'm engaged to Danika Sherlock?" he finally said.

"You're not?"

"No."

"Were you ever?"

"No."

I boggled, flabbergasted. "Then she's absolutely bat-shit crazy. Did you date her?"

He shook his head *no*. "Who told you we were engaged?" He leaned forward. "Was it Harry?"

"Harry never lies to me. Never," I said absolutely. "Danika said it. In Buffalo, after the shooting, at the hospital."

"That was seven, eight weeks ago?"

"Six weeks, two days."

"I just met her. Mid-November. Three weeks ago."

There was a confused twinge scrunching up the front of my brain. I put my ice water to my forehead and let the coolness from the plastic cup spread into my skin. "OK, hold on. I'm missing something."

"What happened in the hospital?"

"She brought me yellow roses. Told me she was your fiancée. Said she hoped I felt better soon. She went to the vending machine for me and got me a Dr. Pepper. I remember it distinctly because she wouldn't let me pay her for it."

"How did she know you were in the hospital?"

I smiled at him sourly. "You mean if she didn't see it on TV or hear it at the office? She is, or was, a second degree clairvoyant. Retrocognition. She can perceive past events, people, places, objects from a distance. If she wanted to know where I was, all she had to do was meditate on it."

"Why did she make up being engaged to me when she hadn't met me yet? And why didn't you just ask me if it was true or not?"

Because I'm a fucking coward. I sank sadly in my pillows. This had nothing to do with Batten. This woman hated my guts, and not because I'd had sex with some Fed. This was personal. Batten was a weapon used to hurt me. What I couldn't imagine was *why*. What the hell had I done to incur homicidal wrath? Was this about taking Harry? Or was that also just a way to hurt me?

Batten clued in. "She came to see you at your worst. Injured. Prone, in the hospital."

"She must have searched the events of my recent past for something that was making me happy." My eyes strayed to his lap and I dragged them away, blushing gloomily. "So she could take it away, kick me when I was down."

I avoided his gaze but felt it searching me. If he didn't know why I was so pissed at him before, he knew now. All this time, I'd been furious for no reason. He wasn't a liar, or a cheat, or a jackass. Well, he might be a jackass, the jury was still out on that one. But I didn't have the hots for a lying cheater; maybe my taste in men wasn't as horrible as I thought. It was too much to think about. I resolved to deal with it later.

I hurried on: "She must have convinced herself it was true in that demented little skull of hers. Three weeks later, she shows up in your life for real."

"She came to Virginia with her lawyers, asking about getting some footage in and around Quantico for her reality TV show. We turned her down; she hadn't done work for the PCU at that time. But it was amicable."

"Those pictures you showed me this morning," I pointed out. "She was there."

"We called GD&C on our flight in. They said they had a psychic living in Denver, said she could be there in 15 minutes. I assumed they meant you. She showed. We made her leave her TV crew in the van. She wasn't pleased, but she did it."

"She's been living in Colorado?"

"Think you better tell me exactly what happened in that motel room."

I didn't want to get you fired so I got myself stabbed.

"Please." I shook my head, pushing my water aside. "I'm sick of hearing myself say it."

"You went to the Ten Springs Motor Inn because Sherlock called and said she had a clue ..." he encouraged, but his eyes had narrowed in on something in my face, reaching *shrewd* with alarming rapidity.

"The End. Please. I've over-explained to two men already."

"Sheriff Hood," he listed.

"And Harry."

"You said two men. Harry's not a man." He could never resist.

"Well, I know for a fact he has a penis," I pointed out, feeling petty. "I've seen it about eight hundred thousand times. Penis still equals male, right?" A little white lie; I've never seen Harry naked, not once in ten years together. Harry would never get caught with his pants down.

"He's not human."

"He's human-*ish,*" I established. I didn't like getting sucked in, and Batten's jaw was starting to do his clench-y thing; he didn't seem in the mood to let it go. "Why not date Sherlock?"

As always, there was a disturbing lack of feeling in his corner, like I was facing a projection of a person but not the real thing, an empty wall with a handsome reflection.

"She's too ..." His lips puckered in a bizarre imitation and he cupped his hands in front of his chest. The result was so ridiculous that I nearly choked on surprised laughter. I huddled up protectively around the pain and slapped the spare white hospital blanket.

"Stop!" I gasped. "Don't make me laugh, tool."

"Sorry," he said, but a slow smile had spread across his mouth, reaching his eyes: a genuine Mark Batten smile, just for me. "You don't think she looks a bit ...overdone?"

"Guys love her." I informed him sternly. "You're breaking ancient traditional man-rules by not being completely senseless about her."

"Sorry. When I grab an ass I like it to have some—" He broke off with a cough as the door opened and a nurse came in.

I grinned at him steadily as the nurse came to the bed side with a tray.

"Yes, Agent Batten? By all means, finish that intriguing sentence."

"A discussion for another time, Miss Baranuik," he replied smoothly, his face perfectly blank, easily business-like. An unexpected memory slid into my brain thick and sweet like honey, the sound of him going over the brink, panting *oh baby, oh fuck yes,* hotly into the crook of my neck while the bathroom door slammed repeatedly against drywall. I dropped my eyes to his crotch to look for signs of stirring. He gave me a warning glare behind the nurse's back, stood up suddenly and went to finger the curtains open to look down at the rear parking lot, glittering with ice under a full winter moon.

The nurse prepared to take blood and I said, "Uh, nurse, wrong vials. You need gold caps for mine."

To her credit, the nurse's eyes widened only momentarily then she said, "All righty, hun, I'll be right back then. Don't you go anywhere."

I gave the required polite chuckle. When the nurse had gone, Batten asked, "Gold caps?"

"Anyone who feeds a revenant directly from the vein gets residual saliva in their system. Undead saliva contains a minute amount of their telomerase. The medical community still thinks they need to keep those samples conspicuously marked and separate from "normal" blood from "normal" people. Didn't you wonder why I'm stuck at the end of ICU in isolation? You watch: she'll come back in a Hazmat suit."

"I'm sure I should know what telomerase is? Vampire disease?"

"I'd give you a bio-chem lesson if I thought there was any chance you were honestly interested." He nodded without a dig, which surprised the truth out of me. "When normal human cells divide, the chromosomes lose telomeres at the ends. This is related to aging, the loss of telomeres. Revenant telomer*ase* is a protein complex which replaces the tips, halting deterioration of chromosomes during cell division, a supernatural version of the regular stuff found in human cells, produced in the gastrosanguinem in their stomachs. It flows through their bodies when they feed. It's why they never change, one source of their immortality."

Batten's lip curled slightly. "And this stuff is in you?"

"Tiny bits, yeah. It's like when you swig from a can of Coke, and there's backwash left behind. When Harry feeds," I felt suddenly exposed, "He leaves traces of it in my veins. End of lesson."

The nurse came back in, and to her credit she neither hesitated or slowed her stride. She hadn't even doubled up on the latex gloves. After taking my blood, she got out the cuffs to take my blood pressure.

Batten stared out the window at the dark parking lot for a long time while the nurse pumped up the cuff and put a stethoscope to the inside of my elbow. Nearby in my purse, my cell phone started grinding out Bobby Brown's My Prerogative. Horrified, I snatched the bag and frantically dug for the illusive noise maker.

The nurse's eyebrow wanted to creep up but she got it under control. "You'll have to turn that off."

Batten smirked at me over his shoulder, like he'd somehow figured out my dirtiest secret. I flipped the phone shut, wishing Harry would stop messing with my ringtones; if he wore underwear I would give him the a wedgie of a lifetime.

Batten said, "This shit shouldn't have happened."

"I didn't pick the ringtone," I told him.

"I meant the altercation. You should have called me. You had no business going out there."

Altercation? That sounded a lot like a tango, for which two parties were needed. A mysterious valve slapped open in my stomach dumping acid like a breached dam. "I gotta call you before I leave my house, now?"

"When it has to do with me or my job, yes."

"You don't get it."

"Fill me in," he said tightly, folding his big forearms over his chest. My jaw clacked shut, and I backtracked.

"I thought it was the capital-R right thing."

"Right thing for who?"

You, jackass! "Everyone."

"Fail to see how getting stabbed was the right thing for you."

"Oh, I suppose you would have saw that coming?"

"You're supposed to be psychic!" he shouted, ignoring the nurse's tearing Velcro and alarmed retreat. Guess my blood pressure reading would have to wait.

"I'm not that kind of psychic."

"You should have called me."

"I called Chapel!"

"I would have asked better questions," he threw in my face. "Like: "where are you?"" *Point: Batten.*

"This wasn't my fault!"

"I never said it was," he belted back, his voice vaulting octaves. "Why do you fight me about every goddamned thing?"

"Because the minute you open your mouth, you turn into a ginormous dill hole."

"And you turn into a neurotic little twerp." He paced. "Just hear what I'm actually saying, Marnie, without imagining insults between the lines."

"I don't do that!"

"You never actually listen to me."

"Well, right back at ya, jackass." I settled back against my pillows carefully, ignoring the pull of stitches here and staples there.

Batten stalked back to the window, speechless with glittery-eyed anger. The silence that followed was a mire of unspoken questions, unexpressed feelings, and I understood none of it. He finally said, "You're not done hating me, obviously."

I think I preferred hating him; it was a lot less complicated. "I don't like cheats and liars, especially ones I can't read."

"You can't read me?"

I'd told him that already, more than once. I didn't know why he needed to hear it again. "After what Sherlock said, I thought you were a sleaze-ball."

He didn't turn around to face me. "Don't know me as well as you think."

An ugly truth. We'd known one another only a week before we drove each other into a frothing argument that got twisted into clutching, thieving, frenetic sex up against a bathroom door. That's *so* not me. If he hadn't taken that first rushing stride towards me with his hand out, I'd have had time to remember that I don't screw guys I don't know. But his hungry forward motion sparked something primitive in the non-thinking animal part of my brain, and touching him back seemed like the next obvious step. Of course, my version of touching him back was an attempted slap across his face, but it quickly turned into an eager pull to my open mouth, my lips quivering for contact. Guess my "oh no ya don't" needs some work. *Sexual chemistry: one. Self-control: zilch.*

Between that romp and the next, we barely spoke two words to one another that weren't directly related to the case, and even then it was tight and sparing. We pretended we were focused on the job, stake-outs done in strained silence, neither of us trusting ourselves to say the right thing. I thought he was trying to make believe it didn't happen.

"After she visited, I was sure you didn't return my calls or come to see me in the hospital in Buffalo because you'd been busted."

He spun around, frowning. "I *was* there. Three days, then the PCU got called to Philadelphia and we had to go."

"I didn't see you," I argued.

"They had you on some pretty heavy drugs. Don't remember any yellow roses in your room. Chapel brought you Godiva chocolates. Was hoping you'd sober up enough to offer me one, but you never opened them."

"I was awake?" What had I said? *Oh God.*

"We had a few odd talks. You weren't making a lot of sense. Ranting about Barbary pirates, and lazarettos in Venice, and vampires behind the scenes of the Velvet Revolution. Figured you were out of it." He jerked a thumb behind at the door. "Are you going to remember that I was here tonight, or should I write a note on the back of your hand?"

"All right," I snapped. "It's irrelevant, I guess. It's better this way."

It wasn't at all better. Better was exactly the wrong word for it. But it was the only thing that made sense.

Batten quietly showed me the back of his head. What he was thinking, or staring at through the glass, I couldn't imagine. But he was still here and that was something. "This hostility toward me, you sure it's all yours?" he asked carefully.

"What the hell does that mean?"

"Harry's back."

"My emotions are entirely my own."

He made a noise like he wasn't so sure. "You seem determined to write me off. I'm sure Harry's on board with that idea. Maybe the idea's his."

"It hardly matters; the Feds aren't going to dissolve their fraternization rules any time soon." *Then again, if Sherlock carries through with her threat to expose our fling, neither of us have a career to worry about.*

If I could touch him again without getting him in trouble, or without getting hurt ...I distracted myself from that dangerous line of thinking with a brief revenge fantasy, during which I carved a hunk slowly out of Sherlock's impossibly tiny ass. I felt my lips curl up, and it felt ugly, cruel. But can you blame me? I had staples in my guts because of her. Having her arrested wasn't going to be nearly so satisfying.

"Speaking of rules," Batten started. "When Harry was in the hall before, I think I made a gaffe."

"Shocking," I deadpanned. "You keep jerkin' his chain, I will let him eat you."

"I asked if he was here for a snack. He seemed upset."

"Ya think?" I pointed my straw at him. "Harry's got indescribable patience, born of four centuries tolerating people's quirks. But when that patience runs out, he holds a grudge like nobody else. He'll either thrive on it, or chew your chest open. Neither will be pleasant."

He ignored that. "He said: "even if I were so selfish, it is not allowed." What'd he mean by that?"

"If your DaySitter can't provide you with enough while maintaining their own health, it's more honourable for the revenant to go hungry."

He snorted softly. "There's an honourable way to use someone as food?"

"As a matter of fact there is, smartass. You've killed how many immortals? You still don't know a goddamned thing about them." I glowered. "Noob."

Batten scratched along the underside of his chin, where an evening beard was shadowy. "Tell me."

"The Bonded revenant must consider the DaySitter's well-being before his own. They've been known to go into starvation mode if their partner is ill, and boy is that ugly."

"Uglier than ..." He let it go with a chesty rattle followed by a cough. "Ugly how?"

I folded my arms and waited until the argument had gone out of his face completely, until I thought he was ready to be civil. Caesar Millan would have called it a calm submissive state. I wondered if there was a Jackass Whisperer.

"A starving revenant enters lich-form, shrivels up, gets all ropey and sinewy. Think Harry's a monster now? Tie him up and don't feed him, then you'll see monster."

"I wouldn't do that." He must have thought it necessary to point that out to me. I nodded that I accepted his word.

"I've seen a sketch of a starving rev. It was like a human died weeks ago and someone forgot to tell it to lie down."

"Sketch, you mean an artist's interpretation?"

"In a doctor's file. A sketch because you can't take photographs of revs, they don't show up on film, and they tend to fry digitals. This patient was starving because his DaySitter was in a coma and he had become depressed, refused to feed from anyone else."

"So give him something for the depression?

"That would have worked, if he had fed."

"Animal blood?"

"Doesn't cut it. Only human blood works. Once a revenant feeds, he has a circulatory system. But how is Prozac going to help if you have no working circulatory system?" I pointed out. "Starving can drive them completely, irreversibly insane. A lich-form revenant gone too long without resting and feeding becomes like a rabid animal. Or he goes the other way, becomes melancholy, suicidal."

"So what happened to the sketch vamp?"

"When his DaySitter died in hospital without ever regaining consciousness, he ..." Thinking of my Harry, I remembered my manners ... "Antony Brossard Ledesma walked to the nearest baseball diamond, six miles from the hospital in Pittsburg, sat on the pitcher's mound in the snow, and waited for sunrise."

A flicker of sadness crossed Batten's eyes. I said nothing, lest I break the bubble of momentary empathy I saw. Maybe there was hope for him yet. He rubbed his mouth with one hand, deep in thought.

"Antony was eight hundred years old," I continued carefully. "In that time, he'd observed the invention of the printing press, the microscope, the first steam engines, submarines and hot-air balloons, vaccines, batteries, rockets and locomotives, the pianoforte and friction matches, sewing machines and streetcars, ether and nitroglycerine, dynamite and typewriters ..." I drifted, but there was no lack of fascination in the vampire hunter's gaze; in fact, he looked like he'd never thought such things. I gave him a chance to disappoint me. He didn't. Encouraged, I added with an envious smile: "Steam turbines, combustion engines, telephones, microphones, fountain pens and elevators, X-rays and airplanes, motion pictures and neon. Helicopters. Microwaves. Nuclear energy. In the end, none of it meant a damn thing to him, not when he lost his Bond. Antony sat in the cold Pittsburg night waiting; he had hours to reconsider. When the sun rose, the eyes that had witnessed both the invention of the steam turbine in 1629 and high-temperature superconductors in 1986 lasted less than a minute. He was a waist-high pillar of ash in 25 seconds. According to witnesses, his final shriek could be heard for twelve blocks."

"Were you there?"

I hadn't been, but I'd met him once, in Portland, when his DaySitter Kathy worked 2nd Floor. I didn't think I wanted to share that with Kill-Notch Batten, so I told him instead: "Immortals don't talk of suicide by daylight; they say "he cast no shadow that morning." Harry told me that, the evening after Antony's death."

He looked away from me. When he spoke, his voice was thick. "Vamps all do this lich-form thing?"

"There's a healthy option: wraith-state, a big feed followed by a long sleep, like a hibernating bear. Their casket is absolutely necessary for this kind of rest, and soil from their rebirthing, the place they were turned. Harry would chose that option, if he felt it necessary to deny himself for a long period, he'd never risk going lich. Besides, Harry clings to long-forgotten tenets. He's an Olympic-grade clinger."

"Are there many other vampire etiquette rules?"

"How do you not know this? Of course revenants have rules." I wiggled my fingers towards the water pitcher with a request in my eyes. He obliged, refilling my cup. "Even packs of pink-assed baboons have rules among the members of the troop."

"Who sets these laws?"

"If I remember high school biology correctly, the baboon with the biggest, pinkest ass."

He sighed impatiently. I grinned around my straw, sucked frigid water. "The upper echelon. Immortal hierarchy. They have a royal family. You knew that."

"Tell me."

"Okay fine, play stupid. Very convincing, by the way. There's the father of the revenant race, the Overlord."

"He got a name?"

"Yeah, but it's creepy and I don't think it's a good idea to say it while I have open wounds."

Batten's left eyebrow danced upward as it was prone to do. "What kind of sense does that make?"

"Superstitious nonsensical sense," I agreed with a shrug. "Everyone's allowed to have shit they won't do because it gives them the willies. Like you and spiders. You pound wood through revenant chest cavities without blinking, but you panic and drop your Fries Supreme in your lap when an itty bitty dangles in front of your face? Seriously, what's the dealio?"

"The Overlord, Baranuik ...?" Batten urged, putting his elbow on the arm of the chair and resting his chin in his palm. I couldn't not smile at the regret I saw in his face. He'd inadvertently shown me a moment of abject terror, sandwiched between all his macho posturing and genuine badass heroics. In his horror-struck moment, I had quietly reached across the front seat of the unmarked car and pinched the spider between thumb and forefinger, flicking the smudge of remains into a Kleenex, rolling my eyes while he struggled to regain composure. "The Overlord rules from where?"

I side-stepped. "The Overlord leaves the ruling to a king, the First Turned, who also has a name I don't like to say out loud. And then there are those whom the king made first, the four princes."

He rocketed forward to the edge of his seat. "Just four? Are you sure?"

"So Harry says," I said cautiously, not liking his sudden eager lean.

"Males, all?"

I frowned in thought. "Harry's never mentioned any females, so I guess so. I'm not sure Harry was even supposed to tell me that much, but sometimes I drink absinthe before feeding him to get him drunk off his ass and probe him for secrets."

"A whole royal society of the undead, hunh?" he prodded.

"None you'd wanna meet. Creatures so old, they predate human history."

"How's that possible?" His face had been tuned to *dig for dirt*, and I expected more vamp-bashing was on the back of his tongue waiting for a change to spring out.

I debated telling him. He always seemed to maintain a detachment from reality. In the face of a demon, I had no doubt that Mark Batten could maintain that he didn't believe in demons. I'm sure when he blew the heads off werewolves with silver bullets, he was sure there were no such things.

So why not tell him that the original revenant, the progenitor of undeath, was a fallen angel who had flanked Satan in the War in Heaven before the Dark Mother rose beside God, her Consort, and backhanded a third of the angelic host from heaven?

Because I didn't need Kill-Notch Batten armed with the knowledge that the ancestral source of Harry's power, passed down blood-to-blood, was actually a demonic, soul-devouring school chummy of the devil, that's why. My Wiccan power was blessed and light, but Harry's immortality was hell-wrought; though he avoided using it for evil, it was miles from petunias and puppy tails. Sounded like an opportunity for a messy spiritual debate with a man I would peg as an atheist anyway. How could Batten listen to the truth about immortals, without considering then the possibility of things he'd always shunned? He barely bought the whole Blue Sense/psychic power thing, and I hadn't yet been able to impress him with it, since I couldn't read him at all. He certainly thought my witchcraft was irrational baloney. Now he wanted the history of the primeval powers without me going into the mystical? Impossible.

Batten rubbed his face, looking as tired as I felt. "So who's this Overlord?"

The Overlord's true demon name sprang to the tip of my tongue then; it stung like hot cinnamon candies on Valentine's Day, sweet and excruciating, the kind that make your spit into lava and blister the inside of your cheeks. It niggled the front of my skull, writhed like a maggot preparing to molt. I crammed my eyes shut.

Dear heavens, is He listening? I saw the word forming on the insides of my eyelids, lighting up like a sparkler scrawling in near darkness, capital *A,* capital *S* ...I forced my mind onto something neutral: macaroni and cheese. There. Thoughts of comfort carbs, the ultimate demon-be-gone.

"Can we talk about it another time, please? These painkillers are making me seriously loopy."

"Sure. We'll have plenty of time."

I didn't have time to ask what the hell he meant by that. Harry swept into the room; the sight of my Star Trek thermos in his hand cheered me up; the night was finally looking up.

C11

Harry was smiling, showing lots of white teeth, no fang. Batten averted his eyes like he always did; I think he was afraid that if he saw fangs he'd have no choice but to face that, no matter how many revenants he'd dusted, he was intimidated by this one. I'm not sure he could live with that. Or maybe he sensed Harry might try to mindfuck him with his unearthly gaze; Batten should know I wouldn't allow that. Not in public, anyway.

As though egged-on by Batten's discomfort, Harry's aura did a cold boil, a visible phenomenon. More than just his otherworldly presence filled the room: as always I could smell menthol cigarettes under his light, clean-smelling 4711 cologne. As he approached the bed with impossible refinement, I knew he was showing off. Harry didn't have to move like that. It was a conscious choice and he was making a point: here comes power infernal and immortal. How could any human compare?

Harry was dressed like he'd been back on his Kawasaki so I guessed it wasn't impounded. Big motorcycle boots, this time the leather as shiny and clean as the buckles. I wondered how long he'd been in the lobby shining the street salt off of them. His mid-length over coat flapped open to reveal black Levis hugging lean powerful legs. Black leather biking gloves looked so startlingly like part of a murderer's kill kit on his death-pale hands that I could all but feel them squeezing my throat. A grey cashmere scarf snaked several times around his neck reflected the battleship grey of his eyes. I wondered where his helmet was. Undead or not, you crack your skull open and sandpaper the road with brain tissue, story-time's over.

"Agent Batten. *Bon nuit, trou du cul,*" Harry greeted, mock-tipping an invisible hat. I couldn't be sure, as my French is not good, but I thought Harry called Batten an asshole. He turned and performed a low, sweeping bow at the bed. "How does my lady?"

"I does spiffy, and you?"

"Apart from being heartily distressed by your atrocious grammar, I do very well indeed. As visiting hours have long flown, I cannot stay long. It is pure luck the nurse let me in at all."

Luck, my ass. It was more likely terror; it wasn't like Harry was putting any effort into blending in. The poor nurse was probably twisting security's arms to come flush him back out. I wondered if there had ever been a revenant in this hospital before. Or any hospital in

Colorado for that matter; revenant emergencies don't require human doctors.

Harry handed me the thermos, and palmed two round white vitamins into my hand. "*Doppio* espresso macchiato, dash of cinnamon."

"And suddenly, life is fabulous."

"Because of me, or because of the caffeine?" He knew exactly how relieved I was to see that he was 100% intact and healthy.

I humoured him anyway, downing my pills then beaming up at him. Having his answer, he put his hand inside his coat and pulled out a jubilant bouquet of tulips in a rainbow of petal pink, spring yellow and the vivid orange of tangerine peels.

"Tulips in January?" I exclaimed.

He laid them beside the bed. "For my beloved pet, most anything is possible. Surely fetching her favourite flower is no great task. Am I ...interrupting?" Harry aimed the bristly indictment in Batten's direction.

"Whether you're here or not makes no difference to me, vamp." Batten propped his elbows on the chair's arms and steepled his fingers in front of his mouth.

"After some examination of the evidence, I should think you'll discover how little I care about your existence as well, young man."

"Funny," Batten said with a calm smile. "Got the impression you're threatened by me."

Harry threw back his head and laughed with gusto. The sound of it rose goose bumps and then rubbed them with velvet. Despite the smiling and laughing, the moment was anything but friendly.

Baboons, I observed. One with a big gun and the other with a big mouth, and both with alpha-sized, flaming pink asses.

"Is there anything left of the cabin, Harry?" I interjected, disconcerted nerves jangling: they were as much Harry's as mine. "Was she there?"

"Our home is perfectly well and good," he replied. "Unfortunately, fifteen officers of the law trod all over before I could tell if anyone else had been there but for the two of us and your morning visitors." He aimed another brief accusatory glance at Batten.

"What about inside?" I asked.

"Agent Chapel was the only one brave enough to venture within. He's there now, and shall stay until we are ready to take you home."

I struggled to sit straighter. A nagging, dull pain was starting in my lower back, right hand side. "He's an FBI agent, not a house sitter. He can't be watching soap operas and watering the orchids."

Harry put a hand up. "Agent Chapel assures me that you are his top priority at this point in time."

"That's ridiculous," I said. "He's got better things to do."

"Agent Chapel also said if you didn't take my word for it, you could call home," Harry said, offering me the phone beside the bed. "And he'll tell you as much himself."

I glared at the phone, and then at my companion. I was no longer charmed by the accent, nor the naked devotion in his eyes, nor the almost-smile on his pale lips.

Harry didn't blink in the face of my glare. "Lay your fair head down. You are not going anywhere until the doctor allows, ducky."

"Quack." I turned on Batten. "Tell Harry that you guys have a murder to solve, and it makes no sense for you to be stuck at my house."

"We're looking at Sherlock for the murder of Kristin Davis," Batten told me, watching my reaction closely.

I didn't know what to think of that. At first, I couldn't wrap my brain around the barest possibility. I rubbed my left temple. "You think Danika moved to Denver to stalk me, and when that didn't blow up her skirt, she beheaded a twelve year old girl, made it look like a revenant kill, so that you'd call GD & C, who would then call her, and she could show up and … what?"

"Lure you to the scene?" Batten suggested. "Maybe she didn't feel confident in her ability to face you with your vampire around."

"*Revenant*. And I'm retired. GD & C called *her* to your crime scene, not me."

"She counted on the fact that I'd still go to you," Batten said. "And she was right."

Hot damn. Heat zinged through my chest and flushed my cheeks. Even though I was not supposed to be lusting after Mark.

"When you came, I sent you away," I said, trying to imagine Sherlock's thought processes that day, her scheming. "And you peeled out like a maniac with your testicles in a knot."

Harry coughed to cover a laugh, turning discretely to make a show of checking my vitals on the monitors.

Batten squared his shoulders at me. "She watched me leave," he supposed.

"She guessed I'd told you no." I got the momentary willies: was she looking at me while I shoveled my snow and answered her call? How cringeworthy. "To take Harry, she had to break our Bond first; that meant luring me out and…" I left it hanging, trying not to get a vivid Technicolour flashback.

Inching two fingers to explore the lower back wound out of morbid curiosity was a dumb idea. It throbbed continuously and I wondered how long it would be until I could have more meds. "I touched the knife and got a clear impression."

"That knife is evidence," Batten groaned. "It's been bagged and tagged, it's going to have your fingerprints all over it."

My stitches were under a dressing, and the area seemed a lot smaller length-wise than it felt pain-wise. "My DNA and fingerprints were already smeared all over it. I had to Grope it. Her feelings had re-focused towards Harry: want, need, loneliness, mixed with the belief that she could now take my place. Harry, I need my notebooks. I need to write this down."

Harry said so quietly I almost didn't hear: "Oh, ducky, whatever for?" He touched the back of my hand with his cool fingertips.

I recalled: "She really did think you were hers, Batten, that I'd stolen you away. And she thought she deserved to have Harry, that I deserved to lose him, that it was fair turnabout. Someone else told her that, someone she trusted. Mixed in all that were confused feelings about her revenant companion, George, missing him, needing him, jealousy. I didn't really get the connection. But her plan was destined to fail. Once Harry knew what she'd done to clear the plate for herself ..."

"I'd have torn her in half stem to stern and had her guts for garters," Harry agreed, "But you didn't hear that, Agent."

"You think it surprises me?" Batten murmured, but his thoughts were elsewhere, his gaze past the window glass and into the distant night. "You talk of rules and law. You think I don't know you could kill at the drop of a hat?"

"For my DaySitter," Harry said, staring a hole in Batten's back, and the edge in his voice tingled all along my right arm, where he hovered. "I'd kill for MJ. You really ought not judge me too harshly, lad, for I suspect you'd do the same."

"And before DaySitters? How many innocent people did you drain dry in those years? A thousand? Ten thousand?"

"This is not the time," I warned. "I'm trying to connect the dots and you're pointing fingers in each other's faces like a couple of drunk knuckleheads at a bar."

"There is no doubt in my DaySitter's mind that you have killed more than I, Agent Batten." Harry dropped his voice, as though he regretted having to point it out. "Ask her which one of us is more a danger to her well-being."

"Hey, baboons?" I clapped once, hard, to get their attention. "This is truly fascinating in a Discovery Channel sort of way, but I'm switching off now. It's ... well, they took my watch, but it's gotta be after midnight. Get out."

"It is only 10:00, love, but surely you must be exhausted after surgery." Harry motioned to the door at Batten. "I'll have a few minutes alone with my DaySitter now, if you don't mind."

It was a dismissal. I'd love to say that Harry wasn't doing the big dog thing, marking his territory, but he wasn't even trying to be subtle about it. The effect was immediate; I didn't need any psychic powers to read the stiff, hot irritation flashing from across the room.

"I'll be with Chapel at your place, Baranuik."

Ah, back to Baranuik, just one of the guys. Punishment for Harry's lordly manner, I guessed. I nodded at him mock-formally.

"Very well, Special Agent Batten, sir," I said crisply, adding a salute. If he got it, he didn't indicate, and like always I couldn't feel anything from his side of the room. "Tell Chapel I'll be home tomorrow." Both men started to object, Batten with an exasperated exhale, Harry with a ruffled-feather squawk. I cut them off. "I'm not staying here a minute longer than I have to. It's not safe for either of us. Tomorrow, I sign papers and ditch this dump."

Their voices in unison became a cacophony of objections, all more than a little insulting yet admittedly valid. I closed my eyes and settled back into my pillows so I could ignore it. I yawned, long and loud behind my hand to make my point. Batten stalked out without another word.

When I cracked an eyelid, Harry was pondering my forehead. My favorite pink calfskin gloves lay limp across his palms, stained but newly stitched where Danika's knife had flayed the palm.

"Harry, these are probably evidence. You took these from the crime scene."

"Perhaps I ought not to have done, only I thought you might want them."

"You sewed them?" I touched them tentatively, brushing just my fingertips across the leather, waiting for an inevitable influx of residual rage, horror, pain. It didn't came. I examined the tiny, tight stitches. "You can sew?"

Harry sniffed with insult. "Don't be absurd, of course I can. I spent two world wars as a field medic with the Royal Army Medical Corps. In 1937..."

Crap. I'd forgotten, and now he was building steam towards his Victoria Cross lecture. I cut him off. "Right! Faithful in Adversity. The Linseed Lancers. I remember."

"One expects that you should." He slid the gloves onto my hands one at a time then reached up to tuck hair away from my temple. "I suggest a hair cut, and you make an appointment with Sweeny Todd."

"Oh God, my hair!" I had forgotten completely. Batten hadn't said a thing about it. Neither had the sheriff. "Bad enough I'm stuck in this horrid hospital gown. What does it look like?"

"It does nothing to hide that the chill affects your nipples," he said frowningly. "Did you not notice the hunter's iniquitous stare? Apparently discretion is a foreign notion to the scoundrel."

"Harry," I wailed. "My *hair!*"

"At least they washed the blood out of it, that looked perfectly frightful. I have seen soldiers in the trenches along the Swiss Frontier with the tops of their heads blown clean off who had less blood in their hair. Of course, you are such a fair and flaxen blonde ..."

"Harry!" I slapped my hands to my head, feeling around. "What does it *look* like?!"

"Quite ..." he wrinkled his nose. "Punk rock. If you had a stronger face, you could pull it off." He scanned my head, disapproval playing across his tight lips as he tapped them with one forefinger. "No, upon consideration, I'm afraid you simply do not have the cheekbones for it. You have been eating far too many biscuits; it has softened the line of your jaw." He reached out and chucked my chin with a cool finger. I swatted him away.

"Knock that off."

"I know you prefer the truth."

"Not the whole truth!" I tugged edges of my bangs down to peer up around my eyebrows at the jagged clumps. "It's that short?"

"Oh, it is gone, love. You look like the young lady who sings that song you like, the one with the demonic clowns in the video? Pink?"

I stared at him with growing horror. "Sherlock gave me a faux-hawk?"

"I shouldn't like to call it that." Harry cocked his head, peering at my skull. "Rather, it appears as though you have, perched atop your crown, an albino hedgehog afflicted with severe jaundice. As I have repeatedly advised, were you to buy shampoo of a better quality, the colour would not be so dreadfully brassy. Furthermore, I fear it is time to have your highlights refreshed."

I exhaled hard, slumping back into the pillows. My defeat was complete, a real trouncing, though I couldn't tell you who'd done more damage: Sherlock, or Harry and his nitpicking. "Sonnuva twatwaffle."

"Always a lady," Harry noted with a wry patience. "If you gel it down so it is not spiking up all over your head, you could hope to look like Twiggy. Only, it is pretty uneven on this side. I shall make you a proper hair appointment with Clarice for a fortnight this Friday, cut and colour?"

"Tomorrow," I corrected. "As soon as I leave, I'm fixing this."

"You are not leaving tomorrow." He chuckled disdainfully. "You have had your viscera stapled. I would wager you cannot walk the measure of the king's own arm without folding like a bad hand."

"You always say, "Keep calm and carry on." That's what I'll do."

"It does not apply in the face of grievous injury. You're dreadfully compromised, my love."

I stared at him knowingly. "You can't be alone in the cabin, Harry."

"I shall be hosting your good man, Agent Chapel, indefinitely."

"Which means Batten will be there too, because there's *no way* he'd trust you alone with Chapel. Batten thinks you're the frigid cross between the boogeyman and a man-eating lion."

Harry smiled fiercely with pleasure, took a long moment to lick his teeth suggestively, teasing with the tip of his tongue the spot behind his canines where his fangs were retracted.

I shook my head. "It's your brilliant idea to be alone with two men without feeding for days on end?"

He nodded, becoming serious. "I have discussed it with Agent Chapel, and he has agreed to stand in as DaySitter while he is at the house, *just,*" He silenced my open-mouthed squawk of objection with a hand, "In the guardian sense: guns and brute strength and the like."

I tried to picture impossibly tall, nerdy Gary Chapel being brutish and strong, and ended up with a mental image of him whapping necrophile beetles with his keyboard, whirling his mouse above-head like a Scottish mace. He must have passed FBI training courses and at one time been somewhat capable, right? Maybe he still was. Maybe he had kickass hidden skills. Maybe he was secretly a superhero or a ninja. My eyes accidentally rolled so far back that I could practically see my optic nerves.

Harry assured me, "I rather fancy a nice long nap. Six, perhaps eight days. Hopefully the criminal stench of your hunter's drug store cologne will not keep me alert."

I rolled my eyes. "You need a big feed before "napping", which is an asinine thing to call it by the way."

"What expression do you prefer?"

"Don't sugar coat, Harry. You're talking about dry hypothermia."

"A perfectly ghastly term, not to mention medically inaccurate."

"I'm not afraid to say the words. If you're going to spend the next week in wraith-state, you need a full belly."

"How attentive of you, my pet; rest assured I have three bags of o-negative in the boathouse freezer and vow I shall drain each of them before I go to casket. Now, keep still a moment." He produced a fingertip, upon which a pale blue bead of nectar, from a tiny poke in his skin, glimmered.

While he slipped his hand under my gown, under the bandage, and dabbed at the stapled wounds, I kept still and did a mental count of the stock in the freezer: steaks, ground beef, chicken drumsticks, a shrimp ring, my sister Carrie's homemade raspberry freezer jam … I didn't think we had blood, but maybe he'd been stockpiling for just such an occasion.

"You're sure, Harry?" I said uncertainly, wincing when he rubbed his numbing blood along a sore spot. "Chapel's been told about Ajax? And the bugs?"

Harry flashed his deep single dimple; that crater, in combination with the cute divot in his chin, totally blew any chance he had of looking fierce. Good thing he could usually keep a straight face when it was time to intimidate.

"Such a fuss you make," he said, removing his healing fingers.

I patted his cheek with my gloved hand. "Fine. Go home to your new manpanions."

He regarded me suspiciously. "That was too easy."

"The last time I was away from home, you baked 43 batches of Snickerdoodles in a nervous fit. I'm assuming I'll come home in a few days to find my Kermit the Frog cookie jar packed to the brim with macaroons."

We had made certain concessions over the years, Harry and me. He didn't smoke in the living room and I didn't pester him to give up tobacco. I didn't sing Monty Python songs off-key in the bathtub anymore, and he entertained me tub-side by crooning lounge-singer love songs in deep baritone. I'd stopped fighting him on the issue of dancing lessons; I let him swing me around the living room and show me how to use my hips to follow his in stride. He baked cookies he couldn't eat, and every now and then I drank his favourite absinth cocktails or brandy in my espresso, so he could enjoy getting tipsy during his feed. I gave up on vocalizing my desire to have sex with him, and he kept his vintage bondage collection tucked out of sight in the cellar. Our life together worked. For two people so radically different, it seemed like life should be more difficult than it was; when it was just him and I, everything was peachy.

Harry was watching emotions cross my face; he sat and let them shower him in turn without seeking them more ardently with preternatural probing. His eyes were a steady, reassuring mortal grey, darker tonight, similar in shade to his cashmere scarf and glossy with the same sheen. I was so content to have him nearby, I could have ignored my wounds completely. It might have had something to do with the drugs. I should have expected him to pick up on that.

"What sort of medication did you say they gave you?"

"I didn't." I crunched ice between my molars. "Probably you can't get any."

"I've recovered your Beretta."

"From the Buick? Are you out of your undead skull? Did you bring my gun *here?"*

He waved that away. "Guns and tranquilizers are not a wise pairing."

"Better than guns and this espresso you brought me," I suggested. "I'm going to be twitchy all night. You can stay, right?"

"Alas, a nurse fast approaches," he confided, wiggling his eyebrows. "Her hips working under her uniform with the allure of fecundity."

"Fecundity. Barf." I grinned. Harry was an ass man.

"No doubt she means to remind me that visiting hours are long gone. I should be getting home to our fine, feathered roost and our nice ..." A flash of teeth. "Warm-bodied guests."

"Harry!" I said warningly.

His face was all innocence, eyes wide and glittering with humour. "Angelcakes?"

"Batten has 105 tiny black tattoos over his heart, one for every revenant he's dusted since he was a zitty preteen twerp riding around on the back of his grandfather's dirt bike. Don't you think he daydreams you're number 106?"

Harry's laugh was merry, but there was a dark, cunning light in his eyes. "No doubt, my pet."

"You don't actually trust him?"

"I am hardly so imprudent. However, I do very much trust your Agent Chapel and his ability to manage their affairs, both personal and professional."

"You trust Chapel with your *life?*"

"As should you, my cherub. Agent Chapel is a formidable ally who keeps us secure inside the scope of his good graces." My Cold Company stood. "Are you reconciled at last to be an active accomplice in Agent Batten's case?"

"Accomplice sounds shifty," I groused. "I'm not reconciled to working with him. But I'll find Sherlock, and she better hope Batten finds her before I do. He won't hoof a woman in the taco. I will."

He *tsk*ed me. "I hardly think it is necessary to get your hands dirty, my doe, or your hooves as the case may be." He rolled his eyes up to the ceiling. "If you would only permit me—"

"Down, boy," I said, though the Dark Lady knew I was sorely tempted to take him up on it, to set him loose on the world, to let Colorado become a rancorous immortal's hunting ground.

Harry acquiesced with his usual gentility, performing for me another exquisite bow, deep and sweeping, his coat dusting the floor. "As my lady wishes. I bid you good night, my only love. I hope you will be home to me soon."

I hoped so too. I watched him sway, pacing gracefully despite clunky motorcycle boots, across the glass-front of the ward, I watched nurses cast worried or perplexed glances at his back. The way they parted out of his path reminded me of spooked horses shuffling, restless to get going. The nurse with the matronly hips shivered. She caught the gaze of another nurse and they grimaced at one another in wordless understanding, shoulders up, a full-body *yikes*.

Though the room eventually warmed by a few degrees in Harry's absence, my heart did the opposite. The days were always long and much too quiet without him.

The nights here would be worse.

C12

Five days. Five days without my espresso machine. Five days without my own roomy, soft bed. Five days without my Cold Company singing acapella in the kitchen with his iPod ear buds in, while I played Name That Tune. Over the past few decades he'd developed vocal magic, what we preternatural biologists called audiomancy. The revenant could adjust the tone of his voice to mimic just about any male singer, and if he turned it on you in just the right way, it tickled down your spine like a fistful of peacock feathers. Sometimes it sounded as though he had two distinct voices, a subtle harmony coming from deep in the throat, a trick of the old ones, like throwing his voice or sending it curling through my belly.

I wondered what treats he'd downloaded since I'd been gone. It could be anything; his taste in music ranged from Mozart to Metallica to Eminem. I secretly preferred when he did John Denver. I'd fallen asleep many a night to Back Home Again as he lingered in the next room, the sound of him shuffling books on our shelves accompanying his soft humming. *Soon,* I promised myself. *Hey it's good to be back home again …*

Every hour on the hour, I unofficially cursed Danika Sherlock's name, not with spells or hexes but with venomous thoughts; I knew better than to speak serious Words against her, but boy did I hope for some nasty cosmic justice to come her way, and may the universe have mercy on the fool who stood between my fist and her mouth. Impotent fantasies of revenge kept me awake long into the nights, and dreaming of the comforts of home and my Cold Company helped me finally get some sleep. I was jerked awake routinely by nightmares—flashing blades, wet fleshy slaps *(Don't you die yet, Marnie—don't you die on me yet, bitch!)* the stench, her vomit and my blood, old pennies and sour milk. Urgency, the urgency—*gun, I have to get the*—fumbling and failing, and then her hate-filled face filled coming at mine again and again in half-shadow.

I wanted strong espresso and homemade cookies warm from the oven, with a cube of soft caramel in the center the way Harry made them. I also wanted Danika Sherlock to choke on a sock full of razor blades while plunging headlong off a cliff into a vast ocean of hydrochloric acid. I wasn't going to get everything I wanted, but the cookies were a distinct possibility.

I was being released today. The phone message the nurse had relayed promised my ride was on its way. The staples had to stay in my stomach for a while yet, and I'd have to come back to have them taken out. As luck would have it, I'd be awake for that procedure: it's nice to have something fun to look forward to. The stitches would dissolve, the surgeon said, and I had to take showers instead of baths for a while. That was gonna suck; lifting my leg to swing it into the old claw foot tub was going to hurt, just like a million little motions I made hurt now, thanks to injuries in mini-muscles I didn't even have names for. Harry's revenant blood had done wonders to speed my healing, but basically, in the necessary lull between painkillers, everything hurt, including just laying here.

It was chilly in the hospital, and the sheets they provided were light, crisp white things topped with scant blankets of bleached cotton. I hadn't slept well. I missed my cabin with its woodstove cranking out heat, big wooly Afghans heavily draped on my bed, fat cozy rag rugs strewn across the wood floors, throw pillows smelling of Harry's cologne that rubbed off the back of his neck. I missed the creak of his footstep up the pantry stairs when he woke for the evening, and the warm spill of contentment I felt when he stirred from his rest, and his weight shifting the deep couch cushions beside me.

Soon, I promised myself again. After I picked Sherlock's teeth out of my knuckles and the case was settled, I wasn't going to leave my home again, I resolved. Not for a long time, not for any reason. I was going to hole-up like a hermit 'til the cookies ran out.

Around noon I saw movement across the big windows; though I didn't look closely (one of the nurses had scored me an old celebrity rag-mag from the nursing station and thankfully I wasn't in it), I got the impression of wide shoulders under nylon jackets, office blues, no-nonsense strides. Only monsters, cops and well-armed thugs have that confident, top-of-the-food-chain strut. My ride was here.

Where Chapel's shoes made a stiff, business-like pace into the room that looked like it hurt when he moved, Batten's made more of an easy, soft-soled swagger. It's not like Batten's pants didn't fit, or his balls were too big (not the way I remembered them). It was the walk he did when he was pleased with something. The Blue Sense had been on overdrive all day, so it was no surprise that I felt Chapel's relief even before he came in the room. I felt nothing from Batten, but I suspected he might feel the same way about my release.

I, on the other hand, was anything but pleased to see two of them.

I slid off the bed. "You're both here. It's broad daylight. Where's Harry?"

"Home." Batten hadn't shaved and his fingers played with the strangely demonic scruff on his chin. "Sheriff Hood dropped by with some questions and offered to stay with him."

Panic shot through my veins.

"You brainless twats!" I cried, grabbing the duffel bag from Chapel's hand. "You left Harry alone with a stranger? Was he resting?"

"Wide awake. He made scones." Batten didn't bother hiding a smirk. Apparently Harry's baking was funny. "Lemon poppy seed."

"They're not alone together, Marnie," Chapel soothed. His hand fluttered up to smooth his necktie but it wasn't there. I'd never seen Chapel without one. "Hood brought his chief deputy."

"How did either of you make it into the FBI when you're so obviously stupid?" I demanded, unzipping the bag vigorously and madly shaking the contents onto the bed. "I hate you both. I really, truly hate you both."

"I see they've lightened up on your pain killers," Batten noted.

"Plunge backwards up your own ass, fucknugget!" I barked, fishing in the pile for matching socks, tossing bras and panties aside in a flurry. "At least I've met Hood. I don't even know this other clown!"

"Neil Dunnachie was a decorated homicide detective before coming out to the Lambert County Sheriff's Department last year, a twenty-year veteran of the Denver PD," Chapel supplied.

"As if his damn name does me any good at this point," I spat. "He could be a lunatic. He could be a pervert. How do I know I can trust him?"

"They were both former homicide detectives," Batten said with the kind of patience one reserves for small children, senile seniors and mental patients. "They're not going to kill somebody."

"You're right. Probably they're not going to kill a *person*." I pointed at him with a pair of pink cotton underpants, flapping them at him. "What about a revenant?"

Batten blinked impassively.

"I understand your concern, Marnie," Chapel said.

"Do you?" I demanded. "Really? Do you know that of the three so-called humanists who staked Danika's companion, two were cops? And not Podunk hotshots making their own rules in the backwoods, either. They were NYPD. They broke into her Manhattan apartment and staked him in broad daylight, for no reason other than he was a revenant. They thought they were doing the right thing. I bet they still think they did the right thing. In their minds, they killed a monster. But instead, they created one."

I thought it would make a grand point, so I disrobed in one swoop, letting the hospital gown flutter to my ankles, displaying ugly twisted stitches, the wounds still an angry red, the dressings around my middle crusted with blood and yellowing ooze. I laid one arm across my bare breasts and glared at them. I should have been embarrassed standing in my underwear before the two of them, but the flinch around their eyes was worth it. The wide, wrapped wound in my gut was impossible to ignore. Chapel's attention didn't stray very far from the bandages. Batten's eyes settled for some reason on the incidental rug burn on my knees. I couldn't tell what he was thinking.

"This is what happens when a DaySitter loses their companion. Do you see what she's been reduced to? What would I do, if I lost Harry? How would I lash out? What kind of maniac would I become?"

"Marnie, that wouldn't happen to you," Chapel assured me.

"Are you kidding?" I shouted, forgetting about covering my boobs and flailing my arms at them. "I'm half-cracked on my best days, and that's *with* Harry. Can you imagine what life would be like for me if …" I felt my spine crawl and turned on my heel to look at Batten head-on. I just stood there for a minute, covering my chest, digesting my thought before voicing it. "You're hoping they will stake him."

His face was blank, unreadable, but his voice was stiff with anger. "What did you say?"

"You heard me. Did you tell them it has to be rowan wood? Or did you have something worse in mind for Harry. Fire, perhaps? Tub full of holy water? Did you leave your kit behind for them? You have a nice alibi, here with me while they do your dirty work."

"You know that's not true."

"I *don't* know. Not when it comes to you, Mark." I felt close to tears and chose anger instead, turning my back on them to struggle into a bra. My hands quivered as I jammed my legs into a pair of jeans. "You're blank. You're an empty elevator shaft. I can't go up, I can't go down, I'm just stuck alone in the middle. I don't know what you think or feel about anything."

"Well, I'm telling you. I don't wish Harry dead. You'll either believe that or you won't."

"I don't," I glanced at Chapel. "And what about you? You want Harry dead?"

"Of course not," he said quickly, his calm façade fading briefly. "Lord Dreppenstedt has been … he's been …" He was watching me try to button my pants near the bandages, his face pinched, pained. "Let me help you, Marnie. Settle down. Can we just …"

I was pulling a long-sleeved t-shirt over my head, impossible to do without tenderness in back and pain in front, tugging at stitches here and there, and I growled frustration at them, an enraged monster trapped in a t-shirt, face pressing cotton. Hands drifted to help me and I slapped them away.

"Try being sane and civil for one goddamned minute?" Batten suggested, easily dodging blows.

"That won't make you go away!" I cried, muffled by cotton.

"The vampire can—"

"Revenant!" I shouted.

"Call that thing whatever the fuck you want, it can take care of itself!" he assured me when my face reappeared.

"If he could, would he need me, shit for brains?" I tapped my temple meaningfully. "What do you think a DaySitter is for?"

"Fuck buddy?" Batten suggested.

I ignored that; none of his business that it was untrue. "Why do you think the old ones have this complicated ritual Bond in place? What if the debt vulture or the beetles ..." I floundered, tears returning; I felt weak, and that tightened my lips in near-fury.

Batten strained to follow. "What the fuck's a debt vulture?"

I pressed a finger to my twitching eyelid. "Oh my God, noob. Seriously? Why do I even talk to you? I have no patience for either of you. I'm calling a fucking cab."

Chapel said quietly, "That's not necessary, Marnie. I promise you, Harry is perfectly fine."

"If he's not ..." I wasn't dumb enough to threaten federal agents with a fate worse than death, especially since there was no way I could deliver on it, so I fixed them both with my best glare, the one my baby brother Wesley always said could melt icebergs. Then I remembered Harry's words: he trusted Chapel with his life. And so should I. "Get me home to him, Gary."

Batten shoveled my things back into my bag and followed at a run. He tried to take my elbow and I wrested it away from him; he was lucky not to get it in the balls.

"Slowly, Marnie," Chapel urged as I propelled down the hall ahead of them, clutching my stomach in one hand. The pain was better than expected, seemingly whisked away by magic just after it reared its tugging, biting head. Chapel fell behind, struggling with a limp of his own. I wondered fleetingly how he'd hurt himself, wondered if Harry was responsible.

"You don't know," I snarled over my shoulder at them. "You don't know all the trouble that could happen. Even if they didn't mean to hurt him. One of them could innocently open a blind and the sun ..." The lobby doors slid open loudly and a dark miserable snowstorm blasted across our path. *Ok, no sun.* "Something could go wrong."

"Take it easy," Batten ordered. "I don't think either of them is going to forget they're in the company of a vampire."

His stubborn use of the V-word nearly made me lose it, but I didn't think my gut could take another strenuous shout. "They could."

"Won't happen," Batten insisted, punctuated by a harsh laugh. "You know what it's like being near that thing. And you're accustomed to it, they're not."

"*Him*, not *it,* not *thing*," I corrected through my teeth.

"This is Hood and Dunnachie's first vamp. Trust me, that *thing* is making quite an impression." He jabbed a thick finger in my face. "Stay."

"Arf," I replied sourly.

I waited at the wide curb beside Chapel. I noticed out of the corner of my eye that one of Chapel's long arms hovered too close to me, inching to support me somehow. I shot him a look. He dropped it.

Batten hurried through the snow towards their rental car. There was barely ten running strides of visibility, then we lost him in the white blur; the snow was tiny grits whipping horizontal with the wind, straight into our faces. It was like going into warp speed on the Starship Enterprise, with the gusts pushing the storm under the hospital's overhang. Chapel and I had to squint against it.

"What did Batten mean by that?" I raised my voice to be heard over the wind and traffic. "That Harry's making an impression?"

Chapel ducked his face nearer to my ear. "Seems Harry wasn't in the mood to pussyfoot around with the are-you-or-aren't-you routine. He answered the door full-on changed, eyes, fangs, vocal tricks, everything."

I choked back a startled laugh. "He mindfucked cops?" I blinked in disbelief. "In front of FBI agents? In our own home?" I wasn't sure which part bothered me the most.

"Briefly," Chapel said; it came out oddly defensive. That struck me as even funnier. I laughed and then winced, wishing I hadn't. Chapel put his briefcase up to block the snow from our faces, though he had to duck a full foot and a half to place his face near to mine. "Somehow he knew two hardcore doubters were at the front step."

"Doubt's an emotion," I reminded. Harry would have picked it up immediately. If Harry was human, they'd call him a true Groper-Feeler, but you didn't use human psychic terms for revenants: revs are just plain revs.

"He turned to me with his hand on the doorknob and said, "how absolutely *maddening* this part is," in that way that he has."

I didn't have to ask. I could imagine all too well Harry's stiff London accent saturated with vexation; he liked to pretend it was a tiresome chore to prove his nature over and over, when in fact it tickled him to make an impression.

Chapel continued, "So he extended his fangs, brightened his irises to …" Gary floundered for a descriptor and settled on "Inhuman, and whipped open the front door. He invited Rob and his chief deputy Neil in for tea and scones in this bizarre voice that sounded like a harmony. They almost didn't come in."

The humour made Chapel's eyes intense in a way I'd never seen before. Maybe part of Agent Chapel had loosened up with the removal of his tie. His top button was still firmly fastened, but baby steps, right? Already I trusted him less to fix my computer.

Chapel continued, "When they remembered how to walk, they stumbled into the hallway, at which point Harry did this thing with his hand, like a walking-pull? I've never seen anything like it. The shadows in the house solidified and fell in a blurry wake behind him, seemed to cover his stride. Then in a blink, he was five steps ahead of where he should have been."

"Shadow stepping," I said, not bothering now to hide my smile. Harry was really enjoying himself today. "A trick of the older ones. You should see him do it in the forest at night. Gave me nightmares for weeks after he showed me. It's pretty fucked up."

Agent Chapel's face paled for a moment and then went pink in the neck. Surely not because of me dropping the f-bomb. I couldn't imagine why else my comment would embarrass him; the effect faded quickly.

"Hood and Dunnachie didn't question Harry's nature for a second after that," he added, his humour gone. He inspected the parking lot through narrowed eyes that missed nothing; I thought it an excuse to look away, rather than a scanning-for-bad-guys.

The SUV pulled up and the heavy back end slid in the slush into the curb. I felt better. The image of Harry dialing-to-monster on Hood and his deputy was satisfying. At least they'd know for certain who and what they were dealing with. It would make them vigilant if not respectful.

After all that, Sheriff Hood still volunteered to be alone in Harry's company? *Point: Hood.* The "I'm-not-afraid-of-the-big-bad-wolf" act, or maybe even genuine bravery. Bravery in the face of the undead and unknown. Had to respect that in a guy. Hood was more than just a pretty face. I might have to put him on my People I Don't Entirely Hate list.

Chapel sounded like he was thinking out loud. "I shudder to think what Harry would have done if they'd asked him for further proof."

"Well it's a good thing they didn't." I paused with the passenger side door open, looking over the hood at him pointedly. "He hasn't had me in five long days. He's bound to be famished by now."

His hazel eyes fell away from mine. Shame. A throat-full of it nearly choked me from his side of the car as the Blue Sense tore into being like an avalanche down a ski hill. I had to grip the dashboard as I ducked into the passenger seat, bewildered by Chapel's rush of feeling. Was he embarrassed by the idea of me feeding Harry? This wasn't news to him, but maybe he was only now realizing what that really meant: that I really did let Harry drink from my veins. Perhaps that shook Chapel up. Maybe it had kept him awake and nervous, while I was away? Maybe watching Harry drink glass after glass of microwaved blood brought the issue home to Chapel in full, stunning colour. Whatever it was, again it was blessedly brief. Unflappable Chapel was nothing if not a master of self-control. By the time I tipped the passenger sun shade down to use the mirror to apply lip gloss, I saw he had his calmly reassuring mask back up. A quick probe of the SUV's emotional atmosphere revealed tight control; any apprehension was dialed-down to nil.

"How much do you know about Hood and Dunnachie? How do you know they're not, you know, like you." I eyeballed Batten, specifically the part of his shirt that hid the kill-notch tats. They might be sort of sexy if they didn't indicate wasted immortals, not that I'd ever admit that aloud.

He checked the rear view mirror for Chapel's level of attention and then said more quietly, "I'm not all bad, am I?"

The tone of his voice hinted at scandalous pleasures, private naked escapades behind closed doors, or in our case, up against them. I fought down the instant responding wave of warmth in my groin that indicated my body was an idiot.

"You're an oversized ass-hat. You hate my housemate. You won't respect that I'm retired. You push me; I don't try to improve *you*."

"Nothin' to improve."

"I don't ask for anything you're not able to give."

"Maybe you should," he suggested; the intimacy I heard had to be my lurid imagination.

"Your FBI shield didn't change the fact that at your core, you're a rule-bending carnage machine. If there weren't revenants to dust, you'd be making a living killing something else."

His jaw ground, a single ripple. "I've never hurt an innocent person."

"Depends on your definition of *innocent* and *person*, I suppose," I drew a deep chest full of air then winced as a stitch pulled low in my back. I heard a sharp inhalation from the back seat, like Chapel had suddenly pulled a muscle. A glance in the make-up mirror showed him staring out the window, lips pinched in a rigid line, brow rutted.

I told Batten quietly, "I don't trust you for a second not to hurt Harry. That's enough of a reason to dislike you."

"Didn't touch a hair on his head," he assured me, his voice still gruffly intimate in the front seat. "Could have. He gave me plenty of opportunity."

My breath caught in my throat. I wasn't remotely convinced by Gary Chapel's new show of focus on his Blackberry, so I lowered my voice. "You snuck into Harry's room?"

"Invited," he replied.

"Big heep hunter accepted an invitation down into an immortal's private lair? Aren't you brave." I shifted to get more comfortable.

There was a heartbeat of quiet, during which I figured he was searching for a non-jerky thing to say. Finally, he offered: "It has a real theatrical flair for decorating."

I felt my lips tug up reluctantly. "His nod to Poe and Wilde."

"Hence the two-faced portrait of perfect Harry and rotten Harry above the fake fireplace? The bust of Pallas above the door? The stuffed raven?" When I nodded he mirrored it. "I dig the bumper stickers inside the lid of its coffin, especially: *What happens in the casket stays in the casket.*"

"You weren't in there when Harry was resting, though. Right?"

"We took turns every afternoon, watching it."

"Watching." My head was starting to throb. Since I couldn't go back in time and make sure they didn't do it, I could only make sure it didn't happen again. "You do know that "watching" isn't a literal requirement? You can watch him just fine from upstairs. It's mostly just making sure critters don't get at him. Or hunters."

A slow smile began to spread over his lips. I didn't get the joke. He shook his head with a surprised chuckle. "Harry said flat-out it was our job to sit in the chair by the casket, like bodyguards. "Sentinels" was his word."

I was about to scoff but then thought it sounded like classic Harry manipulation; what else had he done to amuse himself in my absence?

"So you sat there."

"I sat there."

"For hours. Literally watching him."

"Figured if I didn't do a good job, you'd get pissy."

"Since when do you care what I want?" He didn't answer. "You weren't tempted to drive a stake between his ribs?" No reply. "You just sat there."

"I drank beer and played its video games. Old school Mario."

I tried to get a mental picture of Batten sitting in Harry's black leather video game chair, not ten feet from an immortal lying prone and vulnerable in his casket, and Batten just ...being there. If body snatchers hadn't replaced the real Mark with an alien duplicate, I had no other explanation.

"I don't know what to say," I told him, meaning it. I wasn't used to feeling gratitude toward the hunter. I glanced in the make up mirror. Chapel was still pretending not to listen to us. "Thank you, Mark."

"You're welcome, Marnie," he said easily.

"Now if only we could stop you calling him an *it*."

"Never gonna happen."

We drove on in silence, Batten pushing the car with his usual heavy-footed management but taking the corners with far more prudence than I'd witnessed him use in the past. The bridge at Lambert's Crossing was a death trap; only wide enough for one-way traffic, in the best of times it was tricky to stop on the downward curve or take turns when the road before and following it was glittery with black ice. When we whipped past Askant Mill on Catawampus Creek, the traffic thinned considerably and the incline of the road made the car struggle between gears. Batten gunned it through Ten Springs while I stared at the dashboard, avoiding the bright lights outside the Ten Springs Motor Inn. A flash of flapping yellow in my peripheral told me the police tape was still up around room four. Batten's eyes slid sideways past me, and his jaw did that clenchy thing before his gaze returned grimly to the road.

Close to an hour later we were slowing to round the curve at Shaw's Fist, a mountain lake so small it looked like the Green Man had hocked a loogie. The lake was ringed by a huddling cluster of eighteen summer cottages, most of which were closed up until spring. Since I bought the cabin from my sister Carrie in October, I hadn't had a chance to meet the couple of neighbours who had winterized their cabins to live there year-round. I wasn't sure I needed to. Maybe my life would be a whole lot easier if it didn't have any people in it. Maybe Harry and I should just get 45 cats and call it a day.

My phone went off in the trunk, muffled. I had finally changed it from Harry's idea of a joke; it now played the Inspector Gadget theme song.

Agent Chapel's Blackberry summoned almost simultaneously. I checked the state of my lip gloss in the make-up mirror so I could see him glance at the text display. His mouth fell open ever so slightly and his professional calm faltered. Seconds later, Batten's went off. He slipped it off his waistband and glanced down at it, then hurriedly shoved it in his pocket. The car lurched forward down the last few miles of road, plunging off the paved section and onto snow-packed grit and gravel.

Uncertainty stole my words. Instead of asking, I ate at the inside of my cheeks. *(You and me. We finish it. Together.)* Probably they had to drop me off and rush to some far-off emergency. Right?

Through whipping snow and the bare trees thrashing in the wind and sprawling branches of cedar and pine, red and blue spinning lights flared off the cabin's frosted windows. *(You had what's mine. Gonna have what's yours.)* My throat constricted. The first car I saw, a Ford Explorer parked askew in the middle of the road with one door cranked open to the snow, said **SHERIFF** across the side in big black lettering.

C13

I tumbled from the car in a mad panic while it was still in motion. Stumbled, skinned my knees on the icy gravel but launched back to full-on sprint feeling no pain at all. There were too many men in my way—*deputiesfiremenEMS,* the siren of my brain screamed--too many obstacles to dodge. Plunging through them, their orders ignored, I pelted past the fire truck toward the porch, a quarterback with the barest of padding, clutching one arm across my bandages. Batten's bellowed command sounded acres away. My boots slid on the snow, plunging me to the ground again. I rolled once and vaulted to my feet.

I couldn't breathe. The world spun and I rocketed through it. A deputy with a roll of that damn yellow tape. Someone shouting about a civilian. I ducked a swinging arm, propelled into an EMS guy, put my shoulder in him, bashing him into the wall. Steel clattered, rubber tubing snake-coiled like spilled entrails, packs of gauze fluttered madly to the floor. The hallway swam. I threw my gloved hands and caught a wall to slide-run along it while my vision slid sideways. There was a gurney half-in half-out of my office. My voice sounded impossibly small, as I called out Harry's name over and over.

Another medic knelt in front of my kitchen table. A strange man sat there before him, a dark-haired doppelganger of Richard Belzer whose face didn't compute. Lingering in the threshold of the pantry, Harry stood in morning dress: dove grey flannel trousers, white shirt and a red apron, grey felt spats over his patent Oxfords. His ankles were crossed casually and his face was calm, but one of his suspenders had fallen off his shoulder and he didn't seem to notice. His hair stuck up at the front. I took two running steps towards him and he seized me by the biceps, holding me at arm's length.

Choked with relief, no one else mattering, I reached out to touch him, to check him: face, chest, shoulders, intact, uninjured. I patted him until he shook me.

"Stop," he said. "Settle down. You're going to injure yourself."

"You're alive! What happened? What …who?" I couldn't see everything in the kitchen at once or get my breath. Harry took my elbow and wheeled me into the bedroom like you'd take aside a misbehaving child, smiling an apology to the injured stranger at my kitchen table as he shut the bedroom door.

"Do sit. Let me see your bandages."

"Harry, please." I sat obediently. "You're okay, right?"

"I smell blood. You've gone and buggered something up. What have you done, here?" He knelt before the bed, his eyes shuttered. "May

I have my face back? I would appreciate it if you would please stop pawing me."

The collective emotions in the house from so many people on alert made my throat squeeze, and my usually limp empathic powers surged. My stomach did a sluggish twist like an old-fashioned wringer washer.

"Someone's hurt." My brain reported *Chapel's hurt,* but that didn't make sense, was obviously wrong, so I ignored it.

"Deputy Dunnachie was bitten by a necrophile beetle, but he'll be off to the hospital directly for antivenom and a round of IV-antibiotics."

Harry read my wordless confusion loud and clear, but was in no hurry to explain. He yanked at the heels of my boots.

"But necro-beetles only show up for dead things," I said, stupidly. "You weren't at rest with the local cops here, right?"

"You trod snow and slush into my kitchen," he informed me coolly. "This rug shall need washing, as well." My socks came off next, and my toes curled from the chill touch of his fingers. "Clearly I should not have let Agent Batten pack your clothing. These boots are wholly unsuitable to the weather. They are dress boots, not meant for—"

"Holy rolling shitballs, Batface, just spill it!" I exploded.

His gaze crept up to mine. Under his curved and thrice-pierced brow, I watched the unhurried, unnerving liquid-mercury shift as his irises bled to luminous platinum around pinprick black pupils; I was more than a little surprised to find this display was still capable of silencing me after all these years. I squelched a shudder.

"OK revenant, I'm suitably intimidated." I hurried him on with hand motions. "Come on."

"When you are calm," he promised.

"I am calm, see?" I said, breathing deliberately slow to show him. Funny thing, it convinced me too. I wasn't sure whether it was his solid presence, or the hushed familiarity of my bedroom, or the measured breathing, but it was better. My hammering heart slowed, the room stopped buzzing, sounds started to filter back in as adrenalin fled. I realized that under the collective murmur of male voices and the scuffle-thud of big boots on my weathered linoleum floors, something was playing on the CD player on the kitchen counter. A real big band. Someone crooning, the song I knew but the smooth voice one I didn't recognize.

"I'm better. What beetle? What happened? You're sure you're not hurt?"

"One question at a time please," he sang. "Now, are you going to vomit?"

I blinked, not understanding. "Why would I ..." Then I thought about it, shaking badly, my gut in knots. Now that he mentioned it, I might just. Swallowing hard, I slowed my breathing further through pursed lips, nice and deep. "I don't think so. But answers would help."

"When you are truly calm," he repeated tolerantly, "And I have made perfectly sure that you've not cocked up your stitches. The abdomen is fine. Let me check your lower back. Something is bleeding."

"Probably it's just old blood on the bandage."

"Please." He sounded offended. "One smells nothing like the other." When he finished his inspection, he nodded once and shuffled two knee-steps to Carrie's old hand-me-down cedar dresser to rummage. He fished out my softest angora socks and came back.

"It is just weeping, it should stop. The music is Michael Bublé doing "I've Got You Under My Skin." What do you think?" He went to grab my ankle.

"I think I can put on my own damn socks."

He laid them across my lap. "By all means."

I drew my knee up and bent over. The staples in my stomach yanked and I let out a hiss. I wasn't the only one in pain; in the kitchen, someone (I assumed it was Dunnachie) groaned loudly and then threw up, hopefully in the sink. Harry started to hum along with the song, tapping his fingers on his knee, watching my progress with an astute lift of eyebrows.

"Michael Bublé, hunh? He's good." I tried again and failed. "Uh, can you gimme a hand?"

"How inconsiderate of me not to have offered, my darling." He placed one of my feet on his bent knee and worked the sock on. "You owe Agent Chapel an apology; you have cut him to the quick."

"What's that supposed to mean?"

Harry opened his mouth and then shut it again like a trap. Then he said, "Only, your ridiculous banshee hollering frightened him; he is one who is not accustomed to being so badly startled out of his emotional restraint. He must be growing attached to you."

My companion allowed himself a private self-satisfied smile and I wondered what the hell it meant.

"I didn't mean to be overdramatic," I said. "I thought you were dust."

"If you'd kept a calm head and thought about it, you would have *felt* me in here, safe and sound and entertained by all the action."

Entertained? "Well, I'm glad my shooting, my stalker and my stab wounds are as much fun for you as they've been for me, Lord Dreppenstedt. I dig when we can share stuff, ya know?"

"Oh, MJ, I am hardly the heartless cad you take me for." His chuckle turned into a frown that matched mine. "You can feel that, my love? That I am teasing you?"

I shook my head. "I can't feel anything right now. Or, it's more like I can feel a jumble of everything, but no one stronger than another. I'm not sure there's anything I'm *not* feeling, but no, I can't focus on you. Guess I'm too wired."

"Wired or not, you should still be able to filter them out and focus on me ," he said sternly. "We are inexorably linked by our Bond. Beloved, I have my hands on your bare skin." He demonstrated by moving his hand to my cheek, cupping my chin and stroking one thumb along my jaw to the length of my throat. If he could have avoided stroking atop my jugular, he would have, but his hand moved without his permission and he was forced to swallowed hard. "I can feel your distress. Can you not sense what I am feeling?"

"No. But I think it's normal for me to be a bit scrambled, Harry. We wouldn't know, because last time I was this traumatized you were in Portland and I was in Buffalo." He flinched, and I hurried to explain. "What I mean is, we couldn't have experienced this kind of disconnect due to stress before. We're just noticing it now because we're together."

He didn't look at all mollified by that. "No, I was correct when I presumed that your half of our Bond is damaged. We must remedy this."

"After you tell me what happened?" I pressed.

He gave me an impatient flutter of sandy lashes. "The sheriff and his somber chief deputy accepted my invitation to tea. I sent your agents away on chauffeur duty."

"That was bonehead-stupid."

"I was bored stiff by the agents' company. Despite what your badge bunny hormones may mislead you to believe, officers of the law are dreadfully dull; why, even your much-ballyhooed hunter induced yawns. I am afraid his reputation may, in fact, be based on rumour and innuendo," he said innocently.

I chewed back an angry accusation: he'd been hoping someone would challenge him. Batten hadn't lived up to Harry's expectations, I guess. Neither had the local cops.

"We were having a pleasant chat when the mail truck arrived. Deputy Dunnachie asked if I cared to pause our question-and-answer period so I might fetch the mail. I explained that I rarely went out during the afternoon. Deputy Dunnachie wondered aloud, with a marked degree of audacity, if I was indeed capable of venturing out of doors during the afternoon. Naturally, I was inclined to demonstrate."

"Naturally," I deadpanned.

"We went out together, and while I waited under the shelter of the weeping cedar by the end of the drive, Deputy Dunnachie went to the fence to fetch the mail."

"And then of course …" I felt my forehead pinch. "There were corpse beetles in my mailbox?"

Harry smiled, but it was unpleasant; I braced for it even as he hesitated. "I expect the beetles were attracted to the severed human head secreted within."

I stared until my eyes felt dry. Then I remembered to blink. Harry seemed perfectly content to wait while the gears in my skull ground to a halt and caught once again. "A head."

"A head, dearheart."

"Like, a skull? A dry, dug-up, formerly gross but now completely clean and polished …no? How about a plaster cast? A medical school learning tool skull? That kind of head?" Harry was shaking his head slowly back and forth. "So an actual …with flesh and hair and …brains and … I should sit down."

"You are sitting down, my love."

"Oh, good. I'll have less distance to fall when I pass out. Whose head is it?" *Don't say Kristin Davis. Don't say Kristin Davis.*

"That which at one time belonged to a young lady. It may possibly be the one your FBI gents are missing."

"Why my mailbox?" I cried. Unless Davis' murderer was Sherlock, and she wanted to congratulate my narrowly escaping death by delivering hacked up body parts. I stood. "I guess they need my help."

His lips crooked into a half-smile and he made a soothing noise with them, part way between a shush and a cluck. "In your current mental condition that is neither sensible nor prudent."

"Mental condition!" I huffed, but it was sort of silly to argue since I'd just thrown a major snit-fit in front of 20 or so strangers. "Did you see it?"

"But of course. I rushed forward to help the deputy and," He displayed his hand, upon which a big red welt was swelling between thumb and forefinger. "I was forced to kill the poor, faultless creatures."

"You rushed into the sun?" I grabbed for his hand and he dropped it out of my reach. "They bit you. You're lucky they didn't get to an orifice, or you'd be short a few million brain cells."

"It is of no consequence, as I explained to the medics. You know I am neither vulnerable to crypt plague nor to the venom in their bite." He shrugged with a lopsided, self-deprecating smile. "I feel far worse for the beetles. We disturbed them from their feast."

Feast. *Blerg.* "What about the head?"

"The head has been left *in situ*, right where the deputy discovered it."

"Crammed atop my Christmas cards?"

"Who sends a witch Christmas cards?" Harry cocked his head in consideration. "Perhaps the head was an early holiday gift?"

"Drooling semi-digested grey matter on my gas bill and attracting brain-eating zombie beetles, some gift." I wondered how much the average flamethrower cost, and if I could find one on EBay. "You know what follows *necrophila noveboracensis,* Harry, if they don't clear them all out before the adults lay their larvae." The larvae of the necrophile beetle had only one known natural predator: spitting carrion spiders. "*Scytodes rugulosum* are the rabbits of the spider world. We'll have eight million of the little fuckers before you know it."

"I do so enjoy when you teach me lessons I learned centuries before your birth. It is indescribably endearing."

"Can the sarcasm. Once they get in, it's hell trying to clear them out. I'll have to re-caulk around all the windows to make sure they don't sneak inside and make a big ole web in your casket."

"Leave it all to the professionals, dearest philomel." He put his hands on me, to ease me back to sitting. I fought it for a moment. His hands insisted.

"Philo'*what?*"

"You tried the forensic work and decided it was a one-time thing. Furthermore, no one is asking for your assist—"

"Baranuik, I need you," Batten called from the kitchen.

Harry's lips tightened into a line. "Shruff and cinders, how I detest that man. Have I mentioned?"

"I'll let you eat him later."

His eyes flashed. "Promise?"

"Nah. But I will let you tell him about the spiders." I grinned. "He's phobic."

"If you are prepared to dally with him, be off then. Your reckless, self-punishing determination to be close to that rodgering ne'er do well is most unfortunate. Let it be said, lest you've forgotten." He pointed at the bedroom door, the back of which was decorated with a poster of Captain Jean-Luc Picard's profile against a backdrop of the Starship Enterprise. "That man makes you miserable more often than not."

"That's a terrible thing to say about Patrick Stewart," I chided, laying a hand on Harry's cheek. I stroked him there, where his smooth cheek dotted with the barest of stubble around his dimple. It was a literary myth that a revenant's hair no longer grew. As long as they were well-fed, it was all systems a-go in many ways. Harry shaved every single evening. He swore he only used his straight-edge, but had a not-so-secret habit of swiping my Gillette Venus razors and apricot-scented shave gel. My eyes were drawn almost helplessly, just for a minute, to the forbidden curve of his lips.

"Baranuik!" Batten barked again. I saw temptation flash across my companion's face like the warning flare of heat lightning.

"Don't do it, Dreppenstedt," I cautioned. "Whatever you're about to say, just don't."

"Would it kill him, then, to think the two of us were having a congenial personal reunion?"

"If "congenial personal reunion" means screwing, we don't. And even if we did, he might wonder why that occurred at the same time as the discovery of a severed head." I felt my eyebrows pucker together. "Hacked-up body parts should be a definite turn-off for any couple, Harry."

"I am already the penultimate evil in his books," Harry said without expression. "Malevolence embodied, sin personified. It is perfectly likely that I am a suspect in this crime, and can do no worse in his eyes. I expect that Agent Batten will never think a fraction more highly of me, no matter how I attempt to redeem myself, therefore I do not intend to waste any concern as to what impression I make with that particular gent."

It was a sad but realistic assessment; Batten would be hard pressed to see Harry as anything but a fiend.

"So you're just going to be yourself and if Batten doesn't like it he can go choke on a cockroach?"

"Or something ever so slightly more delicately phrased." Harry assented with the barest of nods. Then attentively: "Is Agent Batten truly afraid of spiders?"

I winked at my Cold Company and whisked open the bedroom door.

C14

The kitchen had emptied-out. Something in the way Batten stood in the epicenter of the room, hip cocked, legs firmly planted, said he didn't like calling on me, or needing me, or needing anyone else for that matter. Tension quivered along the solid line of his shoulders, and his forearms, crossed over his chest, bulged like they were chiseled from rock. He was dying to act, needed to act, but had no one yet to stake. His kit was propped open on my table, exposing his weapons brazenly like a male stripper flashes cock for dollars. Rowan wood, hand carved, laced the inside of the lid. Four green bottles of Brut cologne stamped with a black cross atop red wax seals were strapped deep inside and I understood in a rush: Batten didn't wear watered-down cologne ... he wore holy water that he just happened to keep in old Brut bottles. When he glared at me, it was clear didn't want to ask for my help. Which was great, because I didn't particularly wanna give him any.

"Where is everyone?" I asked.

Batten's dark blue eyes were veiled. "Chapel's managing the scene. Hood went with the bus and his man."

"Detective Munchie?"

"Deputy Dunnachie."

"Right." I shoved my hands in my jeans pockets. "He does look a lot like Richard Belzer ... dunked in mint jelly. He gonna be okay?"

"Hood said he's been green since early this morning, fighting flu. Add the shock of a vampire and beetles hollowing out a kid's skull and I'm not sure any of us wouldn't be green."

Hollowing out. *Eeeeuuuuww.* Zombie beetles: all about efficiency. "Did you spray the rest of the bugs? Spray won't kill them, but it'll daze them enough so we can flick them aside and burn them."

He gave a single nod. "Already taken care of."

I took the long gaze down the hall. The front door had been left open, the door mat crumpled to one side kicked under the draft guard. I could hear their radios crackling back and forth, competing in volume across the yard through the storm—codes bantered, orders given, requests made—very coordinated, everything well in hand, not a single one of them seeming shocked at the sight peeking out of the mailbox. They sure as hell didn't look like they needed my help.

Batten's face was carefully blank. "Got in touch with the mail carrier. The head wasn't there when he dropped off the mail."

"Just the kind of thing an unbalanced head-toting mailman would say."

"Means in the minutes between the truck leaving and Dunnachie going to the mailbox, the head was placed there."

"Wonder how long someone hunkered in the forest with a severed head, waiting for the mail truck to come and go," I mused. Then I thought: if the beetles were close, they probably found the head before Sherlock could get it in the mailbox, and may have swarmed her. "Check the ERs for anyone else admitted with beetle bites in or around her orifices, or the early symptoms of crypt plague caused by *yersinia sanguinaria*: massive headache, plummeting body temp, black blooms under her skin, especially in and around the lymph nodes, as well as incoherence. Then again, if it's Danika, her coherence isn't great to begin with."

I saw Harry out of the corner of my eye, lingering in the bedroom doorway.

"K9's ten minutes out," Batten said.

"K9's useless," I sighed, feeling the frustration tightening my shoulders until they matched his. "The dog's going to hone in on Harry's scent, and once it does it won't be interested in anything else. You know they haven't been able to train K9 dogs to ignore the undead yet."

"Then I guess we could use your Talents here," he said.

"Well, as fascinating as body parts in a mailbox might sound to you, Harry's right: I retired for a reason. I am a spaz, and when I stick my neck out, I get clobbered." I turned away from him to the kitchen sink to draw water into the old-fashioned whistle kettle for tea; then I put the tea pot in the sink with some hot water inside to warm the china. "The Marnie Baranuik Blue Sense vending machine is officially unplugged."

"Quitting is Harry's idea, then?"

"No, but I'm grateful for the reminder. This is your case, not mine."

"So you said. But then you went bumbling off to chase down clues on your own." Batten continued, his voice raising through the octaves. "Without calling me for backup."

"We've been over this. I was trying to do the right thing, but it was a mistake, I admit that. Working this case at all would be a mistake. It would be a disaster. Like last time. Like Buffalo." *Except in Buffalo we fucked like two sex addicts after an unsuccessful support group meeting.*

"If you're talking about Prost," he growled, "We were only on that case a couple weeks. We barely gave it a shot."

"I gave it a shot, all right. Two .38s, shoulder and spine, and it was about as much fun as a club up the ass."

His perceptive eyes narrowed to slits. "Thought you said quitting had nothing to do with the shooting."

He had me there. I wasn't about to confess I retired so I didn't have to see him again. I stuttered around in my brain for a clever retort and gave up, chucking tea bags into the pot—two, four, seven, not even counting anymore.

"Talk to me, Baranuik, stop running." Batten jabbed a finger at me. "You're not this cowardly, deep down. I know you."

"You don't know shit," I snapped, pointing back. "You're all job. When it comes to me, you're fuckin' clueless."

"You talk awful big for such a tiny woman." Batten scowled at me, advancing, his square-shouldered form looming over me.

"Go ahead, remind me of my size. See what good that macho bullshit does you."

"You need to do more than this, to get rid of me."

Harry came to lean against the counter, enjoying the show; loud and clear I got the impression that part of him agreed with Batten, which only served to irritate me further.

"I'm not trained for FBI shit. I'm just an ex-pro psychic. I should set up a quaint little magic shop, flip tarot cards and self-publish erotic poetry like old Ruby Valli."

That drew Harry stiffly upright. "Poetry?"

"Hey, I know Ruby Valli." Batten took a step toward me, drawing himself up to his full six feet. "I've worked with Ruby Valli. She's 93 years old, half lame and still plays paintball with people half her age. Unlike you, she's earned her retirement, but she'd be all-in if I asked for her. The fact that she's arthritic, half-deaf, and mostly blind wouldn't stop her for a second."

"Fine, so put *her* in the PCU!" I sputtered. "She's precognitive, she probably already knows the outcome!"

"Out-gamed by a little old blind lady with a bum knee, how's that feeling in your gut, Baranuik?"

"You mean the guts that are held together with titanium staples? It hurts too much in there to separate shame from agony. Maybe when it heals, I'll be able to tell the difference." I stared him down, crossing my arms over my injuries when the whistle on the tea kettle summoned; I whisked it off the element and poured boiling water into the teapot. "I'm not the Great White Shark of psychic investigations, no matter how many papers print it. I'm not a kickass crime fighting superhero." Except in my daydreams, when I aim the blow dryer at the bathroom mirror. "I'm just an ex-Groper with bad hair and a sweet tooth. What do you want from me?"

Batten yanked on his earlobe. I'd seen him do it before. I didn't think he was aware that he did it. He gave it another long tug and lowered his voice to an almost reluctant tone. If I didn't know better, I'd have thought something gentle and kind was about to come out of his mouth. Except his face hardened instead of softened, and I tensed in response.

"I have your permission then, after Sherlock stakes Harry, to remind you that you decided not to help me?"

I jabbed a finger at his face. "You have absolutely no idea how much I hate you for saying that."

"We started off hating each other. Might as well end on the same note."

"I got no problem with that," I snarled.

"For fuck's sake, Baranuik, go out there and Grope that head."

I practically heard Harry's flinch; he came to stand behind me, backing me up.

"You want me to put my bare hands on it?" In all honesty didn't know how could I go out there and actually *do* that; he'd never asked me to touch a body before. My psychic consulting had been limited to getting emotional impressions from the scene, and touching evidence but *not* remains; clothing scraps and shoe prints in mud, and broken glass stuck in tires. If I touched it, not only would I have to see the killing, not only would I be swallowed up by empathic vibrations of the victim's scrambling feelings, her desperate panic and the horrible knowledge that she was about to die, but in Groping it I'd also be assaulted by the physical memory of what happened: the pain, the touch of death. It was bad enough to have waking nightmares of what Danika did to *me*. I didn't really want to grapple with the sights, sounds and feelings of a young girl's flayed, glistening spine exposed at the neck.

Then again, I also didn't want to wait around for another victim to get dumped, or another body part on my property. I hunched my shoulders up around my collar. "You insensitive prick. You have no idea what you're asking me to do, what it would feel like …"

"Harry's a Groper," Batten suggested to me. "Right? Your psychic shit comes from him? Maybe Harry should do it."

"Well, lad," Harry exclaimed. "Aren't you full of pithy insights and vapid ideas this afternoon."

I pounced, "You're not using my companion in broad daylight, douchebag. Every time he actively uses psychometry, he draws on—" I clenched my leather-clad fists, not wanting to give Batten the satisfaction of the whole story. Harry avoided using his Talents purposefully, because he believed they tainted what little good there was left in his soul; Harry was an immortal who believed in redemption.

"Marnie, we've got no leads. No trace. Chapel said prints so far have been a bust. We even fumed the body. DNA on the blood at the scene's a long shot at best. No witnesses saw the dump. No one's come forward to say they saw or heard the abduction. If Danika Sherlock decapitated that young girl, you can tell me right this minute," he said. "Then Chapel and I can take the steps necessary to prove it."

"Why don't you get out there and do your goddamned job, without falling back on a psychic to make it easier for you?"

"Because I don't want her to fuckin' kill you, Marnie!" he exploded. He uncrossed his arms and motioned at the door. "Beat work takes time, time you might not have. Even Harry can see the sense in that!"

"Oh yes, even I," Harry murmured, but without fight; again, I sensed he agreed with Batten.

"She's already stabbed you once, Marnie," Batten said. "She's not fucking around, here, she wants you dead."

He hated me, but he didn't want me dead. How terribly romantic; probably the closest I was ever gonna get with Jerkface. I prodded my temple with a gloved finger. "You just don't stop, do you?"

Batten pointed in the direction of the noise and draft from the front porch. "I'll stop. When you get out there and Grope that head. Won't ask you for another thing."

I hesitated; that sounded awfully final. Did I *never* want to see him again? I thought that's why I quit working with the FBI in the first place. But I knew now that the engagement had been a lie, a delusion in Sherlock's sick little mind. Did it change anything, make our tryst any less casual? Not really.

He was still using me, with no regard to how it might put me at risk or how damaged I already was. I studied his piercing, angry eyes. Demanding. God, he was such an asshole. So why did I want to throw him on the kitchen floor and wrestle him out of his pants? I plucked Harry's cell phone off the kitchen counter, and texted Chapel's Blackberry: *Groping evidence in ten.*

"Groping won't work well," I warned Batten, taking one last shot at saving my sanity. "Too many people out there. K9 is coming. Dogs barking, cops shouting …impossible."

Chapel texted back, *Stay inside please. Too bright. Unsafe*. It took me a frowning moment to realize, he thought it was Harry texting. I tried again: *MB Groping evidence in ten.*

"I'll get rid of the distractions," Batten said resolutely.

"The body part belongs to the coroner. I can't go near it without his nod."

"Let me deal with the details, Baranuik. You do whatever it is you do."

"I'd step it up a notch if I thought you had my back," I admitted quietly. "We're not all as brave as you, you know. Some of us have stuff left to lose."

Batten recoiled, but his cop face compensated by going blank, deflecting whatever shot I'd gotten in. "You're not going out there alone," he assured me. "Whatever you need, you got. You coming?"

I glanced down at Chapel's reply: *Good to have you back. Whenever you're ready.*

"You win, but don't get all cocky about it or I'll give you a fat lip." I looked up into Harry's gloomy eyes as he scanned my face unhappily. "Looks like I'm going back to work, Harry. When I'm done, I'm going to need soap, lots of it, in a nice hot bath."

"Shower," Harry reminded gently, his hand landing on my shoulder. "And you'll go no where until you've had your vitamins."

"Whatever." I vaguely registered the pill bottle that appeared like magic in Harry's hand. "I want pizza, and Dr. Pepper, and I want to watch old Dr. Who with my companion, my big furry blanket and a hot water bottle."

Distress shadowed Harry's stare. "We can just start the DVD now and call for delivery. Green olives and extra pineapple?" He attempted a smile but its curve didn't quite make the dimple. "You don't have to do this."

"It looks like my only option, if I want Kill-Notch to go away." I planted my hands on my hips and turned to crane up a whole foot at Batten's scruffy chin. "Can I have your big fancy gun?"

His head did a slow crawl. "Not on your life."

"Fine," I sighed. "But you're not my best friend any more."

C15

Getting rid of the crowd was not possible. I figured it had been a stretch, the first of many promises Batten couldn't keep. The cops did retreat to the warmth of their vehicles, and the firemen decided they weren't needed after all. Their truck rumbled away after some difficulty turning around on the narrow dead-end street. A sheriff's deputy had to move his Explorer into the mouth of a snowmobile trail and it was briefly stuck in a snow drift.

I could still hear radios squawking across the yard, even from my office, muffled through the window. The coroner's van was running, and two attendants were leaning against it having a smoke and talking, their heads slightly together, oblivious to the exhaust around them. I saw a face I recognized and squinted, putting my nose up to the window pane; Robert-not-Robin Hood was back, sitting half-in half-out of a Range Rover, one lean leg stretched way out. Shouldn't he be with Dunnachie at the hospital? Maybe he couldn't resist the show; I sure as hell didn't want Hood watching me out there.

I waited in my office by the window, peering through the blinds with my nose in the slats, watching Batten stride across the front lawn to talk at the different groups, managing the scene, his pointing and gesturing authoritative. I could tell he was pissing people off and wondered if he cared. Chapel was much better at this sort of thing, but he was no where to be seen. I could sense, stronger than usual, Chapel's unique energy, that calm, resolute vigor, unbendable, as though we had a different connection, lately: full signal, five bars. I sensed Chapel's expectation close enough to be palpable but not so close as to pinpoint his location.

Batten knew he'd be able to wear me down with words, the dick. I'd known it too; fighting it was wholly necessary, but the truth was Mark Batten could sell me snake oil, aluminum siding, oceanfront property in Idaho and a 5 year subscription to a Rice Cake of the Week club. If he took his shirt off, he could sell me my own ass.

But now that he was getting what he wanted, his way, was he happy? No. Jerkface looked even more pissed than usual, his dark brows pulled down, his body vibrating with tension. Was there no pleasing him? And why, I wondered for the first time, was he such a hardass in the first place? Watching him tromp across the yard, I understood it wasn't just me, *saw* it wasn't so: he was a jerk to everyone in equal measure. That should have made me feel better. It didn't. There was damage, there, that I hadn't seen before, and the realization came as a one-two punch: because on its heels was the certainty that no matter what happened between us, Kill-Notch Batten would never in a million years confide in me the source of his pain. The cologne bottles meant something. His grandfather's, perhaps. It was his grandfather's kit. Clues, but no answers. I'd never get answers. And with Batten being a psychic null to me, I'd never sneak the answers, either.

Behind me in the dim, I heard the swish of the rug as Harry tossed it aside. "Almost ready?"

I came around the desk to stare down at the white pentagram painted on the floor of my office, 6 feet in diameter, the five points adorned with hand-drawn symbols: spirit, water, fire earth, air. In the center, my artistic sister Carrie had painted for me a spreading tree and three snowy white owls.

"Brilliant." Harry said with a clap of his hands. "Strip."

"Right. I'm getting skyclad with a double-clutch of cops on my lawn."

Harry's lips tightened. "I suppose the nudity isn't strictly compulsory."

"None of this is necessary," I pointed out. "I don't need witchcraft to do a little Groping. All I need is you."

Harry knelt and placed a gold votive at each point of the pentacle. "I'm afraid I insist today, love."

"But ..." There was little sun through the snow-clouds, but I turned the blinds to the complete room-darkening option, blocking all view. My voice dropped an octave without me meaning to do it. "*He* doesn't like me."

Harry laughed. "He likes you just fine."

"I'm still thrumming from Aradia's necromimesis. I pulled too much and haven't thanked Her. Neither will be too thrilled with me." I wrung my hands and felt the leather gloves bunch in my palms. "I've got it all wrong, lately. I'm too wound up. I'll infect the whole spell and things will turn out degraded and wonky."

Harry's head shook. "This is your chance to set things right with both of them."

"Lock the office door behind you, then," I sighed, whipping off my gloves and tossing them behind me on the swivel chair. "At least if I flash some tit, He might listen." I held out my hand and he slapped the athame into it like a nurse gives a surgeon a scalpel. "Good bye, Harry."

"I thought I should assist."

"Out." I unbuttoned my jeans.

He had taken his apron down from his neck and the strap hung low on his waist. He moved it now to its proper place, tightened the cord at the back. It looked out of place atop his tux. "Fancy a post-spell boost?"

"Please. Double espresso."

Harry bowed and closed the door behind him. I waited for his essence to join him, for the air in the office to stop its cool eddy and flow. Icy currents purled around me. When it stopped, I slid my shirt over my head, suppressing a shiver. I unlocked the gun safe under my desk to retrieve my book of shadows, and my eyes fell on the jar of newt eyes. I'd thought there were only 13, but a quick count showed 15, two of them damaged; they lurked in the bottom like filmy angel fish fins, whitish-orange with a trace of vein. Screwing off the lid, I fished one out to examine it closer, and the Blue Sense flared so strongly that, for a second, my vision blurred. The eye flew out of my hand to the desk top with a small wet *plip* and I let it go gladly, shaking my hands clean. I didn't have time to wonder about it. There was a soft tap at the door and whisked the eye up, shoved it in my jeans pocket, covered my bare B-cups with one arm and tiptoed behind the door.

"Who is it?"

Harry's exhale was forced, unnatural and medically unnecessary, but it made his point: I should know when it's him. I cracked the door. A plucked yellow orchid blossom slipped in through the crack, pinched in his well-manicured fingers. "For Her."

"Ah! Thanks."

"You're welcome. The *phalaenopsis* on the kitchen window ledge is now naked." I felt a wash of unexpected heat from him and he cleared his throat. "I had better check on my scones." He shut the door and I relocked it.

Heat? From my Cold Company? I hadn't had a chance to feed Harry yet since I'd come back from the hospital. Where was he getting warmth from, if not from blood? Then I remembered: the freezer in the boathouse. Harry had told me about the o-negative supply. At the time, I wasn't sure he was telling me the whole truth, but it sure felt like he'd just fed so it must be true.

Using Earth magic to strengthen myself against the negative energy that could very well be lurking like a rabid toad in Kristin Davis' fumigated skull would require His blessing. When a psychic of unknown practices is after you, you take any and all precautions available.

I removed the gold votives from the pentagram's points, cut the athame over it to break the fledgling circle mounting there. Listlessly, it dissipated. There was a low mirrored bowl on the shelf beside my desk. When I set it in the center of the tree I tucked the orchid in it, placed the silver candle at the spirit position and put match to wick. A slip of dried white sage came from my top drawer but my hand faltered; where had I left my bolline?

The boathouse. I hadn't cut herbs since November and the bolline was still out on the potting table with the old clay herb pots and bags of triple-mix. I let out an annoyed moan. Did I really want to get dressed, trudge out to the back yard in the calf-deep snow with a flashlight in my mouth to search the unheated boathouse for a curved knife, then come back here and strip down again, just so I could cut some damned sage? Could I just this once use the athame for cutting herbs?

I glanced down at the pentagram and felt a ripple of apprehension. I knew better than to screw with procedure when everything else was already iffy.

Half way to the boathouse I cursed myself for not grabbing a coat and my gloves. I was vulnerable to all sorts of things with my hands "out" in the world like this. The boathouse doorknob was frosted. I wasn't used to touching surfaces with my skin, and definitely not wintry metal. Inside, the boathouse was still and hushed. The potting table was beside the freezer under a shaft of light populated by colonies of swimming dust motes. I steadied myself with a hand on the freezer's grimy top, reached up high and *...He hasn't touched it ...* took down the bolline from its hook, staring in wonderment at the impression I Groped from the freezer.

Harry hadn't been out here. The dust coating its lid only reinforced this. If I lifted the top, I would find no bags of o-negative blood. He lied to me.

That couldn't be. Ashamed, I was about to march right back to the house but my feet stayed rooted to the gravel floor, daring me to check again. Taunting me with the possibilities of betrayal. Could it be? I put my bare palm out to taste the air, naked fingers flickering out in an ever-growing circle. My scalp prickled. Nothing felt like my Harry. The whole place lacked his familiar energy, his signature. I moved deeper into the boathouse, back behind his carefully-stored, covered sports car, then back to the door. Cobwebs in the corner of the door added visual proof that I resented.

But he's fed. He's felt warm, on and off. I refused to even think the question that was burbling in the back of my brain, and focused on the angry realization: Harry had lied at the hospital and was, today, still lying to me. He was taking directly from the vein. And not mine.

I opened the freezer and fished around. No blood. I sunk a bare hand into its frigid depths and touched the ice. I knew the feel of my own signature and the last person to touch this was definitely me. I spread both palms flat, hovered them in the space just above the freezer. Under my hands the Blue Sense tingled, and I let it fall again, licking at the chilled air. Nothing but traces of myself in the freezer.

If I was honest with myself, I had known he was lying to me back in the hospital. I'd known, deep down, that he intended to feed on some warm body. A blinding red wave of fury rose in me; I squelched it carefully. This would have to wait. I shoved the bolline in the waistline of my pants, careful of the bandages around my middle. My back ached, a dull throb threatening to go to full roar unless I took some of those expensive painkillers I'd been given a prescription for.

I shouldn't *need* painkillers. I shouldn't *be* injured. Harry shouldn't have needed to drink deeply from someone else's veins. I should have ignored her call. I should have hung up in Danika's ear. Next time someone begged me for help, I'd let them fend for themselves. And as for Batten, he could fend for his own stupid career. My path back to the house was tromped: The Red Wrath Shuffle. I kicked snow out of my way harder than was necessary, as though it had fallen to offend me and I had to show it the error of its ways. It was official. I hated everyone and everything. The first person to get in my way was going to be real sorry.

Batten waited just inside the back door, leaning one lean hip against the washing machine in the mudroom. He pushed away with a frown.

"What the hell is taking you so long? I've had to explain to three different services—"

I grabbed him by the face with both naked hands and pulled him into a rough, open-mouthed kiss. For a moment, his spine went rigid. I dug my fingernails into the back of his head and forced him to remain in place. Not that he was fighting it. He should have been. *Tsk tsk, fraternization*, I thought. *Screw it.* Fraternization was delicious. I sank into the kiss, fed off it, drawing sudden sexual heat into my belly and letting it spread in all directions through my body, overwriting the rage. Under my bare palms, I felt things stirring in his cheek, budding impressions of his morning shave, the filling in his left molar, the sweetness of the French toast he'd had for breakfast. Actual impressions from the blank face. Heady with need, I let the sensations ride through my brain, welcomed them.

In a heady rush up against the washing machine, Batten melted into my body and his tongue slid across mine hungrily. Backing me up against the machine, he eagerly pressed his hips against my core, his knee finding the spot between mine and parting them.

I broke the kiss and gave him a good hard slap across the face. He gave me the silent, glazed beware-of-lunatic assessment for the hundredth time.

"Gonna have me arrested for assaulting a federal agent?" I asked. He shook his head, no. "That's a shame. Three hots and a cot sounds real good right about now."

He found his voice. "You okay?"

"Don't pretend you give a shit. I'm a tool to you. You're using me. Maybe I'll feel better about it if I start using you back." I pointed into the meat of his broad, immovable chest. "Parasites: you, Chapel, Harry, all of you, every last one. Now leave me alone while I prepare myself."

"I was wrong, Baranuik," he called to my retreating back. "You *are* half-cracked."

"You have no idea, Agent Batten. No fuckin' idea."

Harry was in my path through the kitchen and I breezed by him, letting him taste a dollop of my pain at his treachery, releasing a mere trickle of it from my control so it could lash him. Startled, his eyes went large and he drifted silently back against the kitchen counter.

Showing the wisdom of his age, the revenant said nothing.

C16

My heart still jack-hammering, I took a deep breath into my lungs to settle down. The fresh-cut white sage dropped into the mirrored bowl atop the yellow orchid blossom.

"Hail Aradia, Queen of Light/ Stand I naked in Thy sight/Through You all things take their flight/In the darkness of the night."

I relit the silver candle, feeling the rise of arcane power ride up my arms. I dropped cautiously to my bare knees in the middle of the circle. After inviting the four guardian elements of the Watchtower inside a tight saltwater circle, I focused my intent on their blessings.

The Watchtower responded. The essence of the divine swelled, palpable under my touch. There was always a point in casting where I was distinctly aware that I was no longer alone, when the Four rushed in towards the circle to fill a void, to pave the way for a visit from the goddess. I meditated on the small bending flame of the silver candle and banished all the negative feelings I'd been having. Any time an ill thought cropped up I slapped it back down into silence. Gruesome murder? Nope, down ya go. Jealousy? No thanks. Justice? Ok, maybe a little of that would be nice. Infidelity? Deception? My stomach rolled sickly and I pushed that away. No negative thoughts would touch me right now. I willed radiant thoughts to overwhelm the shadows in the corners of my mind: comfort, safety, love, devotion. Things would be better. I'd help them be better. I'd focus on the good. Unworthy as I was, I'd shepherd in the light.

The flame licked hard towards me, then steadied. I was ready.

"Hecate hear Your humble slave/ Grateful for the life You saved/ I ask of You a simple wish/ accept the offering from my dish." It was clumsy, but it was hurried off the top of my head. I put match to wick on another gold candle and set it in the center of the circle next to the silver.

"Lady, I call thy Consort underground/Cernunnos, Horned One, Wild Unbound/ Hunter and Hunted, stand for me/ An' it harm none, so mote it be."

The flames flickered once, violently to the south. "I call Thy consort, Mother of the Sky," I breathed out hard from my nostrils. Nothing. I hopped to my feet to fetch my Book of Shadows, a small leather-bound grimoire bound with twine. A bundle of dried Vervain was tied to it. I used the bolline to carve an upward arrow in the side of the silver candle, anointed it with consecrated oil and rolled it in powdered rue before re-lighting it and returning it to the pentagram.

"Goddess of Power," I invited. "I depend upon the grace and blessing of Your consort. Will You call to Him on my behalf?"

Nothing. "I knew it. The Green Man hates me." I took a break, remaining in the circle, gently stretching my torn and battered self, rolling my shoulders, turning my stiff neck from one side to the other. For good measure, I cracked my knuckles, trying to give the impression of Serious Business. I leaned over to scan the grimoire for hints as to how to improve when the gold candle licked up into the air, hitting me directly in the nipple.

"Mother*fucker*!" I shrieked, slapping a hand to cup protectively. Crawling away from the candle, I tasted the air.

There was a change inside the circle, then, an invasion of sun-warmed fur and fresh air, hinting of sweet thick blood, of dark crumbling earth and fecundity, of gritty pitted limestone and fat spitting in a fire. I was not alone.

"The Big Dog's up in here, hunh? Showing me how it's done?" I pulled myself to my feet, tentatively drew aside the bandage on my belly. "That was my tit, Sir. Apparently flowers aren't Your thing. This what You were looking for?"

One of my fingernails swirled around the edges of my wound, fingering its edge. As His blessing curled up my spine I welcomed it, a pound strike to echo my slamming pulse. I opened my arms and felt filled, channeled it towards the earth point. The currents swam under one of my palms and I let my hand ride the new heat in the air, playing along its waves like a palm frond in the ocean breeze.

"Why so shy?" I murmured, crooking my hip at the flame invitingly. "Ok, I admit: I've been bitchy with the penis-people lately. I've been relying strictly on girl power." I nodded as ideas began flashing through my mind, seeing things from different perspectives, as though the lens of my mind were refracting energy in fresh directions. "That's not accomplishing anything, is it? I running on half power. I've got big troubles, and today I see that You're the one I need. Let's make nicey-nice, whatever it takes." I took the athame and slid it along the far edge of my belly wound, drawing fresh blood. For a minute the feeling of its warmth running down to my hip bone was almost sensual, made me writhe. I dipped a finger in, approached the gold candle.

"Green Man, Sun God, Might of Earth and Strength of Righteousness, accept this offering from Your supplicant." I fed the fire a cautious taste. *"God of War, hear me. General of the Sky, stand with me. With blood I call You from the Forest. With blood I call You from Cave and Chasm. With blood I call You from the Edge. Everlasting One, brace me with Your resilience, shelter me with Your undying power. Hear me,*

mighty Consort, and be satisfied." I dropped my bloodied fingertip into the tongue of the flame.

Heat spiked through my spine and I jerked with a gasp. Pouring into my veins, the Green Man invaded, laid claim, exploring my wounds and not gently; He discovered and roamed like an experienced lover's eager hands, finding strengths and weaknesses, calculating, measuring, He knew me. I felt overrun. Swaying, I put one hand out to seize the desk but it was just out of reach and I pitched, listing near the edge of my circle. Fortified by the spirit of the Green Man, I reveled in the molten-stone surge of potency and supremacy that burbled now just beneath the surface of my being.

It was, in a word, breathtaking.

"With gratitude and grace/ I mark Thy ancient place/Welcome Thy ward upon me, Mighty One/and in a blink the spell be done."

Quickly I blew the candles out, broke the circle and pressed the bandage back tight to the leaking wound. Wham, bam, thank you Sir. In and out. Probably I should learn from Him, and keep all my dealing with the savage sex swift and sweet.

When I came out of the office tucking my shirt into my pants, Harry was at the table spreading raspberry jam on a quarter of scone for Batten. They both glanced up from what might otherwise be a lovely afternoon tea, if the guest was James Dean with a badge, and the host was the bulletproof love child of Fred Astaire and Martha Stewart.

"Blood magic," was all Harry said, but his eyes spoke conflicted volumes; appetite, desire, worry, disapproval. I knew that, secreted away behind his tense lips, his fangs were extended.

I glared until my companion looked away. "Agent Batten, there's a head waiting for me?"

He didn't look like he was interested in showing me anymore, but he got up from the table and zipped his jacket halfway. I knew this was to leave access to his gun, though he couldn't believe that Sherlock was still out there with the yard full of cops and now a K9 unit, the dog straining at the leash and lifting its nose in the direction of the house.

"Are you sure Chapel cooked all the beetles?"

The last of the scone popped in his mouth. "We'll find out." He dusted the crumbs from his lip and nodded thanks at Harry.

"On this single matter we may be in complete agreement, Agent Batten," Harry called to us as we stepped onto the porch. "She might, in fact, be quite mad already."

C17

Bending in half to tie a double knot in the shoelaces on my Keds hurt my stapled gut like a motherfucker, but Batten was watching, so I had to keep a stiff upper lip. While I exchanged my light gloves for heavy tan fur-lined lambskin ones, I heard the impatient shuffle of standard issue boots behind me. I realized too late that there was still a mushed-up newt eyeball in the right front pocket of my jeans, making a conspicuous wet smear, but there was nothing I could do about it in front of Agent Batten. Twisting into my puffy pink parka, I was an acrobat twisting on the trapeze, and zipping it up right to the hood made me feel like a gladiator strapping on armor. I'd put the innerpants holster in my jeans and the Beretta Cougar mini was now tucked near my butt-crack. *Look out, Sherlock: Marnie Baranuik has gone badass.* I turned to face Batten, all business.

His eyebrows were puckered hard with dismay, as if he were witnessing a ridiculous act that both aroused him and hurt his head. I jerked the ties on my hood, which nearly swallowed my head in a perfect padded pink circle.

Batten folded his arms across his chest. "You look like a marshmallow Peep."

"If she's out there, I don't want her to see me," I explained from within.

"You're the only five-foot female who would be at this cabin fondling dismembered body parts."

"Don't say the word dismembered, it's major *blech.* And I'm 5'3"."

"In three inch heels, maybe. You're not fooling anyone with the hood." When I opened my mouth to object he waved me quiet. "What the hell is that?"

He reached around me like he was playing grab-ass, and jerked the gun out from behind my back. I nodded at it. "Right. That. I thought I should pack heat."

His lips twitched into a barely-contained smirk. "Is it loaded?"

"Only if the bullet fairy did it when I wasn't looking."

"Put it away."

"But what if she's out there?"

"She's not out there," he said tiredly. "Even if she is, there are nearly twenty law enforcement and emergency personnel out there trained to use firearms. *Loaded* firearms."

"Do you honestly think a nutcase would leave a severed head in a mailbox and not hang around to watch the fall-out?"

"They're long gone. It's possible the mailbox and the murder wasn't Sherlock at all," he reminded me. "No proof yet that she murdered Davis."

"I'm sorry. You're right." I swallowed hard and shook my head, passing the Beretta butt-first to Harry, who verified that it was unloaded before returning it to my bedroom. "I'm letting my anger affect my work."

I stopped on the porch, looking down the length of the drive at the mailbox. It had always seemed charming before, listing slightly off center, dented in the back as though the mailman woke up on the wrong side of the bed one morning and punched into it. Now it seemed like a time bomb, ticking off the seconds before it went off. I felt Harry's cool presence return, an icy ward that had the opposite effect on my shoulders than the cold air did: I felt the muscles melt, and knew Harry was pushing his feelings of comfort and confidence through the Bond at me, either to buck me up for the job ahead, or for his own agenda. I couldn't tell which.

"Better to think of it as an *it* and not a *she,*" Batten advised at my shoulder. It wasn't the first time he'd given me that advice. I thought, rather miserably, it might not be the last, and the trepidation of seeing a wasted life again hung its hooks in my heart, dragging me down.

"If Ms. Sherlock is out there, you had best not stand so close to my DaySitter, Agent Batten," Harry said from the safety of the shaded hallway, and touched the door further closed, so that it blocked more of the late afternoon sun.

"Let her see," Batten growled. "I don't give a shit what she wants. Or what you want, vampire."

It dawned on me that Batten was playing pretty fast and loose with what was still my life. I wasn't about to play worm on a hook; I'd seen Danika Sherlock's snarling hate enough for one lifetime.

"*I* give a shit," I hissed at him. "Let's not jerk her around more than we need to. Stand away from me, Agent Batten. And when I go to the mailbox, you stay here."

He crammed his hands in his pockets and shuffled aside with an impatient sigh. I took one step forward and my heel hit ice. It slid out from me too fast, but Harry had me under the armpits before I knew what had happened.

Apparently Batten hadn't seen him move; he grunted with surprise. I straightened while Harry melted back into the hallway, and adjusted my coat with a proud jerk. My companion gave the Fed a sweeping frown of disgust, as if he'd expected Batten's reflexes to be better.

Rather than sort out their brewing tiff, I focused on the mailbox, avoiding all the eyes that followed my determined approach, wishing I'd spruced myself up a bit so at least I'd have the armor of desirability on my side to offset the shitstorm of doubt. Bravely to the police do-not-cross tape I marched, a spare yellow vein in the otherwise colourless yard, fluttering in the cold wind around the ramshackle fence by the mailbox. Psychically pummeled by their qualms, buffeted by their distaste, I pulled up my chin, alert so as not to trip over my feet, not wanting to glance around and see derisive sneers or rolling eyes or silent laughter. There were few things I find more degrading than the blatant disbelief of men I admire: cops, firemen, medics, they're all heroes to me, doing brave work. I know they don't feel the same about me, and sometimes it made me wonder why I bothered. Even if I was successful with this effort, I couldn't prove what I saw. No one had to believe me.

Oh well, screw it. I'd do this, and we'd solve the case, and everyone would go away, right? *Riiight.* I could keep telling myself that, but I was sorely convinced that Batten was determined to be a part of my life, even as he railed against the science of psi, even as he disapproved of my living situation and my Talents. Even if he thought my having a gun was amusing at best and tragedy-in-waiting at worst.

I unclenched my teeth long enough to mutter under my breath, "Jerk", putting them all out of my mind. Nothing mattered now but the head in my mailbox, its original owner, and the person who put it there; this was my task. Finding out what it felt like to be decapitated ranked real low on my list of Things to Do, but maybe nailing Sherlock's ass would balance it out? I ducked under the tape line with my shoulders scrinched up around my neck in anticipation.

Maybe it was the cold that took my breath away. By the time I rounded the box I could barely draw air. My other artsy sister, Claire, had painted for Carrie morning glory flowers creeping up the sides of the box, heather-blue cupped blossoms open to greet the sun. The lid was down. The cheerful bright red flag was up. *Delivery!* it proclaimed cheerily. The thought of trying to cleanse the death out of this box seemed about as possible as reaching up and caressing the moon's big round bottom. I'd need bleach and lavender, a full roll of paper towels, rubber gloves, a HAZMAT suit, and in the end a new mailbox, because there was just no way I'd ever be able to make it feel clean. Maybe I should consider a tidy slot in my storm door *...so Danika can slip severed body parts directly into the hallway?* OK, maybe not.

For the second time today I took off my gloves and bared the fragile pale skin of my naked hand. It hurt, so unused to the fresh winter air was my flesh; I didn't let it show on my face. I glanced over the box to the porch. Batten stood with his arms crossed, his legs in a wide authoritative stance, the one that made his tight butt look fucking marvelous if memory served. He was surveying the men to make sure no one interfered. His jaw was doing its clench-unclench routine. I tried to mimic his confident body language, setting my shoulders back. Harry was barely visible over his shoulder, safely tucked in the dim hallway, one pale slender hand holding the door ajar. I could tell by the half turn of Batten's face that the hunter had the revenant guardedly locked in his peripheral vision.

The heavy weight of the Sun God's protective ward vibrated down my arm, strengthening my resolve. I made an experimental poke of the metal lid.

Images flashed immediately: *the mailman's bare hand. Calluses, big knuckles, early rheumatoid pain.* Attempting a psychic link to him as a warm up exercise, I caught a whiff of the pot he'd smoked with his wife that morning during breakfast of eggs and cheap side bacon, how he disliked cheap bacon streaked with too much fat and wished she'd buy the better, meatier stuff; even when he gave her extra money for groceries she'd still buy the cheap stuff, but it was a minor thing. He was a mellow man who picked his battles prudently. He was a man who loved his wife, despite or even because of her thriftiness, and all her other faults. His name was Jacob. No one called him Jake, just Jacob.

I tried once more, rubbing the metal and closing my eyes. I saw him again, a slightly portly man in his early 40s, those thick calluses from playing bass guitar, his habit of masturbating during his long drive out to Shaw's Fist. He'd pull off on one of the quieter roads and have what he considered a little "stress-busting tug". Sometimes he didn't--couldn't really--wash his hands afterward. I felt myself blushing but didn't break the link. Inside the box, there were a lot worse things than a microscopic hint of residual semen from an otherwise happily-married man.

Thinking about that made the head a bit less ghastly when I finally opened the lid. Because out there, not everyone was off-their-tits crazy. Sometimes they were only mildly loopy. Maybe life with people in it wasn't all that bad. Maybe knowing something more about them made tolerating them easier, not harder. It was something I'd never considered, but the fact remained: I was staring at this poor girl's head, and knowing the mailman masturbated in his truck so he wouldn't make his wife feel like she wasn't doing enough to please him made looking at the dead girl somehow less horrid. I couldn't have explained it. But there it was, and I was calm enough to notice details without barfing on my Keds in front of the cops. Always a plus.

The hair was brunette with soft natural hints of auburn. Her mouth was closed, which was good. I'd been to a crime scene where one of Jeremiah Prost's victims had died with a scream frozen on his jaw, his toddler mouth open in a silent wail. It had made the scene a hundred times worse, had kept drawing my eyes back in horror-struck, sympathetic wonder to the frail bloodless corpse forever crying out for his mother.

I closed my eyes, squeezed them to erase Jeremiah's history written across my memory banks then focused on Davis.

There were dark sunglasses propped on her ... *"it"*, I corrected. I would be damned if I was going to touch them. I didn't want to see if her eyes were brown, blue or green, open, closed or missing. There were cotton plugs in her nostrils, shredded by beetle pincers and dangling, smudged with fluids.

There was a ripple of conversation between those watching me. Radios had been turned down slightly, enough so they could hear them and I could barely. I appreciated that. But their voices were distracting me from going deeper, and I jerked my chin at Batten in a summons.

He stalked across the snow-covered lawn like he was expecting a fight, brow lowered and shoulders forward.

"Chill out, Cro-Mag," I said when he got close enough. "They've fallen back. That's great. But they're still making too much noise. If you can quiet them, I'll try again."

A nod. He turned around to go talk to the clustered groups. I was drawn to the flicker of impatience from the coroner's attendants, who were sharing a lighter and having their third cigarette. The doctor had long gone and was waiting for them at the morgue in Denver with the rest of the body. The attendants couldn't leave without the head. It was their "property" technically, from now until the funeral home reclaimed it for the family after the autopsy. They were being good sports as a favor to the FBI but the attendants didn't appreciate having to wait. They figured they'd already waited in the cold too long. I tried to focus past their foot-shuffling irritation. Again the image of the mailman's sticky fingers teased the outer reaches of my awareness. I told myself, just because it was often on his hands doesn't mean it transferred to the metal. Besides, he kept Kleenex in his truck. In the glove box next to the well-read Busty Babes magazine.

I pinched my lips together to deny myself the outrageously inappropriate grin that tickled and threatened the corners of my mouth. No no *no*, I was not going to start giggling like a harebrained nutcase in front of the collective departments of sheriff, fire and rescue guys. Marnie Baranuik didn't giggle. Ever. Especially not when faced with gore. I succeeded in making it look like Serious Business instead of lunatic laughter by pulling down a dour grimace. *Point: me.*

Batten was getting heightened resistance, now. The coroner's attendants had had enough, and I couldn't blame them. I glanced at the porch and raised my eyebrows at Harry. He cocked his head in consideration, looking, as he often did, for my permission to step in. This time, I shrugged a *why not* in silent approval.

Harry never failed to make every motion appear salacious, and crooking one long finger seductively at the forest was no exception. His long fingers coiled and curled through the air as though he was weaving electric invitations through the atmosphere, lifting from his side toward the danger of the open yard, the setting sun, creeping in the direction of peril. I'd seen his do this before, still it had the power to take my breath away. I didn't think that anything could resist the lure of that invitation, not once they beheld the potent force of energy behind his luminous eyes. Even the inanimate craved his governance. Now, it hurried to obey.

As though she were a hesitant lover given over to wicked seduction, the woods offered up her darkest secrets to him in a rush. Filmy shade peeled out from under the trees, misting as it raced across the snow-covered lawn like an inky wave, picking up pricks of frost in its swift, slinking purl around him, shrouding the porch. He raised both hands only slightly, palms up, commanding the sanctuary of the shadows in an ever-growing spiral drawn up the length of him until it cloaked his head.

At first no one noticed the immortal on the covered veranda manipulating 100 foot shadows clear across the yard. Then someone let out a guttural exclamation. Another cursed, drawing the attention of the rest. Nervous laughter punctuated by the backpedaling of heels on hard-packed snow, men putting space between themselves and what they were witnessing with well-wide eyes. Hood vaulted from his truck, rigid with attention while the K9 dog went bat-shit berserk, flipping out at the very end of his tether. Batten's stern decree ordered someone to put up his weapon, which meant a trigger-happy nincompoop was drawing down on my Cold Company. *Dirty Harry vs. Dracula*, I thought. Not that it would matter. Bullets couldn't kill a revenant unless you blew their entire head right off. These cops carried mostly standard issue Glock 9mm, and though bullets caused as much pain to revenants as it did to humans, their high-tech Tupperware wasn't likely to accomplish anything but slowing a revenant down or plain pissing him off.

The wind coughed, just enough to stir the hair from behind Harry's ears; it tousled from its perfect style. I knew that would bother him if he wasn't fully concentrating on marking each of his steps with deeper and deeper shadow, his asylum torn from the forest. He had made it all the way to the bottom step, shielding himself from the setting sun by sheer will, his power sizzling darkly within a sharply contained space. My own bravery wavered a moment and worry rattled through my jaw, making my teeth chatter: one slip of his focus and his shelter would whiff away, and the sun, full enough even though it was setting, would discharge him to ash in seconds.

One long finger pointed from beneath the cuff of Harry's wool coat and he rolled his voice at us across the lawn. Though he said it in flawless velvety French for effect, I knew it would stroke inside their ears in English; the marked disagreement between their ears and their brain would strip away any residual ballsy human folly.

"*Silence enfants ... maintenant.*" Silence children ... now.

I struggled to keep a straight face. Harry at his theatrical best, pulling out the Bela Lugosi eyebrow arch and everything. Oh, he was the perfect debonair Hollywood monster, his black coat stirring around his ankles suggesting an opera cape, his show-stopping eyes bright and flashing unnatural, lambent silver. Of course, the cops didn't notice him chewing Juicy Fruit, or see the square hint of the Nintendo DSI in his coat pocket. Probably would have ruined the effect.

Dead silence. Better. *Point: Harry*, to add to his total of eleventy-billion.

I snuck a peek at Batten, who was standing now with Chapel and Hood by the Explorer. I bet Batten noticed the gum. And the gaming system. And the platinum eyebrow rings that were the only indication that Harry wasn't lingering in a fantastic literary time warp.

Batten's colour was high and mottled, his fists clenched. Tough titties. If he didn't want me to call out the big guns (or the weird guns anyway) then he should have done the job right. Pretty simple concept. If I wanted to track Sherlock and knock her teeth out, I was going to have to use what I had.

Harry looked at me expectantly. He snapped his Juicy Fruit.

I mouthed *thank you*, gratefully, as he retreated to safety indoors. It occurred to me for the first time that Harry and I made a pretty efficient pair, that perhaps he and I could solve this problem, or all problems, without the Feds.

I turned my attention back to the carefully-dressed head in my mailbox for second impressions. The cotton nose plugs were not a whim: this was something funereal, it had meaning to whoever tucked them there. The sunglasses were for shock value. I was supposed to whisk them away and be distraught by what I found, which told me her eyes were probably damaged or sewn shut or gone altogether. I really didn't want to be the one to find out which it was, but no one else had disturbed them yet.

I didn't have to touch it to know this head once belonged to Kristin Davis. There simply weren't that many missing heads to offer options in that department. What kind of nutcase would kill a twelve year old girl to put her head in my mailbox? Did said nutcase know her beforehand? How did the nutcase find Kristin, and was Kristin special for some reason, or just an opportunity that presented itself? Was the nutcase Danika Sherlock, or some other squirrel-brain?

I felt Batten closing in on my position as I reached out, my bare fingers inching towards the skin of her cheek. I brushed it softly, feeling the hard chill of frozen flesh just before the electric shock of the Blue Sense threw open a new window in my mind.

Everything went completely black. I inhaled sharply, jolted, but left my fingers stubbornly on the apple of her cheek. I saw nothing at all: not the lawn, or the head in the mailbox, or my own arm, or the winter-wrapped world that was my yard. I saw black.

"Blindfolded?" I asked myself. I tried to probe her last moments. "Are you blindfolded, honey?"

She didn't have anything to say to me. The dead never did, not in so many words. I can't see spirits in the Realm or talk to ghosts or loved ones long-passed: no human being can. Mediums are frauds. The ability to see and hear the dead, that ability belongs to the dead alone. No living person can pierce that veil. All revenants can, through the dead's natural affinity for the dead, but this was one Talent they could not share.

The memories, however, the unlocked secrets marked on her remains, were mine to shuffle through; places, scenes and secrets that could not be hidden from me were disappearing like pencil marks being erased with each minute that went by. If she was hovering there now in spirit to tell me what happened, she could cry out, howl and beat her ethereal breast, but I'd never know it.

"She didn't know who was touching her, drawing her away, into a vehicle but she trusted …because she had an idea that it was someone who knew her? ... she fought only when she sensed danger. By then it was too late and she knew it, was angry at her self for being trusting. She was too close to the curb when she started to put up a fight, and she stumbled, twisting her ankle badly. She was dragged into the car. Van, maybe? SUV? Higher than a car. I can't see. I can't see anything. The vehicle smells funny to her, spicy. No faces, no places. She knows which bus stop she's at, though."

Batten was at my elbow. "Bus stop?"

"Coming home from school. Special bus stop, right outside of the building. That's significant, don't know why. She's so accustomed to it that she doesn't give it any thought, takes it for granted that they pick her up next to the front door. It's not a regular school. She was late. She was alone, none of the other students remained. She must be blindfolded, because all I see is black."

"A hand over her face? A cloth? Enforced? Drugged?"

"I don't know, I don't know. It was all black before she was approached." I couldn't see, I could only feel lost in the dark.

"A scary black?"

It was the perfect question, completely enlightening. "No. A familiar black. Comfortable. Not strange at all." I struggled to understand. "It's all she knows."

"What do you mean?" Batten said, but his tone said he already knew.

"Kristin Davis was blind. Why didn't you tell me?"

I thought he was going to have a good answer to that--something other than "I was saving that tidbit back to test you"--but before he could say anything, a flood of impressions collided into my brain. Overlapping, fighting to assert themselves: perfume, light and floral, rough hands on her arms holding her down, small hands but cruel without a trace of hesitation, wax and cat piss, an old musty cellar. Then sharp pain, sudden and searing along the front of my throat, savage, so unexpected and excruciating that I let out a gurgling scream and broke contact, flailing back onto my ass in the boot-churned slush.

Batten scrambled to help me up. I shoved his hands away angrily.

"I just forgot," I hissed, embarrassed. "People are watching. Don't touch me."

"Your stitches," Batten reminded, stubbornly offering his hand. I didn't want to touch him without my gloves on; I fished in my pocket for lambskin and yanked it on with a quick tug. He waited.

"Forgot what?" he asked, pulling me to my feet.

"To brace for the pain of decapitation," I snapped, cramming my eyes closed, unable to focus with his voice in the mix. "But there was something else."

"Before? After?"

"Do me a favour," I said. "Shut the fuck up."

It made no sense at all, the pain in her eyes *after* the throat slash. If her head was off, her eyes shouldn't be capable of pain, as she should be dead. Unless her head was off and her eyes were still alive to feel pain. But how? Why? That boggled my brain; if it were true, I didn't really want to know the details. Brushing snow off my jeans before it could melt into them, I took a bracing breath before approaching the lid again.

I knew I wouldn't feel anything through my gloves, but that didn't make me any more confident, frankly. My fingers trembled as reached for the sunglasses, slipping them down from the pale, finely-veined eyelids resting limply closed, strangely saggy.

The decapitated head of Kristin Davis opened its jaw with an audible crack. A wretched sloppy noise followed an icy hiss. Toppling to one side, its eyelids flew open accusingly; where her eyes used to be, ragged red holes gaped. What was left of her throat wetly gurgled at me.

I vaulted backwards with a shriek.

C18

"Fuck*shit*--" Batten's reaction time was too slow. I took the fall hard on the back of my head. Impacting the frozen ground made me nip the side of my tongue but I forced myself not to react. I lay in the snow, still, faking a faint, clutching my plastic piece of the prize.

Ice crunched under running boots, holsters creaking and keys jostling, coins in pockets, heavy huffing in frosty air. The K9's German shepherd was going ape-shit nearby. I hoped it didn't get loose and snap someone's arm off; too much undead activity for the poor animal to handle.

"She tipped it over!"

"It moved, I saw it. *It moved.* Fuck me!"

"She moved it, dumbass."

"Back off. Don't touch her," Batten barked. His steamy breath bathed the side of my face.

One man said, "Yeah, like I want to touch the bloodsucking vamp's creepy psychic wife?"

Another piped up: "I swear it opened its mouth."

"It was bullshit, that's what it was." Whoever said it didn't bother to lower his voice or soften the disgust.

"Where are the sunglasses?"

"She broke them. There's a lens missing."

"This is tampering with evidence, Agent Batten." A gruff voice, demanding an explanation, accustomed to being in control. "Does the PCU regularly break evidence in the course of your investigations, or it just this particular civilian you have trouble controlling?"

"Calm down, Jack." Sheriff Hood's voice. "I'm sure it was an accident."

"Marnie?" Chapel summoned calmly. I felt the back of his hand on my cheek, and the blue Sense instantly ripped me a new vision, of worry blended with excitement. "What happened, Mark?"

"The mouth opened. Made a sound. Then she fainted, the glasses went flying."

"We should get her in near to Harry. I understand that might help," Chapel suggested.

"What might help is if we don't let civilians have access to the crime scene," the Jack guy said, snarky.

"What did this accomplish?" the gruff voice demanded.

"Are we about finished, now?" A coroner's assistant.

"Take it away," Batten said.

"It didn't actually move, right?" The other assistant. Forced laughter.

"Missing the lens, Agent Batten."

"We'll find it," Batten assured them. "Fan out, it can't be far."

"She's not coming-to." Chapel, concerned and not hiding it well for a change.

Quietly, the second coroner's assistant: "No way it could fucking open its mouth."

The first assistant, with a smoker's cough. "Well it ain't moving now. C'mon."

My fingers worked with minuscule motion along my side, worked at tucking the missing lens in my waistband, praying that I wasn't being watched.

"Let's get her out of the cold at least," Chapel said.

"With that *thing* in there?" one of the men scoffed.

Another man made a guttural sound. "Fuck that noise. He ain't human. You saw what he did."

"I seen one of those things get both arms torn off and still manage to kill three SWAT guys in Juarez. True story."

"Yeah but how old was it? See, that matters."

"It don't matter, all them monsters the same," Juarez-guy said.

"Telling you, it matters. The older ones are worse. I heard it right from the FBI seminar."

"I don't care what you heard from no damn seminar, schoolboy, I seen it with my own eyes," Juarez said.

"Yeah but how old was the thing?" Mr. Seminar demanded.

"This guy's American, right?" Another voice, quieter. "That means he's younger, and he can't do shit like that. Not like one of those fucking old-as-dirt European ones."

"I ain't finding out today …are you?"

Hood talked around something in his mouth but I didn't smell smoke. "Put the lady in the van with the head, we'll take her into town, going by the hospital anyway."

"Won't be necessary. I got her." Batten's arms hoisted me easily. Being jostled against his chest was nice; I resolved to enjoy it while I could.

I thought about what the cops had been saying: if people did mistake Harry for American, then he wouldn't be as grand a prize. Why did Danika want him so badly? Did she hate me because she coveted Harry, or did she covet Harry because she hated me? Chicken and egg time. Why us? There were plenty of other young psychics worldwide, far more successful than I, with more powerful revenant companions with better Talents to covet, plenty of others to hate.

"Agent Chapel, we need you!" one of the coroner's assistants called, voice climbing a full octave. The other yelled:

"Oh fuck. Oh *fuck!*" A plastic sound, rustling. "Thing's squirming, oh God. Oh Christ!"

"It's *revenant,*" Batten said to no one in particular, total delayed reaction. "And she's not his wife."

I doubted anyone heard him; the men had fled to watch the rustling bag with the reanimated head inside. He started towards the house, hard exhale from his nostrils moving what was left of my hair.

C19

The lens of the sunglasses was digging into my lower back painfully as I lay recovering on the couch; it was my own fault for swiping it in the first place then tucking it so near my stitches. Sometimes having people think you're the fainting type works in your favor; that Batten thought I was a fainter was vaguely irritating, but I guess Sherlock was right. I'm a great little actress.

"Would it have mattered?" Batten wanted to know.

"You knew she was blind," I accused, moving to rest on my elbow. "And that her eyes were gouged out. Right? This was some sort of test. You still don't believe I'm psychic."

"I believe that *you* believe you're psychic. Tell me what think you saw."

Riiight. "Could you reword that so it's a bit *more* insulting?"

"Tell me, Baranuik."

"What exactly would be the point?"

Harry, humming a vaguely recognizable tune, brought me a shot of espresso, a No. 2 and a Moleskine, and the cordless home phone. The cops and others had gone, and if it weren't for Mark and I fighting (*did we ever do anything but?*) the night would've been peaceful at last. I sank my chin into the arm of the couch and listened as Harry's voice hit each note with soft precision; after a minute I was calm. Harry tried to hand me the phone.

"Who is it?" I whispered.

Disapproval thinned his lips. "Vivaldi. Opera No. 7 concerto No. 7 in D minor. Have I in fact taught you nothing at all, in the end?"

I had to smile, which grew into a tired chuckle. "I meant, who's on the phone, doofus."

He looked down at the item in his hand, seeming surprised to see it. "Ah yes, how foolish of me. T'is your sister on the line."

"Crapsicles. Not now." Being the oldest of seven is not always a blessing. "Which one?"

"The one that does not entirely despise you," Harry remarked flippantly, urging me to take the phone. When I didn't, his frown deepened. "Do take this, lollygagger, I've a delivery from Shield at the door that simply cannot wait. Is the American Express card in your purse?"

"My nightstand, the blue wallet." I said.

Did Shield, a local blood donor organization that Harry uses once in a figurative blue moon, explain his warmth, I wondered? My gut said he was attempting to pull a fast one, manufacturing a cover-up story on account of my suspicions. *Suuuuure*, he'd been getting deliveries. He sure as hell hadn't stored them in the boathouse freezer.

I glanced at Chapel to gauge whether he had witnessed one of these deliveries while guarding Harry this past week and a half: I read Gary as curious, the name and idea of Shield seeming foreign to him.

Disappointed, I said into the phone: "Carrie?"

"My infamous sister is alive and well!" Carrie sang. "Well, halleluiah. You ever think some of us might like a phone call when your world goes tits-up?"

She knows nothing, she knows nothing. I made my free hand useful, jotting the psychic impression I'd gotten outside at the mailbox in my notebook, while I kept my voice light, casual.

"What the heck are you even talking about, kiddo?"

"You've made the dinner-hour news. Did Lord Billionbucks forget to pay your cable bill?"

I dropped the notebook and strode across the room to grab the remote from the mantle, flipping the channels until it landed on CNN. Horror gurgled from my throat. "That's my face!"

"I know. Don't you ever wear make up?" Carrie said. "You're too pale to walk around without mascara. Eyeliner. Blush. You can afford make up, you know."

The entire Baranuik family had profited from Grandma Vi's death, and from Harry's generosity. After Harry paid Carrie three times what this little cabin was worth *and* bought her an overpriced townhouse in posh Niagara-on-the-Lake near Mum and Dad's Virgil farm, still she was bitter where Harry's money was concerned.

"Why am I on TV?" I demanded, as though it was her doing.

"They said you were in the hospital again. Is that true? Why didn't you call?" Harder now, with frost in her voice, "Why didn't "Harry" call us?"

Harry, in audible air quotes. Like it maybe wasn't his real name. Like he was an enemy spy on a mission of infiltration or something. Still, of my siblings, she was the only one who didn't outright despise us, so I let it go.

"It wasn't necessary to call because I'm perfectly fine, really."

"Oh my God," she said, the panic in her voice causing the Blue Sense to nearly explode in my ear: *dread, worry, anger*. "You're really hurt!"

"Nope. A scratch." I *pshaw*-ed, dredging up whatever psychic wall I could manage.

"This has nothing to do with the shooting, it's a new injury," Carrie guessed, her breath quickening. "Did that serial killer from New York track you down? Did he come back? I told you you're not cut out for police shit!"

"You're way off now. Stop it. Jeremiah Prost is in the wind. Just calm down."

"That's it. You're moving back to Canada. I'm coming to get you."

"I'm not going anywhere."

"It's not safe down there with all the crazy vampires."

"Carrie, you know damn well there are more revenants in Canada than in the US," I lied, flapping my arm as though she could see it. "And not all revenants are crazy killers." I saw Batten's head came up sharply and ignored it. "OK, no more than half of them. Could you calm down?"

"As you can plainly see, dramatic overreaction is entrenched in the Baranuik genes," Harry commented to Chapel and Batten as he returned to the room with a dark indigo wine goblet in his hand. "Never have I known a conversation between Baranuiks to be touched by either peace or civility."

I felt Chapel's flush of discomfort as he put 2 and 2 together and figured out what was in Harry's goblet, what Shield must be. Flicking a glare at Harry, who had recommenced humming doleful Vivaldi, I turned up the volume on the TV.

"Carrie, honey," I soothed, "You know how the media blows shit out of proportion when there's no real news. Oh Lord and Lady, I look like I'm dying of Consumption. Couldn't they have gotten better pictures of me?"

"Do better pictures of you exist?"

"You meant that in a nice way," I deadpanned. "Right?"

"All that pretty blond hair and you drag it back into a boring ponytail."

Not anymore. "Have you and Harry been trading critiques of my 'do?"

"Yeah, right, on our nightly phone chats," she sneered. "You look like a drowned albino rat. On a lighter note, who's the delicious hard-bodied hottie bossing you around? Look at those shoulders, those arms. Yowza, that's a big man, right there. Yum."

The snapshot frozen in the corner of the screen was from Buffalo. The delicious hard-bodied hottie was Batten. He was pointing at a dumpster, his brow furrowed, his lips curled up exposing one pointy-yet-human canine. I remembered the argument, the exasperation in his voice. We'd been driving back to the police station at half past 3 am from a 16 hour strained and silent stake out, the day after our first vertical romp. He'd stopped behind the station to toss out our leftovers while I was asleep. I woke up hungry when he parked, and when I'd found out my food was gone, I lost it. He'd been telling me where I could find the rest of my burrito. I'd been telling him where to go. The photographer had caught me in a flash-framed double-shot, half way to enthusiastically flipping Batten the bird with both hands.

"Uh, that's just a cop." I coughed discretely. "An indescribably annoying Fed."

"Oh my god, it's *him,* the one you told me about. You had sex with that guy?" Carrie shouted into the phone. "Holy shit, you lucky slut!"

"Voice down," I begged, acutely aware I wasn't alone in the room. "Seriously, I'm just fine."

"Forget what I said before, I *do* want details," my sister laughed. "Tell me about his body. Every inch. Start at the shoulders and work your way down. Don't skip a freckle."

"You're over reacting. Dramatically. " I smiled at Harry then stole a glance at Batten, who was watching my end of the conversation with one eye while monitoring CNN with the other. "We'll talk about this another time. Give my love to mum and dad ..."

"He's there," she guessed. I could picture her swinging her knees up in the chair and settling in for a juicy chat in her sunny family room. "He came to see you. Did I interrupt? My God, you were about to fuck."

"*No!*" My cheeks burned. The screen on the TV changed. "Holy hell, that's my office. Why is CNN at my friggin' office?"

"Someone forgot to water your plants," Carrie noted. "Probably it was you. You never were good at keeping things alive. Well, except for "Harry", but how hard is that? Any one of us could have done it."

I bit my tongue. That huge thorn in my family's side had not withered over the years: why me and not any of them? Vi's last wishes had named me, but it wasn't written in stone. Harry and I both had the ability to walk away. My family assumed we'd refuse one another. Sitting in the lawyer's office that bizarre evening, buzzing with nervous anticipation, not knowing what to expect, considering one another for the very first time: me a shy 17 yr old Canadian puzzle fanatic in dark-rimmed glasses and ash blonde braids, he a cultured centuries-old British aristocrat. I guessed he would bow out gracefully with an apology, that the apology would be the last I'd hear from Lord Guy Harrick Dreppenstedt of London, England. At the same time, an immediate understanding resonated in me: if he wanted me, I would accept, and on some level, I was already his. Harry could have chosen instead to Bond my father, as everyone expected. Roger Baranuik had been studying for this eventuality, and would have made an excellent guardian, an educated companion. Or, Harry could have gone back to Europe, to his own familiar corner of the world. Instead, he offered me the Bond. And I accepted instantly and unequivocally, plunging the rest of the Baranuik clan into bewildered fury. Together, we had borne their disapproval.

Now, Harry was looking at me steadily from his wingback chair, aware of my reminiscing, eyelids heavy with unspoken pleasure, his gaze wistful. He swirled the contents of his goblet, but his hungry stare yearned for someone warm wiggling beneath him; a shiver tickled my spine and I had to look away.

"All those lovely philodendron, dead." Carried *tsk*ed in my phone ear. "Always surrounding yourself with death. At least you made it with one living guy. That FBI guy looks like one angry SOB. I bet he fucks like a jackhammer. Am I right?"

My cheeks flamed anew. Harry, with his exceptional preternatural hearing, had heard every word my sister said, and his attention was again pulled from the TV to check my face curiously.

"I'm not going to discuss cases with you, Carrie," I said carefully. "It's unprofessional and probably illegal."

On TV, a journalist in navy pencil skirt and wildly impractical high heels was talking to a vaguely familiar public relations guy at Gold-Drake & Cross about the spare office beside my former secretary John's desk. The cameraman took a long shot of a door that still bore my nameplate in silver and then for some reason went to black and white like some old detective show. I half-expected the score for Dragnet to start up. "*Ladies and Gentlemen, the story you are about to see is true* ..." The door swung shut. The producers were creating some theatrical metaphor for my career and didn't even realize. If I dared to look at anyone else in the room now, I'd collapse into a smoldering ruin of shame.

"Why this particular psychic?" the journalist wanted to know.

Public Relations smiled his promotion grin: conservative estimated orthodontic cost, eight thousand dollars. "It's the girl-next-door phenomenon. She's an every day person, relatable, touchable."

"Hear that?" Carrie teased. "You're touchable. Like quilted toilet paper."

"Splendid," I said sourly. "Must be why the world wipes its ass with me."

Carrie groaned at the public relations guy's expanding on my popularity, and I wasn't sure which made me cringe more: his flattery or my sister's disgust. "Your first and only case ended with you getting shot and a vampire serial killer in the wind," she said, as if I needed a reminder. "He's somewhere draining more kids because when it came time to take action, you choked."

I'd said much worse about my own self, but to hear it from Carrie ... I know she thought I agreed. We'd discussed how I felt about it. It didn't make it any easier to hear her flippant remarks. I stiffened defensively and out of the corner of my eye, I saw Harry sit up. I felt my jaws doing the Mark Batten Angry Dance while I chewed back comments I'd surely regret saying to the only quasi-friendly sibling I had left.

"As you know, Nancy," PR guy said on TV, "I can't discuss the details of open investigations with you, or reveal any personal medical information. What I can tell you is that our star psychic will have a ton of fan mail to go through when she returns to us."

He touched open the door of the spare office, the paint a soothing blue-green. The mail was unbelievable, postcards and envelopes spilling from boxes and plastic shopping bags, propped in the chairs, covering an old unused desk. Parcels were kicked under chairs, stacked in piles on a window ledge. Flowers, teddy bears, cards of condolence. Even jewelry: Public Relations displayed in his palm a necklace with a big heart locket encrusted with blood-red garnets, bearing the sepia-toned picture of the gift-giver inside—a gothed-up young man who couldn't have been more than 16 with black lipstick and a severely staged-debonair facial expression. The dude had drawn a bleeding heart in the corner in what I sincerely hoped was red marker. I reeled back a step with a horrified *urk!*

Carrie made a snort of disgust. "Look, that punk is infatuated with you. He wants to be your little fake-vamp love-bunny."

Harry startled into a hoot of delighted laughter that made Batten and Chapel jolt with alarm. Harry doubled over in the chair, clutching his sides. I'd never seen him laugh so hard; I thought he might actually be breathing. He had to set his goblet down on the coffee table.

For some reason, the music CDs bothered me the most.

"Jeez, mixed CDs. I wonder what's on them. Oh that's right, laugh it up, Dreppenstedt!" I picked up a throw cushion from the couch and whipped it at him.

When Harry tried to stop, a ludicrous snort-laugh combo escaped him, setting Batten off at last. Laughing at me in unison: a baby step up from wanting to murder each other.

I cut my eyes to Chapel warningly, but he was keeping a straight face. Good ole Gary Unflappable Chapel, always under complete control. He had his Blackberry out and was thumbing furiously, hazel eyes darting behind his glasses.

I said tersely, "Maybe all psychics get fan mail, ever think of that?"

"Jesus, Marnie." The laughter had left Carrie's voice and now her tone held something entirely new. The antagonism was gone. It wasn't envy. It wasn't worry. I couldn't diagnose the remarkable sound in my sister's voice. I slipped off my lambskin gloves and tossed them on the coffee table so I could fold my bare fingers around the phone.

It was *awe*. From thousands of miles away, I felt it as crisply as if she was standing in front of me, looking at me like a scientist discovering a new species of insect. She had made a discovery, and it quickened in her chest. Like a gold miner polishing a solid clump of mud and finding a nugget of possibility, Carrie was for the first time wondering if maybe I was special after all.

My sister believed.

C20

My throat was thick. “Who else is seeing this? Is dad …”

“Dad’s sick in bed,” Carrie said. Translation: he’s off the wagon, barfing his guts out. I didn’t wanna deal with that, so I didn’t ask. Avoidance, thy name is Marnie. “Margot’s in Paris, big surprise. Rena is back up north, hunting. Wes is …Wes.” I could hear the shrug over the phone line; my baby brother was migratory, never in one place long; we never knew where he was until he popped up asking for money. “The rest of the Baranuik clan is probably choking on their Sunday night chicken carbonara.”

“Can I call you back later?”

“On one condition,” Carrie sighed. “I want every single dirty detail about Delicious Hard-bodied Hottie. In exchange, I won’t tell mom about any of this. Deal?”

Harry’s eyes were laser beams burning a hole through the side of my face. I said, “You win. I’ll email you later, ok?”

“If you have any explicit pictures of his—“

I hung up on my sister before she could finish the sentiment. Harry wasted no time; though his giggle-fit had settled, he barely hid his teasing grin behind the rim of his goblet.

“My pet, it seems you are universally adored as the darling psychic of this generation. I had no idea.” He sat forward, his lips still twitching. Something illicit swam behind his platinum gaze. “You have suitors a’ courting. I am duly enraged.”

“You’re anything but.” I rolled my eyes. “I’d like to know what changed. When did they give me an office full of fan mail? I don’t even work there anymore.”

Batten steepled his fingers in front of his mouth. “A gamble. GD & C were willing to go with the subterfuge. For your part, you’ve got to keep it up.”

“You did this.” At least the fake fan mail made sense now. “I shouldn’t be surprised.”

“I am more astonished that the lad knows a full-sized word like subterfuge,” Harry said.

Agent Chapel clearly had no idea what was going on. “Mark?”

Batten explained: “To pressure Sherlock out of the woodwork, I leaked to some contacts in the press that the Great White Shark was back to work. With the Davis family’s permission, I revealed that we’ve retained the nation’s “star psychic” to assist the FBI with the Davis case. The PCU’s official comment on this is: “Marnie Baranuik is the best choice for the job, and we have complete confidence in her ability to help us solve it.'"

I winced. "Jeez, why don't you just publically cockslap Sherlock in the face?"

"Always a lady," Harry observed wryly.

"So you're using me as bait to draw a lunatic out of hiding?"

"We didn't discuss this ..." Chapel's fingers were poised over his keyboard looking twitchy, like he needed to find a solution but couldn't think of how to begin. "Marnie, I apologize. I'd never have approved this."

"Which is why I didn't run it by you," Batten defended. "This had to be done."

Harry sat forward. "Are you so blind to the peril inherent in taunting a deranged maniac who has terrorized my DaySitter?"

"Sure, let's wind the nutjob into a tizzy. My luck, she'll show up with a crazed glint in her eyes and a flamethrower in her hands." I squared my shoulders at Batten. "What about the fan mail? Was that your doing too?"

Batten sat back in his chair, his knees falling open. "That's all you."

"How long have you been receiving fan mail?" Chapel asked.

"I got one letter, *one* ..." I wracked my brain. "Eight months ago? Way before Buffalo. I did a missing person's case in Florida. Nothing preternatural about it. Parental abduction. I wasn't much help. The kid was recovered because of an amber alert and solid police work, not because of what I did. When I got back to Oregon, the fan letter arrived. It seemed ridiculous, so I told John to put it somewhere. I guess he kept it."

"And all that followed. That's what he told reporters the last time they ran a clip about Gold-Drake & Cross," Chapel swung his laptop around to show us streaming footage of a news cast about the Jeremiah Prost case as it was going *kablooie*. The same spare office behind his desk, and the same bags of mail waiting for me. The date was October 13, 2009. The day Batten and I nearly ruined a motel bathroom door with our heaving naked bodies, and four days before I was shot.

"This is why she hates me." I chewed the inside of my mouth. "She's the gorgeous reality star, she's spent Lord knows how much money and effort getting that way, but I'm the one with the office dedicated to fan mail. I'm surprised everyone at GD&C doesn't hate my guts."

Chapel intoned. “I came across one of the earliest cases Sherlock assisted Gold-Drake & Cross with. It was a PCU case, in her home town of Stillwater, Oklahoma.”

Chapel pulled up a different video clip on his laptop. It showed an almost unrecognizable Danika Sherlock (then Danielle Smith-Watson) in shapeless denim coveralls and big rubber boots, baseball cap turned backwards, tracking through a field with a search party. Directly in front of her, leading the way, was a younger and less permanently-annoyed version of Batten with longer, fuller hair and a trim goatee. The look of puppy-dog adoration was naked on her face when he turned to point into a stand of tall grass and bark orders at her team. Ah, young Batten, that same wide-legged authoritative stance, the same hard ass, literally and figuratively. As the groups split off, young Danielle cast more than one glance over her shoulder to watch Batten walk away. Then she slipped on a pair of sunglasses and I thought, *are they the same ones?*

I slid my gloveless hand into the back of the waistband of my pants, reaching, fingering the stolen lens carefully. It slipped deeper and settled in the crack of my ass. *Frig.* Harry was watching my hand moving behind my back with subtle amusement.

On the couch, Batten cocked his head and studied the video. “I don’t remember this.”

Chapel said, “May 1999. Missing persons case turned suspected lycanthrope kill. We lead three major search parties before we found the remains. Turned out the young man in question was the victim of a hate crime, not a werewolf.”

“1999,” I said, squirming, trying to skillfully dig the sunglass lens out of my panties without anyone becoming wiser. “GD&C let Ville Aaman go for conduct unbecoming and he’d started doing his freelance precognition seminars. A year and a half later, he’d blow the lid off the psychic-revenant connection and lay claim to coining the term DaySitter.”

“Vamps called you bleeders before,” Batten said low, without looking at either Harry or me.

“Uh, no. No revenant ever called their companion that. Bleeders is slang for bodies-for-hire, blood hookers; it was taken out of context and used by hunters to add credence their cause,” I said. “Back in 1999 GD&C was supplying psychic support to law enforcement but the laws were still fuzzy, and it was done quietly, without a lot of media promotion. They’d send out groups of them at a time, young psychics in training with a senior investigator.”

"Right. Stillwater," Batten remarked, nodding. "Ruby Valli was our senior psychic investigator on the scene."

I squinted at the video. Ruby Valli didn't look familiar, but then I'd never met her; she'd left GD&C by the time I was out of training.

Batten continued, "Precognitive. Ruby saw the location of the eventual arrest but couldn't identify the criminals. The vic was a transsexual, had his first operation. When we found the gouge marks on him, we though werewolf. But some of the local punks had targeted him. Tied him to a fence and went at him with meat hooks."

Harry murmured softly, "And you call me a monster."

"You do realize that junior psychic in training behind the old lady is Danika Sherlock, pre-Hollywood," I pointed out, glad both Feds were glued to the laptop as I wriggled against the lens in my panties. "And that she's majorly crushing on Bulletproof Batten."

Batten didn't react, other than a slight tightening around the eyes.

The Blue Sense sputtered between my fingertips and the lens briefly, and then dissipated like smoke.

Harry supplied for me, "You do not seem to be paying the least bit attention to young Ms. Watson, Agent Batten. You're almost pointedly ignoring her."

"We had three psychics on loan from GD&C. I steered clear of them," Batten told him. "Working part time hunting vamps, coordinating with search and rescue, I probably didn't even know she was one of the psychics. Didn't want to know. Didn't want to have anything to do with DaySitters or their vamps."

"Did she start hating me before she had the crush on you, or after?" I wondered aloud. "Maybe this *is* about you, after all."

"Are you sure the person you saw gouging the head was Danika Sherlock?" Chapel turned to me. "That she's involved in both your attack and the Davis murder?"

"I didn't see any face in relation to the head," I said honestly, stroking the lens with my fingertips. "Because I couldn't see anything through Davis' blind eyes. But I know what Sherlock's hands felt like on me, in violence. I think those hands were on Kristin Davis. I didn't get a whiff of a revenant. I think Sherlock faked bite marks on the body to get you PCU guys out, but there was a reason behind her choosing Kristin Davis specifically as a victim."

Harry stared through the indigo glass, all laughter gone now.

"You're sure the bite marks are faked?" Chapel took off his tortoise rim glasses and squinted at them. He put them back on without cleaning them. "Could Sherlock be harboring a new companion?"

I asked Chapel, "Tox screen show any ms-lipotropin in Davis' throat tissue?"

"No."

"V-telomerase?"

"No. Nothing." Chapel passed me the files once more, open to the toxicology report.

"How far apart were the so-called fangs?" I asked, scanning for the answer but knowing he'd have it.

"Quarter inch."

"That's pretty close together," I remarked, holding up an invisible ruler to my eye and imagining the space between. "Too close. Even for a new, small-bodied revenant, a turned adolescent."

"I've never seen fangs less than two centimeters apart," Harry offered. "It would be an exceptionally diminutive mouth."

"Two centimeters is, what, almost three quarters of an inch? About the norm," I said with a nod. "How wide were the fangs themselves? Pin pricks? Or did they have girth."

"If they didn't have some girth, they would not be fang marks at all," Harry reasoned. "Fangs are teeth, they are not needles. Teeth make irregular marks, not perfect circles, and there would be some tearing at the edges, no matter how small the fangs or how gentle the revenant."

"What if it were a child vamp?" Batten said it.

"No such thing," I brushed off.

"How can you be so sure?" Chapel wanted to know. Again his pen was poised, but his gaze settled on Harry, not me.

"It cannot be done," Harry said. "There was a time, many centuries ago, when the blood of children was highly prized. "Love by the dram," was the phrase bandied about in the darkest taverns of Amsterdam, where to this day an immortal can find just about anything he fancies. These unfortunate partners were killed outright, even if their revenant was willing to try and turn them."

"Partners," Batten said contemptuously.

"Orphans, Agent Batten, in some cases sick children who would have otherwise been left to starve in the gutters by the humans around them. I do not defend the practice, nor have I ever indulged in such a loathsome act; I am only recounting the unfortunate facts."

I interrupted, throwing a bucket of cool science on the fire. "There are limitations in the hypothalamus. Before puberty hits, the human body does not excrete enough human growth hormone to reactivate the vestigial organ that parcels out ingested blood, the gastrosanguinem, re-grown during the three day period of transformation from alive to undead."

"If you tried to turn a child," Harry said, "By spending three days feeding that child the nectar of a revenant's veins, the only result would be the death of the child."

Batten said, "You sound pretty sure about that."

"Again, I've certainly never tried it myself," Harry huffed, his eyes taking on a hurt sheen. "Nor would I, even if I were sufficiently old enough to turn humans with an assurance of success."

"You're not?" Batten asked, giving Harry a thorough once-over, as though he'd never seen him before. "Thought all vamps could turn humans."

"Your noob is showing, Kill-Notch," I snort-laughed, shaking my head.

"So Kristin Davis' head didn't move because she's been turned?" Chapel asked.

I gave Chapel a pointed look. "A moving revenant *head?* Impossible. If you decapitate a revenant, he's ash."

Harry agreed. "I am surprised that your preternatural crimes unit does not already know this information. Are you not trained in such matters?"

"We do courses when budget allows," Chapel said, a little defensively. I reached out my hand to touch Gary's forearm apologetically and felt an immediate flicker of annoyance wrapped in shame from his side of the couch, followed closely by hope and curiosity of an almost painful strain. *Hope?* There was one for my notebook. I broke contact quickly, pretending I'd sensed nothing, feeling embarrassed like I'd walked in on him in the bathroom.

"I know someone," Harry suggested, "Who knows quite a lot about the subject, if you require private tutoring."

No, I mouthed at him across the room, biting the word off. Harry smiled placidly.

Batten stood. "It's nearly seven. We're due at the morgue for the post at eight. The pathologist is putting this case at the head of the line."

Chapel put his laptop in its case and clicked his pen closed. "Will you two be all right tonight if we go? We may be a few hours."

"Of course." There was a cracked sunglass lens in my underpants and I was very aware of its jagged edge. "I've got my Cold Company for protection."

"When we get back we'll discuss our next move." Batten looked at me when he said it. I boggled, struggling to comprehend this massive shift in Batten's attitude. Did he actually have faith in me? Since when?

"What did you have in mind?"

"The Davis funeral. I want you front and center with me and the family, if it's ok with them. The more eye-catching you are, the better."

"And by eye-catching you mean ..."

Harry supplied, "Jaw-dropping, delectable, sumptuous?"

I gaped at them both. "You want me to hike my skirt up in shameless self promotion?"

Batten's eyes took on a salacious heat I hadn't seen in a while. "Hell, yes."

"I meant, for the case."

He just smiled.

"Harry?" I said

Harry swirled the dregs of his meal in his goblet. "This was bound to happen, ducky," he answered enigmatically.

"Just get out there and draw attention," Chapel agreed reluctantly. "We'll be sure to nab her the second she sticks her neck out, Marnie. It's risky, but ..."

"Piffle." Harry swung his one leg on the arm of the chair and smirked. "I shall of course be in attendance, at the viewing if not the church service. How successful do you think someone would be if they tried to cross me to get to my DaySitter, Agent Chapel?"

He seemed to mean something else, and his gaze towards the Fed was solemn, intense. It may have been my imagination, but the temperature in the room seemed to plummet ten degrees further, until an arctic brand of tension crackled like glacier movement under the ticking of Harry's grandfather clock. It sounded like a warning, and dialed Chapel immediately to *uncomfortable*. While Batten put on his coat, Chapel touched his necktie and looked at Harry's centuries-old portrait above the mantel, then sharply away.

"I think your DaySitter has in you an invaluable weapon, Lord Dreppenstedt, if she chose to use you."

The revenant's answering gaze was inscrutable.

Chapel said, "We'll be back after nine."

Then they were gone, and I was left scratching my head.

C21

"You look tired," Harry said. "Come lay your head upon my shoulder."

"I need to jot down all these impressions before I forget them. My memory doesn't seem to be working well lately. If I could get some sleep ..."

"You memory will work better when you're safely tucked into my arms, ducky."

I cocked my head at him. His lips were blue.

Grandma Vi had passed along a journal in her will, one that had followed all of Harry's DaySitters like an owner's manual. It had been started by his first, a young woman named Marie-Pierrette D'Elissalde. I couldn't pronounce Marie-Pierrette with the proper French accent, or not without sounding like my tongue was tied in a knot and shoved down my throat, so I'd long ago taken to calling her Mary-Perry, something Harry barely tolerated. Mary-Perry had made rules for all those who might follow her, suggestions we all followed. Each DaySitter but me had added their own touch to the journal, and Vi was no exception.

Second Cannon from Marie-Pierrette's journal was a biggie, and it strummed in my head: *a warm vampire is a fair and gentle companion.* When she'd written this, vampire was the accepted term, though it was about as cringe-worthy for me to read this as it was to read the N-word in my grandfather's old Jokes and Quips For Every Occasion book. Scrawled beneath this advice in my grandmother's flowery handwriting, an unusual opinion: *always keep your Cold Company comfortable.* So far, it was as Harry would put it "spot-on".

Notes forgotten, I went to his chair with a blanket and curled up in his lap. He trembled once, violently. "Jesus, Harry. When you're ready for a nice warm feed ..." I reminded him. He shook his head, running his fingers through my shorn hair. I wondered what he was thinking. "Harry, if a DaySitter were to leave their Cold Company, would that revenant go nuts?"

"Don't go, my only love," he said quietly, closing his eyes and putting his chin on top of my head.

"I'm not going anywhere," I said with the "duh" heavily implied. "I'm just thinking out loud."

"There is so much that we still do not understand about undeath, but there does seem to be a myriad of mental health issues tied to the dissolution of the Bond. I would venture a guess and say yes, separation from one's living DaySitter could cause a revenant to become quite mad, and go rogue. T'would be a perilous state of affairs." He moved the blanket to cover his knees. "You speak now of Mr. Jeremiah Prost, one presumes?"

"The one that got away," I mused. "I can't be around Batten and not think of my last day on the case, watching him turn, seeing the gun, not understanding it, feeling the bullets."

"I imagine being in your society does always remind Agent Batten of that dreadful day as well. He certainly projects a measure of sadness when he sees you, more than an ounce of loss, of regret."

"You feel Batten?" I blinked with surprise. "Empathically?"

"Queen Anne's dead." He said it quickly as he did sometimes, *QueenAnnesdead*. "I feel everyone."

"I can't feel him at all."

"He is a null for you, a neutral." He brushed a pale hand through the air. "This is a human failing. No revenant has a null. Would that it were; it is dreadfully uncomfortable for me to be in his society."

"Did Jeremiah have a DaySitter who left him, or died?" I wondered. "How would we find out?"

"I thought we were finished with Mr. Prost. Do you imagine his crimes could be linked to Danika Sherlock in some way?"

"I don't know, I wish I'd kept my files," I said under my breath. "It was stupid to burn them." And all because I'd written along the margins explicit sex notes about my romp with Batten, and couldn't bear to look at them.

Harry rubbed his hand up and down along his arm, an old throwback human habit; he had no circulation to stir into warmth under that skin.

"Why does this matter to you, my darling? What she did in the past is not in the least relevant. T'is enough to know that Ms. Sherlock is a violent sociopath who needs to be stopped."

"You're not telling me anything new, Harry. She stabbed me repeatedly, of course she's a psycho."

"I did not say psychopath, ducky. I said sociopath."

"Same diff."

"Do be serious, pet. To get rid of her, you must find her. To find her, you must understand her. Ms. Sherlock's pattern is nothing new. It is the stuff of human history: scare people and grab power. Sociopaths have been doing this since caveman brain overlapped animal brain overlapped lizard brain".

"You lost me."

"You might find that does not entirely surprise me."

I knocked him in the chest with my knuckles. "I know a certain smarty-pants rev who'll be pretty hungry by morning if he doesn't drop the attitude."

"Your mighty fist is formidable, dearheart." He managed a straight face. "I must of course submit to your will."

We enjoyed one another's companionable silence for a stretch. My head was starting to whirl and a throbbing at my lower back reminded me that it was almost time to take my painkillers.

"I think you need to put this nuisance out of your mind for a while." Harry touched my hair again, played absently with the jagged edges. "We should pick out your outfit for the funeral."

"What's to pick out? It's a funeral, I'm not going to wear a tutu. Black pants, black shirt, gun, black jacket, black shoes."

Harry's soft chuckle tickled my ear. "Agent Batten believes Ms. Sherlock will be watching, and that you should be gorgeous enough to make her lash out in spiteful passion."

Gorgeous? "Baring a miracle, I don't see that happening."

"Short skirt, fitted shirt, tailored jacket, high heels, push-up brassier. Lots of leg, lots of cleavage."

"It's winter," I protested. "Harry, it's a kid's funeral! You're both off your rockers if you think I'm showing skin."

"Surely, if Agent Batten recommended the short skirt, its sole purpose serves to solve the case." He hid the sarcasm by smiling against the back of my head. "I am quite certain I have something suitable for you in my wardrobe. Of course, when weighing one's haute couture options, one must always consider the collections of Jean Paul Gaultier. You'll be pleased to know I have several new frocks for you to try."

"I told you to stop buying clothes I'll never wear," I gave him a pinch on the forearm. "Besides, what would Chapel think?"

"In my experience, men who are surprised into a state of arousal by a pleasurable sight or sensation are rarely critical of its source."

I lifted my head from his chest to study him, feeling that he meant more. His expression revealed little. "Is that so?"

"Oh, absolutely," he confirmed; a dark, wicked light blazed through his eyes, though to what he was confessing was still a mystery to me.

"I need to go outside and set up a ward," I said. "So no one can bust in here without us knowing about it."

"You will not go outside without your gloves, surely?"

I went to my coat and patted my pockets and found no gloves. I didn't remember anyone removing my lambskin gloves when I "fainted", or where I'd left my pink calfskin ones. No matter: I had gloves everywhere.

I went into the office and opened the cabinet on the east wall, frowning at the obvious lack of a certain hat box. "Harry, did you take back a hat box from the office cupboard?"

"In your bedroom."

I passed through the dimly lit kitchen and into the small bedroom that was tucked between living room and bathroom. I'd never liked the two bedrooms upstairs with their tiny connecting bathroom, their steeply sloping claustrophobic ceilings and round windows like glaring Cyclops eyes tucked into the eaves. The bedroom off the kitchen was far more cheerful with its Irish lace curtains and pastel rag rug, and much closer to my espresso maker. As a bonus, on the other side of the kitchen was the pantry, and within the pantry's packed shelves was a discrete and narrow cellar door. In an emergency, it was ten running steps across kitchen and pantry, and twelve precipitous stairs down to the safety of Harry's casket; he'd made me practice this drill a hundred thousand times since we moved in.

I laid flat on my abdomen to peer under the bed, cautious of my belly wounds. The pain was much better than it had been earlier; being around Harry's palpable energy was definitely speeding my healing, and whenever I did feel the jarring tug of pain, somehow it was whisked away. I had too much on my mind to wonder why. I was just glad it was working out that way.

The jar of newt eyes was near the back wall. "You hid my bits and pieces."

"You took my hat box," Harry parried.

"Well, I figured you didn't ..." I glanced up at him, read his pursed lips as though they had words written across them. "Harry, may I please borrow the empty hat box in your closet?"

"Of course, my angel. I shall fetch it directly."

I rolled my eyes into the underside of my bed. "Why did you move my newt bits here? They were okay in the cabinet."

"I wasn't sure your agents wouldn't snoop, or understand why you'd need such things." His face was carefully blank. "To be honest, I am not sure I understand the need, either. Using animal body parts does not seem like white magic."

"Well, it's not black magic."

He blinked once, pointedly.

"It might be sort of ... off-white?" I amended.

"And the people who removed the eyes from the newts?"

"Oh that's bad mojo on them," I said emphatically. At the downward tilt of the corners of his mouth I said, "They did it, not me. I've never hurt an animal, dead or alive. You know I wouldn't."

"You simply must be more careful, my love."

"Said the demon descendent."

"My point exactly. Your soul is still very much up for grabs. Furthermore, I have an abiding faith that my own soul is not irredeemable. I am intimately linked to the infernal by my immortality, and you, my darling one, are intimately and forever linked to me." Something passed over his face then, a shadow of an emotion I didn't have a name for. If our Bond wasn't bungled, I could have plucked it out of him easily, but as it was I had to take a wild stab at it and call it regret. "How easy it would be for a woman of your class to slide from murky *demimonde* to the downright forsaken, and take me sliding with you."

"I meant to use them for good, not evil. I found an online supplier. After the order went through, I thought it was pretty paranoid to think I'd ever need such a thing. Now I'm glad I bought them, they're exactly what I need."

He trailed a finger over my nightstand and then lifted his pale fingertip to examine the dust. "You did not use your usual supplier?"

"Thrice Around The Circle wouldn't have anything like this."

"That should have been your first clue that it was a foul deed." He looked angry now, my dusty room forgotten. "You purchased them online, with no earthly idea of what caliber of person might be behind the site."

I saw his point. "I get it. Seventh Cannon: know whom you're dealing with." Harry inclined his head, waiting for me to expand on the thought. It irritated me. "But Harry, you don't understand: the person or people I'm defending us from don't play by fucking rules, they don't respect laws and don't adhere to cannons. They're not confined to using one type of magic or another. They've got the universe to hurl at me. Am I just supposed to—'

"Yes," he said crisply, drawing himself straight, his eyes daring me to argue.

"You don't even know what I was—"

"Yes."

"Stop that." I returned to my stomach, dragged the jar forward. The lid gave my bare hands a tentative tug at the Blue Sense. I blocked whatever vision or linkage was starting to form; I really didn't need to know about the people who touched this jar, pre-delivery. I stayed on my knees to rummage through my night stand drawer for gloves. There weren't any.

I peered at the clear liquid bobbing with eyes, pretty much the last thing in the world I wanted to be touching. The punctured one lay on the bottom, a deflated and inverted blob, a piece of onion-thin tissue floating like mermaid hair in the alcohol. I remembered I had the other one in my jeans pocket still, probably dried-stuck to the fabric by now. I'd have to send for a credit to my account.

"Harry? I can't find any of my gloves. Did you move them someplace?"

Apprehension flashed across his face. "No, my love. You have pairs in your bedroom, in the office, in the hall stand ..."

"Gone. All of them."

"*Mais c'est impossible.* You have near thirty pair at last count."

"I just had some on, before I fainted. They were with me when I was at the mailbox, on my hands. The lambskin ones with the extra-fuzzy lining." I double-checked the pocket of my parka and found only an old menthol cough drop in a crinkly wrapper. "They were just in the living room, on the coffee table, I'm sure I took them off while I was on the phone with Carrie."

"The only people to be in this house since then were your agents," Harry said. "Perhaps we should check the bedrooms upstairs, where they have stored their overnight bags."

"Why would Jerkface take my gloves?" I frowned, outright discounting the possibility of Chapel taking them. "If he thought they needed them for evidence or something, he would have just said "Yo, give me those" or something equally pushy and moronic."

"One would certainly expect so." His troubled face scanned the kitchen with concern.

"Besides, I *just* had some. Two pair. Lambskin and the pink ones."

"It would be a mistake to ignore this. I fear it indicates a larger problem."

Great. Just what I needed: more problems. "I don't have time for this. The sun is practically gone. I need to do this warding spell before full dark."

I collected some items from the office (nail polish, dried legumes, tiny mirrored discs, Liquid Paper corrector fluid) and swept the jar up, cradling it between my elbow and belly, careful not to let it touch my bare hands. I could open the lid, and block what I didn't need or want to see, but not for more than a moment; the Blue Sense was much too strong to be ignored for long.

Kicking the front door shut with the sole of my navy Ked, I stopped short to stare at the front gate and its fluttering yellow tape.

C22

It had taken a therapist from Gold-Drake & Cross to point out that I had gone from one extreme to the other, where my attitude towards death was concerned, following the shooting in Buffalo. One minute, death was the sheltering care of my Cold Company, the strength that lay beside me on nights that I needed not to be alone, loyal and protective, radiating strength. It was the elegant creature with enormous intuition who fed from my veins and spoke in soft, posh cadence in my ear. Death wasn't a scary thing. Death was just Harry, resting in proper morning dress, or charming in a shadbelly coat, astute and quirky. My Harry, intelligent and witty, using his big words like abstemious and frigorific. My Harry, splendidly-groomed and smelling fantastic.

An unrealistic view, I know, but that's what death was to me before Buffalo. Sure, I'd seen bodies, I'd been to funerals, including Vi's, but death couldn't touch me. Not really. I couldn't die: I believed, right down to my very core, that Harry would simply not allow it. If he couldn't protect me from it, he'd at least turn me (*I refused to accept that he couldn't, or wouldn't*). I'd be at his side for eternity, that was the only thing that made sense. With Harry, I was invincible.

The next thing I knew, death's face had changed radically. It had only taken a heartbeat for death to storm down an alleyway—*a rogue revenant, a bullet, a stinking pile of sludge* –to plummet into my flesh in excess of 700 feet per second, a shocking violation, the slap of an unwanted wake-up call.

I had withdrawn after that, the only defense I could muster, coiled up to lick my wounds. We'd retreated to the only place I could think of: Carrie's quiet remote cabin. But nothing could fix that I'd seen the other face of death. Death wasn't my graceful companion, and death wasn't on my side. Death was everywhere, and I could no longer pretend it wasn't going to get me, one way or another.

And now, as the sun sank into the dark acres of wild forest west of the cabin, death might be waiting in the yard for me. I stood on the porch, feeling the reassuring weight of Harry's hunger behind me in the warm cabin. It was dim enough that he could join me outside without exhausting himself with shadow manipulation, but I thought I'd better face this alone.

If Danika Sherlock had been in my cabin to steal my gloves, surely someone would have noticed. When I'm asleep, Harry's awake, and his eyesight and earshot are far better than mine. She's not the

Invisible Woman. As far as I knew, she wasn't even a practicing witch. So if she didn't take my gloves, who did? And why?

Taking the gloves was an indication of a desire to make me suffer: I wore them to protect myself from the constant input of images, scenes, thoughts, feelings, link-ups and hook-ups with every single residual signature around me. Harry had centuries of practice filtering these things out. I had only ten years and was fairly inept at blocking. Without the gloves, I'd be walking around with my hands in the air like a fresh-scrubbed surgeon, unable to use them for fear of going bonkers. Taking my gloves stunk of something Danika Sherlock would do. Except, would she step down from stabbing me to an act of petty theft? Why not just shoot me?

But here I was, rooted to my porch, staring at the empty front yard while the sun disappeared, again assuming it was all Danika's doing. I had to stop that, because Batten was right: there could be someone else behind everything. If I focused on her, I might miss something.

I marched out to the front gate while I still had a bit of twilight remaining. Shade was dappling the corners of the property, where large black pines cloistered the yard, blocking any view of the neighbour on the east side. CSI had taken the entire mailbox, wood stand and all, and it had left a crater in the icy ground like gums after an extracted tooth, earth wounded and torn. I avoided the taped area, stalking the front line of the property, abandoning the jar's metal lid behind me. From my pocket I withdrew the sachet and began sprinkling its contents as I went. Each time I reached a place where the English Ivy parted to expose a bare spot on the wood, I tucked an eye of newt.

I pulled out from my pocket a handful of *abrus precatorius*, a psychedelic legume, the raw seeds containing one of the deadliest toxins known to the plant world. When I cast them outward in a line they made bright red spots in the snow, some landing with their black dots staring up at me like lethal watchers. I'd never needed the black-watch spell, but I'd secretly memorized it long ago, hoping it would never be used. Keeping most of the ingredients hadn't been a chore, except for the eyes.

I intoned softly, "*Abrus a chapelet, black-watch for me*," and went another foot. "*Hedera helix, blessed bindwood/ bind my spell to this line,/ fall to earth and rise again,/ flow to me and all that's mine.*" I rooted in the jar for another newt eyeball and placed it in a nest of ivy leaves.

"*All-seeing eye of the crone and sage, blessed be the sacrifice of your creatures. All-seeing eye, black-watch for me*," I breathed, misting the cold night air. I felt something crawl along the nape of my neck. A warning. I whipped around to look at the empty yard.

The wind had picked up. Something *oogy* thrummed along my spine like slippery squid tentacles. The black-watch spell in its infancy was beginning to warn me of detrimental influences nearby but I could see nothing except the fair bulk of Ajax the debt vulture sleeping in a nearby tree. It was a subtle change, but the sound of the breeze lifting through the woods nearby was like an injured cow moaning in a barn. I clutched the jar a little tighter to my chest, swallowing the lump in my throat.

Apotropaism, the need to protect from evil, was more my speed than actual confrontation; I still believed that my actions in the Motor Inn had been the better of two choices. I could have killed Sherlock. Most people would say that killing her would have given me the only sure shot at surviving in the long run. But the fate of my soul was as important to me as it was to Harry, who guarded it with his constant reminders to "keep true" on the right hand path. Killing Danika would have screwed my karma. I might be impulsive but my intentions are usually good. I resisted out of fear, but did the capital-R Right thing in the end. I could rely on that. Did it make me predictable? Highly likely. Too predictable? I hoped not. Again, I scanned the empty yard. There were no footprints that hadn't been obliterated by the rising wind, including my own; it was like I'd levitated to the spot by the mailbox.

I took a small mirrored disk out of my other pocket and turned my back on the yard to place the disc where the fence cornered. Again, my skin crawled; I hunched against it and continued. The wood of the fence had aged to the point of crumbling. Long nails browned with old rust hung ineffectually in wide gaps, dangled where they had relinquished their hold. The joints no longer connected properly. It didn't matter. The fence's physical strength wasn't going to thrust evil out.

Was Danika out here, watching me? I saw nothing over my shoulder when I stole a furtive glance. I saw only swelling, deepening shadows; any one of them could mask her presence. I would never inherit Harry's perfect night vision. Much of a revenant's Talent was not transferable to his human DaySitter: the ability to sense the undead or smell blood at a fair distance, night vision, immortality, audiomancy. *If only*, I thought with a lopsided smile, and then took it back: I bungled enough shit without adding to my repertoire of ridiculousness a major power like the ability to sway someone's mind.

I wriggled the mirrored disc in until it was wedged good and tight into the joint.

"Oh silvered glass confound my enemy/ magic mirror black-watch for me./ Return, return, return thrice fold/ Each reflection, for me to behold."

This should prevent her or anyone from psychically spying on me by mystical methods, if that's what she was doing, if she was even capable of that. It would also report to me if a force was flitting around unseen, by reflecting it into my home mirrors. It was the wiccan version of security cameras for unnatural forces.

I used the bolline to clip several evergreen vines from the English ivy and set the jar of newt eyes aside so I could braid the vines together. On one strand, I used Liquid Paper corrector to coat white for peace. Another, I used my Revlon "All Fired Up" nail polish to coat with red for vigor. It should have been blood, but I'd had enough of that lately, and it was the intention that mattered. The third vine, I left its natural woody brown for strength. I wound the braid into the ivy at the corner of the fence, effectively hiding one mirrored disk there. I flicked Harry's monogrammed lighter and held it aloft so I could better watch the way the wind was playing on the dense, dark green foliage clinging stubbornly to the fence.

"Hail fair moon in the wake of night/guard me and mine in dark and light/The laws of magic I abide/sacred elements by my side." I ran a bare hand along the old wood of the fence, honoured its aged crevices and cracks, its abiding strength returning with the sacred infusion. *"Ye who guard the Watchtower, return/Your ancient lessons shall I learn/Welcome here, your splendor and might/Let your charm light up the night."*

Power flared brilliant orange in the dark like dragon's breath and raced in a blazing hot ripple along the entire length of the ivy-coated fence. A stray spark zinged out and bounced off the jar lid, attracted by the metal. The heat created by the union melted the snow and the lid sank out of sight.

"Just you and me tonight, Lady Mine," I breathed. "I hope you remember I'm your most humble servant." Then I smirked. "Ok, maybe humble isn't the right word. But devotion I got in spades."

I reached down to pick up the jar of newt eyes and a sharp cramp doubled me over in the gut. I let out a pained squawk and went to my knees in the hard pack snow. Whistling air in and out through pursed lips, I had to wait until the pain settled before I could begin to straighten. The front door opened, spilling hospitable light onto the porch, Harry silhouetted in its bright warm aura. His concern carried over the space between us.

"Do you require assistance, beloved?"

"Coming," I gasped. "I'm fine. Just a stitch." I touched the newt jar with a bare finger, just a brush, and it cracked loudly. A large chunk of its glass body toppled forward, spilling the remaining imperfect eye remains into the snow along with the sharp stink of preservatives and alcohol.

Eeeeuuuuww. I scooped it up, shuddering at the slimy consistency of it, as the broken filament slipped between my fingers. I wiped it into my jeans pocket with the other one, thinking again about a refund for shoddy merchandise.

As I turned to return to the house, my eyes fell on the Buick, which sagged to one side in a funny way. I cocked my head and studied it, giving it a wide berth, moving to the nose to see better. Both tires on the driver's side had been deeply slashed deeply; thick rubber lay like a dead seal flayed in the snow.

"Curses and cuntfungus!" I hurried with dread to the black vinyl cover thrown over Harry's Kawasaki near the front porch, knowing before I lifted it what I'd see. Both wheels were torn to the rims. I scanned the yard; the feeling of being watched intensified, like cockroaches crawling under my collar, until scurrying inside to my Cold Company was the only thing that made sense.

C23

I found Harry lingering at the kitchen sink, plunging his hands into the hot soapy water of the sink, using a dirty spoon as a pretext for warming his arms up to the elbow. "Agent Chapel rang round on the telephone, my fawn," he started.

"Harry, our tires are slashed."

His head came up. "The Buick?"

"Now, don't freak out ..."

"My *bike?*" he roared, shaking the water from his hands. I put my hands on his chest; it quivered under my touch, and his fists vibrated at his sides.

"Nothing we can do about it at this time of night, Harry, so just chill. I'll get it fixed tomorrow."

"We are trapped here alone, then?" he clarified. I didn't like the way he said it, and a shiver tripped up my spine. I waited for the horror movie lightening and thunder, but it didn't come: the night was still and empty.

"Just stuck for a night." I tried to smile. "Batten and Chapel will be back soon."

Some dark thought slithered through the ash grey of his eyes like a fat black leach grabbing hold. His fangs were fully extended now, and I marveled, not for the first time, how clandestinely he could go from just-Harry to lethal preternatural force with little outward hint.

"Did you lock the door properly?" he asked.

I'd double-checked it, so I nodded. When I was sure he wasn't going to bolt, I dropped my hands. "What were you saying about Chapel?"

"Agent Chapel reports that the Davis family is reluctant to have you at the funeral at St. George Anglican in Ten Springs."

Slighted, I huffed. "Fine. I didn't want to see those poopyheads anyway."

"The very sentiment uttered by Sultan Mehmet II before he fled Prince Tepes and Wallachia," Harry said agreeably.

"No doubt."

"Fear not, my snubbed sugarplum, your industrious agents have instead secured for you an invitation to the funeral home to pay respects before the funeral. Agent Batten suggests we arrive in style." Harry returned his arms to the warm haven of the sink, closing his eyes with pleasure. "Deputy Dunnachie and Sheriff Hood will watch the mourners in the church afterward on our behalf."

"I don't wanna go at all," I said, glad at least that I didn't have to bring Harry anywhere near a church; the last time we'd come within a block of a house of worship, smoke had started rising from his hair and he smelt like charred road-kill for days.

Dropping the broken jar pieces and singed lid in the recycling bin in the mudroom, I washed my hands thoroughly, grabbed a Ziploc bag from a kitchen drawer and stuffed it in my clean pocket. Standing shoulder to shoulder with him at the sink, I sighed. "You know, the funeral home is going to be awful, too. Maybe you better stay here. The family's priest will probably be there. You can't go near a man of God; he'll give you hives."

"Your agents believe it is for the best that you make an official appearance, and I will not have you so exposed without my protection."

He was right, I knew, but I didn't like putting him at risk. "I need cookies," I sighed. "Pretty sure I've never needed a cookie this badly."

"Without biscuits, there is no happiness in my pet's life."

"Truer words were never spoken," I agreed.

"I thought you wanted: shower, Dr. Pepper and a sitcom to go with your supper of pizza?"

"I want all those things. But first I need a sugar boost. You know, to get the energy to pig out."

"Hmm, yes." He kissed my forehead, a rare occurrence and one that made my lips twitch up. "Pigging out requires great fortitude."

"Batten's a crapweasel for using me like this."

He hung his head. "Please do not make me defend his actions."

I blinked in disbelief. "How can you?"

"I trust you are not honestly surprised by his actions."

"He wants to finish this, I get that. I'm just surprised that you're on his side," I said. "Chapel was pissed. Do you think the case is Chapel's main concern, or does he actually have my best interests in mind?"

I glanced up at him, feeling Harry's hesitation, the flinching in his arms, a reflexive drawing-away. Doubt. Guilt. An answer to an unspoken question came to me as glass fresh-splintering clear across a mirror, so obvious, so indisputable that I should have seen it at once. It seemed unreal but once it occurred to me, it was the only thing that made sense. When I considered Chapel's guilt, the blushing, the way he was sometimes missing his necktie, (which I would no doubt find downstairs in Harry's basement bed chamber if I cared to go hunting for it), Chapel's confusion and disappointment about Harry's delivery from Shield, it all made sense now. Gary Chapel wanted to feed Harry. Had he already? Was Chapel the source of Harry's warmth? Of all people, Gary?!

Of course it was Gary. Chapel had done what he promised: he'd stood in for me as Harry's daytime protection, but in truth he'd become DaySitter in every sense of the word as it applied to Harry's well-being, except for the Bond. He was there when we needed him, but he'd gone ahead and fed my companion from his own veins. I hadn't asked him to and I'd never have approved if anyone had asked me. Maybe that's why they hadn't. Could it have been Gary's agenda all along? Above and beyond the call of duty, indeed. I wondered if either of them would admit it.

And now Harry could scarcely wait for Gary Chapel to come home to us, pulling away from me when I mentioned Chapel's motivations. Why, when I was standing right here in his arms? Was Chapel a more ideal protector? A better partner? Was I no longer Harry's priority? Had I been usurped? Or was I just being paranoid?

I felt a flush of irritation and pulled away, rummaging for Oreos in the pantry. When I couldn't find them on their usual shelf between the Cheez Doodles and the peanut butter, my right eyelid started to twitch. I had to press on it to make it stop.

"Where …" I heard my voice drop to deadly quiet. "Are my Double-fucking-Stuf Oreos?"

"I believe they were set on the kitchen table earlier."

"Those are my cookies to give, not yours. Mine."

"If I have trespassed against you in some way, I do sincerely apologize," he said calmly.

"It's strange how you're wrong about that, when you *think* you're always right about stuff."

"That is a head-scratcher," Harry agreed. "How can we reconcile this seeming incongruity?"

"Who exactly ate them? As if I need to ask."

Harry's chair creaked as he sat back, unrolling his sleeves and refastening his cufflinks. "I am many things, darling: I am your instrument of reckoning; my reach, your retribution; the sound of my voice, your enemy's death knell; the reach of my hand, his final ruin. 'Ere I tread, his doom shall follow." He flashed a brilliant smile, teasing. "I am not, however, the monitor of this home's cookie intake, my spirited little sparrow. No man living or dead could manage such a task."

I started running more hot water in the sink, turning my back on him. "It was Chapel, wasn't it? He took my cookies."

Harry was quiet for a long beat; when he answered his voice held a cautious lilt. "It's possible?"

"Well, how dare he?" I threw the sponge into the water angrily. "He comes swaggering right up into my personal space, *my personal space*, where he wasn't invited ..."

"Was he not?"

"I didn't ask him to come here and shove pictures of headless corpses in my face then damn well move in with me! Then he opens his fat yap and swipes my goodies?" I rinsed the teapot carefully and set it in the drainer so I wouldn't chuck it through the window over the sink.

"Judging by your fury, I'm surprised he walked away from this act alive," Harry said with a wary trace of sarcasm.

"What choice do I have? I can't blink my eyes and turn him into a smoldering ruin."

"Hmm," Harry agreed guardedly. "Dearheart, are you quite sure you're not projecting? Is it in fact Agent Chapel that is causing this sudden fury, young Gary and his felonious pilfering of your biscuits?"

"I am a law-abiding woman, and it's a damn good thing too, because he has some pretty big delusions, the deconstruction of which I would have heartily relished."

Harry fingered his empty goblet. "I always suspected that Agent Chapel had some serious defects and was not to be trusted. Thank you for exposing the squirrel's true nature." Now the sarcasm was liberally applied. My face heated.

"You're not taking this seriously at all," I accused.

"Should I be? The Agents are human. They do need to eat."

"They need to eat." My throat felt full of bile. "*They* do. *They've* got lots of needs, don't they? What about me? What about you? Is nothing sacred around here?"

"A revenant does not eat biscuits," Harry said, looking confused at his need to point out the obvious. "What is it about their needs that has you so upset?"

"Just because he's here doesn't mean he can help himself to whatever is mine, help himself to everything!" I sloshed soapy water around with the sponge, scrubbing the teapot more vigorously than tea stains required. "Why doesn't he just throw on my lingerie and traipse around waving my sex toys while he's at it!"

"Lord and Lady," Harry choked back a surprised laugh. "That's not a pretty picture to paint!" After a beat. "You own sex toys?"

"No!"

"You do not, then, refer to the purple apparatus in your night table that I was surprised to discover next to your wallet?"

"That's a foot massager!" I fibbed, turning to scowl at him.

His face was carefully blank, tasting the lie with a heavy-lidded gaze. "I thought *I* was your foot massager."

"Sometimes you're unavailable. And my foot massager isn't for Gary-blasted-Chapel to touch either!"

Harry's eyeballs crawled backwards as though he were searching for answers to my malfunction on the inside of his skull. "Brace yourself for further betrayal, darling. I believe your young hunter had several biscuits as well."

"Well, of course he did. Batten I expect to annoy me. Batten can't help it. Batten was born to aggravate me. His very existence is punishment for me, probably for horrid things I did in a past life. But Gary? *Gary?*" I waggled the wet sponge at him and dripped all over the floor. Harry watched the soapy mess with raising distress. "I suppose we should get his name tattooed on our wrists, since it seems he owns everything else in this damn house."

"What sense does that make?" Harry pushed back from the table, now, rising. The kitchen filled with his anxiety, and despite the breakdown of our Bond, I felt it hit me in the solar plexus.

"Stop that!" I shot back. "It makes perfect sense. Angry sense!"

"As one can clearly see." He swallowed hard. "Perhaps you should retire for the evening. You have had quite enough excitement for one day."

"And another thing." I balled the sponge and tossed it back in the sink. "I want a fucking bath! Not a shower, a bath!"

"Well, you cannot have a bath," he said calmly. "Doctor's orders."

I pointed at him hard. "*You bother me!*"

"Is there anything that is not bothering you at the moment, my love? Perhaps I can help you sort things out."

I exhaled hard, squeezing my eyes shut to stop weary tears. "Oh Harry. I'm sorry. I'm ..."

"Overwrought?"

My shoulders fell. "If stress were water, I'd be dog paddling the Pacific."

"Such a fuss you make. Come to me." He stood and beckoned me to his embrace with arms open. Despite my suspicions, I stepped into the shelter of his familiar clinch and let myself melt against his body, the well-fed warmth of which I stubbornly ignored. "Oh, the crown of my comfort, the spring to my bumbershoot, the very laces of my boot. How I do abhor the song of your distress."

"Gosh. Never been called someone's bootlace before. I don't know what to say," I muttered into the revenant's chest.

"I may know what you need, my quivering quail." His hand slid down one of my arms, his lingering touch raising all the hairs at the nape of my neck.

"I don't think I'm ready for that just yet."

"Mm hmm," he said as though he didn't believe me. "You're a tough little bird."

"I'll hurt something."

"We shall have to be gentle then, won't we?" he promised, tipping my chin up to face the twinkle in his eyes. "I'll go slip into the appropriate attire and meet you in the living room in ten, shall I?"

"There's no way I can talk you out of it?"

"Tut, tut," he chided. "Surely you recognize that I know what is best for my pet?"

C24

"You're going to have to do better than that," Harry reprimanded.

"But it hurts."

He *tsk*ed at me. "You're not injured here."

His graceful, supple body moved in to faultless alignment alongside mine, close enough to touch. The fine sandy hair across his perfectly sculpted chest tickled my bare shoulder as he leaned in closer. The lithe, taut line of the revenant's belly put me to shame, reminding me how very out of shape I'd let myself become.

"You're just stiff and out of practice," he said, his mouth brushing my ear.

"You're calling me stiff?" I huffed. "Don't make me state the obvious, dead guy."

Harry's cool hand landed firmly on my shoulder. "You can do it."

I groaned, reaching for my heel. "I don't think I can."

"Do not crank your ankle, you will injure yourself. Come now, ducky, this is a simple position. You mastered this long ago."

He helped me slide my ankle onto my knee in lotus position and then patted high on my thigh. So intimate were his long, even strokes kneading my muscles with familiarity, if anyone had peered through the frost-covered glass of the living room window, spying me in padmasana and Harry in yoga pants and bare chest, they might assume he was both my personal trainer and my lover. *If only.*

"Better," he encouraged. "Breathe. Don't slouch."

"I couldn't slouch if I tried," I snarled.

"Less whining, more focus. Straighten your spine. Now we are only going to do a half-twist. Stop when you feel pressure right here." His agile hand lit across my belly.

Yoga massage with Harry always involved a lot of coaching. He'd been limber for the better part of two centuries and I was just learning. Exercise is vital for revenants; their muscular systems don't work the same way as ours and fall flaccid quickly without daily upkeep, which eventually affects their preternatural might. Being undead doesn't negate the effects of a sedentary lifestyle, quite the opposite in fact. One look at 800 pound Fat Dracula on YouTube should explain why revenants stick to human blood: all ingested food becomes permanently stored fat in a revenant body, which is why Harry's only indulgence is the odd roll of Polo Mints he brought back from London.

Even after Fat Dracula's liposuction, his weight had ballooned right back up, because he refused to give up bacon double cheese burgers. I sympathized: nothin' like a good bacon double cheeseburger.

"Nope, this is too much," I reported, wincing.

"All right; Stop, stop, stop." He put his hands on my hips. "Move to ardha matsyendrasana. Is this better?" He didn't wait for my answer; his hands were on my body and he knew exactly how I felt. "Breathe. Twist on exhale. Lift your ribcage. Gently, love, gently."

We moved together with his hands rubbing my muscles until I could do no more without hurting. He patted my knee to wordlessly release me from exercising. I went into rest pose and his feet touched my shoulders, softly pressing down. His fingers slid under my neck and pulled along under my ears in gentle waves. Once I was relaxed, he moved onto his own more strenuous routine. I didn't have to wonder if he was as hard as he looked; Harry's workout regimen kept him strong and flexible.

I spent the next ten minutes on my back watching him work out: proud warrior, tree pose, downward dog, sun salutations, he made it all look easy. When he started inversions and forearm stands, I grinned at him.

"Show-off."

"If I wanted to blow my own horn, love, I would be doing this in the nude."

"Thanks. I'll never get that image out of my head," I grumbled, moving to the couch.

"At long last, I have you all to myself," Harry said with a contented growl, sliding behind me on the couch. "Are you quite sure you are well enough for a feed? I would still be willing to wait a few more days."

I stiffened, not wanting to confront his deception about Gary but not sure I could keep my tongue from betraying me. Lies lay in my gut like spoiled tuna salad. He tried to pull me closer and I tensed.

"Oh, how clumsy of me," he breathed. "I have upset you. What have I done wrong?"

"No, nothing," I said.

"Did we overdo the yoga?"

"No, I'm fine." I forced myself to relax against him, the cool curve of his body familiar. "It's time for your feed."

"You are uneasy, pet, restless. One should think it is the ideal time for us to unwind together." His crisp and refined English tongue lilted with confusion as he continued his line of reasoning. "Everyone has left us. The special delivery has been taken away. You have charged the warden vine at the gate to warn us of any intrusion. Agent Chapel has left me one of his guns for self-defense."

"He did what?"

"His Springfield XD tactical."

Chapel's favorite sidearm. I guess my little Beretta mini wasn't manly enough for Harry.

"Soon enough, your agents will return. They've been splendid watchdogs."

"I bet they have." I didn't intend for it to come out sounding so bitter.

"We're perfectly safe," he insisted.

I agreed. "Any time now the knot in my stomach will unclench."

Harry wrestled something from behind a pillow. "What do you make of these fanciful things, eh pet? I bought them for a future occasion but since you cannot find your others, I thought it best not to wait."

A new pair of gloves appeared from behind a couch cushion, soft as a calf's ear, in a light tan colour. They had tiny, cheerful green frogs embroidered around the cuff. I couldn't not brighten.

"Where in the world did you find these?"

He beamed, pleased at my reaction. "I think you'll find that if one spends enough money on Savile Row and Jermyn Street, one can find an accommodating tailor who will make anything. And I've been through generations of bespoke tailors and haberdashers."

Knowing the extensive size of his wardrobe (his closet used to be a cold cellar and was three times as big as mine) I wondered how much money he'd spent on upscale clothing in 400 years; stylish neckties from Hermes and white linen cravats in the style of Beau Brummell; cashmere scarves and seven-fold silk neckties, the "*non plus ultra*" of tie-making; hound's-tooth jackets, coats of herringbone and cheviot worsted wool; monk strap buckled shoes and welted Oxfords made by Foster & Son; Devonshire bowlers, pork-pie and top hats from Christies and Lock & Co Hatters. When his Oliver Brown Royal Ascot Tall topper was damaged, he mourned it for a week. He was currently waiting, not at all patiently, for a delivery of two dozen shirts from Turnbull & Asser custom-fitted on his last trip to England. I couldn't begin to imagine the cost. Even when he'd purchased the yoga pants he was wearing, he had ferreted out what company made the very best ones.

"Oh Harry, thank you. They're nifty, I love them."

"You are most welcome, of course."

He threw his arm along the back of the couch. I felt his pulse speed up to match mine, felt the slow evenness of his breath against the back of my head. He required neither a pulse nor breath; both were affectations to put humans at ease. They worked. If I ignored the coolness of him, I could almost pretend he was still a man, that he wasn't the elegant reanimated dead.

He was hungry, but he'd wait until I was ready, until I was comfortable. It was our routine. Harry did not like his feed to be rushed; he always said that anticipation was, in itself, a sensory delight to be savoured, and would spend a good half hour just smelling my neck if I let him. Tonight I wished he'd just get it over with. I felt hurried by the anticipation of Batten or Chapel returning while we weren't quite finished. Feeding Harry wasn't exactly a clandestine affair, but I didn't want an audience; being watched was an intrusion. Now that I thought about it, I didn't want Harry not to feed. I wanted Batten and Chapel not to come back.

I must have been having a serious hate-on for humanity because Harry misread my feelings and said low, "I'll hunt her down and break her if you want me to."

I almost didn't hear it. He went very still, and I knew he was serious. "I shall scent her down like a bloodhound, and when I find her, I shall put my thumbs in her and tear her open like a bag of onions."

What do you say to something like that? Thank you very much? It's not necessary this time, but I'll take a rain check?

"Not what you wanted to hear," he said, more a comment than a question. While he pulled the fuzzy blanket off the back of the couch to lay it across my lap, he forgot to breathe, and the steady false beat of his heart faltered. "I do wish you would let me handle this."

"You've got my back, I get it," I acknowledged. I figured it was safest thing to say. "But I don't want—"

"Slaughter and carnage. I can promise you, there wouldn't be anything left of her to get us into trouble."

"Harry, I can't listen to this," I warned him. "I'm not worried about getting myself into trouble. You can't risk it. Your hands must be 100% clean; you don't think Batten's chomping at the bit to watch you fuck up? He'd be the first one in line with a stake."

"No doubt," Harry said with a chuckle.

"And it's not what I meant to feel, anyway. I just don't want anyone but us to be here right now."

He ran his fingers through my hair fondly. "Why's that, love?"

Thinking of Chapel, I said: "Guess I just want you all to myself."

There was little difference to Harry between "make people go away" and "make people go away forever". As soon as it came, that underlying menace inherent in the revenant dissipated, and he was back to being just Harry, fake-breathing and fake-pulsing behind me. He might have dropped it for now, but I knew the idea was still squatting in his mind like a poisonous toad. The consummate predator, he'd fixated on his prey and would not likely forget it. And he didn't give two shits about the law, necessarily. Only the concern for the final destination of his soul, that lingering hope that he might redeem himself, kept him from stalking her right this minute, I imagined.

"Harry, it's time for your feed," I reminded. So much stalling. Did he think I was still too weak, or was he more interested in his new ... I stopped myself before even thinking the word *bleeder*.

"What do they call this haircut, again?" he murmured. "A fairy?"

"A pixie cut." Our hairdresser, Clarice, had done the best she could, considering she'd made a house call to the hospital. God bless small town folk. I'd taken to avoiding the mirror in my room, and in a way I'd been robbed of my true reflection just like a revenant. How long had it been since Harry had been able to see his human face in the glass, to see what we saw when we looked at him? I wondered what it was he really did see-I knew it wasn't *nothing*. It was probably best that the candid reflection did not appear to the human eye in mirrors or film.

"No, go back go back," he urged, pointing at the TV. I thumbed down on the remote and saw a scene I didn't recognize in an old black and white movie. "Dracula, Bela Lugosi, 1931. It just started."

"Ok, ok. We'll watch it *again*," I sighed, but in truth it had been years.

"Fancy some popcorn, my pet?" he offered.

I made a negative noise. "I'm too tired to eat." Something I knew he was never too tired to do. As if reading my mind, he brushed his cool lips against my cheek, and a forelock of his hair teased my temple. He rested his chin on my shoulder from behind me. Hunger quivered through him but he said nothing about it.

"So?" I prodded.

"So what?"

"What do you think of the pixie haircut?"

"If I ever get my hands on the butcher that did it, I'll show her why they call them boning sheers." I shivered and Harry chuckled, his mouth close to my ear. "Too much?"

"Boning shears. Uber-*blech*."

"Since when are you squeamish?" he said with genuine astonishment.

"Since the surgeon told me they had to put staples in my gut wound and I got a vivid mental image of my insides closed up by little metal claws. I repeat: *blech*."

"Whatever shall we do with all our CSI DVDs? And Bones. Oh, farewell to Dexter," he teased. "Think I could get a fair price for them on EBay?"

"Gimme some time. I'll get over it," I said, shifting until I was contentedly surrounded by the width of him, crooked up into a nook in his arms.

His chin sank questioningly to my neck and I put my hand on the back of his, our go-ahead signal. He barely whispered, "Only if you are certain, my Own?"

I patted his hand there, where his knuckles rose in soft, gentle peaks, traced the delicate lines of his strong wrist. I heard the slightest wet *snick* as his fangs extended.

When he pierced my skin, there was no Hollywood movie prop sound, no Foley-artist-puncturing-watermelon-with-spike noise. There was no sound now at all, nor pain. Harry slid gradually in, worked his way tenderly, sensitive of his pressure like a gentleman making love to his new bride. When that first flood of warm blood hit Harry's tongue, he sighed and I sank further into his embrace. His arms trembled and tightened, not out of fear that I'd try to leave but in unutterable ecstasy. He drank deep, and I felt him becoming rapidly dizzy from the heady, exhilarating torrent of hot life into his veins.

"The Bond's not entirely kaput," I said softly. "I can still feel your hunger."

But I hadn't guessed how famished he still was. Sure, he'd lied about the blood in the freezer, but even still, he'd had almost nothing for nearly a week, now, except a covert feed from Chapel and a sip or two from Shield. And clearly that wasn't enough.

"O-neg my ass," I said, grabbing the remote from my lap. I turned up the volume. "There wasn't any blood in the boathouse. You're busted, mister."

Harry's response was a low moan against my skin. I felt the eager suckling and wondered how he'd managed to fool me. I'd felt his suspicious warmth, but how I had missed the signs of deprivation? I eyeballed him over my shoulder. The shadows under his eyes were quickly fading; I hadn't seen them before now. Close up, I could see beige smudges on his flesh.

"Are you wearing my make up?" I asked, incredulous.

"I did not wish to worry you, love," he murmured, coming up for a breath before sinking in for another long drink. This new breath was real and necessary, not an affectation; as my blood flushed through the veins supplying his lungs, they renewed with vigor and energy, responding to autonomic nervous impulses. For the remainder of his feed, Harry's lungs would, like a newborn's, rattle with fresh life. Oxygen would be rushed back through the gastrosanguinem, producing massive excretions of telomerase and a heady dose of dizzying euphoria.

"Did they know you were starving?" I asked, meaning Batten and mostly Chapel.

Harry chuckled with his mouth muffled by throat flesh, and I knew he found the term starving ridiculous.

"No, of course they didn't," I answered myself. "Batten in particular wouldn't give it a second thought." I considered asking flat-out about Chapel then let it go. Maybe it was a one-time thing and I should stop being ... was I jealous?

Harry's body temperature warmed where our bodies touched. I patted his hand affectionately. The flesh there had flushed pink. For the next few hours he'd pass well for human, with the exception of that nameless otherness that marked the undead as exceptional. Finally, I felt his erection stiffen against my lower back. Not anything to be flattered about, just a natural reaction to such a deep feed. It had taken me literally years to get over the hardening manhood after every big feed. Now it was just a sign that he was nearly full. If a revenant could ever be truly full ... highly debatable.

He pulled out as gently as he had entered me. Like a cat cleaning its kitten, he lovingly licked the wound in quick, flickering lashes and then lingered for a while, amusing himself with the tiny pricks. His chilly tongue had flushed hot with life. I closed my eyes while, onscreen, Dracula shied away from Van Helsing's exposed cross.

"Our guests have returned," he said against the skin at the nape of my neck. "Will my fresh marks upon you bother them much?"

Thinking of Chapel, I murmured, "Frankly, my dear Harry, I don't give a rat's ass."

C25

I was hoping a night in my own bed would bring deep and blissful sleep, but I was foiled again.

Watching Batten pace and Chapel write on his portable white board late into the night had given me a form of exhaustion I didn't have words for, one that did not induce sleep. My brain was trying to tell me something, like I had a nugget of truth buried in the mudslide that was my mental state. Skimming through all the notebooks in my office and bedroom only revealed a sub-clinical compulsion to make notes that meant nothing to anyone but me, sometimes not even to me. What did "that's the promise" mean? I had scrawled it, possibly while under a heavy drug haze, in the hospital.

Trying to link to Danika Sherlock again and again through the cracked sunglass lens surreptitiously in my bedroom had drained me, since every time I started to open a psi-bridge I got psychically bitch-slapped away into dizzying darkness. My efforts came at a high cost; I had the mother of all psychic headaches, and no drug could touch it. There was indisputably a malicious force guarding Sherlock's lens, locking its secrets just out of reach, though it didn't taste like *her,* not exactly. If Sherlock had help, and I was beginning to think she did, then I had to find out what sort of magic this other person might wield. It was only a matter of time before I managed to out-maneuver the lens, but it was going to require some more assistance of a green magic sort, and I was wary to do any more spells until I was fully healed. The black-watch spell had left me with cramps and a broken jar, which could have been a broken hand or worse if I'd been wearing any sort of metal rings or bracelets for the spell to react against.

Hours of flipping through every single one of my textbooks and scouring the internet for reference to "blind eyes" or "beheadings" had brought of a ton of icky stuff I hoped never to be subjected to again. But it hadn't offered concrete leads on a spell in any form of magic that might tell us why Kristin Davis had been chosen to die. I had combed through disturbing websites and bewildering serial killer fan sites, and had tried to run down hints and whispers of reanimation spells and flesh magic, mostly of a Haitian vodou zombie-flavor, but these sorts of things (thankfully) were not widely available to the general public in detail. YouTube had one promising video to offer, something entitled witch-walking, using blind eyes. I'd never heard of it. The video was gone when I went to show Chapel. He was working with the company to trace its user.

I'd need a more reliable source anyway, but I hadn't come up with one. The costs of flesh magic were high, and its results, from what I remembered from school, were unreliable. Flesh magic spells could be interrupted, or jump-started, or amplified by water and fire, which is why you never, *ever* set a black witch on a flaming pyre unless you want a very angry, crispy version of a black witch removing burnt ropes and chasing you around said burning pyre. Witchcraft trials had seen thousands of white witches burned to death, but not a single black witch; sadly ironic, when you consider the inherent non-violence of most white witches.

Speaking of torture, I was finding that living with Batten was a rare form of sexual torment. Knowing he was upstairs undressing at night robbed me of the necessary relaxation for sleep. Picturing him in my guest bed, easily able to drum up images of his familiar hard body splayed under the sheets, wondering if a leg was peeking out from under a blanket, wondering if he wore pajamas, wondering why in the world I wasn't tiptoeing up those stairs to find out, why my hands weren't roaming under those sheets across that wonderfully hard, thick, manly ... yes, it was making me restless and fidgety. Knowing that my sudden appearance beside his bed would probably be welcomed by Jerkface as the continuation of our not-so-secret tryst, made it ten times harder not to go to him. I'd spent the night wishing Mr. Buzz the purple vibrator was quiet enough to use with relative assurance of privacy in a house full of men trained in attention to detail.

When morning made its rude approach, I'd barely slept, a tossing-turning sexually frustrated half-doze that shouldn't even count. I showered, taking an extra ten minutes with my expert soapy hand, but it wasn't nearly enough. By the time Harry retired for the day to his casket, and Chapel shouted he was running to the precinct to meet with Hood and Dunnachie, my brain had long given up hope of getting lucky and had settled into a hormone-sickened blur. With my crudely shorn hair in a towel, my robe cinched tight, I padded barefoot to the mudroom to toss a load in the washing machine.

Harry had a load of angora socks in the delicate cycle. I chucked them in the dryer (probably the wrong thing to do) and dumped my own small load of delicates in with a bit of Woolite. I heard the old fridge *click-clunk* open behind me, glanced back to see a sleepyhead version of Batten in stretchy black boxer briefs and not a stitch else, standing in the glow of the interior light, blinking and scanning the shelves.

My belly contracted. I must have made an audible intake of breath, because his fresh-shaved chin turned in my direction. I side-stepped behind the mudroom door a heartbeat too late.

His voice was full of laughter as one of his fingers pulled the mudroom door wide open. "Hiding?"

"I thought it best, since you're clothing impaired."

His eyes took in my robe with growing heat. "And you're not?"

"I'm impaired in so many, many ways," I agreed.

Batten stalked toward me and I found myself retreating helplessly. My butt brushed up against the hot, tumbling dryer.

"I see you're not very smart in the morning," I noted.

His eyes gathered heat, and the absolute worst thing he could have said came in a low, husky voice from the mouth I couldn't stop staring at. "We're alone. No one would know."

My knees weakened. "My luck, it'd be on CNN tomorrow."

"You can't hide from me forever."

"Yeah, I'm adding that to my list of reasons to hate you."

"Maybe you should just stop running."

"Listen ..." I tried to sound convincing, but my breath was coming faster, and when my tongue swiped out to wet my lips, his eyes fixated on them. "Despite what you might think, I'm not desperate for your flesh kabob." *Lies, lies!*

His eyebrow crooked up just before his lips spread in a roguish grin that was downright lewd. "I seem to recall you enjoyed it."

"Nuh-uh. My left ass cheek fell asleep."

"Not the Kebob's fault; it hasn't had anything to do with your ass."

I ignored the *yet* heavily implied. "I got a kink in my neck that bothered me for days."

"No one told you to fling backward like a trapeze artist."

"I don't control my arching when things get out of control!" I protested.

"Lucky I caught you before you fell off the table. Could have cracked your head open."

The dryer's heat caused static in my robe and it clung to the back of my thighs. I cinched the tie tighter with trembling fingers.

"I'm not a plaything you can strip and moisten whenever you want," I told him.

"Good. If I wanted a hooker, I'd get one."

"Well, what the hell do you want?"

For a moment, he looked serious. "Let me in a little. Can't you do that?"

Oh crap on a rake. This was emotional. Back to shallow! Back to shallow! "I let you in as far as you'd go. To the hilt. Twice."

He backed me up bodily against the dryer, his pupils dilating rapidly, his chest rising and falling heavily. Swallowing hard, he nodded. "Wasn't what I meant, but thanks for the reminder."

"Shit," I exhaled, aware that one of my hands had disobeyed a direct order and landed on the fine trail of hair beneath his belly button. The hard abs underneath his skin were mind-numbingly warm and all I could think was how nice they'd feel if his body was grinding against mine.

Batten's voice had thickened, gone husky: "Are you wearing anything under that robe?"

I shook my head back and forth as though imparting very bad news indeed.

"Shit," he seconded. He put both hands on either side of me as though he needed to make sure I wasn't going to bolt. 105 black marks on one tanned pectoral, four and a slash for five, marched over and over inches from my mouth. His lean arms were covered with a dusting of fine hair, and shook slightly as his face descended toward mine. He groaned, "God, I wanna taste you again—"

The front door slammed open and Chapel's voice stabbed the air. "Someone slashed the SUV's tires!"

"Fucka*nut!*" I exploded, and this time I meant it. I could have throttled Gary Chapel to death with my bare hands. Batten's mouth tightened unhappily. In a flash, reality rushed back into his face.

"Next time you decide to waltz around half naked," he said sternly, "Make sure I'm not home."

I called at his retreating back: "Next time I nearly give in to your lurid advances, do me a favor and shoot me in the head."

C26

It hadn't been a day since my release from the hospital, much too soon for a bath; by four in the afternoon I really didn't give a flying fig. Let the water spill in and fill my abdominal cavity, if it would. Damn the torpedoes! Let me sink tragically like the Titanic in my claw foot tub. Let Leviathan Himself come to gobble my scrumptious soul. Ok, I took that last one back; the demon king Leviathan would totally get his serpentine nose out of joint if I lured Him all the way from the abyssopelagic zone in the Bermuda triangle for a snack, only to renege at the last minute.

I lurked near the bubble line like a sunken hippo, only my slit eyes showing. After much dispute and scathing condemnation, a surly, early-awoken Harry had decided to allow me my bitter soak. Probably, he figured he'd helped me heal enough. I was going on my third hot water refill and my second bubble addition, and 40 whole minutes of soaking delight.

"So, you intend to stay in there and prune?" Harry confirmed.

"I'm not pruning, I'm hiding. Psychos can't kill you in the bathroom," I replied sagely. "Hard and fast rule."

"Tell that to Norman Bates," he pointed out. "And Janet Leigh."

"I'm never getting out of the bath. I'll just stay here forever."

"I see." Harry studied me expectantly with the Bela Lugosi brow arch; I ignored it. "We have an important viewing to attend. You promised." He tried the impatient toe tapping; I ignored that too. "Agent Batten will be sorely disappointed."

"When have I *not* disappointed Mark Batten?"

He clipped a thumbnail and murmured disapprovingly under his breath, "I can think of at least once."

"Twice. Shows how much you know." I disregarded the nail brush he passed me, and the sea salt body scrub and pumice stone. This was a sulking soak, not a primping one. I stared at my freshly painted toenails, curled on the far edge of the tub, and used them to flick bubbles at the wall. "And you're damn right, I was fantastic."

At last he sighed grandly and put away the clippers, picking up his nail file instead. "You do realize this calls for a dramatic rescue of Herculean proportions," he warned. "I shall not be held accountable for any ensuing affront or grievance."

I watched him suspiciously out of the corner of my eye.

He continued, "But of course, I would do anything for you, my merry grig. Consequently, at great personal risk to my image, here goes the Marnie Baranuik theme song ..."

To the best of my knowledge, I didn't have a theme song. I braced for the worst. He cleared his throat. Raising his voice to a nasal falsetto, he did a bang-on impression of Lou Christie and started trilling:

"I don't want the world to kno-ow. I don't want my heart to sho-ow!" He fluttered his eyelashes, and gathered steam. "Two faces have Iiiiii, ah-*Iiii! Yii-yii-yii-yii yi-ah-i.*"

"Harry!"

"*Yii-yii-yii-yii yi-ah-ii.*" His pitch bounced off the tile walls and reverberated in my head. I gulped a deep breath and sunk under the water. I saw him leaning above between the bubbles, smiling around full fang. His audiomancy would not be buffered by mere water. Through it, his voice carried perfectly and I heard him even louder than before: "*Yii-yii-yii-yii yi-ah-ii.*"

I exploded up out of the bathwater. "You burst my eardrum, you're paying for it, you preternatural pain in the ass!"

"I could go higher if you like ..." he filed his thumbnail, tapping his foot along to the beat in his head. He bumped it up an octave. "Two face have I! Oh no no no. One to laugh and one to cry!"

"I'm begging you, *begging* you ..."

"Two faces have I! *Ooooone* to laugh and one to cry! Ah-ah-ah-*iii.*"

"OKAY! Uncle! Uncle!" I whipped out of the bath water in a shower of bubbles. "I'm going to have that flippin' song stuck in my head for hours. If I start humming it at the funeral home, it's your damn fault."

Harry handed me a bath towel. He dropped his voice down a few octaves and crooned mock-sorrowfully in his lounge singer voice: "Will I ever laugh again ... he'll never see me cry. Will I walk with a smile on my face, knowing I live a lie-*iii-ii!*" His voice shot up 4 octaves to a shrill noise that cracked the bathroom mirror clear across. I jumped in surprise, clasping my towel around my chest.

Batten bellowed from somewhere deep in the cabin: "Jesus H. Christ!"

I wriggled a finger in my ear, smirking conspiratorially. "That one hurt."

"It did, rather." He cringed apologetically. "I may have given myself a hernia."

"Sounded like you had your dick in a Cuisinart." I grinned. "How the hell is that *my* song, anyway?" I toweled-off.

"You really don't know?" He blinked at me in mock-astonishment. I swatted at him and he danced away in a blink-step, grinning and unreachable. He lifted one finger into the air. "And now, to the wardrobe!"

I let my shoulders fall in defeat. "Yes, Alfred, to the bat cave."

I'm one of those fair ash blondes who look best in pastels. Though I've never been able to pull off "girly-girl" in act, deed or dulcet speech, clothing in the tones closest to petal pink are most flattering on me.

Unfortunately, my companion had chosen a clingy, low-cut silk blouse in hot magenta that made me look like a freshly smashed pomegranate. The curling frill along the bust line made my cleavage itchy and I'd never mastered the art of the inconspicuous tit scratch. I couldn't have possibly drawn more attention to my breasts without a neon sign. The skirt was barely there, flippy as opposed to tight, deep black against my winter-light legs. Not that I was ever tanned outside my least realistic daydreams; I burn, blister, freckle and go right back to pasty. For that, I blame my mother's Nordic stock.

Now, as the limo took the turn at Lambert's Crossing, I put some Shalimar perfume on to cover the pungent scent of a brand new leather jacket and tucked the tiny trial-sized vial into the pocket with my pink pearl lip gloss, emergency condom and a plastic baggy containing one of the squished newt eyeballs. After the viewing, while respectable folks went to the funeral, I'd pop into the store to find a suitable envelope to mail it back with the sternly-worded letter I'd jotted explaining the defect. Probably I shouldn't be sending ruined animal body parts through the mail, but I'd figured out the cost to be approximately eighteen dollars per eye of newt. I didn't need the money, but that wasn't the point. For eighteen bucks each, you'd think I'd get usable eyeballs, not deflated stringy goop; in fact, the site had guaranteed perfection. I didn't like it when people broke their promises to me. That was grounds for full-on bitch mode.

Harry ran a cool hand along the fringe of my hair, ran his fingertips through, finger-styling until the look pleased him.

"Nice as nine pence," he judged, which I assumed was a good thing. "What are you thinking, my pet?"

"That this skirt is way too short," I warned him, covering my bare thighs with my hands. "How will I sit down in the funeral home?"

"Like a lady," Harry sighed. "You can manage that, can't you?"

"Yeah sure, like a lady flashing her gitchies to the world."

"A lady who should perhaps stand all night."

"A lady who can barely stand upright in these slut heels someone forced her to wear." I displayed 4 inch heels in the same retina-melting magenta silk as the shirt.

"A lady who should have worn some dark knickers under her clothing, if that is the case." Harry's eyes rolled up to search the roof of the limo for patience.

"A lady who's already wearing the panties her companion picked out."

"A lady who shouldn't say the word *panties* quite so vociferously in mixed company," he said quietly in my ear, eyeing the chauffer.

"A lady packin' heat, Professor Higgins, check this." I gave a little flip of my jacket to demonstrate how it hid the holstered Beretta Cougar. "And don't try to talk me out of it. I'm sick of being the only one who isn't dangerous."

"Dangerous." He blinked as though the word didn't compute when used in relation to me. He rubbed a hand across his forehead. "Flames and ether, give me strength."

"Let Sherlock come at me with a knife, now, see what happens."

Harry rubbed his forehead some more. If he'd been human, I'd have guessed he was getting a headache. "Is your little hand cannon loaded this time?"

"I put a clip in just before we left. Maybe I even did it properly."

He surveyed me. "You're right-handed, you are aware?"

I glared at him. "Think you're so smart."

"If Agent Batten catches you with the gun holstered on the wrong side, he will not be impressed." He stared long out the window into the darkness. "If he catches you with it at all, he may have you in shackles before the night is through."

Batten putting me in his handcuffs might not be such a bad thing, I thought, but did not say. I turned my face to the window so he wouldn't see my private smile, and felt a swell of helpless arousal that I tried to stamp down, knowing my Cold Company would pick up on it immediately. *How about Batten in the handcuffs? All naked and at my mercy …*

Below the chill that Harry always carried with him I felt a breeze on bare skin and yanked the shirt further down around my freshly-applied bandages.

Harry sputtered, "For heaven's sake, stop giving your blouse the Picard maneuver, you will ruin the silk."

"You're miserable," I accused. "What's your malfunction?"

"Such insolence." His lips set in a tight line. "Sometimes I wonder why I tolerate that pretty mouth of yours at all."

Stunned by his moodiness, I settled back into the seat and scowled at the back of the chauffer's black hat, wondering if revenants got PMS. Harry went back to staring out the window and gave me a full-on cold shoulder, a proper chilly silence, until the limo glided to a stop in front of the funeral home.

Up on the big white stairs above a crowd of milling mourners and photographers, Batten and Chapel waited expectantly in funereal black, creases crisp, shoes shined. The looked like G-men waiting for the president.

"Do try not to shock the cameramen like an incoherent starlet, my pet?" Harry suggested quietly as we waited for the chauffer to open his door. I slid closer to him and touched the back of his hand.

"If the gun is the problem, I'll leave it in here under the seat."

He didn't answer.

"Ok, if my mouth is the problem, Harry, I can leave *it* in the limo. Or I could just slap a bandage over it. Maybe the limo driver has some duct tape ..."

"Forgive me, my love. You are not the problem." He hung his head. "I'll try harder to block it."

"Block what?" I asked.

When he refrained from answering, I closed my eyes, tried to focus on his emotional signature and felt nothing. Stupid broken Bond. As soon as the chauffer had the door cracked Harry was out and comfortably bathed in the flashing of cameras. Immortals not only didn't show on film but almost always overexposed digital images, especially if they got close to the camera; Harry didn't have anything to worry about there. Unlike me, who had every reason to worry about film.

I flipped out of the limo like a performing seal, lost in a graceless tangle of bare limbs. I nearly broke an ankle twisting my high heel on the curb. The madly clutching hand I threw out to catch myself landed in Harry's crotch. Harry quickly caught me by the elbow and hauled me upright, his grip squeezing hard both for my safety and with barely contained irritation. I wobbled against him, venturing a peek at his blank face. I followed his gaze up to see Batten's lips writhe in a hard-squelched grin.

Harry sighed, wrapping his arm around my waist and covering the tell-tale bulge caused by the holstered Beretta with his hand.

"Always a lady," he noted with forced cheer, nodding in greeting at Chapel.

C27

My father's endless supply of prose, compulsively scribbled in his own Moleskine notebooks, may have been useful here at Pennywick Funeral Home in Ten Springs; I was at a total loss. There were never good words at a funeral. Good coffee, maybe. Good flowers. Good squares, if you got there early. Never good words. Just stale stock phrases that meant nothing, said to soothe the mourner's discomfort more than to buoy the family. At a funeral following a particularly horrific end, like Kristin Davis', there weren't words at all. Hallmark sympathy card writers would have been stricken mute.

Harry left my side, disappeared into the press of people in search of comfort. Why his mood had suddenly become so foul, I could only guess: no one liked burying a kid, I suppose, even when that kid is a stranger. Or maybe I had really put my foot in it, in the limo.

I joined Batten beside the guest book set up by a massive spray of doleful stargazer lilies. I hate lilies: the smell of them, the way their colour fades from flamingo to a sickly, wilted grey-pink. They remind me of sudden goodbyes, and of Grandma Vi, and of the massive bouquets that had been Harry's outpouring of misery, dwarfing her small bronze urn. It had seemed impossible that such a big personality like Vi's could be condensed into an urn that fit so neatly in Harry's trembling hands, as he'd helped my mother set Vi in a hole in the ground. It had felt so wrong to turn and walk away, so wrong to leave Vi alone where she'd stay, sequestered in a lonesome cemetery, never to come away with us again, to the warmth of indoor heating, music, laughter. At the time, it had seemed impossible to close the gulf between this strange Lord Guy Harrick Dreppenstedt and me, in the back seat of my father's car, his head turned away to get one last glimpse of the cemetery. He would never return, for fear of keeping her spirit chained to Earth with the dead's affinity for the dead.

I caught my breath as the memory pricked my heart, and searched for Harry's reassuring silhouette. No taller than most women, Harry would nonetheless stand out by the old-fashioned cut of his over coat swinging cape-like at ankle-length, or his graceful glide across the quiet carpeting, silent as a creeping shadow, or the diplomatic inclination of his head as he politely answered the curious and uneasy glances of mortals. But I didn't see him.

Batten was scanning the guest book, looking at the names. He glanced over and did a double-take at my skirt.

"Too short?" I asked.

He maintained his blank cop-face. "Fortunately, yes."

"I told Harry it was inappropriate. He insisted that his opinion trumped mine."

"Well, God bless Harry." He looked sideways at me. "How much for ten minutes in the handicapped stall?"

"You shouldn't say shit like that to me, dumbass. You're going to get us both in trouble."

His lips did a lewd curl. "Not gonna pay for back-talk."

I tried not to smile back, shaking my head. "Fuck you: *not* an invitation."

"Jacket new?"

"You hardly know me well enough to be familiar with my whole wardrobe," I reminded him. "I could be a leather jacket kind of girl."

"And a push-up bra kind of girl," Batten noted.

"I'm not pushing-up. This is just how my boobs go," I lied. "Besides, Harry said you wanted "saucy vixen"."

Batten's mouth opened and then snapped shut. "Dead guy knows me better than I thought."

"He gave me a choice," I confessed. "This, or the tiniest plaid kilt you ever saw."

"I have totally misjudged Harry. He has fantastic taste."

"Dick." I wobbled closer to the table so I could lean on it. "I'm very uncomfortable."

"Somewhere there's a barefoot hooker who'd appreciate her shoes back."

I ignored the jab, since the gleam in his eyes told me he liked the whole outfit just fine. I straightened my skirt and smoothed it behind me with one hand, mostly to check that I wasn't flashing my gitchies at the senior citizens behind me. "I don't see Sherlock."

"It's more important that she sees you, so go mingle. Be professional. Smooth."

"Smooth, professional mingling would require walking without flipping on my face, right? Don't see it happening." I looked around the room and did a headcount, trying not to make direct eye contact. I had effectively garnered an alarming amount of attention just standing here in the far corner, but that might have been the skirt; if the furnace went on while I was standing here by the vent I was in serious jeopardy of having a Marilyn Monroe moment, only far less glamorous.

"I'm glad I'm going to miss the church part," I said.

"You, sitting on a church pew, in that skirt? In front of God-fearing church folk?" Batten shook his head, raising his gaze to search the mourners. I did the same.

"Chapel's here somewhere?" Batten nodded. Funerals made some people ramble on to fill the silence and struck others dumb. I was the nervous babbling type. "Was the limo your idea? It was show-off-y." Met with silence, I answered myself: "Guess that's the idea." Then: "What if she doesn't show?" And: "I need a cookie."

Something about the way Batten stood, legs spread wide and sturdy, owning his space with a military bearing, shoulders back, jaw tight, made me wanna hit him with a hammer then sit in his lap and suck his tongue a little. As complicated as my feelings for Jerkface may be, it's kinda hard to hide that you're thinking about sucking someone's face when you're staring right at them; I had to look away.

"Where's Harry?" he asked.

"He went to see if they were putting out another tray of cookies at some point. We missed the first batch."

"What is it with you and cookies?"

"Some people drink when they're stressed. Some smoke. Some bone their psychic consultants."

Batten adjusted his earpiece then folded his hands in front of the aforementioned boner. "Consultant, singular."

"Until my metabolism hits the skids, I'll eat as many cookies as I damn well please."

As if I'd spoken of the devil himself, Harry arrived with a little paper plate piled with cookies and gooey squares.

"Sugar for your scowl, my livid little nightingale?" He set the plate in my hand. "Why is it, Agent Batten, that whenever I disrupt the pair of you, my pet has an aggravated look on her face?"

"Another tuxedo." Batten scanned Harry from head to toe. "You look like the damn phantom of the opera. Doesn't bother you to stand out?"

"I couldn't possibly *not* stand out," Harry pointed out with a shrug, and though it sounded arrogant it was also true. "Mortal eyes are helplessly drawn to undying grace."

Batten rolled his eyes. "You could try toning it down."

"Wardrobe advice from a man who dresses like a stud farmer." Harry gave him a clearly critical head-to-toe inspection. "How comical."

"Not here, you two, not now," I whispered, wavering on my heels like a newborn foal taking its first steps. "Please."

"Don't look now, I think our vampire just called me a stud," Batten said.

Harry smiled unpleasantly. "You could raid a Wal-Mart and upgrade what passes for your style, Agent Batten."

I took Harry by the elbow and wheeled him away, landing us both beside the coffee urn. "Hear that?"

"Hmm, yes. "Our" vampire." Harry inclined his head. "Agent Batten ought to watch his choice of phrases. People will think he's in love with me."

"Not that," I shushed, although I had heard the "our" and noted it with a mixture of interest and suspicion. "The piano."

"It is a video in the next room," he said in the funeral-home hushed voice that is an unspoken law. "Miss Davis was taking piano lessons and had an ear for music from the sounds of it. Yes." He cocked his head slightly. "There's talent there ...a shame she had only taken to the ivories two months before. Her father said that Beethoven was her favorite."

"You spoke to Mr. Davis?"

"He too finds comfort in a biscuit."

I drew coffee from the urn and doctored it sweet. "There they are, now."

Nothing would restore a sense of normalcy to the Davis family, not even vengeance; they were beyond saving, and it showed in their sallow cheeks, Mrs. Davis' blush standing out too bright on her pale cheeks like spots of warning, lips that hung heavy in the corners. Three years before Mrs. Davis had had a stroke and she had limited movement on her left side. Her wheelchair was the best money could buy, her shoes were Christian Lacroix and her Belgian-cut diamonds must have cost more than my Buick. Today their money would only serve to lift the financial burden of the services. Relief from the emotional burden couldn't be bought, unless you counted the sedatives that were dampening what I could feel from Mrs. Davis, psychically, across the room.

I knew I couldn't stall much longer. I had to introduce myself. I sipped nervously at my coffee and completely missed my mouth. Coffee splattered my breast at the nipple, an unfortunate perfect circle, an Arabica bean areola.

Harry sucked his teeth disapprovingly. "T'is a very good thing that you are gentle, my angel."

"Why's that?" I dabbed fruitlessly at my tit with a napkin.

"A gentle hazard is always preferable to the alternative."

My cheeks flamed; instantly his hand shot out to take my hand.

"Such flippant condemnations should never cross a gentleman's lips. I do apologize." I dabbed more furiously. He took my napkin away. "That's quite enough, Lady Macbeth, the spot is not coming out without the handiwork of a dry cleaner."

I sighed deeply, and confessed: "I'm pretty sure I flashed the cameras earlier like a drunk celebrity getting out of the limo."

"You very nearly tore off my bollocks."

I winced. "And yet, you people still try to get me to leave the house!"

Harry advised: "While your coffee mishap dries, perhaps you should practice speaking to other people without tripping over your tongue? There's a familiar face."

He motioned with his chin subtly to a corner, where a frail elderly lady was sitting in an upholstered chair, sipping hesitantly from a Styrofoam cup. Her white hair glowed like a soft halo under discrete track lighting. On the wall directly above her was a large oil painting, a still life of fruit in a bowl done in deep jewel tones. It loomed over her in its heavy cherry wood frame that matched the deep reddish wood of the gleaming casket—I was guessing the best that money could buy—sitting ten feet from her.

"Is that Ruby Valli?" I whispered. "What's she doing here?"

"Paying respects, I should imagine. I understand she is the organist at the church the Davis' attend, and was Kristin's piano teacher."

That didn't sound right. Mrs. Valli was a precognitive, an ex-senior psychic investigator from First Floor at GD&C who had a reputation for dabbling in the dark arts, why work in a Christian church? Perhaps the black magic mumbo jumbo was just a moldy old rumour that bore no merit. Or perhaps, I had just found a possible source for information about the flesh magic that reanimated Kristin Davis' skull in my mailbox. Would it be dreadfully impolite to ask about dismemberment at the funeral of the victim of the crime? Probably I couldn't ask here. Ruby Valli looked directly at me through the crowded room. I smiled faintly, the restrained half-smile that you give at funerals, and approached her.

"Mrs. Valli?" She didn't seem to hear so well, from the frowning enquiry on her face, so I bent closer to her, spoke louder and introduced myself. When she shook her head in confusion, I explained: "We both worked at Gold-Drake & Cross. Well, actually, I came just after your retirement party. But I've heard so much about you over the years, I feel like we're colleagues."

A beautiful, warm smile lit her face. "Oh, honey, that's sweet of you to say. What a terrible night this is. I wish we could have met under different circumstances." And then, losing interest in me quite suddenly, she dismissed, "Well, it was nice to meet you, dear."

I got the idea that if she'd been ambulatory, she'd have turned on her sensible heels and left me standing in open-mouthed rejection. As it was, I hovered, sure I'd been shooed by someone who wanted nothing to do with me, awkwardly wavering in my slut shoes. I glanced uncertainly over my shoulder at Harry, who frowned encouragement at me.

"I, uh, I wonder if I could come visit you at your shop, Mrs. Valli? We could have a talk. Would that be okay?"

"My shop, dear?" She looked surprised that I was still standing there. Her eyes scanned me from head to toe through thick glasses, clearly not impressed with what she saw. "You don't come to my shop."

"I don't?" I blinked. "When don't I?" I heard myself and shook my head. "I'd be wearing pants. What I mean is …" I lowered my voice. "Mrs. Valli, have you seen my future?"

"My shop burns down, dear," she told me simply, as though she were discussing the weather, or the war in the Mid-East. "I learned a long time ago not to interfere with the visions I might be blessed with. I'm going to stay with my nephew in San Bernardino next week while I look for the new house. I find a nice little place on the West coast. Green vinyl siding."

I didn't know what to say. Speaking to precognitives was always eerily confusing. Seers creep-out the rest of us: the Gropers, the Feelers, no one really likes to hear about what was coming. Before I could open my mouth again, Ruby Valli motioned to Hood and Dunnachie by the doorway with Batten. "There's one you need to watch more carefully, dear."

"What do you mean?" I turned so my hips covered her view and they wouldn't see her talking about them. "Which one? Why?"

"The hunter, of course. I see fire from him. Fire and alcohol, the instruments of the devil. Not to mention dishonesty. He deceives you." She looked up at me and blinked through her glasses. "Please keep clear of the shop. The bones are cast, but the future is fluid. I'd hate for anyone to get hurt on my account." Ruby Valli struggled out of the chair to her feet and took two experimental, shuffling steps aside with the help of her cane, leaving me looking at the back of her curly-haired head.

Avoiding the grieving parents and keeping my jacket yanked over the warm, damp coffee stain, I strut over to where Hood and Dunnachie had been left standing post. I found if I walked quickly and confidently enough, my ankles didn't have time to buckle and I wasn't in as much danger of doing a face-plant. Hood watched me approach with a mix of uncertainty and poorly concealed amusement, his one hand leaving his side in case he had to catch me. Dunnachie's long, morose hawk face was barren of expression.

Hood nodded a hello. "Those shoes are murder on your arches. Better hope you don't have to dash off."

"I am painfully aware of their limitations," I assured him, accidentally getting caught in the swampy gaze that was still, I discovered happily, a blend of sympathetic and skeptical. *Skeptathetic.* Handsome; not in a cocky badass way like Batten, more of a corn-fed, clear-eyed cowboy way. "No Danika Sherlock yet."

To his partner, Hood said, "Sweeping back entrance again."

Deputy Dunnachie nodded, ignoring me completely. I followed the path of his gaze, tracing Harry's every elegant move across the room.

I asked Dunnachie: "The beetle bites didn't cause any lasting damage, I hope?"

"If the vampire hadn't been there, there wouldn't have been necrophile beetles in the first place."

I'd never heard his voice before. He sounded like he'd had a hedgehog squatting in his voice box for the last decade that periodically tried to claw its way out. If he wasn't a whiskey drinking chain smoker, I'd eat my frog-print underpants.

"Well, that's debatable. There still would have been a severed head," I said cautiously. "If that revenant hadn't squished the necrophile beetles, they'd have burrowed into your brain."

I thought he was going to argue, but he surprised me with, "You have a very quick-thinking monster roommate."

"Thanks," I said, before I realized he was being glib. "I should tell you, in case you're wasting effort pursuing this: Harry didn't kill Kristin Davis."

"Says you." He didn't turn that long face of his down to look at me.

"Well, yeah." Clearly, my word wasn't going to carry much water with this particular cop. "If it makes you happy to watch him, go for it. He is fascinating to look at. If you're trying to figure out why, it's the *otherworldliness.*"

His Adam's apple bobbed; his eyes were flat and unafraid like a well-fed alligator in a Florida gator farm. "Predators often revisit their victims."

"The hell you say," I gasped, feigning shock.

Irritation buckled his eyebrows. "This viewing is the perfect place for him to relive his crime."

"I know all that junk. I work with Supervisory Special Agent Know-it-all," I said. "But you're wrong about Harry. He had no intention of coming. He's only here to guard me."

"And why are you here?"

"*I'm* a suspect?" I laughed, but it quickly died. "The only thing I've ever been accused of killing is a good time and a plate of cookies. The PCU wanted me here. Normally, I'd do the opposite of what everyone wants me to do, but since I have PMS and needed to come out for chocolate anyways, here I am."

He finally looked down at me. Everything about Neil Dunnachie was sharp and craggy, from his aquiline nose to his high Spock-like eyebrows, to the worn, over-suntanned skin, making him look a lot older than he was. There were faint acne scars pitting his chin. I think that's why he grew a scruff of a goatee over it. A full beard would have worked better. Still, despite the odd angles and worn appearance, or maybe because of them, he was interesting to look at. He had not only a cop's competence and natural resilience, but something deeper, more personal, a bullshit-resistance inside hard eyes that had seen unspeakable things. Not a guy who got rattled easily. I had a feeling that no amount of feminine wiles would sway this man once he set his mind on something, and right now his mind was set on *monster equals murder*.

He asked me, "You got some place you'd rather be?"

"Chernobyl? A super-max prison yard? Up Shit Creek? Anywhere but here. Being here reminds me of my grandmother's funeral. My father giving me the silent treatment. My mother collapsed in a folding chair. My siblings bickering and being generally stupid. And in the middle of it all, oblivious to his new family, Harry ... pale, cold and utterly devastated." I didn't know why I was bothering to share, but the words came anyway. "Harry hung at my mother's side. I think she was the only one who felt the same degree of pain as he did about Vi's passing. The grandchildren rarely saw her. My father was too self-interested to care. Harry ... he seemed lost."

I remembered my brand new Mary-Janes blistering and rubbing my heel. I remembered watching this stylish creature I'd inherited, wondering what exactly that meant, what he truly was—down to the science, although at the time, science wasn't my strong suit—how this was going to work. I remembered Vi's urn, and trying not to imagine her body being burnt into ashes on a slab ...an urn, Harry had explained quietly, because she'd spent enough time in caskets. Her companion's casket, where she spent her days, sleeping curled at his side so they could be awake all night together. I remember thinking I might have to quit school, or take night classes, and would I ever have a job? Get married? Have children? Vi had a child: my mother. Harry was not the father; revenants have dead sperm. So was Harry ok with her sleeping with other men? With my grandfather, Matts? There had been so many questions I hadn't felt comfortable asking, competing for attention with my broken heart.

Dunnachie interrupted my thoughts. "He doesn't seem lost tonight."

"Well, it's less personal, but he feels their sorrow, their devastation. Harry's an empathic revenant, that's one of his Talents. He's not even attempting to block it the way I am." I needed another cookie, but the platter had been cleared away. I couldn't even get crumbs. "He's trying to alter the distress he's exposed to, by making the Davis' feel better. In that way, he's more charitable than I am. I just want to go home and be done with this. I haven't even been able to go meet them yet, to shake their hands and say how sorry I am for their loss." I rubbed my ungloved hands on my skirt to dry the sweat and left a smudge on the silk. I looked around for Harry. He was standing directly behind me and I jerked guiltily.

"Pardon us, officer." He pulled me aside. "You are perspiring. Shall I take your coat?" He slid it off my shoulders and I made sure my silk shirt was covering my gun. It didn't cover it *well,* but no one would notice unless they looked right at my bum. "Agent Batten would like a word, and then I do believe we're taking our leave."

"Thank the Lady," I whispered. "I feel like we've been here all night. You know, Ruby Valli didn't want to talk to me. She didn't want me coming to her store, either."

"Chances are, at her age, she does not have the energy for the pandemonium your company guarantees." He looked like he completely understood; I elbowed him.

"She also said her store was going to burn down."

Harry breathed a soft laugh out of his nose. "Seers make announcements. T'is their only charge in life. Were she always right, she would be holding grand seminars like Ville Aaman, not turning tarot cards and selling tumbled stones in a magic shop."

Batten's voice was a harsh hiss at the back of my head. "Are you wearing a fucking gun?"

I jumped guiltily again, set my lips in a line and craned over my shoulder. "Why are you looking at my butt?"

"You'll pass it to me, nice and slow," he told me. "Then go make your condolences and go home."

I took exception to the word "home", like it was *our* place, not mine. I also took exception to relinquishing the only thing that was giving me a measure of confidence.

"No," I shushed. "I've learned my lesson. My life sucks so bad that I need to be constantly armed. That's just a fact. I'm over it. I suggest you get over it, too. My gun doesn't leave my hip."

"That's the dumbest thing I've heard you say," Batten said low. "Give me the damn thing before you shoot yourself in the ass."

"If you had allowed MJ a gun in Buffalo, she may not have been placed in such peril, may not in fact have been wounded at all," Harry spoke up. The icy shadow of his body close to mine was familiar and comforting, but as Batten stepped closer on the other side of me, I could feel the impatient huff of steamy air as Mark took a deep breath and exhaled angrily. I was a hot n' cold sandwich.

"*You* could have come to Buffalo," Batten reminded Harry. "You chose to stay in Portland. It may have helped to have you there."

Harry stiffened; Batten had finally found the thorn in his side.

"Buffalo. The Armpit of America. Too right, I could have prevented much had I been there. A pity." After a meaningful glare, he stalked away. Batten watched him go with new interest.

"I hit a nerve with Tall, Limp and Pasty?"

"Don't call him that," I floundered. "He's not tall." *And he's not always limp.*

"All right," Batten agreed, sliding his hand to my hip, taking the gun. His lake-bottom blue eyes dared me to argue as he tucked my gun somewhere behind him. "Does Lord Fancy Pants have a problem with Buffalo?"

"Specifically with Cheektowaga," I said pointedly.

Batten's voice was a low growl. "I'm fond of Cheektowaga. Had the best 20 minutes of my life there."

"20 minutes?" To avoid blushing hard, I performed a text-book emotional door slam. "More like five."

"Harsh."

"Honest." I straightened my shirt, watching Mr. Davis walking out with some relatives, leaving his wife alone, forlorn in her chair. "You'd be wise to never mention Buffalo again. Harry knows damn well that he could have sheltered us from the mindfuck in the alley. He shoulders half the blame for the shooting."

"And the other half of the blame?"

"You, jaggoff."

Batten accepted this silently, as if he agreed. "You're not to blame for any of it?"

"Not in his books."

"Why not?"

I watched as Harry noticed Mrs. Davis sitting alone, and move to fill the void. He bent slightly at the waist, made soft and comforting small talk with Mrs. Davis beside the casket, holding my leather jacket draped over one of his arm like a sommelier with wine and a napkin. She gazed up at him from her wheelchair with naked appreciation, tears glistening, one hand hovering protectively near her heart.

"Harry expects me to make bad choices," I said finally.

Batten was opening his mouth, maybe to agree, when the closed lid of the casket blew open. In a sawdust cyclone of reaching, rotted arms, metal hinges cartwheeled through the air, screws clattered into the walls, wood shattered, shards spinning. A patchwork creature wrenched up out of her satin bedding and keened, her agonized tongue lolling in the air.

Harry sidestepped across the floor in a whirl of coat, putting himself in the line of sight between the casket and the grieving mother. He was too late. Mrs. Davis had seen, in violent Technicolour, the thing that used to be Kristin with her butter-yellow funeral dress clinging wetly to putrid skin.

Mrs. Davis rocketed backward, her wheelchair hitting the wall with a thud as the crowd's screaming chorus drowned out her shocked objection. Her dead daughter threw her stitched-up chin back and wailed. Mrs. Davis' horrific shrill rose to an octave only me and dogs could hear.

Dead Kristin's head whipped around.

OK: me, dogs and ghouls.

C28

Nothing I had ever seen in textbooks or online could have prepared me for the grotesquely rotted horror of Kristin Davis' ghoul scuttling on the Berber carpet, her skinless fingers coated in the slime of rapid decay. *Too rapid*, my brain noted, just before she looked up at Harry with eyelids sewn shut and my mental processes screamed to a halt, leaving all notion of sane thought behind in its wake.

Harry stared unblinking at her lids, achieving a sphinx-like stillness. The ghoul scrambled to snatch at my jacket in Harry's arms; Harry never flinched. He relinquished to the ghoul my leather jacket, melting slightly from solid statue to liquid motion, backing away with cat-like fluidity.

I vaguely heard Chapel ordering: "Get these people out, *get the family out!*".

Dunnachie and Hood became heavily armed sheep dogs, their barking full of authority, their big arms ushering toward safety as the Big Bad Wolf keened, a ragingly terrible sound, as she stood knocked-kneed, rolling her head, tongue ululating.

Two things happened abruptly at once, then. Batten holstered his gun and took off from where he'd fallen to one knee, bolting like an Olympic sprinter for the rear exit, I hoped to get his kit. At the same time, a shoving, sobbing stampede crushed out the front doors, leaving only the group of us squaring off against the fetid monster, and Mrs. Davis mindlessly moaning in her chair, waving her pointer finger, lost without sensible words. No one had thought to wheel the grieving mother out.

Impossible. This wasn't happening. Kristin was dead, yes, but she had been embalmed and tidy, her body stitched up carefully, intact and pristine in her brand new, first time off the lot casket.

With difficulty, the ghoul forced open her sutured eyelids to reveal yawning holes full of brown-stained cotton between thick threads. She roared with frustration as the threads pulled at her flesh then ripped. She eagerly tore my jacket apart, seams flaying. Small polished gemstones thudded with my lip gloss, my pink Moleskine mini and emergency condom in a rain of personality on the carpet. A little plastic Ziploc bag with the ruined newt eye fell with a plop to the floor.

The ghoul dug frantically at the bag like a puppy at a burrow until the plastic split; she snatched up the eye, really just a stringy pinkish filament of sclera now, and, pulling out the cotton in her sockets, pressed it there into her useless, gaping hole.

Ok, not a newt eye. I had a brief image of the ghoul digging at my entrails the way she'd dug open the Ziploc, saw stars in the swirling black of my head, felt like I was pitching backward. *Nope, blacking out now would be bad.*

Mrs. Davis was chanting: "*She had Krissie's eye, she had Krissie's eye!!*" over and over in revulsion from behind her hands.

"I didn't know," I said, mostly to myself.

I drew fierce focus on the perfectly smooth oblong stone by the ghoul's foot, a red jasper, and I felt suddenly clearer. Dead Kristin was wearing patent leather flats, now dotted with gobs of meat. I dragged my gaze away from them and back to the red jasper. If only I could get to it, without getting close to it … her? I didn't know what to call her anymore. This was not Kristin Davis, and yet it was; I had no doubt that the young girl's spirit was trapped inside it.

I heard wheezing sounds coming out of my mouth, heard words forming. Incredibly, I was making sense.

"She shouldn't be rotting, why is she rotting?" No one needed to hear that now, but I couldn't make myself stop saying it. "Why is she rotting so fast?" I had a light bulb moment, a rare 100 watt one. "Exothermic reaction. Heat. Flesh magic." And then, as all the hair on my scalp pricked straight up: "Demon."

"What is that thing?" Batten demanded behind me, throwing his kit open in a clatter on the floor. Green bottles of Brut cologne and holy water jostled with silver chains that caught the overhead lights. "Marnie, what is it? A zombie?"

The ghoul withdrew its soiled fingers from the muck of her face and bayed in seeming pain. Paralyzed now, I could only stare, pulling with my lungs but getting no air. Something else was stirring, just beneath the surface of reality, an awful perfume worse than death, black magic encountering and bruising the underside of my own grey power. The ghoul felt it too, and knew its source.

Dead Kristin's head wobbled atop a ruined spine as it creaked in my direction, held upright only by infernal magic, vertebrae grinding audibly.

Batten barked, "Marnie, get out!" but Harry was already moving toward me, pointing at the front door commandingly.

"Harry, get Mrs. Davis!" I ordered. As Harry came away from her, Mrs. Davis lost it. She wailed hysterically,

"My baby. My baby! *Get away from my baby you monsters!"* reaching, grabbing Kristin's elbow.

The skin sloughed off in her hand in a long wet sheet. Mrs. Davis' gurgling scream raised my hackles. The ghoul took two more loping strides toward me and I shouted:

"...Carna come unlock the door/Remove the boundaries I implore!"

When it happened, I felt it: blinking disappearance, sudden incorporeal lift, flinging bodily through the sludge of limbo-space, appearing in a windless shock in the opposite corner. I didn't look to see how my little jump had affected anyone but the ghoul. She stopped, trained in on me again, lifted those melting lips off her teeth and snarled frustration.

Mrs. Davis teetered face-first out of her chair; Harry changed directions mid-stride. With eye-blurring speed he swooped her up and whisked her out the front door, where ambulances were starting to noisily arrive.

Dunnachie hissed, "Witch," at me, and crossed himself.

"You can roast me later, if you think that'll make your version of God happy," I said distractedly, not taking my eyes off the ghoul. Dunnachie made a strangled noise.

Hood choked on the stench as the thing wafted past him, "Tell us what you need us to do, here, Baranuik."

I'd stepped up to bat. Sometimes I'm stupid like that. One half of my brain said, *Fuck this noise*, and tried to convince me to run for it. I really wanted to listen to that part. The other half said calmly, aloud, "This is not a zombie. This is a ghoul. It doesn't want to be here any more than we want it. It is enslaved by a demon."

"So what can we do?" Hood demanded.

"No sudden movements." I jerked my head in the direction of the front door. "Nice and easy, get the fuck out of here. And tell those EMS guys to stay out. Treat it like a fire: you don't send a bunch of extra bodies rushing in."

Dunnachie was drawing down on it with a massive horse of a gun, some kind I'd never seen but definitely a force to contend with, while his mouth moved silently. I was betting he was reciting the Lord's Prayer. Fat lot of good the prayer or the gun would do him, tonight. The ghoul itself was under the direct control of a lesser demon, and she didn't want Dunnachie. The ghoul didn't notice anyone now but me. Yay me!

While Beethoven for beginners played in the next room, the young girl who would never play again gave my ruined jacket a long sniff and then writhed along the floor in my direction, her shoulders undulating slowly like a puma in a cage at the zoo, padding with otherworldly precision. So much for music soothing the savage breast. The smell she shed in her wake was a rank heavy wave; my stomach lurched as bile stung and churned high in the back of my throat.

Hold it together, Marnie, I thought as I stepped backward inch by inch, nodding. "That's right, sweetheart. This way." I kept my voice steady, pointing at Dunnachie and Hood. "Mark, clunk Curly and Larry's heads together and get them the fuck out of here, so we can deal."

Batten wrested several long, sharpened stakes out of elasticized slots in his kit.

"Mark ... are you listening? That shit isn't gonna help," I said, shedding my high heels in case I had to bolt in my stocking feet. I abruptly ran out of space again up against a corner. I didn't think another spell to lift me through limbo-space was such a brilliant idea, since I was getting angry red hives all up the inside of my arms from the not-so-white magic.

The ghoul stopped for a minute and shuddered long and hard like it was preparing to vomit. Batten was creeping up behind it, the preternatural incarnation of the Crocodile Hunter.

"Hey dicksmack," I barked. "Try listening!"

Sightless, the ghoul nonetheless stalked me as I sidled right. I tried a feint left, and it matched me easily; her muscles tensed like a cat getting ready to leap. I went for the Beretta, knowing it was pointless, wanting it anyways ... and found it missing. *Fuckanut.* I heard Chapel to my left check his clip and cock his gun.

Out of reasonable options, I bellowed: *"Harry?"*

The revenant returned too fast for human eyes to track, blowing past them in a blur of billowing coat and pale flesh. Dunnachie fired off two rounds in rapid succession, hitting Harry in the back. Flesh and cloth flew from his wound.

Harry grunted, "Father, shield her!" and cast his hand at Chapel.

Harry's coat fluttered over him like a descending murder of crows on an abandoned dirt road. Too shocked, what I cried out wasn't a word. Chapel made a short, horrified bellow of agony, doubling over. Batten shouted something I couldn't make out. The ghoul ignored it all, encroached on my personal space another stalking, creeping step.

"Restless spirit, I implore you!" I cried. "I do not have anything else for you! Harry? Harry, answer me! Mark, help him!"

The ghoul reared up, bent fingers scrabbling at the terrible stitches all around the bloat in its delicate yellowing throat. Fat goblets of bruise-blue and greenish flesh rained down from the chin as it shook her head madly, gurgling. Something that looked like bloody snot poured out of its nose. Half of its scalp slid forward, auburn hair a sticky mat.

Harry writhed, relentlessly pressing forward across the stained Berber despite an inhuman howl brewing in the back of his throat. He held up a warding hand as Batten circled with a stake. How he knew that Batten was fixed on the ghoul and not on finally staking a wounded adversary, I didn't know, but Harry rasped with full confidence, "She will turn on you. Please do be careful, lad."

Batten said, "Hope you mean the ghoul."

Hood regained the ability to speak. "Baranuik, how do we kill it?"

"Fire," I answered. "Shoot it a hundred times, or cut it in a million pieces, it will just keep coming. Only fire, or the one who raised it, can end this."

"So what do I do?" Batten snapped, knuckles white on the stakes. "Get a fuckin' flamethrower?"

I heard Harry's wry, muffled, "Shruff and cinders."

"You let me deal with it, for fuck's sake," I snapped, balling my fists. And under my breath, I called to her. "Kristin. *Krissie*."

The ghoul came around to face me again, and this time Chapel fired, from the ground, two pops that sounded fake, but which took a piece of Dead Kristin's shoulder off in a spray of bone chips. She ignored it, lifting her parched lips off pale gums and snarled at me, flashing plaque-packed metal braces. As she gnashed her teeth together, enamel snapped and she spit the bits. I slid as far as possible into the corner, pressing my back into the wall hard. Her skin had slipped off some more and now half of her face was just so much raw meat. One socket, crammed with the clear fleshy shred of a ruined eye like a pile of scrambled egg white, attempted to blink at me. The other cavity just goggled, raw and open, waiting.

"Krissie, I didn't know it was your eye, I swear," I breathed. "I don't have the other one with me." I showed the sightless creature my shaking hands. "See?" *Of course it doesn't see, stupid. Does it?* "I don't have it. Look!"

I focused hard on my palms, an idea forming. It was crazy, but even as I thought that, my fingertips spread and cupped to form a wide bowl.

Drawing down the moon was a long shot, but as my lips started to move, nascent light immediately shimmered to life between my fingertips. It grew quickly, flashing in roping lines across the skin of my palms. There, written on my flesh, was the promise of the Goddess. When I doubted, She did not, and it was time to trust Her opinion.

It got heavy all of the sudden and I nearly dropped it; the muscles in my forearms snapped to attention to hold it still in exactly the position it began, and my fingers curled into near-claws to contain the power spilling through me into the bowl of my palms.

"*By the count of one, the spell's begun,*" Last chance to opt out. If I stopped halfway through or otherwise cocked it up, I'd call the full heat of the sun, which could only end in a massive Marnie-*kafoomf*. I'd lose my eyebrows. Again.

"*By the count of two, my blessing's due/ By the count of three, suffer my need/ By the count of four, Dark Lady's lore,*" My voice thickened and I had to shove it out. "*By the count of five, the spell's alive/ By the count of six, my force be fix'd/ By the count of seven, so lightly given/ By the count of eight...*"

That's when I drew a blank. Out of the corner of my eye, I saw Harry jerk like I'd slapped him. Forgetting his promise to restrain himself, he lunged up.

"Harry, no!" I commanded, but he would not hear. He was a visual blur, a crow drawn in black finger-paint streaks, as he stole Dunnachie's baton from his utility belt, whipping it around overhead and coming at the ghoul. The ghoul reached for him. Harry swung the baton up and under her arm, flipping her around in a submissive hold that twisted her to one knee. Bullet wounds or not, with superhuman strength, the two undead creatures set against one another, straining with set grimaces. I could hear Dead Kristin's joints cracking. Harry officially crossed legal lines with a determined, fangs-out hiss, putting his preternatural weight behind his clinch. The ghoul's shoulder joint buckled outward with a wet, warning pop. I had to stop him.

The moon's gentle glow filled my hands as Hecate's power raced in to reclaim the ground She had lost to my dabbling with limbo-space. It flickered like a candle near-snuffed by a draft and I shouted: "*By the count of eight, the divine awaits/ By the count of nine, Her light be mine!*"

As the glow swelled, I rushed forward, swinging it at the ghoul's face. A taut sphere of the divine captured in a witch's blessed hands, it bubbled up against the poker-hot black sludge of the demon's handle on Dead Kristin's ghoul. One touch was enough.

The ghoul swiped at me with its free arm, hitting me just the wrong way, fist connecting with my cheekbone and pelting me over hard. With a throaty grind the ghouls' head rocked back, knocking Harry's chin and breaking the revenant's hold. Whipping to her feet,

Dead Kristin launched across her own shattered casket, pouring liquid-smooth through the air, surprisingly agile for a decomposing slab of meat. The ghoul landed like a jungle cat on all fours on the other side, limbs rebounding flexibly despite their injuries. Harry spun after her in a soaring arc of cold, savage energy. Batten tore through the space with a stake raised, and his approach was accepted by the wide-wing outstretch of the ghoul's embrace; she flung wide her arms to catch him like a child caught by a father playing toss-the-baby.

The stake sank in between her ribs and snapped in his hand but the response was lightning quick: she whipped him through the room like he was made of balled paper, then shoved past a horrified Rob Hood, flailing him aside.

Harry made a dismayed snarl and sprang back to his feet despite the bullets imbedded in his ribs, rocketing towards the ghoul. At the same time Harry's baton rose again to strike, Kristin Davis' badly spoiled cadaver fell under Harry's swoop, disappearing into a back room, clattering furniture down and shrieking as she went, leaving behind a trail of hot sick.

Harry and Chapel went after it like a shot. Dunnachie lowered his gun and looked to me for an explanation, eyebrows puckered in a twist. Hood was wiping, wiping, wiping his arm with his hand, his pasty face quickly greening to match the tone of the quivering gunk stuck to him.

"You shot him," I accused Dunnachie, who looked genuinely baffled. "You humungous asshole. You shot Harry."

Dunnachie's mouth worked impotently, then said: "I thought ..."

Batten dropped to a knee beside me. "Marnie, your stitches. Are you all right?"

I thought about it. There was putrefied ghoul sludge on my cheek and hands. It smelled like someone had dumped a rancid box of meat in an old cheese factory.

"Excuse me," I gulped, bolting. I used my elbows to bang open the bathroom doors and shove the faucets on. Running water over the jiggling feculent goo didn't cut it or remove it. I pumped soap madly from the dispenser with my bare hands; the Blue Sense flared into unexpected vivid reaction. As nausea blared in my gut, I tried to force up a psychic wall to block it, but caught the faintest whiff of a sordid mind, a trace of black magic on the soap pump. I slammed my eyelids shut and tried to block it. Images squeezed into my brain like cold fingers nonetheless—*need want hunger rage*—and I scrubbed harder between my fingers until the vision began to lift.

Carefully breathing through my mouth, I checked my hands front and back to see if they were clean. An experimental sniff told me they were definitely not. I washed them again. And again. After the fifth wash I found a paper-thin strip of overripe tissue stuck under my fingernails that wouldn't come out.

I didn't know whether to cry or barf. So I did both.

C29

"Explain to me," Batten said from the front seat of their SUV, "Why you had Davis' eyeball in a Ziploc bag in your pocket?"

"I thought it belonged to a newt." I sniffed at my fingernails. They smelled vile, so bad I couldn't believe it and had to check again.

Batten inhaled deeply through his nostrils, exhaling nice and slow. One of his hands stroked his forehead. "Tell me."

"I saw these filmy things in my jar, which should have only contained eyes of newt. I suppose the fact that I had 15 should have tipped me off, or size of them, right? But they were broken, and I didn't really inspect them. I assumed." I sighed. "And you know what they say about when you assume."

"You make an ass of u and me, and accidentally raise a ghoul at her own funeral?" Batten finished with unexpected grim humour.

Beside me, Harry reached for my hand, noticed me sniffing it, and changed his mind. His nose scrunched as he searched his pockets for his monogrammed handkerchief.

"How did Kristin Davis' eye get in your jar?" Batten asked.

"All in favor of going another round with the Demented Mailman theory?"

"Don't toy with me, MJ," he said.

I froze with alarm. Harry abruptly stopped rubbing the gunshot wounds in his back against the seat like a cat against its master's legs. He craned sideways at me ever so slightly, his neck stiffening with displeasure.

"Only Harry calls me MJ, Agent Batten," I said quickly. "You may call me Snickerdoodle."

Batten whipped around in his seat and blinked at me in disbelief.

"What? I like Snickerdoodles."

Batten repeated unhappily, "How did Kristin Davis' eyeballs get into a jar in your home?"

"Actually, I have a theory about that," I told him. He didn't seem impressed. He should have been; I so rarely have workable theories. "A ghoul isn't raised by accident, and it isn't easy. Someone was planning it, but I don't think they intended it to rise during the funeral. That part *was* accidental. I think the plan was to conjure Davis in ghoul form after the funeral, using the eyes at my house as a lure to attack us."

For a moment, I imagined the ghoul rummaging through my bedroom looking for her eye while I slept, and had to re-launch my heart by giving my chest a thump. “Unfortunately I took one of the eyes out of the jar, planning on mailing it back for a refund. I got too close to the casket with it and jump-started the spell.” And all of the sudden, the reanimation of Davis’ head in the mailbox made a whole lot more sense: I’d had a broken eye in my pocket.

“So this was witchcraft?”

“Black witchcraft. Flesh magic. The spell used was exothermic, belching out heat from an internal, infernal source, and sloughing off her skin as the heat was liberated.”

“All that bloating,” Batten agreed. “There shouldn’t have been gases like that in an embalmed body.”

I wrinkled my nose, and hugged myself. “Thank the Dark Lady it wasn’t summer or she’d be covered in flies.”

“Do we think this was Danika Sherlock?” Batten asked.

“Danika’s a fucking lunatic,” I reminded him. “Question is, would she have the mental resources to do this?”

“I am inclined to suppose this business requires the wherewithal of a far more stable mind, an organized psyche,” Harry said, almost to himself. “Ms. Sherlock’s iniquitous attack at the Ten Springs Motor Inn was possessed and near-mortal, but out of control.”

“She must have control, if she’s doing complex magic,” I said.

Harry shook his head. “Upon no account should I like to think Ms. Sherlock capable of turning out complex magic. Why, only yesterday you said the barmy fraud was not a witch at all, that she was all gall and wormwood; barking mad and due Skeffington’s gyves, granted, but not in the least keen with a bolline.”

Batten looked around as though he’d tripped through a portal into an alien land. I estimated Mark understood about 30% of what Harry said at the best of times, and this was not one of those times.

“Yes Harry,” I said wryly, “Word for word, that’s exactly what I said.”

“Was it English?” Batten asked.

Harry pursed his lips. “Do not furnish me with your cheek, young man. I’m sure you will agree, Ms. Sherlock may be red in tooth and claw but when it comes to multifarious conjurations of a malevolent manner, she is hardly worth a tinker’s cuss.”

“Thanks for clearing that up,” Batten’s shoulders shook with silent laughter. “Maybe you just don’t know what she’s capable of?”

“Oh, lad.” Harry gave a scolding cluck of his tongue. “I am a 435 yr old man. It is safe for you to suppose I have more than a basic working knowledge of both the normal and abnormal psychology of mortal *homo sapiens* and all of which they should ever be capable."

Chapel broke his silence. "Let's get back to the subject."

"Gotta sort the data," I suggested. Lost without a No. 2 and Moleskine, I used my fingers to list off facts. "Kristin was raised a ghoul, not a zombie, so we're looking at black witchcraft, not Haitian vodou."

"Explain," Batten ordered.

I complied, fishing out my Shalimar purse spray and dousing my fingertips, rubbing the dribbles directly up under my nails. Now they smelled like velvety Oriental vanilla ghoul scum. Not exactly the improvement I was hoping for.

"A zombie is raised as a servant by a bokor," I said. "A Haitian necromancer. Zombies are mindless slaves to the bokor; without direct orders they merely shamble about looking for yummy snacks."

Batten looked reluctant to even say the word out loud. "Brains."

"A popular misconception," I told him, leaning my tired head against the rear driver's side door and closing my eyes. "Any chewy bits will do: tongues, livers, gall bladders, spleens. A nice mushy heart. Zombies' jaw joints tend to give them trouble, and most of the time they lose teeth when their gums retract after death. They're slow like morbid constipation and not overly bright, but the bokor's magic combined with the byproduct of *yersinia sarcophaginae*, their active bacterial infection, gives them incredible strength. They'll rip doors off hinges, bash through ribcages, crack your skull open like a shell to get to the nibbly parts."

"The ghoul moved fast." Chapel glanced in his rear view mirror at me.

"No faster than a human. It had extraordinary strength but not supernatural speed. It just wasn't what you expected from the dead."

"It outran Harry," Chapel pointed out.

"But Harry is healing two massive bullet wounds to the back. I'd like to see *you* whip up preternatural speed while you're holding a couple of .45s in your broken ribs."

"The ghoul still seemed really fast," Chapel argued.

"Because you expected shambling zombie-speed. Any human can outrun a zombie. Just pop behind a tree or dive in a bush. Zombies are dumb as stumps. They won't think to look there unless the bokor orders it. Kids know: pulling your blankets up over your head fools some monsters. If they can't see you, they give up and stumble off down the hall to eat your parents."

Harry said, "I would not suggest that as a wise course of action in the case of a ghoul in your bedroom."

I felt suddenly ill. *A ghoul in my bedroom*. Fetching her other eyeball. All at once, I knew where Kristin Davis' remains were hurrying off to.

"Go on," Batten urged.

I gave a queasy smile and hesitated before saying: "Fact: raising ghouls and poltergeists requires goetic summoning via the lesser key of Solomon. One needs the cooperation of a lesser demon, and that means flesh magic."

"You thought the reanimation of the skull in the mailbox was also done with some form of flesh magic," Chapel said.

"Yes. The good news is, we can totally find our bad guy now. They'll either be having an abnormally-long orgasm while speaking in tongues ... or they'll be missing exactly one pound of flesh from their own body, and probably a digit. A finger or toe. That might be hard to miss, even for us."

"Poltergeists are spirits." Batten drummed his fingers on the headrest. "Like a ghost? So, what exactly is a ghoul and how is it made and ordered around? Was there someone at the funeral with a magic remote control? Did we miss the shoes sticking out from behind the curtains by the coffee urn?"

"Hilarious," I sighed, but something nagged me when he said it, and I knew I was forgetting something. Something I had seen, or heard, or felt. Harry noted my frustration through the Bond and tapped the back of my hand in question. I smiled him away and he went back to contemplating the night through the car window.

"A poltergeist is not a ghost," I said. "A ghost lingers after its body has died because it's lost. They're confused, often melancholy, but not hurtful to the living. A poltergeist on the other hand is the angry, uncooperative and incorporeal remains of a person raised very soon after death against their will by a demon. It's basically a soul that is prevented from rightfully ascending to heaven. The demon kinda plucks it out of the light, and holds it here on Earth in spirit form for a bit. Poltergeists are crankyass bitches. They were almost in perfect peace and now they're stuck here with only a demon for company. If they're kept here long enough—and that would require the goetic witch, I might add, continually feeding the demon pound after pound of her own flesh to keep the *demon* cooperative—the poltergeists gain strength and bulk, and can actually affect their environment: knock over chairs, shove people, scrawl things on your mirror in lipstick. You have to keep the demon happy to keep the poltergeist here. Once the demon flees back to its cosy nook in the third circle of hell, the poltergeist is free to go join their ancestors."

"Sounds like a lot of work," Batten said. "That's not regular witchcraft, like what you do."

"Dark Lady, no," Harry gasped from beside me, and clutched for my hand, forgetting the smell of it. "Do not for a moment think I would allow such monstrous acts from my DaySitter. I'm not happy about the space-hopping, either." He turned my arm so he could see the hives along the inside, and gave me a long penetrating look. "If she wishes to dabble in a bit of candle magic or kitchen witchery, fine. Flesh magic, or any other black magic, is absolutely forbidden. I will not have demons in my home."

Forbidden? I felt my eyebrows hit my hairline but left it alone.

"Anyways," I continued, "A ghoul like the one we just saw is a similar story to the poltergeist, except it's corporeal. It's the literal raising of the dead, but unlike a zombie who obeys a bokor's commands, a ghoul is much less controllable and reasonably sentient. Once it's set loose, it's free-thinking and reactive to its environment. It'll adhere to its original task, given by the witch through the demon, but it'll take detours if it chooses."

"Does it have to be a specific demon at work?" Batten asked.

"There are two types of demons that do this work. Judging by the appearance of the ghoul I'd say the witch used exothermic flesh magic to call a wrath demon, rather than sex magic, which is endothermic, to call a lust demon. Although," I reconsidered, "The head in the mailbox wasn't sloughing skin and rotting quickly. Of course, it was cold and possibly frozen beforehand ..."

"Sex magic?" Batten's brow almost went up in interest, but he kept it in check. *Eyebrow magic.*

"Never mind." I crossed my arms over my chest, wishing I still had my jacket. I scratched distractedly at the hives.

"If the information would help us," Chapel requested.

"You just wanna hear me talk dirty," I accused. The glance Chapel gave me in the rearview mirror was not amused. "Sex magic involves laborious rituals rarely used any more, except by horny noobs, involving a 9 foot circle and lots of nudity. The witch conjures the lesser demon with the promise of possession: he or she literally allows the demon to enter their body, after which ..." I shrugged. "Classic goetic magic has a witch and her sexual partner in the circle of power, but there's a lot of battery-powered magic in those circles now. Who has time to find a partner who'd be into orgasm under the influence of demons? Probably Craig's List doesn't have a subcategory for that."

"I would not be so sure, my darling," Harry said dryly.

Eeeeuuuuww. I pressed my back further into the seat. "People are freaks."

Batten cleared his throat. "Why a lesser demon?"

Harry and I exchanged looks in the dark safety of the back seat. I had to laugh. "Uh, because you might be able to conjure a greater demon against its wishes but it would not be controllable once it arrived. It would eat you alive. A superior demon might listen if it chose to, but would probably be pissed off at your audacity, and would eat you alive. Last but not least, a demon king wouldn't deign to hear you at all. Try all you like to conjure one, they've got better things to do than obey the call of humans."

"Agent Chapel and I lost track of the ghoul, my love. Will it return to its demon master, or should we search for it before it cuts a swath through town?" Harry asked.

"No need," I informed them. "Since the first thing it did was reclaim that eye, I'm assuming it was raised with the task to get its eyes back and destroy anything that tries to prevent it. Safe to say, it's going to get its other eye."

Batten muttered, "Where is Kristin Davis' other eye, Marnie?"

"Pretty sure I left it under my bed in a sandwich baggie," I sighed, defeated. "And I thought I told you to call me Snickerdoodle."

C30

Some nights I wish I was five again, wearing my fuzzy blue Smurfs pajamas with the loud slipper feet, curled up under my father's desk while he worked away at his poetry and chain smoked unfiltered cigarettes he bought tax-free in big bags on the First Nations reservation. A frustrated artist, starving only because he regularly forgot to eat, Dad was never the best at providing for his family. But then, he figured since my mother, Vi's only child, had no interest in feeding an immortal, that *he'd* be inheriting Harry (and Harry's considerable wealth) one day, a misconception that freed him from the burden of making more money than the bare minimum while he bided his time. After days in our family greenhouse, father focused on his true love: the written word. Driven to distraction, my father would stare at the pages in silence, at times struck mute and wordless for hours. One of his sock feet would tap the carpet earnestly. His pen would thump the legal pad while he struggled to fit the lyrical images in his head into verse that pleased his ear. Sometimes, real low, I would hear him muttering a stanza over and over, twisting it backward, or cut in two, playing with the language until it sounded fresh. Perfect.

I'd known then that if I made a peep, I'd be asked to leave, so I'd stick to eating my Cheetos (in retrospect, probably not the quietest snack to be covertly munching) and reading Garfield comics. When Garfield was particularly goofy, I'd cover my giggles by slapping both hands over my mouth. Looking back, I'm sure my father must have heard my snorted-back laughter. Maybe his child's hilarity inspired him rather than hindered. I was rarely shooed from the study the way Carrie was.

The world was all right, then. No one ever fought, not in the world when I was five. We didn't have a lot, but we had our passions. No one said a hurtful word, for words were sacred tools in my parent's house; Roget's thesaurus lived on our coffee table and we were encouraged to use the best word we could for every occasion. "Ghoul-bait" was never a winner, but it was the one I was thinking now, as Chapel eased their SUV into my driveway and headlights swept the slim figure standing on my front porch.

His too-long, white-blond hair roped down along his shoulders in odd dreadlocks as his chin hung low, and even after he must have heard tires crunch frozen gravel he did not raise his face to us. It didn't matter. I recognized the build immediately through that spooky familial bond that lets you pin-point your own kin in a crowd.

Except he wasn't in a crowd. He was standing vulnerable and alone, blanched by my Halogen porch light, in worn jeans and a tattered red and black plaid jacket that didn't look warm enough for a Rocky Mountain winter, hands shoved into his pockets, a navy blue baseball hat tucked under his arm rather than on his head where it might have held in at least some heat. An oily sort of fear slid through me. He was still skinny to the point of being scrawny, and while all Baranuiks are built light-weight, he looked underfed and unhealthy, and I thought with disappointment but not surprise: *drugs*.

I felt rather than saw Batten in the front seat putting a hand on the butt of his gun and I said, "You shoot my baby brother, Batten, and I'll feed you to my ghoul-friend in barbequed chunks."

"Brother," Chapel said questioningly. He sat up straighter but didn't take his eyes off the young man in front of the SUV's grill. "I thought you had five sisters."

"And Wesley, the unexpected gift from God," I said, hating that my voice had become snide. *Jealous, me?* "Mother's singular angel. She made me take his picture to art class once when we were studying Bernini's Apollo and Daphne. Under all that hair he's wearing, the likeness to Apollo is ... " I struggled to find an adjective that didn't make me sound like a bitch *(Nauseating? Teeth-grindingly disgusting? True, but ...)* and finally settled on: "Striking."

Harry touched my arm and opened his mouth to say something, warning swimming in his eyes. Something had raised his hackles; his eyes had that luminous, unearthly sheen to them. Then, ostensibly defeated by some emotion I was not privy to through our broken Bond, he shook his head and opened the car door.

"Harry, what is it?" I asked.

He shrugged wearily. "At least the media is not here to capture this."

We poured out of the SUV in unison, Harry mindful of the bullets still lodged in his rapidly-healing back and visibly unhappy to see our guest.

Wesley looked up, his face so pale that his freckles stood out in odd dots like they were plopped on by a drunken doll maker. His narrow waist ended in hips that hadn't grown up with him, still boxy and adolescent though he was twenty now. If you ignored the hair and clothing, everything else about him was without flaw, as though painted by a master's adoring brush strokes, from his high chiseled cheeks, across the fine narrow nose to the softly rounded chin. Bright blue Nordic sled dog eyes were framed by playfully arching blond brows and too many lashes. He would have made a beautiful girl, Dad always said;

in retrospect, not the kindest sentiment towards your only son. Probably why Wesley didn't spend a lot of time at home.

As I paced up the walkway, walking fast so I didn't have yet another flip-out in the ridiculous heels, I noticed the path and the drive had been freshly shoveled. My high heels clicked a fast rhythm as I closed the distance.

When I got close enough to my brother I felt a rare influx of power, un-requested, from behind me, from Harry. He never pushed the Blue Sense into action without my appeal, but I felt he was trying to show me something. My psychic empathy extended out to my brother and after a brief struggle trying to hone in past anyone else's jumbled, tossed-salad of feelings, I felt Wes trying to cram down tremors of apprehension and regret, uncertainty blended with a spike of pleasure and relief. Then in typical Baranuik fashion, Wes dredged up some steel.

"Christ," he exclaimed, giving me the once-over. "Where are you shopping, Hookers R' Us?"

"It's not safe out here, Wesley." I reached out to him with one gloved hand and he shrank away from me. I tottered on my heels without his support, flapped to gain balance. "What are you doing here, in Colorado, out of the blue, dressed like you just crawled out of a ditch in Utah?" *He needs money*, I suspected. He'll clean up, flirt with us all for a while, toss around his winning smiles, pour on the charm, make us laugh, make us feel good, and then mention how he's been down on his luck, and wait for a sucker to nurture him. This was Wesley's game.

I looked past him to the front door standing wide open and my eyes nearly popped out. "And how did you get in?"

"It was like that when I got here," he said, and then more defensively: "I didn't ransack the place."

The ghoul. I glanced over my shoulder, past Harry, at the Feds, hanging back, giving us space. Batten was watching us closely. Chapel was scanning the yard, his eyes everywhere. Despite an incongruous nighttime bird fight somewhere in the naked trees, the yard was deserted and windless.

I said to Wes, "How did you get here?" There was no car. I looked down at his big sloppy work boots. There was a scuff so deep it was threatening to become a hole in the left toe. "You just show up at your sister's place one night, hang around on the porch, shovel the walk, take in the scenery?"

Wes' Husky dog eyes flickered past me to the SUV and the FBI agents. His teasing smile appeared, slipped to lopsided.

"You're welcome, bitch. Next time I won't bother. You can just get your big ass stuck in the snow drift."

"*Big ass?*" I repeated, clenching both fists and stepping up in his face. Somewhere above, Ajax the debt vulture echoed my angry cry.

Behind me, Harry cleared his throat unhappily. "I see time and age has improved neither the lad's vocabulary nor gentility."

"Baranuik," Batten barked. "Continue this inside, maybe?"

Wes bit his bottom lip, turning his gaze from the Feds to consider Harry at last. I saw plain male thoughts creeping through his gaze. "Jesus, sis, exactly how many guys you fuckin' now?"

Harry's hand flew before I could react, a blur too fast to see; the jarring smack as the back of Harry's tensed hand made impact with my little brother's cheekbone snapped Wes' head to the side, but he didn't go over. He should have gone over. He didn't even stumble. Like an iron rod had been shoved up his spine, Wes took the blow, closed his eyes for a beat as though he were thinking, pondering a fitting response to the revenant. I saw Wes' tongue run under his lips along the front of his teeth, checking for blood perhaps. I wondered if the impact had broke skin inside his mouth. If so, he was lucky that's all it was. Harry must have pulled the strike or Wes would be on his ass.

My brother had always been a hothead, getting thrown out of bars when he mouthed-off to the odd bouncer who wouldn't accept his fake ID, or tussling with guys hitting on the girl he'd set his eyes on. I fully expected Wes to forget he was facing a 435 year old revenant and blow his lid, at which point Harry would have no choice but to put him on the ground.

But when Wesley's head craned slowly back to face us, there was no fight in his expression, and when he opened his eyes they had gone a disquieting ice-violet, a sickly unnatural warning.

I shouldn't have shrieked. That was a mistake, in that it brought the Feds running. I flung back in horror as Harry's hands closed in on my biceps to keep me from hitting the ground. Batten's boots beat the frozen gravel fast, but I was already struggling to surge forward again, livid now, out of Harry's cupping grasp, making fists to beat my brother's chest.

"What have you done, *what have you done!*" I bellowed.

Again, Wes took the assault, just stood there as I pummeled him, fuming. He didn't have to brace his stance or flinch from the blows. It felt like I was hitting a flat plane of bricks. Cold, immovable bricks.

Harry's hand shot up to warn Chapel and Batten off. "Go inside, agents, but be aware that the door was open when Mr. Baranuik arrived, and the ... escapee may already be within."

"You didn't! You didn't!" I shouted in my brother's face, "You couldn't! How could you? No no *NO!*" and all the while Wesley stood unblinking, unflinching as I fell apart on him. All of a sudden, I couldn't bear to look at those abnormal eyes a second longer. I twisted to flee deep into the dark of the yard, but the smell of ghoul scum on the wind made my gag reflex react, so I spun toward my porch. I couldn't go there either, to face the Feds and their inevitable questions, not now, not yet. I couldn't stay out here. I couldn't look at my brother. Lost, with nowhere to run, I pulled back into the shelter of Harry. Closing my eyes against the hot influx of shocked tears, I realized that my falling apart was not helping anyone, and quickly pulled my shit together.

I raised my voice and called: "Is the house clear?"

Batten came to the threshold. "It's pretty bad in here. Something tore through. I'll call it in ..."

"Don't," I snapped. "Please. What the hell are the cops gonna do? Put an APB out on a skinless twelve year old with no eyes?"

Wes blinked in surprise and his perfect face twisted in a grimace in horror.

I pointed into his chest hard. "Yeah, you heard me. Betcha thought you were the only one with problems. It's about to get nasty around here, a lot nastier than you can imagine. If you can handle it, then get in the fucking house. If not, then go back to ..." I waved my hands at his clothes and hair. "Whatever Rastafarian vampire lumberjack cult you must have escaped from."

Harry softly corrected, "Revenant."

"Marnie," Wes goggled at me. "What the hot, bloody fuck—"

"Fade your irises!" I shouted, jamming my finger into his immovable chest. "I won't have this conversation while you're beaming me with your freaky wilted-pansy eyes. So back down."

"I don't know how," he whispered, and licked his lips. Tiny fang tips protruded. His eyes cut to Harry, not in question but in bashful admission. Harry did not display his amusement, but I felt him shudder against me with a repressed chuckle.

"Fine, listen up: I have a lunatic psychic trying to kill me, and a ghoul trashing my life to reclaim her eyeballs. That being said, are you staying or not, Wesley?"

My baby brother went still. To my dismay, I realized it was that stillness of the undead; the dreaded cudgel of reality hammered home the undeniable truth. I also realized he hadn't had to learn this skill, it was just the result of no longer breathing, blinking, twitching, scratching, sniffing, adjusting, all those things that put human beings, *living* human beings, in constant motion.

He nodded once, seriously. "If you'll have me, sis?"

Soooooo tempting to refuse, and send him on his way North to Mom, but a colder welcome would await him there; I knew that from personal experience. Harry swept past us up the stairs, already assuming I was going to bring my brother inside. He lingered to speak low to Batten on his way into the house, their heads bent together in a rare show of consultation between the tiger and the panther. Both of them turned to look at me, and I squinted warningly at them to bugger off, while I reached out to grab hold of my brother's sleeve to drag him into the cabin.

Wes pulled back at the door. "Uh, Marnie ..."

"God, it reeks in here," I gagged, letting him go. "Are you sure the house is clear? Did Chapel just barf on my bed?"

Harry hung up his overcoat. "My love, you must to invite your brother inside." One long finger pointed meaningfully behind me at the door.

My shoulders fell. I squeezed my eyes shut. "He's not really undead," I attempted to convince everyone, including me. "He bought some funky contact lenses to freak me out. He's not a revenant. He can't be. He's not that stupid."

"I beg you would excuse me, dearheart, but perhaps you could explain why there is a debt vulture fighting with my own in the Aspen, if young Wesley is not, in fact, undead?" Harry asked me politely, cocking his head. "Do enlighten us, doctor Baranuik."

"That's low," I accused. "Appealing to my science. If I wasn't already pissed off at Wesley ..." and the ghoul's mastermind, not to mention irritated that somewhere Chapel was losing his lunch in my house, I'd have sharpened my tongue on my companion. But of course he was right; Ajax was fighting off another *debitum naturae* for territorial rights. Ajax had 400 years seniority, but both birds were immortal, so it was bound to be a long, noisy night unless they could learn to share a tree.

I craned my neck to look at Wesley standing forlornly under the porch light, his eyes still pulsing with that unsightly non-shade where barest lilac met blue-white on a paint chip. If you painted a room that colour, you'd only be able to see the purple tint if the room was nearly dark, like the tone was sitting on the fence, lacking the conviction of its colour.

"Stop beaming at me," I demanded, slamming my purse on the hat stand.

"I can't," he snarled back, throwing his baseball hat on the step. "I already told you, I don't know how!"

I considered another heartbeat before saying: "Wesley Alexander Baranuik, you are welcome in my home."

"Uh …" He reached one hand up to scratch at his scalp. "That's not my name anymore. I took his."

"Harry, I'm going to need to smoke one of your damn cigarettes in a minute." I put one gloved hand to my head and left it there, pressing on the throbbing in my frontal lobe.

"Darling, many immortals take their maker's surnames," Harry reminded. "It is fairly universal."

"My baby brother is not immortal! He's a stupid fucking moron, but he's a living breathing stupid fucking moron!"

"Denial is self-defeating, my sweet," Harry said gently, taking my elbow. "If you are ill-equipped to handle this, I could …"

"You can't, we didn't put you on the title," I surrendered. "Wesley, whatever your new name is, you can come in."

"You must invite him by his new name precisely and in its entirety," Harry said.

Somewhere inside, I heard Chapel retch again, and half-turned my head in that direction. "Can you go check on him?"

Harry nodded once. "Yes, of course, if you wish it, my Own. Do be kind to your brother." He lowered his voice, though it was sort of pointless; if Wesley was a revenant, his supernatural hearing would pick up anything the elder whispered to me. "He came to you for a reason, MJ. One can only imagine why he chose *you*, but perhaps he had legitimate grounds? You must consider the lad may yet be suffering untold distress if the transition is fresh."

"Harry, are you sure this is a smart idea?"

"Love," he admonished, "If you have so steeled your own heart as to render it unfathomable, search *my* heart for your answer."

"I would, but I'm afraid of the dark," I sighed. As Harry drifted off to check on Chapel, I folded my arms and just looked at my mother's angel: all of twenty and never to age another day, washed-out from above by the high motion-sensor porch light, and in the circle of deathly-pale light it looked as though heaven itself was pointing out the joke.

Wes shifted his weight from one scuffed boot to the other, a very human gesture of discomfort, drumming up a hopeful smile for his sister. "I'm called Wasp now. Wasp Baranuik Strickland."

After being clobbered by one surprise after another, this one broke the bank.

"Why?" I grinned openly. "Because you have all of Sting's greatest hits?"

My mother's perfect angel lost his smile. "No. Because I'm part of master Strickland's swarm now."

"*Swarm?*" I couldn't help it: the guffaw brayed out of my chest, doubled me over, and I had to grasp the door jamb so as not to trip forward off my heels. Wes was the one folding his arms now, jutting his chin up, daring me to cast aspersions against his chosen name. I felt my head shaking slowly back and forth, as if , in denying the absurdity of his name, I could render it less funny. It didn't work. I pictured my old poster of the Police in my childhood bedroom and it set me off again. I kicked off my heels and, still shaking with laughter, padded outside across the cold porch in my stocking feet. With one gloved hand, I grabbed my brother by the shirt front.

"Wasp Baranuik Strickland, you have the stupidest name in revenant history, and are welcome in my home," I said, pulling him hard into the house and slamming the door. "But that's the last fucking time I call you *that,* dickweed."

C31

A shower was required before I could do any more mind-wrangling. The smell in the house wasn't as bad as Chapel's vomiting let on; luckily, he'd made it to the bathroom before the events of the evening forced his dinner up. He looked like he was in serious pain, though he hadn't been injured. It was rather humanizing to watch calm, steady Unflappable Chapel lose his cool. I hadn't thought that was possible. After he picked himself up off my bathroom floor and disappeared (hopefully to find his toothbrush) I turned on the shower full blast and stood under it for longer than strictly necessary, letting the water pulse down on my scalp, tilting my head back so that hot water ran in rivers down my face, over my closed eyelids, down my cheekbones, drumming off the point of my chin.

When I finally stepped out, I was thankful. The ghoul might have ransacked my house and slimed a trail that even Mr. Clean wouldn't cut without a ton of elbow grease, but it wasn't still in here. Didn't know where it was, but it wasn't lurking under my bed, so that was a big bonus. My brother might look like the undead cast of Cool Runnings 3: Vikings Take Jamaica, but he wasn't *dead*-dead. Batten's endurance might be slipping but he was still vigorous enough to argue with Harry.

From the shelter of my bedroom, I could hear the two bickering, Batten's voice hard and full of distaste, Harry's playful and jousting. Ah, all my boys were home. I pulled fresh bandages taut on my belly, making sure they stuck on my shower-damp skin, then slid a pair of faded jeans on and a simple white t-shirt, forgoing the bra; the underwire push-up one I'd worn to the funeral had left dig-marks under my armpits against my ribs and I'm small enough to get away with not wearing one. Probably no one would notice but Harry, and he'd be far more distressed about the threadbare jeans.

My wet hair I toweled dry—the only good thing about Sherlock's hack-job was that I didn't have to style my hair any more. It just sorta stuck up in its own peculiar fashion. I told myself I liked it that way, that I was hip enough to warrant a haircut like this, and I almost believed it. Almost.

The din in the living room rose as I put on the only pair of gloves I still owned. I couldn't imagine what they'd chosen to fight about this time. Maybe Wes had said something to set them off. It felt later than the clock said it was. We'd had an atrocious night. Maybe I should just shut off my light and go to bed. I'd performed for them at the funeral. Not *well*, perhaps, but it was over and done with. The media had captured not only images of my underpants, but of me "working" with the FBI. I had effectively vaulted back up on the proverbial horse. I'd scared off Dead Kristin so she wasn't pillaging through Ten Springs in search of her body parts. I'd all but painted a big target on my forehead for whoever started that ghoul's spell. Hadn't I earned some peace and quiet? I whipped open my bedroom door.

"Ok, shut your pie holes or I'll put some knuckles in em!" I shouted on my way out of the bedroom. Wouldn't my father be proud? "Where's White Bob Marley?"

Harry waved vaguely toward the pantry. "I sent your brother to rest in my chambers, to lay in the woolen. He has been travelling and needs to time to adjust to his new surroundings."

Batten made an exclamation under his breath, the gist of which I got without hearing the words; I touched the hollow of my throat and realized the t-shirt I'd chosen didn't cover the marks from Harry's earlier feeding. I didn't like being made to feel like a red-cheeked teenager caught with her panties down, and hated him for it.

Harry's gaze followed my hand, his eyes heavy-lidded, his sensual contentment tinged with smugness.

"Speaking of images I'll need therapy to get out of my head ..." Batten muttered, turning his attention back to the revenant lounging by the fire, who was shirtless now in his grey flannel pants, waiting for me to pry two .45 caliber bullets out of his back. There was a pair of needle-nose pliers on the coffee table, not too far from a glistening patch of slime. That's my life: non-stop glamour and ghoul scum.

Batten was asking Harry: "I thought you said something about self-restraint?"

"And I thought you knew how things worked in this house," Harry volleyed back, laying a large trade paper book to rest in his lap. He seemed to be thoroughly enjoying his position.

"You have no shame, do you?" Batten accused.

One of Harry's fingers went up to smooth his eyebrow until he got to the three small platinum loop piercings. His dark-lit gaze was so intense, so deceptively alive, and the flush of his feeding still coloured his cheeks.

"I've yet to do anything about which I should feel shame. But I assure you," His eyes gleamed meaningfully. "I am thinking about it."

Batten tossed his nylon jacket on the back of the couch. "If that's a threat, bloodsucker, bring it on. I'm not the least bit afraid of you."

Harry chuckled. "Then my DaySitter was right: you *are* as stupid as you look."

"I didn't say that!" I chirped, hands flying up like I was caught in the floodlights during a prison break. "Not recently, or in those exact words. At least, not behind your back."

"Any time you're ready," Batten invited flatly, motioning at Harry with one hand.

I rolled my eyes and picked up the pliers. "Harry, it's not polite to play with your food."

"But doll face," Harry's was the delighted smile of the birthday boy surveying his pile of presents. "He started it."

"This is how much you've matured in 400 plus years? "*He started it*"?"

"Be a shame not to see it through." Harry abruptly swung his leg down from the arm of the chair and Batten flinched; Harry's smile grew tenfold as he swept a pack of menthols from the coffee table, and showed it to Batten as if to say*: See? Just grabbing this. No need to panic.*

"Hold still," I ground out of clenched teeth as I surveyed Harry's back. The edges of his wounds were already softening, progressing towards healing. I'm no expert in ballistic trauma, or the dynamics of bullets, but I knew enough to prod my companion's shoulder with my fingers to check for shrapnel or shattered bone; I could feel nothing but the hard nub under his flesh. It should have been the most disgusting thing I'd encountered all night, but it didn't come close. Compared to Dead Kristin, the gaping blue-tinged gunshot wounds were tidy.

"Look at the poor thing, so eager for confrontation: fists clenched, jaw tight, heart pounding. He really wants a piece of me, and he thinks he has a fair shot." Harry's unearthly platinum eyes pleaded with me. "Oh, do let me school the boy."

"We might need Agent Batten's brains fully intact for a while longer," I lectured. I made an exploratory poke at the first bullet wound with the pliers; Harry didn't even flinch as he lit his cig and snapped his lighter closed. "If you're a good boy, you can eat him later."

"You promised that before but it was all a big tease." Harry looked Batten up and down hungrily, his etiquette having flown the coop. "What do you say, Agent Batten? Shall we go outside and see about putting you in your place? You sorely need it."

Chapel finally spoke up. "I don't think that's going to happen tonight."

"Yeah, pull it together," I agreed. "You're acting like a couple of low-swinging dicks and we've got serious business on deck."

Harry blew a perfect smoke ring and watched it. "When he comes in snorting like a speared bull, any man in my position would be prone to grabbing the nearest red sheet."

"You're not a man," Batten snarled.

"Ah, you are correct, lad! A man cannot smell the abscissin that triggers the fall of leaves in autumn, but I can. I can taste the mulberries the *Bombyx mori* silk moths devoured before they were steamed to death for the silk threads of my seven-fold tie. I can feel the ache of my DaySitter's ingrown toenail. If I touch her arm, I can discern exactly where she longs to be touched next. Can you?"

Batten's jaw did his clenchy thing. Harry tapped ash into an empty mug.

"I feel her, Agent Batten, and I feel you, too: every flicker of doubt, every lurid desire, every hurried thud of your reckless heart. You cling to the belief that I am not a man." Harry dropped his voice to a conspiratorial murmur. "And I do understand why you need to convince yourself of that, boy. Truly I do." The smile reappeared, bursting through like bright white sunshine on a field of snow. It was followed by a hearty laugh. Batten turned angry cartoon bull-red.

"Can the innuendo, fool," I reprimanded, swatting at Harry's pale bare shoulder. "And hold on, this might hurt."

"Do try not to be melodramatic, ducky," Harry admonished, and lengthened his neck, tipping his head forward so as not to cast my work in shadow. He opened his book again and brushed the page with a free finger.

I took a deep breath and eyeballed Chapel out of the corner of my eye. "If your stomach is still bugging you, you might wanna go elsewhere for this."

When neither Fed made a move to leave, I rolled my fingertips around along the sides of the wound until I could feel where the hard nub of bullet was. "It didn't go in very far," I commented. "Are you the man of steel?"

"Superman is bulletproof," Batten said flatly.

"No," I argued. "He's faster than a speeding bullet. Harry would be too, if he'd thought for a second Dunnachie would shoot him in the back."

"No," Batten argued back, "Bullets bounce off Superman, like they did in Superman Returns."

The pliers closed in on the first bullet and when I pulled it out, Harry hissed into his chest. He said, "I had no idea you were a nerd, Agent Batten."

"Harry," I sighed. "We don't have time for pissing contests."

"Revenants do not urinate," Harry waved away with his smoking hand, then motioned to his second wound as I put the first bullet on the coffee table. Harry's pale blue blood bubbled against the mushroomed slug in a slippery mound.

Batten inched forward to look, hands-off, at the bullet. "Jacketed hollow point, but that's not copper or steel. Looks like silver."

"Naturally, it would be," Harry confirmed softly. "Do you like riddles, Agent Batten?"

I exhaled hard. Clenching my teeth, I ground out: *"Lord Dreppenstedt."*

Batten supplied easily enough, "No."

"Evidently, you do," Harry corrected. "That's why you seek out mysteries to solve. When hunting innocent immortals with jolly old Jack Batten got boring, you joined the force. When police work wasn't challenging enough, you joined the FBI. When that failed to blow your skirt up, you joined Agent Chapel's PCU. And now there's the riddle of my pet: will she or won't she, before you get her killed?"

"Bit off-side, don't you think?" Batten charged.

"If you get her into danger, she needs you, but blames you. If you get her out of danger, she no longer needs you. If you work with her, you cannot have her. If you do not work with her, you cannot see her. Therein lies the rub."

"Harry, stop," I said flatly, digging for the second bullet a little less carefully than the first. Foam rose from the wound as the silver in the slug reacted with Harry's pale blue blood. Chapel was pretending to ignore us again, but his shoulders bunched and he looked uncomfortable.

"I'd never do anything to put her at risk," Batten said angrily. "And the fact that she needs you is the only reason you're not a pile of ash."

Harry considered for a moment, then nodded slowly in acquiescence. The second bullet hit the coffee table with a metallic clunk, and Harry folded out of his chair like nothing had happened. He stubbed out his cigarette butt.

"I will give you this, Agent Batten: You endure torment with a brand of patience I have only ever seen in my own kind. You've got bottle, sir." He rose nimbly and Batten jerked again. After a wide, cocky smile, Harry padded barefoot from the room in a very human strut, not bothering to pull out the dizzying slip-glide of the old ones. Guess he figured he'd riled the Fed enough.

"Is bottle a compliment?" Batten asked me, settling onto the couch.

I shrugged. "Hell if I know. That's a new one on me." I glanced at Harry's book: Bed and Breakfast Ownership. *Talk about your bad ideas.* I tossed it into the woodstove and watched it catch.

"I could take him."

It was one of the more childish things I'd ever heard come out of Batten mouth, so ridiculous and so unlike him that it hurt my brain. I felt my eyebrows pucker.

"Sure. And Agent Chapel here could last three rounds of Ultimate Fighting in the octagon with Chuck "the Iceman" Liddell." I rolled my eyes grandly. "Wait, lemme call my bookie and put some money on it."

"Don't think that's a fair comparison," Batten said.

"You're right. Because Chuck Liddell can't gnaw open people's chest cavities to eat their hearts, last I checked. I mean, get real, Batten. Harry's been amassing preternatural clout for four centuries, and you're only human. If he wanted you dead, you'd last one eighth of a second."

"You see him kill someone before?"

I had, but there was no way I trusted Batten enough to share. I blocked the memory completely so the answer wouldn't show on my face and said, "Don't be an ass-hat."

Unhappily, I perched on the chair that Harry had vacated, scooting it a bit further back from the woodstove so I wouldn't get quite the same blasting of heat. Quiet layered disquiet until it was a veritable discomfort lasagna without the yummy ricotta. It was late and I was hungry. I had the lens of the murdered girl's sunglasses (or the murderer's, maybe) in my bedside table drawer, hiding under an old issue of Cosmo that I kept for the *50 new ways to blow your lover's mind!* article. I hadn't completely given up hope that someday I might have a lover whose mind needed to be blown.

Batten's eyes were veiled again, his cop face, and he avoided looking at me. I wondered what he was thinking as he stared gloomily at the small square window of the woodstove, flames licking sooty glass. There was a long silence filled only with Chapel's fingers tapping on his keyboard. No one had made a move to clean up the ghoul's rampage, and I sure as hell didn't want to do it. I hadn't asked for any of this. I wondered if I could get Harry to hire a cleaning service tomorrow. Did Molly Maid know how to get ghoul-stink out of carpets? Could I live with goo overnight, or should I get a pail and soap?

I curled up in Harry's oxblood Cetus leather wingback chair and laid my head in the crook of my arm, curling my gloved hands into loose fists. Harry came back fully dressed, in his fine grey flannel trousers and a proper white dress shirt, rolled up to the elbows to expose my name tattooed on his wrist.

"I trust you gentlemen are staying the night."

I moaned into the crook of my elbow: "They're not staying."

"Thank you," Batten confirmed, to the revenant not me.

"Why do you need to be here? I'm home. I don't need you to watch Harry." And I sure didn't want Kill-Notch Batten around my baby brother right now.

"Someone's trying to kill you, a ghoul has been through here looking for her other eye, and we don't know whether both will come back," he said flatly.

"She didn't get the eye. She'll come back. Fat lot of good you'll be when she does," I said under my breath, punctuated by Harry's disapproving teeth-suck.

Chapel said from behind his keyboard. "Mark and I accepted Harry's earlier invitation. We'll be here until this business is sorted." There was steel in his voice, like he was telling me, not asking me. For once, Chapel did not sound polite. I didn't particularly like it, but I respected it.

Batten cut his deep blue eyes to me with a look that shot hot flutters into my belly: *he has intentions.* I didn't know what intentions (*to talk? to argue? to fuck me senseless?)* but it came across clearly that he was planning something.

"Well now, since we have guests, I should get busy in the kitchen," Harry suggested.

"Don't go to any trouble, Lord Dreppenstedt."

Harry held up a hand. "Don't be ridiculous, Agent Chapel, it's no trouble at all. I've already defrosted my loin for you."

My head came up to witness Chapel's blush. He touched his throat for reassurance but the necktie was missing.

"Pork loin," I amended. "Harry, don't tease."

"*Moi*? Tease? I never tease." Harry frowned as though he couldn't comprehend what I was saying. He smiled pleasantly as he watched Chapel leave the room. "I am afraid I do not have any beer left, Agent Batten, but if you're off-duty could I offer you some spirits?"

"Gin, if you have it." Batten was still drilling me with his gaze like he was trying to send me telepathic signals or something; it was starting to rub against the grain.

"Ah," Harry recalled wistfully. "I remember three pennies for a glass of gin in East end of London back when Saucy Jack was gutting prossies in Whitechapel. Now killers take the heads of little girls clean off and gin's five whole dollars a bottle. What is the world coming to?"

"Harry, what the hell are you doing?" I asked.

"Being a good host, ducky. You should perhaps try it sometime. So, Agent Batten, how do you keep life interesting while you are on the job? I mean, other than incessantly trying to plant yourself between my DaySitter's lovely thighs."

"Harry!" I wadded up a napkin and fired it at his head. It bounced off ineffectually; Harry ignored it.

Batten parried: "The job's interesting enough."

"Oh yes," Harry said. "Ghouls, goblins and goetic magic. I am curious: when first you came to Denver, what exactly were your expectations?"

My stomach did a sick flip-flop. I wished I had gone to bed early. I wished Harry had lost his tongue months ago in a tragic bloodsucking accident. I wished Kristin Davis' ghoul would crash through the kitchen window this instant and give us all a gooey, snarly reason to drop it.

Batten's face was unreadable as he pressed his broad back into the couch, staring at the coffee table as though the right answer was written on the bullets in Harry's blue blood. Finally, he looked up at the revenant and said, "There's no such thing as goblins."

"I believe it is time for you to face an unpleasant truth, Agent Batten: in the empire of her heart the rest of you, you mere mortals, are but court jesters for her temporary amusement. There can be only one king, and I am he." His eyes gleamed, luminous, as he summoned his unearthliness to underline his point. "Ask her. She will say as much, I promise you."

Batten put his elbow on the back of the couch, a seemingly casual gesture. "You seem pretty sure of yourself, bloodsucker."

"Play with her if you must. Pleasure her to your heart's content, and to hers. You have my permission."

"Oh?" Batten's smile was fleeting, tinged with incredulity. "Do I? How generous."

"Uh, pardon me while I put these bullets back in," I said, grabbing the pliers and waving them in Harry's direction.

Harry ignored me. "It worries me not, Agent Batten, for you are inconsequential, and her interest in you is transitory. I am forever."

Would he feel this strongly about every man, or did Batten make him bluff and bluster this way? I looked at Harry and knew then that he had put his foot down in a most final way. I would never be married. I would never have children. Vi had been allowed these things, but something had changed in Harry since then. Maybe he saw mistakes in hindsight. This time, his DaySitter would be his alone. There would be no room for any other man, not seriously, not permanently. I had given my only oath, my only vows, my last commitment.

Batten must have seen something in my face. “Marnie?”

I was utterly seized by Harry’s eyes; they were very human grey now, like lead shavings on cashmere, soft and pliable, but beneath that was a solid, immovable thing—a *thing,* not a person, I knew—the limits of its power unknowable. It was the first time I’d ever caught myself thinking of my Cold Company as a monster, more than a man and not at all human. I felt myself nodding.

“Harry knows he’s my number one. I’m not going anywhere,” I said in a daze. It sounded like conviction but felt like defeat.

“Why don’t you just put her in shackles and a chastity belt,” Batten said grimly.

“She chose to spend time with you, however briefly,” Harry reminded him. “She chooses to stay with me.”

“So this territorial pissing is for my benefit? Because it feels like you’re telling her, not me.”

“Revenants don’t urinate,” Harry said for the second time tonight, and brought his gaze back to me. He smiled benevolently.

I did my best to muster up a smile for him in return.

C32

Changing a subject usually requires a clever segue, or at least some understated wordplay. I had neither. Chapel would have been a help, but he had disappeared upstairs without saying good night following Harry's defrosted loins comment. Maybe his nausea had come back. Mine sure had.

Facing off across the coffee table, Harry on his home turf and Batten the invading force, they looked like a biology grad's interpretation of male-male competition for a thesis paper on Cro-Magnon sexual rivalry; neither moved, but both measured, calculated, estimated, subtly without words now, both of them sure they were the superior choice. Since neither of them was an ideal "mate" by any stretch of the imagination, I wasn't sure what the hell we three were doing. Whatever it was, it was damn uncomfortable, and my cleavage was starting to sweat against my t-shirt.

"*Sooooo*, my brother's undead," I said.

Neither blinked, but I thought Batten's face shaded with a measure of amusement.

"I don't know how he's gonna eat. I mean I can't feed him, that's like incest, it's disgusting, it's revolting, I won't even consider it, I can't even—*won't try to*—imagine, it's a big fat no, ugh, yuck." I heard myself babbling but couldn't stop. "So how about Dunnachie shooting you, hunh Harry? Bet you didn't see that coming. I didn't. For a cop, he's either got really bad nerves, a happy trigger finger, or a hefty dislike of revenants. Probably the last. Man, that's one cop who will never set foot in this house again. First the revenant, then zombie beetles biting him, then the ghoul …not to mention he saw the giant pentagram painted on the floor of my office."

Batten blinked first, and the knot in my gut uncoiled a bit. "Dunnachie said he'd stepped into the devil's whorehouse, here." He held up his hands in case he'd offended me. "His words, not mine."

I laughed tiredly, relieved. "He actually said "devil's whorehouse"?"

Harry said tightly, "Satan does not run a bordello. A gambling house in the Court of Hell, yes, but no bordello."

"You'd know," Batten said.

Chapel came downstairs, checking his Windsor knot with one hand; the tie had made a reappearance. So had the laptop. "We may be wrong about tying Danika Sherlock to the murder of Kristin Davis."

"Right, what do I know? I'm not psychic," I sighed. "I'm fake like Sherlock's tits."

Chapel put his hand flat on the table. "What we need is proof."

"Want me to prove I'm psychic?" I made a quick grab for Gary's forearm with my bare hand open wide. He lurched away from me so hard I thought he was going to rocket out of his chair. His tie flew over his shoulder. "No? You don't want me to Grope and tell you what I see, Agent Chapel?"

"I didn't mean proof of your Talent, Marnie," he said reassuringly. His voice was ever steady but some of the self-assurance had fled his eyes. He smoothed his tie. "Gold-Drake & Cross tests you every year."

Not anymore, they don't. "I don't read what people are trying to put out there," I reminded. "I read what they're *not* trying to put out there. Feelings, emotions, desires. What they're driven to. There's no hiding the impulses of the old brain. There's no subtlety there; it wants what it wants, and it fears what it fears, and I Grope it all."

"And what does Danika Sherlock want?"

I went momentarily silent. "Harry."

"Then why kill us all with a ghoul?"

"Because she can't have Harry."

Harry lectured, "It's a hateful act, the mystic's equivalent of shooting a cop with his own gun."

I swear the revenant's grey eyes brightened at the thought only for the space of a heartbeat, as his gaze dropped slightly below Mark's arm to where he had hung his holster on the corner of the couch.

Harry went silently into the kitchen and returned with espresso. He knew the way Gary liked it, which needled me. Then he brought mine, topped with a dash of cinnamon and a drip of Tahitian vanilla.

Ok, I'm still spoiled rotten.

"Kristin Davis' blindness is important. But I don't know why."

"Blind eyes," Harry mused, "*Les yeux de non vue.*"

Usually when Harry slipped into French, I didn't tune in to the words so much as enjoyed the cadence of his voice. This time my skin prickled, but my brain skipped three or four steps ahead. "There aren't a lot of French witches, and a spell in French is rare. Very rare. But that phrase …I just don't know. Dammit, I used to know how to find the answers. I used to be something."

"Still are," Batten told me. I cut my eyes to him, to see if he was joking. He wasn't.

"It would take us a long time to solve this without you, Marnie," Chapel said, "So if you know anything you're holding back ..."

"I don't know shit," I sighed. "And if you're counting on my help, we're all screwed."

"I don't know, you pulled a pretty impressive rabbit out of your hat back there at the funeral home," Batten said.

"Oh, come on. I chased it away," I rolled my eyes. "How many times can I do that? How many times can I run and hide? I'm so tired."

"Well, I hate to break it to you but you're on deck, like it or not," Batten said, his eyes boring into mine. "So batten down the hatches, Snickerdoodle."

I knew damn well the best way to find Danika was to return to room 4 of the Ten Springs Motor Inn and Grope my way around. It was probably a really bad idea, one I didn't offer out loud; they'd hate the idea and prevent me from going, or love the idea and force me to go. Either way, I wasn't sure I could handle being in that room again, so I held my tongue.

"I almost wish the ghoul would hurry up and get here," I said. "I can't bear the idea of it lingering over me when I sleep. Oh crap," I ran a gloved hand over my face tiredly. "I think I just scared myself."

Batten's lips twitched into an almost-smile in my direction. "So how did the head in the mailbox get reanimated?"

I had her punctured eye crammed in my front pocket. I shrugged, keeping it to myself.

"Were they two separate spells?" Batten probed.

I said, "You guys saw Davis' body the day before at the morgue, right? The head had stopped moving? The body wasn't moving by itself?"

"No, it wasn't," Chapel's fingers deftly found the keys, paused while he thought, then typed some more. "It was like a dead body should be ... quiet, and pale, and soft."

Harry paused in his sipping, the goblet completely still in mid-air. "I say, what an awfully strange sentiment, Agent Chapel."

I had to agree, though if Harry hadn't mentioned it, I probably would have let the comment go unnoticed.

"I didn't mean anything by it," Chapel said, blinking rapidly. "I wasn't trying to offend, Lord Dreppenstedt."

"Not at all," Harry said lightly. "Most people wouldn't describe a dead body with such sympathy and sensitivity."

"What you need is a better source," Batten said without hiding his discomfort, effectively bringing the subject back in line. "Marnie," he summoned, and I realized my eyes were drifting closed.

"Hunh? Oh, yes. A source of info. Books on flesh magic are going to be real hard to come by," I said. I finished my espresso and Harry whisked the empty cup out of my hands for a refill before I had it two inches from my mouth.

Chapel tracked Harry's movement; the immortal gave the barest look in return, but in that glance something deeper than polite acknowledgement passed between them.

Chapel, that dirty little nerd, I cursed inwardly. Could it really be true? He'd be the last person I'd have thought would be curious about Harry and the intimate nature of a feeding, but ever since I'd guessed at the possible relationship, I couldn't see past it. It was in their faces, a budding kind of rapport far different than that of two coworkers or casual acquaintances. I realized I was staring suspiciously at the side of Gary's face, and that he was noticing me stare with rising unease. I studied the frogs on my gloves instead. I had to be wrong. I was definitely paranoid. Wasn't I? I wondered where the fang marks were. They weren't on his carotid. That was even more disturbing.

When I looked up, Batten was staring at me trying not to stare at Chapel. I covered a yawn with my gloved hand.

"What was I saying? Yes, I have a few ideas where to start looking for books," I promised him. "Tomorrow. First thing."

I didn't hear Harry cross the room but there he was, touching my hair softly. "Oh, dear, someone is *très fatigué*."

"Exhausted," I agreed, relieved that while I seemed to no longer be able to feel him, there was nothing wrong with Harry's side of our Bond. "It's been an incredibly shitty day but I couldn't possibly sleep now." I'd gone beyond tired into that jittery, dry-eyed, up all night phase. "I've got to take care of Rasta-Thor downstairs and clean up this ghoul sludge and find that other eyeball. Where did I put it? And I should make a list of all the places I need to call tomorrow to find research materials ..."

"Piffle." Harry started shaking his head. "Come along, say goodnight to the nice policemen."

"But the case ..."

"Aren't you considerate to be concerned about the agents' business," Harry expressed, taking my elbow. "Surely, they appreciate that."

"Harry, I'm needed."

"Quite right, your input is of paramount importance," he soothed. "However, I trust the agents will excuse their gravely injured and addled colleague for a brief rest. After all, a dull axe shall chop no wood."

I knew a certain smarmy, condescending revenant who was gonna get a mouth full of fist in a second. He was starting to make me irritable. Again. The fact that he was pulling at my elbow made things worse.

"Come. You tuck in nice and comfy, and I'll be there in a trice after I've made this place fine as five pence."

"You're going to clean up?" I was almost tired enough not to be suspicious. Almost. I studied him sideways. "What's it going to cost me?"

"As I said, five pence." His smooth, pleasant face revealed nothing. "Oh and darling? Do set the nice little girl's eyeball on the back porch before you turn in?" he suggested.

I gave him a withering look and plodded to my room.

C33

My bed smelled like the jealous undead.

Either Harry had spritzed my pillow cases with his 4711 cologne or he'd rolled bodily in my bed like a cat marking its favorite sleeping place; it amused me to think it was the latter. As I changed into heavy pajamas, I pictured him wriggling in the sheets until it struck me as impossibly ridiculous. Almost as ridiculous as the mental picture of him tiptoeing into my room and adding his fragrance to my pillows in ninja stealth-mode. It was nice to be wanted, but what next? Would I catch the revenant scent-marking in all four corners of my room? I laughed alone in my room as I stripped off my gloves then rummaged in Carrie's old hand-me-down dresser for warmer socks.

"Few women can pull off grandfatherly plaid with your inimitable grace."

I jerked; my laugh ended in an unladylike snort. I hadn't heard Harry come in, or felt him get close. Now that my half of our Bond was hinky, I got a taste of how the revenant's sudden soundless appearance affected normal, mundane humans. Would Wesley be able to creep up on me like that? The thought struck me as unfair.

He continued wryly in his crisp London accent, "Well, perhaps "grace" isn't quite the word for it."

"Honestly, it's side-splitting entertainment when you sidle up on other people, but it messes me up when you do it to me. Maybe you could knock it off until the Bond heals."

"Whilst I did not do it on purpose, I do apologize." He cocked his head, taking the fabric of the pajamas between his fingertips for a rub. "Soft."

In his murmur, there was a mix of appreciation and disapproval, like he was willing to live with my choices but had to voice his opinion. I waited for it, tensing; he undoubtedly felt my unease, but he said it anyway.

"Comfort over fashion," he noted blandly. "Evidently, you are too weary to seduce your mortal stud muffin, and I suppose you've no one else to impress this evening."

I exhaled hard. "I get enough criticism from them, Harry. I don't need it from you."

He looked genuinely confused. "If I don't criticize, how will you improve yourself?"

"Maybe I don't need improvement." I turned my back on him to trade my black silk socks for fluffy pink ones.

"That is akin to giving up." He grimaced like I'd just suggested we spend the evening impaling stray cats for fun.

"Back off, could you? For tonight, for right this second, I'm fine the way I am."

His eyes widened; he watched me as though I were dangerously insane. "Whatever has come over you, my fluttering cabbage moth?"

"Did it ever once occur to you in a whole decade of living side by side that you could accept my faults the way I accept yours?"

I expected him to argue that he didn't have any faults, and I was ready with a full mental list of them, from A for arrogance to Z for ... okay, I didn't have a Z one, but I had plenty in between.

Instead he said: "I shan't put you on a pedestal. You are not perfect, and I cannot in good conscience do you the grave disservice of pretending that you are."

"I get it, Harry. Between the dreadful hair and the sloppy wardrobe, and the stupid things I do, and the horrible things I say, and my dysfunctional family and my appalling work, I'm just about as useful to you as a tit on a rooster." *And there's the real reason you won't sleep with me,* I thought, then swallowed it deep into my gut where it settled in a cold, vicious lump.

Harry's mouth worked at making sound, but his head shook like the words he was trying to get out no longer made sense.

"You must either be tired beyond the capacity for reason, or more upset about your brother's turning than I had surmised, for I said nothing of the kind."

"You said it all and more, with act, deed and body language."

His eyes darted up and to the left. "Undoubtedly, my body has been misinterpreted."

My answer was a simmering glare. He didn't move a muscle, but something in him retreated a full measure until there was a palpable distance between us. I wished all at once that I could still sense what he was feeling, even if it was disappointment, or anger, or misery; where our Bond once linked us, there was a fresh psychic gorge, a crumbling trench void of warmth and consuming itself at the edges. I shuddered and hugged myself.

"Whatever part of my body indicated such contemptible things to you," he said, "Consider it duly reprimanded." He forced himself forward toward me as though the air had become thick enough to wade through. "The stars must be in some funny alignment. We so rarely argue."

My chin quivered and I bit my bottom lip to stop it. Harry demanded perfection from himself and others, and I didn't want him to change; at the same time, the high expectations every hour of every day wore on me like a constant grinding, something out of sync winding against a gear, especially since I was clearly incapable of living up to his impossible standards.

I thought to explain it to him, then chewed it back; why should I have to tell him, when he knew it as plainly as he knew his own heart?

He gave me an opening. "What do you need from me, my only love? You have only to ask and it shall be done."

"I need some uncritical affection," I told him. "If you can't manage that, I'll have to seek it elsewhere."

There. It was an ultimatum of sorts, but I trusted him not to back down; if I knew one thing about him, it was that Harry and Devotion were one and the same. My companion was the embodiment of virtues rarely found since the extinction of knightly ways. Having made some internal decision, Harry rose to the occasion like I knew he would, sweeping a bow at me as an excuse to catch my hand in his. He rubbed it with his thumb, his eyes tightly closed, and I watched as his eyes moved under those fair translucent lids, back and forth like they were searching, scanning, reading the lines of an invisible transcript.

"Oh, ducky," he sighed, placing his cool lips to the back of my hand, his eyes tightly closed.

My shoulders fell. He looked sad and unexpectedly every year of his age. My nurturing urge kicked in and I touched his hair as he straightened. His ancient eyes searched mine with four centuries of experience, pegging the expression on my face with expert precision.

"It occurs to me that I may not be entirely pleasant to live with," he said. "Is this true?"

"Wow. You thought you were *entirely* pleasant to live with, Harry?" I smirked at him. "Seriously?"

"Don't joke. You feel ..." He blinked at me in wonder as something occurred to him. "Flames and ether, I have made a beautiful woman feel ugly."

"Let's drop it. I'm sure that Wesley needs us. Maybe I'll go see if I can bribe Chapel and Batten to stay at a hotel."

"I'll thank you to stop that." Harry refused to let go of my hand. Since his immortal grip had the strength to pull the roof off the Buick, I gave up. "I understand when you ward yourself from *them*, but I must insist you stop your cynical wall-building against me."

I avoided his gaze, blinking rapidly to keep my eyes clear of the threatening tears. When he didn't stop staring at me expectantly, I exploded, "What do you wanna hear?"

"A man could get his heart clobbered by you, Marnie Baranuik, if he were so imprudent as to allow himself to be blinded by your looks. If you have no idea how lovely you are, that is all on me. I should be a clear mirror for you, and in that I have failed. " It sounded like a compliment, a rare occurrence indeed, but with calculating aloofness he continued, "But inside, there is nothing in you that is not hard or fortified. The guardian of your heart is a veritable meat grinder. Cerberus would not do a better job of tearing apart intruders."

"You're calling me cold?" I demanded. "*Me?* That's *rich!*"

"I share everything I am with you!" Harry suddenly towered over me in the room, his eyes backlit with rage. "Every morsel of wisdom I've gained, every dollar I've earned, every moment of my night and into every day, no matter how drained I become. I share every ounce of immortality I can possibly spare you. Everything."

"Everything but your--" I clipped off the word *dick,* my breath streaming ardently from my nose, and finished: "Everything but intimacy."

He didn't miss a beat, as though he'd been expecting the issue to crop up. He pounced, pointing hard to the sky, eyes brightening past silver as his pupils expanded to eat the colour up. "If I were to cross that line with you, you know the consequences of that act, regardless of how pleasurable--"

"No I don't!" The tears wouldn't stop now, blurring my vision. "What would the consequences be? Spell it out for me, Harry, because I think you're full of shit, frankly. All this crap about possessiveness and jealousy, it's nonsense."

"And you know everything, is that it?"

"You're hiding something from me."

His accent thickened and his fine English accent became crisp and cutting. "Do take that tone out of your voice and remember to whom you are speaking, DaySitter." His back straightened and his mouth settled into a grim line. "You ask me for uncritical affection and when I get close, you poison me with your accusations like a black widow spider."

"Don't insult me with lies when every other word out of your mouth points to the truth."

"Why then, all of the sudden, do you suggest that I am a fabricator?" The clear bright rage in his eyes dared me to confront the issue. "Out with it. Let's have it!"

When I backed down, he slammed a hand down on the nightstand; the lamp jittered as though startled off its base, toppling to the floor in a tinkle of shattered glass. Lights out. Moonlight poured through Kenmare Irish lace curtains, imprinting the side of the revenant's pale face with an intricate cut work pattern. The new quiet signaled the birth of a dark silence so windless and arctic that I couldn't imagine an end to it.

I stood there frozen in our emotional polar winter, wrestling with the need to scream it, to grab him by the shirt front and shake him silly, unable to get past my fear of the truth. There was another in his life. There was no doubt in my mind. No one was celibate for a decade, certainly no revenant, and the unadulterated truth was there in his eyes, with neither guilt nor shame, instead putting the blame firmly on me. Another eager, willing body stood there lost in the great black void of his pupils, proudly, wantonly, something worse than a mistress. Maybe it was Gary Chapel, or maybe Gary was just one of dozens, men and women, who supplied the revenant with what he truly needed. I squeezed my hands into fists tighter until my fingernails were raking into the flesh of my palms. I had to know for sure. I had to hear him say it. But if it was said aloud ...what if it ruined everything? What if the act of saying it was the last nail in the coffin? The true and final end of our Bond.

"You broke my lamp," I said quietly.

His eyes flicked down to the shards. "It was a tacky little thing."

"I liked it."

His jaw set. "Then I shall scour the world for its duplicate."

"Try reallyuglylamps.com." I needed to swallow but my tongue was thick and hot. Something dry clicked in the back of my throat. "And technically, it's not tacky. It's shabby chic. It matches your snooty hundred year old lace curtains."

Harry's eyes blazed anew with the need to correct me, but he held his comment back behind the wall of his teeth.

So that was it. I wasn't ever going to ask about his indiscretions, or his refusal to have sex with me. If there was a time to do it, it was now, but when the right words poured out of my brain and into my mouth, my heart leapt with terror and I couldn't make my jaw unclench. He was waiting, calmer now, his intensity fading from the room, and he no longer seemed the four hundred year old monster with centuries of manipulation techniques in his arsenal; he was just Harry, covered in lacework shadows, the guy who was handing me a Kleenex.

I took it. I wiped my nose. What could I say?

"Are you still hungry?" he said quietly.

I shook my head, *no*.

"Get some sleep, he suggested. "Call upon me if you need anything at all. I shall be in the kitchen seeing to our guests."

I didn't watch him bow or leave the room, but stared at the curtains as though they were suddenly the most important thing in the world. It occurred to me then that our yelling must have been overheard by my brother's new revenant acuity, and that two FBI agents in the next room got an earful. To their credit, they had given us our privacy, even after they must have heard the lamp shatter.

I bent to look at the mess and my eyes filled with tears like they'd only been waiting for gravity. I pinched my lips inward and swallowed hard. The lamp had fallen into a wiggling spot of ghoul sludge, but that was the least of my problems. I thought about just kicking it under the bed, slippery stuff and all, to worry about it in the morning. There were tiny pieces of light bulb glass winking in the moonlight that streamed through my window. I reached for them stupidly, and hissed when a tiny splinter pricked my fingertip. I couldn't believe I'd gotten into the habit of walking around without my gloves.

The bedroom door opened again almost as soon as it had clicked closed and Harry stormed back in, his presence a cool eddy through the room.

"Is everything all right?" I asked. "Where are Batten and Chapel?"

"They went for a drive," he said curtly, clutching his hands together and then wringing them as he paced. "Stupid, considering what may be waiting outside, but they had one collective leg out the door already, and would not be dissuaded."

"Oh," I said. I had no other words. "And Wesley?"

"Resting. Exhausted." He knew this simply by aiming his focus through the floor.

"Oh."

"This is all wrong," he insisted. "My stomach is an out-and-out knot, and so is yours. It's perfectly insufferable."

He paced, using his middle fingertip to repeatedly smooth his eyebrow to the piercings, and then swung around to gaze down at me, his inhumanly entrancing face inscrutable. I swallowed back heady panic in my chest and tried to convince myself that I didn't feel like vomiting. His calculating measurement said he wasn't going to let it go; the conversation I didn't want to have was coming and there wasn't anything I could do to stop it now.

"Are you quite well?" Harry asked, knowing the answer. "What is the matter with your finger?"

"Just a prick. My painkillers are wearing off again," I side-stepped. "I should have timed them better. I missed my afternoon dose."

"I will help you find comfort with a neck massage." He removed his onyx cufflinks and tossed them on the nightstand. Rolling his French cuffs to the elbow exposed the black calligraphy tattooed on his wrist.

I caught his cool wrist in my hand and turned it to the moonlight. My name. I looked up at him, shaking my head at myself.

"It has not changed." He assessed me seriously. "Did you think that it had, or ever would?"

"I don't know what to think anymore." I closed my eyes tightly so the tears wouldn't return.

"Lay your silly head down, and let me rally round your battlefield." He massaged his knuckles and cracked them, motioning for me to turn to my stomach so he could give me one of his famous neck rubs that melted a body to the core. But I stayed upright, cross-legged in the tangle of blankets, damp-eyed and nervous. If he wanted this confrontation now, I needed to stop being a pansy, pull up my big girl panties and just say it.

"If you really want to help me Harry, then answer this," I said, summoning my courage. "If I lived up to your expectations, if I did everything you wanted and more, if I made myself the perfect DaySitter, then would you make love to me, like you did all the others?"

He measured me with his unblinking gaze, going very still.

"Would you take me to your bed, Harry, or your casket, or the goddamn floor, or your friggin' antique bondage restraints, or wherever the hell you want to do me?"

We stared at one another in silence.

"Is that a no?" I demanded, my voice thick.

Finally, he let his chin fall, and barely above a whisper he told me, "You're not ready."

C34

It wasn't what I expected to hear. I opened my mouth to grill him and he spilled his voice into the bedroom, his words coming quickly and anxiously.

"And when I say that you are not ready, please do not mistake it for inflated ego, for it is concern for your well-being that stays my hand. The repercussions of intimacy could be disastrous, not only physically but psychically, to our Bond, to my very soul and yours, and before you yell at me again, let me promise you that if I could explain better, I would." He nailed me in place with his battleship-serious stare. "If only I could trust you with this responsibility ... yet, it simply is not possible. You are so very unpredictable, stubbornly impulsive. With everything so uncertain in our life right now, to add the element of ... no. It cannot be allowed."

"Element of what?"

"It cannot be allowed." Frustrated with his inability to speak his mind, he huffed like a cold dragon of the grave, and I said softly,

"Don't grind your teeth, you'll snap a fang."

"Nevertheless, I cannot allow you to continue this ridiculous self-punishment routine, can I? Demanding further intimacy from me, blaming my refusal on some imaginary physical dislike, then suffering to waste your sweet, precious attentions on this ham-fisted jugulator, this, this ..." He sniffed indignantly, unable to find words. "Carrion hunter with a chevril conscience and carlot's wardrobe. I've allowed your unchecked, unchided doggerybaw for far too long. Won't you spare us both this madness?"

He scratched the back of his neck and when I didn't respond, he dropped his hand helplessly in his lap. "My only love, there is nothing wrong with you; you are perfectly marvelous in so very many ways. Why do you think I picked you?"

I opened my mouth and tried to catch wind with it, but my lungs seemed to be malfunctioning. "I ...I really have no idea. We all thought you were going to pick my father."

"Violet thought so too," he admitted, reaching for one of my hands, pulling it to his kneecap. "Until that Thanksgiving when we made the trip from Paris on a mini-break to the farmhouse in Virgil, and stayed for the weekend. For Thanksgiving dinner. When you made the pie?"

I remembered making pie once and only once: pumpkin pie from scratch, and it was an unmitigated disaster. I *didn't* remember Harry coming for dinner. Ever. I remembered Grandma Vi coming alone. I searched back, floundering, the memory lost, blocked or stolen. Harry diagnosed the look on my face.

"Oh, I was not invited inside," he explained. "I was not welcome at the time, as your mother was uncomfortable. Violet asked me to wait at the hotel while she had a visit, however my curiosity got the best of me, and I came as far as the back yard. I knew she was discussing me, could hear the dulcet song of her recognizable voice within, in melody with those who sounded fond and familiar to her. I knew that in that sprawling farmhouse, its windows on fire with light and warmth, welcoming to her but not yet to me, there was someone who might serve me in the future, and that Violet would help guide my decision when it came time to figure who that might be."

I shook my head. "I don't understand. Grandma Vi came for dinner, and you waited outside, in October, in the cold and dark, for hours without meeting us?" At his nod, I shook my head some more. "If you didn't come in, how did you know about the pie?"

"At a little after six thirty pm, I was sitting in the chestnut tree in the backyard watching you through the kitchen window." He smiled, shrugged, as though he did such things every day. "The smoke got so thick in the kitchen that you had to open the screen door and fan the air with a dish towel. I remember," He pressed his long pale fingertips to his smiling lips. "That the towel had ducks, little yellow ducks, embroidered on its hem, as did your mother's apron, draped around your bony little waist. Do you remember, dearheart, what you said as you pulled the pie out of the oven?"

"Of course not," I said, beyond confused. "God, it was more than ten years ago. I think I was only fifteen that year, when Vi came. Why would I ..."

"Of course you wouldn't, my love, because as I would come to find out, every other minute of your day is spent cussing a seaman's blue streak at someone or something."

Baffled, I answered his growing smile with one of my own. "I don't get it, Harry. What did I say?"

"What I heard was fragmented, punctuated by angry snapping of your dish towel and soft exasperated muttering, but I quote: "dickshit ratfucker!""

Sounded like me. "Yeah, and ...?"

His smile broadened. "Bezonter me! I laughed so hard, I fell out of the tree and cracked my tailbone. Though the dead may heal quickly, allow me this: it hurt like a cattle prod in the bullocks." His eyes sparkled. "That very moment, in the hard October night, holding my arse in agony and trying not to laugh so loud as to startle you at the kitchen door, I fixed my fancy upon your saucy heart in a way I cannot describe; there would be no other member of the Baranuik family for my future partner. I wanted you, MJ, only you."

My heart softened as the corners of his eyes turned up.

Harry continued, "I told Vi so when she came back to the hotel." He touched his smiling lips again, a naughty boy with a guilty secret discovered. Then he reached out and traced his thumb over my bottom lip fondly, wistfully. "Was she ever angry with me, Lord and Lady, but I would not be dissuaded. I know what I want, and I always get it. Some day, my impatient little imp, I am determined to enjoy you fully. I will reward your fortitude, this I swear."

That sounded promising; the intensity with which he said it made me blush. All of the sudden I couldn't sit still; restless, I needed to be in motion. I swung out of bed and padded into the kitchen to draw a shot of espresso. Harry followed close behind, the weight of him more substantial now, the promise of someday lingering in my mind. Making sure the counter was clean of putrid yellowish blobs of *ick* (thankfully the kitchen looked relatively untouched) I doctored a cup of espresso with a shot of brandy and promptly forgot about it on the counter top.

"So what are you waiting for?" I asked.

He steepled his fingers, dancing the fingertips together gently. "A sign."

"How irritatingly mysterious of you," I dead-panned.

"If I tell you, you'll only ruin it."

"Another vote of confidence." I lifted my fingers and wiggled them in his face. "I'm just supposed to wait until I somehow pass this indefinite, indecipherable test and mystically signal the beginning of a new era in our relationship?"

"That is not even sensible conversation."

"It's entirely senseless, that's my point." I pointed at him. "We're the least sensible couple in revenant-DaySitter history."

"Perhaps there are things I can do to make the waiting easier for you?" he proposed.

I almost made a very filthy suggestion involving his fangs, my underpants and the table behind me, but clamped my lips together to prevent it from escaping. Harry would not approve.

Or would he? He stared at me, unblinking, waiting. When I remained still, silently blushing, he reached out one pale finger and swept the back of my hand, making contact. The Blue Sense flared between us with the heady snap-spark of burnt sugar. Unfortunately, my filthy suggestion was still rattling around in my vivid-red imagination.

His eyes gathered heat until his power ruptured into the close space between us in a breathtaking wave. He moved too fast too see, too quick to react, shoving his hand around me to cup the small of my back, thrusting me up against the hard plane of his body. He laid his face against mine, the familiar rough scratch of his evening beard pressed my cheek. The entire length of my back where he touched me was twitching, pricking with goose bumps and the thrill of being taken fast and hard and held in place by this new sweeping, possessive clutch. This was not at all like when we danced; no, the courtly gentleman had taken his leave and in his place crept a rogue, a fresh face I'd never seen. Harry's chin dipped to my throat and his mouth on my skin was a cool shock as the hard hint of fang pressed against the thudding pulse there. I left my head fall back, a sigh escaping me. His hunger tore through me, tinged with the unfamiliar tug of lust, and I reached for his hand to encourage him.

He didn't wait for my signal. Up against the complaining kitchen table he took my throat roughly in his mouth, bearing down hard enough to draw a ragged cry. His body pressed forward in one sinewy motion, moving in a slow progression like an army across a battlefield, inch by inch claiming space above me, until I found myself on the creaking table. He dominated the space and everything in it. One of his lean thighs pressed between mine, jerked my legs apart so he could settle his weight along my core.

Drawing back to look down on me, wedged hip to hip, master of the territory, lord of his property, Harry seemed immensely pleased with his new throne. I watched his pupils rapidly expand until his irises were only thin silver threads around two deep black holes and I felt like I was wavering very dangerously on the edge of an abyss from which there was no escape, about to plunge headlong into the watery alien crevice. What could be in there, waiting to sharpen its teeth on my sorry bones? Dizzy with surprise, I reached for the comfort of his familiar face, stroked him with my palm, felt the stirring of our Bond, that precious primal link to my immortal partner. It had only been days since I broke our Bond but its absence hurt, and as it trickled back in to fill the void, the push wrung my insides. The glass prick wound in my finger left a faint red smudge of blood on his cheek and he darted his head to take my finger in his velvety mouth, suckled at it tenderly. I couldn't help but imagine his mouth suckling elsewhere. Keeping me captured in his gaze, Harry's unflinching stare made my core twitch to life. Empathically, I felt the window to his emotions thrown open and for a moment I was bombarded by the avalanche of the revenant's pent-up desire, frustrated need of a nearly terrifying grade. Harry felt it too, his eyes widening with surprise.

"I do believe we may have breathed new life into the Bond," he said, his voice husky with desire. All at once, his eyes swam from battleship grey to faint chrome ringed with pitch streaks I'd never seen before cutting the luminous glow. *So this is Harry, horny,* I thought happily. *Hot damn.* His proper manner slipping, his dignity shrugged off like an inconvenient burden, he gave me a look that was all male, a predatory thing deeper than lust, an eternal hunger entirely different than human love.

"Maybe I'm getting the Bond back," I said, surprised that I could still make sound. The unsteadiness in my own voice was foreign. Rather than running from it, I dared myself to turn up the heat. "You should put yourself between my thighs more often."

"Do you suppose it is as simple as all that?"

"Oh no," I said, offering up my open mouth for a kiss. "Probably to fix it totally, you'd have to nail me. Let's test that theory, shall we?"

"Always a lady," he said benevolently, no disapproval in his voice now.

"Well if you're not going to do me on this table, Harry, then just what *are* you planning to do with this impressive erection?" I challenged. Heart an avalanche in my chest, I tilted up against him, my core wriggling against him. His unearthly eyes sank closed in helpless pleasure, dusky lashes fluttering against his pale skin, he groaned, rested propped on his palms like he was doing a push-up above me. He rolled one shoulder as though resisting his urges was causing physical pain, but all I felt radiating off him was the heavy urgent need of a man growing hard.

His mouth sank again to nuzzle under my chin, and his warming tongue darted out to play with his favorite spot along the length of my throat before sinking enamel for more. I heard his lungs rattle to life and he inhaled suddenly, deeply, with pleasure as my hips ground against him again. My hands, always having a mind of their own, wove down the front of him until they found his belt, then ducked along the front of his grey flannel pants to squeeze between our bodies, seeking the exciting new development throbbing there.

He drew back, his eyes soft around the edges, and given the chance I'm sure he would have told me that we'd find middle ground, deal with everything together, as we always did, as a team. That nothing had changed. That he cared for me as much as his little dead heart could.

The kitchen window exploded in a shower of glass shards, tinkling across linoleum, and I was left staring down at the fiery rush of a sizzling Molotov cocktail.

C35

I barked, "Code 6!" but Harry was already bolting to the bathroom, head down.

The stench of burnt sugar meant the blaze had been strong enough to singe him somewhere, causing his revenant healing to flare. I dropped hard to my knees in front of the sink, fished underneath in the cabinet between a box of empty cans for recycling and a bottle of Clorox bleach for the fire extinguisher. Panic made my fingers slippery and fumbling. Not remembering exactly how the damn thing worked I pulled a pin, whipped around, aimed, hoped and sprayed. Foam blasted out.

Another window burst and this jar broke on the bubbling, blistering linoleum, spilling flaming alcohol into the kitchen and belching black, burnt plastic smoke in the air. "Stay down Harry!"

The second Molotov took a lot more work to put out, especially since its flames had caught the rough chipboard underside of the Formica table. The reek of melting plastic singed my eyes and nostrils.

Distantly, the hollow sound of water running into the bathtub told me Harry had taken the precaution of sinking underwater. There he would stay until I came to give him the all-clear.

The kitchen seemed to waver and blur as my eyes filled with tears. *Just the smoke*, I told myself, scrambling on hands and knees, choking on chemical fumes, while another part of me whispered, *Nooo I was getting LUCKY you bitchass motherfuckers!* My crawl was clumsy with the fire extinguisher clutched in one hand. I took cover in the walk-in pantry where the doorway to Harry's basement bed chamber was, and my resting baby brother. I made sure the door was shut tight and sprayed a line of foam along the bottom to protect him. Then I tentatively reached out and poked at a hot shard of glass, to see if I could get a quick trace on who made the thing and who was pitching it into my home.

I got nothing. Closing my eyes, I forced up the Blue Sense, pulling an extra boost from my submerged companion. I started to taste it, but my heart was drumming too hard and my hands were shaking; dizziness interfered, the psi-bridge dissipating like smoke from damp-lit wood. On the plus side my frustration was brushing away fear, and irritation was setting steel into my spine.

At the front of the house another window shattered. My jaw tightened and I thought of Batten's jaw, and then I thought of my cell phone in the front office. *Mark!* I hauled myself up and skidded to a halt just in the threshold of my office. My desk!

Ducking to keep my head out of range of any more flying objects, I aimed a long foaming stream at the flames arching across my rug, the length of my desk, my blackening Sudoku book, my gutted laptop. My book of shadows lit with a flare. Stray No. 2 pencils became perfect kindling, rolling onto the carpet trailing white sparks in their wake.

"Shit shit *shit...*" I layered the foam heavily on the carpet, almost as heavily as the swearing and cursing. *I'm definitely letting Harry buy me a bigger fucking gun now. Maybe an Uzi. Screw it, maybe a couple of big ole cannons mounted on the roof, fore and aft.*

Another Molotov smashed into the office but didn't break. I grabbed the jar, yelled, "Fuck you!" and pitched it right back out.

Fire raced along the floor toward my book case. Alarmed, I let out an unladylike grunt-choke and aimed the fire extinguisher at the licking flames. I knew I wasn't going to be able to keep this up without help. I jerked open the top drawer of my desk, dug out my cell phone and with a shaking thumb dialed Mark's number, hoping their late night ride (read: uncomfortable escape from the Bickersons) hadn't taken them too far away from Shaw's Fist.

"Batten."

I heard a noise behind me in the hall and spun with the fire extinguisher aimed to kill. A very angry, very drippy revenant glared at the damage around me. A bang preceded Wesley into the hall, dry but fully vamped-out, prepared for a brawl. The corner of Harry's lip curled back to reveal full fang.

"Harry, don't!" I begged but he was flying out the back door with a growl. Wesley was his shadow and an echo, seconding his unearthly noises.

"Marnie!" Batten yelled on the phone but his voice was distant, breaking up.

I cried out, "Stay back! I'm warning you! *Dammit.*"

I darted after them, picturing Molotov cocktail meeting dry old revenant and new revenant and going *kapoof* all together in a massive fireball on the back lawn. Faster than the human eye could track, Harry's wet form zigzagged, jerked and shadow-stepped, slipping and curling along the icy darkness at the edge of the lake. Wesley was nowhere near as graceful but the speed and sheer physicality of him took my breath away. I hurried after them, sloppy in the snow in my sock feet, the extinguisher thudding on my thigh.

Harry took a running leap, bounded up the side of the boathouse, a gymnast from the grave. Wood cracked from the impact. He lunged up and through the air and he was gone. I blinked, staring against the gloom of the heavy forest for signs of him or his prey, swinging the fire extinguisher impotently. I heard the roar of an unfamiliar motor across snow. Wesley put his head down into the wind and pole-vaulted without the pole into the forest gloom.

"Vampire Olympics. Now that would be fucking entertainment," I thought aloud, my mouth hanging open.

A voice on the phone pulled me back to it. "Marnie!"

"Being attacked," I told him, grim. "Molotovs."

"Get in the boathouse and lock the door," Batten ordered. "Stay low. We're on the way. Calling fire and rescue."

"Fuck that. I'm sick of being afraid," I snarled and hung up. I flew back into the bedroom and grabbed the Beretta, checked it was loaded, shoved it into the waistband of my jeans. Passing through the kitchen I shoved my toes in my Keds, not bothering with the heels, then yanked Harry's boning shears from the knife block by the sink, and slammed out the back door. If I got the chance, I was gonna stab that bitch right in the head, and to hell with my karma. Gripping the phone in one hand and the shears in the other I bellowed into the wintry quiet:

"Danika Sherlock!"

The bitter night air answered me, burning my lungs, cold enough to whisk my fogging breath away. My nose instantly began to leak. There were lots of footsteps in the snow, swirled and slushed together into a messy gritty sludge pile; it was impossible to tell which ones were new and which ones had happened earlier. Clutching the shears tighter in my hand I trod out into the yard for the edge of the woods.

"Show yourself, you spooge-sucking skank!" I bellowed.

A flurry of soaking fabric brushed before my face out of nothingness; I fell back, throwing my arms up. Harry grabbed my elbow to keep me from falling on my ass.

"Get back in the house," he said hoarsely.

"*You* get back in the house, and where the hell is Wes? You left him out there?" I countered. "Fire plus revenant equals Hindenburg-like disaster."

"*You* will immediately return to the house, for *you* are my concern, not your bloody bothersome brother."

"Screw you. Besides, it's not in my job description to sit on my hands and hide while someone kills you. I'm gonna ..." I clutched the shears until my knuckles were white.

"You will do what?" he challenged. "Bring karmic retribution upon yourself threefold by injuring another?"

I felt my lips tighten into a line.

"Too right, you will do no such thing," he schooled, his grip on my arm tightening.

"You can't break the law, Harry!"

"There is no law here," he roared. "Now get in the sodding house!"

There was blood on his bottom lip. "Did you catch up to her? Did you see her?"

He noticed the phone in my hand. "Whom did you ring? Tell me that you did not summon Agent Batten."

"Only because I thought the house was on fire." It was thin, but he was distracted by noises behind him, and pointed at our home.

"I am not asking you, I am telling you, go inside. When we can, Wesley and I will join you."

"Are you out of your undead mind? I'm not leaving you two out here alone!"

His pupils bled rapidly to luminous chrome. "Your disobedience is most unbecoming, DaySitter."

"Shit," I breathed hoary frost into the air, as his displeasure washed over me, an icy backwash from the grave. "Fine. Want my gun?"

Harry looked unamused by the sight of it in my hand. I fled to the relative safety of my kitchen.

C36

I came away from the mudroom windows when Harry and Wes appeared on the back step. Harry's wet-from-the-bath hair clung in frosty strands to his forehead. He shook out of his damp shirt in the mudroom, threw it on the top of the dryer, glowering, his cool cheeks drained of all colour.

"I failed to catch him. I lost the trail of his bootless attempt in the boscage and undergrowth."

"Bootless?" I asked in a rush. "He? Him? He was barefoot?"

"We," Wesley said, avoiding my eyes. "We couldn't catch him."

"*A man?*" I gaped. "Are you sure?

"I am quite sure I know what a woman smells like. And by bootless, I mean of course cowardly," Harry chided, frustrated, and threw down a backpack that clinked when he drop-kicked it under the kitchen table. "If anyone asks, your brother was resting in my casket this whole time, to where he should now retire."

He didn't look at Wesley, but my brother took the order without argument; Wes went without another word down through the pantry door into the basement.

I nodded in a daze. "What difference does that make?"

"I found this by the boathouse on my way back in."

Wooden stakes stuck out of the open zipper of the sack. I couldn't get breath; the sight of them made tiny spots swirl into my vision. "Those look like real rowan wood."

Harry opened his palm to show me the angry white sores blistering up where he'd clutched one. Two of the welts along the length of his thumb had burst, oozing fluid.

"This was no amateur attempt, my love." Harry's face betrayed such anger that I was glad I couldn't feel him. "Fire, rowan and silver. Someone came here knowing precisely what they were doing. I tracked a snowmobile into the woods and lost him at the water's edge."

"Hunter," I breathed. "Did you see a boat? Canoe?"

"I did not see any vessel on the lake." He whisked up a plain dishtowel and rubbed dry his chest. "And the water is painfully cold, barely 35 degrees. No human could survive in it for long."

I heard boots coming rapidly up the front steps. I looked down at the Beretta held loosely (and let's face it, impotently) in my grip, opened the cutlery drawer and stuffed it under a jumbled pile of spatulas and wooden spoons.

The front door hit the wall. Batten stormed into the house, palpable rage frothing in his wake. I was so startled to actually *feel* something from his direction as he pounded past me that I didn't realize what he was about to do. He took three running strides and lunged at Harry.

Harry's arm shot out and grabbed Batten by the throat. Whipping around, he heaved Batten effortlessly, slammed him against the wall, held him high, pinning him in place.

"Really, Agent Batten," Harry said calmly. "I would have expected a federal agent to have better impulse control."

"Mark, what the fuck?" I shouted.

Batten choked out: "He attacked you."

"What? No!" I flapped a hand at them. "Harry put him down."

Harry's voice was deceptively pleasant. "I should love to, darling, if he will remember his manners in my home."

I saw Harry's knuckles tighten slightly and Mark made a noise that was something between a crude retort and a strangled curse. Batten's boot-tips barely touched the ground; he wasn't about to promise anything, but it took all the strength his arms could afford to wrangle with Harry's half-hearted hold.

Harry wasn't about to let go either, now that he had Mark right where he wanted and with a fair excuse. His lambent eyes dazzled with victory, and he extended his fangs with deliberate slowness.

I stepped forward. "Harry, I mean it. It's a misunderstanding. You have to let Fathead down."

"The very instant that Fathead promises to be on his best behavior, ducky."

I dug the Beretta out of the cutlery drawer and sighted on his immortal posterior. "Don't make me shoot you in the butt cheek, fool. Cuz I will."

"Sure you will," Harry said over his shoulder at me. Fangs peeked out of his wry smile.

"I will," I warned. "And then I'll point and laugh the whole way to the ER."

"There would be no trip to the hospital. As you will recall, it is your duty to remove any bullets in this body, but if you should like to make extra work for yourself, by all means …" Harry said, though the honey dripping from his tongue wasn't in the least bit cordial. It was a reciprocal warning; I should be choosing sides, and I wasn't on the right one.

Chapel rushed in, skidded to a surprised halt, one of his hands going for his Glock. It was then that Harry dropped Batten, stepping out of range of Batten's arms. Mark didn't retaliate; he was too busy massaging the feeling back into his neck muscles and coughing.

Chapel moved to be nearer to Batten, his hand still hovering by his holster. "Marnie, what happened? We were under the impression that Harry was attacking you."

"Batten jumped to conclusions. Probably because he's a raging moron."

"You yelled, "Harry, no!" and said you were being attacked."

What *had* I said? "Someone was throwing Molotov cocktails through my windows. Why would Harry attack me with Molotovs? Hel-*lo?* He's more flammable than I am."

"Doesn't mean you wouldn't burn," Batten told me.

"You know, for a guy who has 105 kills, I gotta tell ya ..." I made a fist and knocked on his forehead. "You're kind of a noob. If Harry was going to kill me, it wouldn't be with fire." I jerked a thumb at the revenant's full fangs. "It'd be with *those*."

In the distance, a fire engine's siren sounded. Again. The sound of them made me suddenly weary. How many times had I heard sirens in the past two weeks? My neighbours were going to petition town hall to get me run out of Shaw's Fist with a torch and pitchfork brigade.

Sheriff Rob Hood blew into the kitchen and came to a boot-shuffling stop, looking rumpled and crazy-eyed. "What the hell happened now?"

"What are you doing all the way out here?" I asked.

"I wasn't far when I heard Chapel's call go out to fire, and I recognized the address." He shook his head. "Can't catch a break, can you?"

I motioned to the bag on the burnt floor tiles, under the singed table. "Rowan wood stakes. Do you know what that means?"

Hood shook his head. "There a difference between rowan wood and other woods?"

"There's a big difference, in that only rowan is lethal to a revenant."

Hood's eyebrows went up; big news, perhaps, to the guy who until last week clung to the delusion that revenants were a myth.

"No amateur hunter," I affirmed. "He hand-whittled these, you can see the strokes of the blade in the wood. There are big fat chains of solid silver links in that backpack, and those things aren't cheap. Even figuring conservatively, that set must have cost well over ten grand."

"Who leaves behind ten thousand dollars worth of silver?" Chapel pondered aloud.

"Someone who knows that they shall be returning to retrieve it," Harry said softly. His words left the kitchen in silence while we each considered the implications.

Batten broke the quiet. "Where is your brother?"

"Resting, downstairs."

"Through all this commotion?"

"It's not like sleep," I reminded. "You can pound a goddamned stake through his chest and he won't wake up. Right, hunter? You don't even have to be clever enough to sneak up on him."

Batten took that with an arched brow and turned on Harry. "And you couldn't catch the suspect, even with your superhuman speed?"

Harry looked at him steadily through unhappy eyes. "No."

I felt a flicker of dishonesty from my companion; I quickly looked away so I wouldn't blatantly search his face. I knew only one person in the room would see a lie on Harry, and that was me.

"So, whose blood is on your lip?" Batten asked.

OK, two people.

"Perhaps I bit the inside of my mouth in excitement whilst I was holding you aloft against the wall, there." Harry shrugged casually; a ridiculous lie, since revenant blood is light blue. Both of them knew it, but Batten didn't voice it. "I enjoyed your struggle quite a bit."

"Did you, now." Batten wasn't amused.

"Indeed, I did. We ought to tussle like that more often."

Batten looked him up and down. "Why are you wet? Go for a swim?"

"The lake water is frigid. T'would be wholly uncomfortable for me to swim in it, Agent Batten, though the low temperature would not kill me."

I supplied, "We have plans for emergencies. Fire is code 6. Revenants of Harry's advanced age are extremely flammable, more so than younger ones. Harry's job is to get wet in the tub and *stay down*." I cast Harry a glare. "My job is to put out the fire and call for help if I need to."

"Is it also part of Harry's job to eat the person who set the fire?"

I felt my eyebrows scrinch. "You got proof of that, or are you just showing your prejudice again, Agent Batten?"

"Just asking a question, Baranuik."

"Uh hunh. You know, if he *had* eaten someone, there'd be a body left. The bones would still be out there." I pointed with the Beretta at the back door. "Why don't you go look for them? Mind the corpse beetles. Ask Dunnachie, those pincers hurt."

He turned on me, losing his cool, and his eyes fell to my hands. "How many of those goddamn mini guns do you own?"

"Just this one. It fits my grip."

"Is it loaded?"

"How should I know?"

"*Put it away!*" he ordered.

I rolled my eyes and went to the gun safe in my office. "Yes, sir, officer, sir," I muttered. In the gun safe, I noticed the small bag of dried goo that was Dead Kristin's missing eye. I left it where it lay, and locked the safe.

When I plodded back, Hood was talking logistics with Agent Chapel. Harry had hauled several large slats of plywood up from the cellar to put over the broken windows until a carpenter could be called in the morning. The firemen were in, doing their due diligence with a sweep, in case I hadn't put out all the fires.

"Did you go running out there?" Batten asked. "I told you to lock yourself in the boathouse and wait for me."

"Yeah, I don't have the energy for your phallocentric bullshit, Batten."

"This has nothing to do with you having a pussy. It has everything to do with you being a dunce."

Sheriff Hood turned smilingly away from the argument without comment, several long nails tucked between his twitching lips, Harry's hammer in his hand.

"Thanks, gonna put that on my new business cards," I told him. "Marnie Baranuik, PhD. Paranormal Biology. Freelance forensic psychometrist, clairempath and professional dunce."

"Amateur dunce," Batten corrected, taking a pull from the beer bottle Harry put in his hand. "There's no way you're a professional *anything*."

"Goes to show you haven't had my very pro blow job yet." I gave him a *neener-neener* smirk and poured myself a Dr. Pepper on ice while Harry choked out about a hundred old English admonishments that no one else in the room understood.

Some of the irritation leaked out of Batten's eyes; now that no one was hurt and the adrenalin was fading, tired humour replaced it. "I'm sure the firemen are enjoying you making a fool of yourself."

"I'll have you know, I haven't even begun to make a fool of myself yet." I gulped my drink and then heard what I'd said. "That sounded a lot better in my head."

I saw Hood's shoulders shaking, while Chapel held the plywood steady over the broken window.

Chapel offered, "Harry, you said there were snowmobile tracks? We'll have CSIU come out right away and take plaster casts."

It was an hour before the windows were all boarded-up and the firemen concluded that everything was sound and stable and safe. In that time, Harry prepared for me an endless line of *carajillo*—espresso with a shot of brandy—in hopes of keeping me awake. I blame the alcohol for my wandering eyes. I watched Batten's lips on the neck of a beer bottle, remembering the sensation of them working at my nipples. One of his fingertips played with the curling edge of the bottle's label, and what sort of cold fish would I be if the gesture didn't remind me of those fingers on my ...

"Welp, I'm done thinking," I announced thickly, standing. "I mean, talking, I'm done talking. I was talked-out hours ago."

Harry served Chapel another coffee, with lots of cream and sugar. "Darling, we were not saying a thing."

"We weren't? Oh. Well, that's a relief. You won't mind if I slip off to bed, then."

"What are the chances you'll be going to bed for good this time, Dr. Dunce?" Batten asked. There was a teasing, casual-yet-suggestive lilt to his voice that was almost an invitation. It made Harry's upper lip tighten.

I swiped Batten's beer bottle cap from the table, folded it tight in my palm and bent close to Batten's ear. Along the soft, vulnerable edge of his lobe I breathed: "*Blessed be this little charm, sleep ye deep and safe from harm*." Then I slid the cap in his jeans pocket. He watched my hand go down the front of his pants without complaint, raising one dark eyebrow.

"Just do me a favor," I said. "Don't take that out until I say so?"

Batten's head fell back and to the side to watch me. He rolled his eyes with a soft snort-laugh. Then his eyes rolled back even further, and he promptly passed out in his chair. Released from their control, his knees fell apart and his long, lean arms plopped into his lap.

I nodded once at Harry and Chapel, satisfied, and picked up what I hoped would be my last cup of carajillo for the night. "Good night, gentlemen."

"Nicely done, my only love," Harry said, beaming.

Chapel scratched the back of his neck and watched without comment as I closed my bedroom door.

C37

"I'll show him Dr. Dunce," I yawned, setting my last *carajillo* on the night stand. My eyelids, despite all the caffeine, alcohol and excitement, were heavy and roared with the hot, dry need to stay closed whenever I dared blink. It was nearly 4 am. I touched the buttons at my chest to change into my pajamas.

It was then that I realized I had been running around putting out fires and arguing with a drippy revenant and a hot FBI agent *already* dressed for bed in my two-sizes-too-big plaid pjs. That's me: smooth like a fresh-made bed of nails.

I flicked off the overhead light and fell into bed with a disgusted splutter, my head spinning. I had to try three times to pull off my gloves and when I went to put them on the nightstand, I missed. I was beginning to suspect that I was drunk. Either that, or the flickering renewal of our Bond had sent me reeling. If I was sexually frustrated before, I was doubly so now that Harry had agreed to meet me half way, whatever that meant; the details were still foggy. If he was even half as hungry for the taste of a woman as Hot-Ass Batten, I could totally handle being the appetizer while waiting for Harry's mysterious "sign" before the main course.

Then again, the evil part of my brain pointed out (because, as I've said before, my brain hates me) Harry's been making love to a multitude of women for 400+ years. *His* experience was not being called into question. My three boyfriends and a two-night stand really didn't measure up. Oh Dark Lady, I was destined to disappoint.

I sat bolt upright in bed, eyes forced back open by near-panic. Finally, that issue of Cosmo was going to come in handy. I yanked open the drawer and fished around in the dark, and my fingers brushed something cool and smooth and plastic. The Blue Sense spiraled white in my mind's eye, the tiny black point opening in the center, widening until it formed a viewing platform. *The lens.* I fingered it out into my palm, bounced it there once, and then brought it into bed with me.

I'd tried a couple times to link to Danika Sherlock through the lens. Each time, I felt pushed back, shoved out by the murky protective shelter around her, a psychic bitch-slap. Maybe this time I was burnt-out enough to really not care at all, drumming up that gossamer wisp that was psi?

Here? I laid in bed, my body screaming *yes, just lay here. Please? Sooo, sooo tired.* But I had no protection in my bedroom, no supplies, few candles. Like Harry always says, if you're going to do magic, do it right …only when he says it, he uses big antique words that hurt my head.

I dragged myself out of bed, opening my door a crack. The kitchen was blessedly empty now, quiet. I could feel Harry nearby, the inexplicable push of the otherworldly. I slipped the lens in the waistband of my pajamas, near the bandages I probably didn't need any more, while another yawn rocked my face. I attempted to tip toe past the living room.

A glance told me Harry was deeply engrossed in a big leather-bound tome; I was guessing Chaucer rather than Shakespeare, but I was wrong. It was a book of poetry, entitled *A Suite Burlesque.* A quick peek at the author revealed him as one G.S Nazaire. The fire was high in the woodstove, and his lap was covered with a blanket. I'm sure he heard, felt and smelled me pass by, but he never turned his head.

In the office, I clicked on the banker's lamp by my laptop. The room stank of scorched wood but at least it didn't reek of ghoul goo. Since it usually smelled like vanilla scented candles, it drove home the reality that someone had actually tried to smoke us out, armed with the tools to get the job done. A *man,* Harry had said. A man? Maybe Sherlock had employed an Igor-type? As if I didn't have enough to worry about.

I opened the cabinet and reached for my dried lavender but hesitated, the Blue Sense flaring hot under my bare palm. Something was wrong. My fingers hung over the sackcloth pouch, itching with suspicion. I grabbed a pencil from the desk, one of the few that survived the fire, and used the tip to open the lavender pouch.

Monkshood. *Holy flaming shitballs.* I narrowed my eyes. *Bitch put monkshood in my lavender sack?* Aconite poisoning through my skin would have been nasty. I poked around with the pencil and also identified wormwood and a poppet meant to represent me. It had short blonde hair shorn in a jagged edge. I squinted at it as though it had personally offended me.

"That's fine," I told it, keeping my voice low. "Do your worst, Skanky McTwatwaffle. I'm done playing."

I ran my hands out into the space around me, palms questing, tasting the region my herbs and candles. My fingers shook and then steadied, nice and calm. Everything else was untouched by the intruder's taint. Rosemary, chamomile, several white candles collected, I shuffled through my gemstones to find blue lace agate for easy energy flow and peridot for improved clarity. I set them on a fair edge of my desk and moved the rug aside with a nudge of my foot.

My gentle pentagram had been vigorously desecrated with slashed black symbols. Struggling to read along one line, I realized it wasn't a language still spoken just before my eyes crossed and fluttered. I nearly fell forward into the circle but caught myself with one palm on the desk.

"Well, fucka*nut*," I barely breathed out. Grabbing white chalk from the cabinet, I stepped out of my pajamas and drew a hurried makeshift circle on the desk top, filling it with a perfect star. I tried not to think of the cursed ugliness splattered across the owls my sister had painted.

I climbed up naked on the desk, and knelt in the circle, pulling my things in with me. Making quiet invitations to the Watchtower, I did deep-breathing exercises while I waited for them to respond. As the worry and stress seeped out of my bare shoulders, they went limp, and a serene smile crept onto my lips. Unable to comprehend the shift in my feelings, I let my fingertips trace my mouth, following the curve up at the corners; yep, I was okay, not crazy, only bordering on happy. Just checking.

Starting with praise helped lift my heavy heart, and as my breath came quicker and stronger, the smell of burnt wood around me no longer seemed a slap in the face; it seemed a victory, a line in the sand. Yes, I had been attacked, more than once.

But this is my place. Here I stay.

"Holy Mother, I remain/ All that serve shall rise again./Vengeance shall not from me flow/From above or from below." I breathed in sweet, clean air and the smell of wood freshened, like I was walking in the forest out back, and with each imaginary step I took, the ground became softer, until it was springy like root-bound ground. I paused in my journey of the mind, traced back into my unclothed body, brought the lens before me, lit the candles.

"Hail Hecate, Eyes of Night/Blade and chalice, dark and light/Lady serve me in this hour/to call upon Thy Ancient Power/That I might have clarity of mind/with truest sight now entwined."

Harry's snap-spark of burning molasses played under my nostrils, scorching sugar, atop my own weaker version of the sugarburn. As our Bond deepened over the years, it would increase in strength like my psychometric power would. The empathic side of our Bond would as well, and possibly let me feel humans as effortlessly as Harry could. I mean, living humans. Until then, I borrowed from him, and knew that he felt me drawing upon the intimidating well of his seemingly infinite power.

I felt no resistance; from the next room, Harry let me have all I could manage in a steady unfaltering stream. As the cool touch of his undead Talent thickened me like a sponge dropped in a full sink, the delicate touch of the Goddess' blessing also brushed across the bare skin of my forehead, travelled down across the bridge of my nose like a feather. I heard a hush, a gentle exhale, and wondered if it was me, Harry or something *other*.

Quivering with power, I brought the stolen lens back into my palm and visualized Harry's influence rising black and cold like a laser beam from a mausoleum. All the little hairs at the nape of my neck pricked up; I sensed Harry hovering just outside the office door now, curious but maintaining his distance.

I looked past Danika Sherlock in the lens, behind her, around her, side-stepping past the blurry, semi-blocked image of her, completely ignoring the pollution of her on the plastic. Taking the back door in, I tried to link to the person who owned the sunglasses before Danika.

The Blue Sense ripped into being like a puma spilling down out of the trees onto prey below; my head rocked back. If my hair wasn't already a spiky ruin, it would have stood on end with crackling energy. The vision was brilliant, sparkling and mind-searing, but I didn't back down. I pulled more from Harry and his immortal clout responded enthusiastically, awash with cold heat. Again, he worked at relaxing his hold to feed me another length of power.

My lips started moving, and blindly I groped for the chalk. Hand moving across the desk top on its own, I linked to the owner of the lens and wrote his name. *His* name, I boggled. His old name, and his new name. Patrick Laurier. Patrick Laurier Nazaire.

Revenant.

The good news was: it wasn't either of *my* revenants. I stroked the lens and let it pour forth its secrets; "*I can't let her* ..." I didn't so much hear Patrick's words as see them forming across the matter of my mind. "*She can't have access ...without the element of ...to add a dimension ...*"

Access to what, I wondered. An element of what? What could terrify an immortal so much that he'd be ... I stopped. He had to prevent ... my mind skipped backward and then forward three steps; psychometry is about as straight and clear as a bowl of scrambled eggs. At some point in the near past, Danika Sherlock had tried to force the Bond on this young revenant, was possibly still trying. He was refusing. Why would he resist?

I rubbed a thumb across the plastic. *So hungry.* They hadn't fed him in weeks, but there had been blood in the room, blood in his face, blood lashed on dirty grey cement. Blood at the drain. Blood on the baskets. Blood in the circle. *They?* I frowned in thought. Who were *they*? What room? What circle?

"Where are you Patrick?" I murmured, sending a tendril of my mind out, opening myself fully to receive the flavour of him. "Where did you come from?"

And then I was assaulted with an erotic scene: Danika stroking him, her small hand firm and insistent on his cock, trying to get Patrick hard for her; since he had been refused blood, this was impossible. She spit on her palm and tried again. He laughed at her, a laugh that said finally, hopelessly, *I'm going to die but heyfuckYOUbitch.* I saw what he feared the most, as Danika tried with cold, malignant determination to beat him into some form of erection: the rowan wood stake in her left hand. And then I saw something worse: Danika was petrified, because if she failed ...

The lens practically jumped in my hand and suddenly it was hers, her sunglasses, and Patrick was gone, I couldn't reach him, he was just gone. Danika tilted the sunglasses back onto her glossy strawberry blond hair, driving. Glad to be away from the storeroom (*what storeroom?*) and away from the revenants (*more than one, how many?*) and hurting. Hurting so badly. Searing pain down her right arm, ending in a hot, severing edge. A needing, hungry emptiness, almost vampiric itself in its intensity. I'd never felt a human with such a gaping maw of need and loneliness before. Fraught with anxiety of a magnitude that was driving her unavoidably insane, she was resolute even in her psychosis. "*I'm gonna get one. That's the promise.*"

I tried to maintain the link to Danika but it slipped away as though I were waking from a light sleep. (*That's the promise.*) Clutching the lens in one hand and the blue lace agate in the other helped to briefly stutter the vision back into being, but all it showed me was black ... black ... black ... and a strange purple light.

"That's the promise," I said aloud, my brain churning, chewing at something that I couldn't bring forward.

When Harry touched the office door open, his silhouette marked the heartbeats in silence before he ventured in. "Do not let Agent Chapel catch you with that item," he said, his voice very low and unhappy. "If he thinks you a common thimble-twister, he will never trust you again."

I scratched an irritated itch in the center of my forehead. "Before I take offense to that, does thimble-twister mean thief?" At his slow meaningful blink, I moved off my knees to the floor to retrieve my pajamas. "Well, if the thimble fits ..."

His face became blank, inscrutable. "I fed you more than I felt necessary, but you were quite apt in your juggling. You have a most agile mind, my pet. T'is rather a nice change to be proud of you."

I smiled wanly. "Thanks, Harry." *I think.* "The original owner of the sunglasses was a revenant named Patrick Laurier. Mean anything to you?"

"I'm afraid it does not." A casual shrug. "Perhaps he is young."

Harry's idea of young varied greatly from mine; Harry thought any revenant under 300 was a veritable puppy. I nodded, thinking I had heard the surname Nazaire before; Ruby Valli's companion, Gregori Nazaire, was over 1400 years old. Certainly old enough to be making little puppy revenants, and a revenant almost always took the surname of his maker. I wondered if Gregori kept in touch with any of his youngers, namely Patrick Laurier. Harry was watching me steadily.

"You are done in and dog-tired, my love," he said. "Will you sleep now?"

"Soon," I promised. He took the hint and excused himself. I locked the lens with the Beretta and the eyeball in the gun safe under my desk, then turned to purse my lips at the pentagram.

"*Hestia of House and Home/Banish the foul dark 'ere it roam!*"

I tipped one of the white candles on its side and watched the hot wax spill down from desk level and hit the painted owls. In a sour green swirling cloud, it consumed whatever foul magic lay there in Latin, and the fire sputtered to an unhealthy end. I blew with pursed lips to dissipate the curse. Then, because I was feeling cheeky, I blew it a kiss and a wink.

"Toodle-oo, sucker."

I grabbed the pencil and my tan Moleskine from the desk drawer, and wrote: *Patrick Laurier, revenant. Nazaire master.* Would Gregori Nazaire know what had happened to Patrick? And how would I get Ruby's permission to talk to Gregori, to ask? This might be tricky. It would take careful wording and social graces: so not my strong suits.

I wrote: *Danika tried to Bond Patrick, he resisted. "She can't have access ...*" That phrase worried me more than the unsuccessful hand job and the sudden disappearance of the link to Patrick. Why was he resisting so strongly? Was it just that she was unsavory? Or that he was unwilling, or not enamored? What did he not want Sherlock having access to, through him? Was his Talent dangerous? Perhaps Patrick Laurier was pyrokinetic. I'd always thought that would be the most kick-ass superpower to possess, a Talent I categorically did not want

Danika Sherlock to seize. As I wrote this possibility down, the lead of my pencil broke and I reached towards the ceramic froggy pencil holder to get another.

And that's when I saw them.

Tiny little black fangs, scribbled on my froggy pencil holder. Ink. *Rats!* I squinted at it, licked my thumb and rubbed them. Permanent ink! *Double-rats!* Did Danika do this? Did the mysterious hunter do it? Did the mischievous glove thief do this? I stopped my bare spit-covered thumb's rubbing and pressed hard, opening my mind again to Grope.

An impish, lopsided grin. A twinkling glitter of wickedness in those lake-bottom blue eyes, his handsome face crinkling with smile lines. A black marker in his tanned, calloused hand.

My jaw dropped. I struggled between outrage and a reluctant smile, felt my eyes narrow down to mere slivers even as my lips twitched upward.

"Hilarious," I drawled, standing to make for the door. "Cheeky-ass hunter thinks he's funny. And you!" Against the wall: the froggy doorstop had big pointy black ink fangs. Likewise, the stuffed frog in the chair with the surprised expression. "Oh he's *so* gonna get it."

C38

The ceiling creaked and a door overhead shut with an audible click. That's the blessing of living in an old, ill-made cabin: lots of noise. I considered the situation as I flossed with Harry's cinnamon waxed: upstairs, directly above my bedroom, Batten the frog-vandal was still awake and moving around. *Maybe undressing*, my cruel imagination suggested, that powerful, limber body reflected in the tarnished mirror above the guest room dresser. Lucky fucking mirror. Was the overhead light on, or just the bedside lamp, casting half of him in shadow? Was his shirt off, revealing the hard abs and broad shoulders that made me hungry like a carnivorous castaway on veggie island? Were his boxers off yet, or would he sleep in them? Since he was so fond of secretive forbidden sex, I could go up and find out for myself ...but would Harry be as tolerant, now that we had come to a "someday more" understanding? I was already amazed that he tolerated Batten as well as he did.

Looking down at the claw foot tub, still filled with cooled water, I worried about my companion, and about Wes. The water would stay in the tub tonight, I decided, just in case of another Molotov attack caused someone to need a dunk. Or in case I needed to cool off to save myself from crawling up the stairs and begging Batten to please put me out of my sex-starved misery.

What the hell was wrong with me? Jerkface defaced my frogs, and here I was thinking about molesting him? Some punishment! Calling myself half a dozen versions of stupid, I kicked out of my socks and crawled into my cool, creaky bed. When my head tucked down, I slid so rapidly into a half-sleep that I almost didn't have the time or stamina to turn my face into the pillow. As my energy systems shut down, I kept a comforting hold on my awareness of Harry in the next room, wrapping the feel of the revenant's solid presence around me like a security blanket until the very last moment.

I knew right away I was dreaming; someone's mouth slowly teased its way up the soft, yielding inside of my thigh, and that almost never happens. Their hot, moist exhale had me shivering with delight, and when the long lick of their tongue flicked out, my toes curled in anticipation. I writhed as my unknown lover teased me in just the right way, intuiting exactly what I wanted and when; that also almost never happens. It was like the head between my legs must be my own, somehow, so well did this lover know my needs.

Then there was the soft press of teeth, gently at first and then nipping. I jumped a little, surprised, thinking naturally of Harry, though he had never fed from the fat superior vena cava running down near my groin. As the mystery lover nipped again, harder this time, I tried to ask them to knock it off, but my voice wouldn't come, and though I knew that this was one of those dreams where you need to speak up and can't, I tried again. Regardless of how easily I tell people off in waking life, in my dream I was struck mute, and perhaps deaf too, because I heard nothing from below, no breathing or noises, no dirty talk. When I tried to lift my head off the pillow to look at my lover, it seemed to weigh ten times what it should; my neck was limp spaghetti, my head a cement block. I was lucid enough in the dream to think that was kind of funny.

Then with over-eager abruptness, the face pressed against me and his tongue, far longer than it should be, plunged inside, invaded deeply, explored but not gently, and not pleasantly. I wriggled and tried again to cry out, to look. My subconscious didn't want me to speak, but it hadn't taken my sight, I thought, so why can't I look down at my lover?

The ghoul's face shot up from between my legs; though rotted by heat and putrefaction, this ghoul's face was instantly recognizable as Mark Batten. His broad chest was pale and discoloured, greenly terrible; gone was the dark splotch of chest hair I'd once curled my fingers into. A yawning hole flapped over his left pectoral, empty of its beating organ, as if it had pressed the emergency eject button.

He stuck out his too-long tongue, slurping at me in the air. The connective tissue in the back of his throat gave way. Let loose, the slab of tongue fell onto my bare belly with a sick plop. I tried to scream and bat it away, but couldn't. My jaw worked, sound trapped in a dumb void. Rotting ghoul hands pressed my hips to the bed, palms slippery with gelid scum, pinning me in place. Vividly, I could feel the unstable flesh moving across the hard immovable bones of his hands, threatening to rub off. I bucked to get away but his arms were like iron bars. *Its not a dream*, my alarm bells clanged. *Something's wrong, it's not a dream!*

After what seemed like an infinity of squishy, slapping struggle, he reared back to show me the dark purple head of his bobbing cock, giving it a squeeze. My eyes widened though I wanted to cram them shut. What glistened at the tip was not semen; bright ruby red, a droplet of blood balanced there before running down the length of his shaft to the edge of his gripping hand. He stroked it once, displaying it for me, and the skin rolled off in his hand. Horror dragged a guttural choking noise from me.

His voice rasped, grated out in a foul gust: "Isn't this what you want, you filthy cunt?"

I broke from the nightmare with a windless gasp that turned into a half-sobbing curse. Flinging out a hand, I shoved all my cool bare sheets off into a jumble. I scrambled upright, coated in sweat, dry-mouthed with revulsion, shoving strands of damp hair off my forehead. I tried to call out for Harry; my petrified voice box was hoarse and words didn't so much belt out as leak thinly. I tried again and failed. Worse yet was the sudden realization, the hole of vacant loneliness, the absolute blankness in the cabin: Harry was gone, everyone was gone, I was completely abandoned to my own resources. Except …

I didn't want to crane over the edge and look, but now I could hear it, closer, and holding my breath I could hear it even louder: talon-like fingers reaching, skittering on the hardwood, *scritch*ing, snagging the rag rug with jagged yellow nails. I felt my mouth form a perfect O. The wood blackened with foul magic, creaking under the ghoul's touch, as though his flesh was super-cooled gas of a poisonous class and the planks were a living organism, infected. Smoky crystals formed in the wood like frost on a window.

"What do you want?" I tried to shout; my voice was barely a whisper. "Where did you come from?"

Wearing icy slivers on ruined flesh, the ghoul tumbled on his back on my floor to show me his face: above a bare strip of lip hanging atop exposed gums and teeth were Gary Chapel's hazel eyes, clouded by death. A wet snarl purled on the back of his tongue. "You brought us here. You did this. You did it."

Goblets of fatty tissue and red flesh dribbled off the ghoul's body onto my rag rug. As I watched, his sockets sagged like melting wax running down the side of a candle, painfully wet-red with unseeing gore, gaping at me, and his eyeballs burst out to spill their contents in a runny ooze. (*You did this.*) His arms were hairless and skinless, shaking with the effort to roll back to his knees. He looked too weak, or too crippled by cold, to move quickly or unfurl his clenched arms. I could see every tendon pulling, every ligament and muscle and vein. It seemed each of its movements tore silent torment from its gaping maw. (*You did it.*)

I backed away, pulling my sheets with me, when it hit me: no smell. Still dreaming. Its hand landed on the side of my bed and hauled up, bringing its eyes level with the mattress. Shitfuck*wakeup!*

Bolting upright, I bit down on my tongue, hard. My mouth watered, and my eyes stung; *awake for real this time.* More evidence my brain hates me: nobody needs to experience a dream like that. Ever.

Without a second thought to things lurking under the bed or anywhere else, I thrust out from under my tangled prison of sheets and ran full-tilt to the living room, where Harry's reassuring cool familiarity was a bobbing buoy in the night sea.

Harry still lounged in his wingback chair, frowning unhappily down through his pince nez at a copy of *Procession*, erotic poetry by Ruby Valli. He did not look up, merely lifted a corner of the blanket from his lap in invitation. When I crawled there eagerly and put my head on his chest, he folded it back, tucking it up around my shoulders.

"That surely must have been an adventuresome dream," he noted quietly. "Your sweet heart is knocking like a Jackson Model C."

My throat still gluey with residual fear, I ground out: "I don't know what that is, Harry."

"I know." He paused in his page turning to stroke a soothing hand across my forehead. "No more dreaming. Sleep tight. Don't let the grave bugs bite."

And I slept.

C39

Morning had slithered into the living room starting with the slightest lift of darkness, easing the nervous press of night. Even before the clock displayed a reasonable hour, the heavy attendance of that black cellophane glaze lurking at the windows traded places with a softer, greyer version. Dawn was made at last official by Harry's silent movement across the room to shut the blinds.

I'd spent the rest of the night where Harry had put me: curled up on the couch wrapped in a tight circle with a hot water bottle tucked into my belly.

I had to cling to the hope it was only Danika Sherlock behind the ghoul. Better the devil you know. If it *wasn't,* then I had somehow managed to drive more than one person to homicidal rage. Goody. I know I'm not exactly charming, but I had no idea I could inspire such malevolence.

A bottle full of butane sat on the coffee table. Harry's engraved lighter sat beside it. I hadn't seen Harry fetch them, but they were, combined, an excellent idea. Ghoul plus fire equals no more ghoul problem. Too bad fire didn't banish nightmares, too.

Harry still sat where he had for the last three hours, in the wingback chair. He had traded Ruby Valli's poetry for another copy of Bed and Breakfast Ownership, with his rimless *pince nez* perched low on the bridge of his nose, delicately licking a fingertip with each page turn. I didn't see how he could be so nonchalant after everything that had happened. I was still vibrating at overload on the angst meter. The memory of standing at the funeral home sink rinsing rotted, slimy matter off my hands flashed back and stars prickled and swam in my vision; I pressed my face into a throw cushion and willed it away.

To change the subject rattling in my head, I groaned, "When's the last time you checked on Botticelli's fallen angel?"

Harry's attention flicked through the floor and he shrugged. "Dead asleep, if you'll pardon the pun."

Since it was my brother he was talking about, the humour fell sour in my throat. "How long is he gonna be out?"

His hand see-sawed. "Days. Perhaps as long as a week. I gave him my supply from Shield to fill him up, now that you are well enough to resume … oh, forgive my dreadful manners, I should not assume. You are still well enough for me, are you not?"

"Whenever you're ready, but I'm warning you: I might fall asleep while you feed."

Harry *tsk*ed. "Please don't. I would be quite bothered to have you wilted and insensible during a feed." His nose wrinkled and it moved his reading glasses. "Objectionable thought."

"You know what's a more objectionable thought?" I asked, pointing at his book. "You, using tourists as your own personal International buffet. We're not opening a bed and breakfast."

He put the book aside without comment and picked up a nursing handbook.

"Way to sidestep one landmine and plunk directly on another," I said tiredly. "That's another *no*."

"I could use some, how do you say, uncritical affection," he told me, echoing my own complaint.

"You've been content to be the idle rich for more than four centuries, why are you looking for a career all of the sudden? Or are you just trying to drive me bonkers?" His caught-out grin behind his fist was all the answer I needed. I growled at him, and he wiggled his eyebrows playfully.

I picked up *Procession,* read a few lines, got bored, and put it aside. On the coffee table was an older book in green cloth binding, with gilt title: *A Suite Burlesque*. A glance inside this one had me reading aloud, perplexed, "What does 'with straining yard' mean, Harry?"

"With turgid member," he translated, to my blank look. "Erect penis."

With a blink, I dropped the book. "Holy crap! Who writes that in a friggin' poem?"

Unhappily, Harry said, "At least one poet and one plagiarist." But he did not elaborate.

When Chapel came downstairs, his long-jawed Great Dane face displayed worry with all the subtlety of a neon beer sign. Considering he was a master of self control, it was with dread that I ventured:

"Problem?"

"Oh no." He straightened his tie and helped himself to coffee from the thermos in front of me. He took it black, and filled my cup without being asked. "Good news, actually. My unit chief approved a request to transfer the PCU headquarters out of our bunker in Quantico and into the new addition to the Boulder field office. We're also adding two branches on the west coast and one in Michigan." His calf-brown eyes scrutinized me from behind his glasses. "Are you all right?"

"I'm fine, just a little tired." *And a little ghoul-sexy*. I played with Harry's lighter. "So a new budget must have come down the line for you?"

Chapel nodded. "Based on the rise in revenant-on-human violence, we've got the go-ahead to hire licensed hunters to augment each team. I've recommended Batten for promotion to handle the Michigan unit."

This was the source of the ripple of stress that again creased Chapel's forehead, I thought. *Batten hadn't said yes.* Maybe he hadn't said an outright no, either. If there was a reason for his hesitation that had anything to do with me, it was probably best I didn't know.

Harry did not look up from his nursing manual. "I am quite sure Agent Batten is a sound choice, and he shall do an adequate job of it."

"Can't be much worse than this, anyway," I said with a shrug, trying not to think about it. Chapel considered me quietly while I blew on the coffee in my Kermit the Frog mug and sipped carefully. "When I pry my tired ass off this couch, I'm going to drive into Boulder and see if Ruby Valli has any books on flesh magic I can borrow." *And see if she'll let me play Truth or Dare with her 1400 year old immortal companion.*

Chapel was still considering me. Dark circles bloomed in the corners of his eyes. "Maybe I should come with you."

"To Ruby's?" I yawned behind my hand. "What for?"

Chapel looked like he was thinking about insisting. His eyes snuck sideways to my silent revenant as though Harry might back him up.

"Look, I know what questions to ask better than you would," I assured him. "And if there's anything I need to know that I forget to ask, Ruby Valli will tell me. She's a rare resource."

Chapel nodded, finished his coffee. "You think my presence might inhibit."

"It always inhibits me," I joked. Chapel surprised me with a half-smile of acknowledgement.

"I'll guard Harry until you return."

I bet you will, I thought, the green-eyed monster tugging in my chest. He excused himself, fingers pressed to his jaw hinge, exploring some pain there that made his forehead wrinkle.

Harry stretched his legs out in front of him and stared at me, calculating, measuring, probably marking off possible signs of temporary insanity on a mental checklist. I gave him my version of the inscrutable revenant gaze, refusing to squirm, cool and unflappable; it lasted a whole three seconds before I cracked.

"Okay, okay," I hissed, slapping my pillow. "I heard it! Michigan! So what?"

"Shall we discuss this, so that you might maintain a scrap of dignity, decency and common sense through this development?" A cello tube of English chocolate-covered digestive cookies appeared as if by magic in his hand and his fingers made quick business of unwrapping one end.

"Oh no. You're not twisting me into a corner with your word play."

Harry's eyebrow rings twitched. "A conversation with your closest companion is not generally considered a trap."

"Which is why it's such a brilliant trap."

"Agent Batten must go to Michigan, MJ." His voice left no room for argument. "The kindest thing you could do now is make it easy for him."

"Well, his momma was paying me to be nice to him, but I suppose I could give her a refund and go full-speed-ahead on the bitch train." I rolled my eyes to him. "Your casket misses you. T-minus ...?"

"Oh, my doe." He smiled tolerantly. "Do not pretend with me."

"Sounds like an impossible task, doesn't it? But I'm up for it."

"You must be more firm. Push him away. Be as stern and unforgiving as the Tyburn tree; it is for his own good, and yours, after all."

"What tree?" My brows puckered, then shook my head so he wouldn't bother explaining. "It's not like I've been warm and fuzzy."

"I am confident that, given this new opportunity, Agent Batten will weigh his options and see that there is really nothing here for him. It would be unfair of you to confuse the situation."

"By pouring on the infamous Marnie Baranuik charm? You know, the charm that has all the fellas clambering into my bed?" I played through memories of me attempting various seduction techniques on highly unimpressed men, most of which ended with me flipping off a couch with arms flailing, or clonking my head on a bedpost. I layered on the sarcasm. "Well, it's true: I'm a sex goddess. That's my cross to bear. But I'll try to keep it under wraps for a bit longer until he's safely away."

Harry lowered his voice discretely. "It is no secret that you and Agent Batten have an unfortunate chemistry; it is an ill wind that can blow no one any good."

He was right, but I didn't have to like it, and there was no point in faking nonchalance. "I vow to be my cheap, wretched, vulgar self, Harry."

He drew himself up straight. "Shruff and cinders, we'll never be free of him!"

"I didn't mean *that*." I exhaled hard, blowing a spiky strand of hair away from my temple where it tickled. "Harry, you're frowning at me again. Everyone's always frowning at me, as if they can change what I'm doing just by pulling their eyebrows into some magic alignment. Stop it."

"You are plotting something. I do wish you would tell me what it is, so I can brace myself for the inevitable cock-up. The last time you ran off without warning, you got yourself mutilated by a knife-wielding lunatic."

I got *myself* mutilated. "How dare I?" I marveled. "Tell me how you really feel, Harry."

"It is not in a revenant's nature to prevaricate. Would you prefer that I do?"

Yes. No. Sometimes. I sighed. "I like knowing where you stand. And yes I'm plotting. I thought I'd swing by the Ten Springs Motor Inn, slip under the yellow tape and go full-tilt on the Blue Sense, see where it takes me."

He appeared to relax. "Gloves off?" When I nodded, he tested the air for lies, and, finding truth, ironed the creases out of his forehead. "Well, don't you take the biscuit."

That sounded like a compliment. "I'm going to have to finish this, Harry. Me. I didn't notice the last time I worked with them how green the PCU is."

"Perhaps the cure to your blindness might have been lifting your head out of Agent Batten's lap?"

It was the other way around, I thought but most definitely did not say. "They're undertrained, underfunded, undereducated. I don't see that they're going to be much help until it's time to make an arrest, and that's never going to happen unless I step it up."

"I'm not sure I'd undervalue these gents quite to that degree, but they do seem to be floundering. To be sure, you are not considering going to the Motor Inn alone?" He contemplated the area of my belly wound. Then his eyes dropped to my hips. "On second thought ...heaven forbid you find your cheap, wretched and vulgar self in a motel room with Agent Batten."

"Oh, I think it'd be pretty safe, what with my blood being the new accent feature of Room 4's decor."

"Please, ducky. Agent Batten misses nothing, but he also seems perfectly capable of overlooking the obvious, dodging reason and common sense when it suits him, including fraternization rules and buckets of blood. He's practically gagging for it."

"My blood?"

"No, goose, that would be me." He reached over and picked up his bookmark, putting the dream of nursing vulnerable humans aside for the day.

"I won't take Batten," I promised, since it seemed like a wise suggestion. Taking Batten to Ruby Valli's to question such an old revenant would be like taking a diabetic kid into an ice cream factory and letting him see how the mint chocolate chip is made. Also, a room with a bed and Beefcake Batten ... well, that would make *me* the poor kid shown what she can't or shouldn't have.

"I'll go alone."

"And if the inimitable Ms. Sherlock is lying in wait?"

"Why would she know where I ..." *Maybe she lied about no longer being clairvoyant, dummy.* "I'll take the Beretta." At his doubtful look, I promised, "I'll even load it."

"You are not telling me everything."

His pupils were soft, human ash grey but that infernal intelligence swam behind them, threatening to surface. I waited him out in silence, a contest of wills with a creature who had all the time in the world to stare unblinkingly back at me. I cocked my head, smiled, and told him:

"Sometimes I just wanna grab your face and give you a big smooch. You're so adorable when you pout, Harry."

Finally, he clipped, "An immortal never pouts." Then: "Perhaps you should take that charming Sheriff Hood with you."

"Interesting. Not Deputy Dunnachie?"

Harry did not pause. "Sheriff Hood makes himself available to you."

"His Doubty McDoubterson vibe would squelch my psi."

"Give him a good bollocking."

I felt my eyebrows pucker. "Yowza. I don't know what that means, but it sounds real dirty."

"You and Agent Batten are both getting on my wick of late."

"Harry, I don't know what *that* means either!"

"Well, clearly I am to be no help here!" He stood, clearly exasperated. "But you listen here: this time, no quarter given. Is that perfectly understood?"

I had no idea what the hell that meant, but he was getting worked up, so I nodded solemnly. He placed a rare kiss on my forehead. "I still think you should consider bringing Sheriff Hood with you. He's a safe pair of hands, and fit as a butcher's dog."

I thought that sounded about right, though I'd never seen a butcher's dog per se. I doubted Hood would enjoy tagging along with me to see Ruby Valli: retired Gold-Drake & Cross employee, present-day curiosity shop owner, 93 yr old paintball enthusiast and rumoured ex-dabbler in the black arts. If she didn't have books on flesh magic to lend me, I was pretty much out of luck. And if she didn't mind me chatting up her revenant, that'd be great, but then again, if he was powerful enough to be awake all the live-long day, I might be placing myself in a bad way; Gregori Nazaire had a rather lusty reputation. Worse: I heard he digs blondes.

"I'm off to casket, love."

"Without a feeding?"

"You're exhausted. T-minus 25 ..."

I made an affirmative noise and watched him sway elegantly out of the room. I finished my cold coffee, yawned again. My imagination tripped up the stairs to where Batten was still in bed, crept in under the door and slipped under the covers for a peek at his sleeping attire. Damn my creeping imagination. Conveniently, said creeping imagination doesn't like underwear and is under the delusion that hot guys are, as a subspecies, breathtakingly stiff 24/7. I didn't need to close my eyes to picture every masculine curve and hard line of his glorious body. I just needed to access the distracting memories of my quicksilver tongue flickering in heart-pounding, light-headed exploration, my hands eagerly cupping his tight, heavy–

"You alive in there?"

I jerked to crisp attention. "What! No I didn't. When?"

My brain came into focus. Hot-cheeked, I wondered how long Batten had been standing there, watching me glazed-over and dizzy with desire and mentally undressing the living room wall with bedroom eyes. Holy hell, was I drooling into the couch cushion?

"You can't prove anything," I huffed, getting to my feet and wiping cookie crumbs off the front of my shirt. His gaze traced the path of my fingertips across my breasts. I wish it hadn't. My nipples contracted in almost painful need of his attention.

He blinked at me. "I'm sorry?"

"You should be." *For even considering Michigan. And for not going sooner…* "Asshole."

I brushed past him, leaving him in baffled silence.

C40

I drove past the Ten Springs Motor Inn, reluctantly slowing; as luck would have it there was an 18 wheeler behind me, closing in fast on the no-pass two-lane blacktop, a fantastic excuse to return to Grope room 4 later. At least, that's what I told my chicken-livered self as I sped on by. The minute I passed the driveway, the knot in my gut relaxed and I felt a bit lighter. I thought, *do the easy part first*, and head for Ruby's.

I swung into Boulder going precisely the speed limit, clutching the steering wheel with my gloved hands, singing to keep myself awake. Pixie Lott's "Here We Go Again" was on repeat in my CD deck, and my head grooved along with it. Other drivers snickered as I mouthed the words but they didn't know how lucky they were: they didn't have to hear my off-key singing. I didn't have to hear it either; I had the volume up just enough so that I could pretend my voice matched hers.

I cruised a quarter mile past the University of Colorado campus area and eventually found three open parking spaces near the Pearl Street Mall so I'd have room to park the Buick without crunching anyone's wee eco-pod car. The thoroughfare was pedestrian-only, but hoofing-it was not a problem: I had plenty of caffeine humming in my veins now, and my navy Keds on for walking comfort. The street was heavily salted and slip-free. I put Harry's favorite herringbone tweed coat over my black cable-knit sweater, the coat that he wore most often, and nestled my nose into the collar for the smell of his smoke and cologne and his body. It instantly made me think of long evenings by a cheery fire, pressed safe, warm and snug against his well-fed midriff; tension I hadn't known I was carrying eased out of my shoulders. Funny how the smell of him could do that. I took my aqua blue mini Moleskine out of the glove box and wrote this down with a smiley-face after it, then tucked the notebook and worn-down golf pencil in his pocket and pulled my froggy-trimmed gloves back on.

I hesitated about the Beretta, uncertain. Is it bad manners to ask for a favor when you're secretly armed? Probably I'd make a better impression if I didn't mosey on in there with the gun on my hip like a Wild West gunslinger. Leaving it behind has gotten me in trouble before. Then again, bringing it has also not worked out so well. I should have taken it into the Ten Springs Motor Inn to face Danicka. It didn't do dick-all at the funeral home, either, since Jerkface took it away from me. There was a tiny chance that I was a crack shot and could totally handle it if I had to shoot somebody. Then again, there was a huge chance I was a mighty bad shot and would blow a hole in my own kneecap somehow.

Since there wasn't likely to be a stab-happy psychic or a flesh-dripping ghoul in the old lady's friendly, brightly-lit shop, my instinct was to toss it under the passenger seat and lock the Buick's doors. That instinct won out.

I called Batten. When he answered, I said: "Sorry about calling you an asshole."

"Is this your way of telling me you're pinned under a transport truck, about to die?"

"I don't have to be on my deathbed to apologize," I assured him with a sniff. "It's rare, granted, and it's usually followed by me asking for a favor."

He made a gruff noise of acknowledgment. "What do you want?"

You. Naked. Strapped to my bed for about a month.

I opened my mouth and then smartly snapped it shut like a trap. "Could you, pretty please with sugar on top, check in on my brother?"

"I'm looking at him right now."

"He's up? About time. Tell him I'll be back in about an hour and a half, and there's another delivery from Shield coming at around ten thirty ..."

"He's not up," Batten interrupted. "I'm on duty, here."

I caught my breath, tried not to picture young Wesley laying prone and completely at the mercy of my houseguests. I shouldn't have left. God, what was I thinking? I saw Wes too pale and far too thin, his features delicate, dead to the world in Harry's casket, his big ugly ropes of blond hair tangled across Harry's white satin pillow, with Kill-Notch Batten looming over him, threat and menace the hunter's natural aura. Batten out-weighed Wes by a good 50 pounds of rock-solid muscle, not that it mattered; it only took a few pounds of pressure to drive rowan wood between ribs and into the heart muscle of a revenant who wasn't conscious to put up a fight.

My family disliked me as it was; when they found out I'd let Mom's perfect angel get undead then *dead*-dead, they were going to put a price on my head.

"Define duty, as it relates to your daily schedule?" I asked, my voice small and pleading.

"Wow," he said, his voice softly teasing. "That's the first time I've ever heard you sound afraid of me."

Don't get used to it, dipshit, I chewed back, my irritation flaring. I breathed deep and waited until I was sure I wasn't going to lip off. "Where's Harry?"

"They're both at rest, Baranuik," he said. "That's what you guys call it, right? "At rest". Not dead?"

"Uh hunh," I said carefully, though the revenants were dead-*like*, except for what we call VK-delta brain waves, those most like human deep sleep. You could not wake an immortal once he had sunk into VK-delta, even if you had a jackhammer to their chest. It might be a brief state (an hour or two at most between two periods of lighter H-delta or human-delta) but VK-delta was as close to death as one could get without the soul fleeing the body; it was when revenants were most vulnerable.

I swallowed reflexively. "Where might Chapel be?" *You know, your boss, the guy who's supposed to keep your bad ass in check?*

"You might want to pick up some beer on the way home." As if he didn't hear me.

I went with it, feigning casual. "I'll buy Coors Light. You look like you need to cut back on the calories."

"I'm hanging up now," he said with a chuckle. There was no threat in it. I clung to that, trying to imagine I really could trust him.

It wasn't like he hadn't watched Harry before, when I was in the hospital, but Wes was there now and he was new dead. The new dead are not the best at resisting the lure of a hot pulse close by, a warm vein, the regular thud of a human heartbeat or the quickening beat of a frightened heart. Not to mention Wes had a temper that tended to explode after little provocation. What if ...

"Out of curiosity, Batten, where's your kit?'

"I'm hanging up now," he repeated, but made no move to actually do so. This time, his voice was a growl.

"Testy. I'm just asking a question."

"It's upstairs."

I nodded, and realized he couldn't see me over the phone. "Whose idea was it to bring it into the house, yours or Chapel's?"

"Your brother is new dead."

"So, your idea."

"No offense, but the new dead tend to be unreliable."

"I didn't say you were wrong." I couldn't believe I was going to say this. "Maybe your kit should be with you, in Harry's room. Just in case."

There was silence on the other end that stretched so long I thought I'd lost my cell signal. I checked the bars then heard him clear his throat.

"Think so?" His cautious voice, like he didn't know what to expect.

"I'm assuming you've hunted revenants when they're awake? Not just the prone ones? Unless those muscles are just for show." I didn't wait for his reply. "You know they're a hell of a lot faster than humans. If there was a problem, you'd never make it upstairs. Blink and you might find jaws at your throat. The kit stays at your side from now on."

"Gee, Baranuik, if I didn't know better I'd think you cared."

"Get your kit, or go stay in a hotel. I hear they got plenty of space at the Ten Springs Motor Inn lately." Just don't pick room 4.

"Wondered how long it would take you. You wanna sneak around behind Chapel's back like we did in Cheektowaga." It wasn't a question.

"Don't flatter yourself, Kill-Notch," I said, a secret smile blossoming despite my words. "I just don't look forward to the day I have to clean your twice-chewed guts off my nice clean floors."

The sound of his knowing laugh vibrated pleasure down my spine and twitched my quickly-warming nether regions.

"Is that the sweetest thing I'm ever going to hear out of your mouth?" he asked.

I shuffled one toe in the snow, kicked my tires, glanced around at the parking area. *Don't flirt with Jerkface! What are you doing*?

"I've said some relatively flattering things to you in the past," I reminded him. I wasn't sure he'd remember my enthusiastic moaning and breathless praise in Buffalo but it only took him a quicksilver second.

"Between that reminder and the apology, I must be doing something right today," he said, and his voice dropped to husky, almost purring in my ear. Again my nether regions got a jolt. He dared me to tell him, "What is it?"

I bit my bottom lip and took a nervous look over my shoulder, as though Straight-Tie Chapel would be there, frowning disapprovingly and reminding me about fraternization rules, about Michigan, about not being a self-interested cock-tease. *Uh oh.* Shouldn't have thought about Batten's teased cock, which was probably stirring into a delightfully thick gift to womanhood right about now. That tended to end with my logic, self-restraint and intelligence (what little I could proudly claim, anyway) jettisoned from my hard head and into a mixed puddle of brain-brine by my Keds.

How about a radical idea? The truth. For a change. While I could still speak English.

"I like having you there," I admitted, "And I know you've got my back. I trust you. More than ... well, more than almost anyone. I also know you can't stay. But while you're here for me, I don't entirely hate having you."

The silence he showed me then was a cautious one, full of unspoken words. There were a ton of serious talks he and I had avoided; the Danika misunderstanding, the forever-Harry thing, the "how the hell could we work together without strangling or stripping each other" thing. Ignoring it and hoping it would all work out by itself was taking a toll, but when we talked things had a way of blowing up. One of us always took offense. It would help if I could Grope past his wall and see the undeclared truth of what he was feeling, whatever it might be. I closed my eyes and pulled at the ethereal wisp of psi, but as always Batten was a mystery to me, largely unavailable to both my Talents.

"Not entirely being hated by you is a lot better than the alternative," he said finally. The warmth in his voice remained, much to my relief. I was afraid that bringing up his "can't stay" status had damaged our tenuous truce, had put an unspoken stop sign on the rocky road of our non-relationship.

"Don't kill anyone unless you have to, today, yes?" I confirmed.

"Is your gun at home, unloaded, in the safe in your office?"

Next to Dead Kristin's squished eyeball and the stolen sunglass lens, and *not* under the seat of my Buick? "Of course."

"Liar. Batten, out." He hung up on me, knowing the conversation could go no further without it turning sour.

C41

Boulder has a hippie vibe, young and liberal and fresh-spirited. I figured it rubbed off from the couch surfing white-water rafters who lingered all summer long. Harry likened it to Amsterdam, but since I'd never been there, I had to take his word for it. We had scoured Carrie's brochures and dreamed together, planned our upcoming springtime while lingering by our merry winter fires. During the summer months, when the farmer's market was open long into the soft dark evenings, the two of us were going to wander 13th street between Arapahoe and Canyon on a Friday night, browsing, spending money willy-nilly, like we used to do at the Portland Saturday market in Oregon. Or maybe we'd catch an evening performance of Hamlet at the University of Colorado. That was the plan, anyways.

When I got to Curiositatem, I saw that Ruby's premonition had been wrong: the magic shop hadn't burned to the ground. In the large round display window there were wrought iron fairy statues on glass shelves, skulls of coloured crystal serving as candle holders, a wide array of incense and brass burners, and two handwritten signs in clear script. One read: **It is illegal to feed deer and elk in Colorado.** The other was bright yellow with black lettering that said: **mountain lion alert, PLEASE don't feed wildlife**!

Inside, Mrs. Valli's shop was a heady goulash of stereotypes. Curiositatem was once a small niche bookstore called Francine's serving specialty genres, murdered in its youth by the big box stores. She had left behind good bones: light alder wood shelving ran the length of her walls, and a glorious dome ceiling of glass and iron let in the sunlight. An odd place for a DaySitter to work, I thought; her revenant would never feel comfortable under this dome.

In one corner perched more wrought iron garden fairies in various thoughtful poses. In another, bright glass garden gazing orbs reminiscent of mystical crystal balls, and fresh potted herbs to delight the kitchen witches. Glass and cherry wood display cases held kitschy things no modern witch would ever need or use, tucked beside genuine artifacts of such value that my fingers itched to grab my Visa. Mrs. Valli had set up a gemstone station, and somewhere under the soft New Age music humming in the store's speaker system, I could hear the dull rumble of a stone tumbler.

Along the back wall marched an army of books, their titles tantalizing promises. An enormously fat grey and white cat with an orange splotch on her nose hunched in a sunspot above the shelves, her hair and dander filtering through the shafts of light and falling around the cash register. This was where Mrs. Valli sat, barely a snowy-haired head looking over the counter.

"Oh, Marlene!" Her scratchy voice was pleased when she spotted me, and she gave me a grandmotherly smile that made me long for Vi. I didn't correct her on my name.

When the smile touched the corners of her cloudy eyes it caused wonderfully deep lines, happy lines telling of a long life of laughter. She struggled to stand, leaning heavily on a wicker chair that gave a rickety protest. I quickened my pace, thinking to help her. She managed alone, and as I got closer to the counter I could see the little basket where she'd set her pale blue pile of knitting down. The knitting needles were an odd shape, long and off-white like old whale bone.

Ruby toddled around from behind the counter, using the glass-topped structure for support. I wondered why she didn't own a cane, or where her walker was, and just how much Windex she needed to keep this place so sparkly clean, with all its glass, crystal and mirrors. From a rod around the cash area, tiny tinkling crystal wind chimes made an eerie, broken kind of music, setting my teeth on edge. I tried to ignore it.

"I was so hoping you'd drop in, Marlene," she said kindly, smoothing the front of a patchwork skirt. "I'm afraid I was a little rude at the funeral home, dear. You must forgive an old woman for not being herself."

"No one's quite themselves at a funeral," I agreed. Thinking of my slutty outfit, I added: "I know I wasn't."

Ruby was wearing big yellow floral Wellingtons, the rubber scuffed at the toe in black lines. They were otherwise clean as a whistle, and I wondered: why boots instead of shoes or slippers? But then, the floral pattern on them, orange and turquoise flowers, matched the faded hem of her skirt. She brought a pair of thick glasses with bright citrus orange rims up to the bridge of her nose and squinted through them. She was adorable.

Ruby said, "I heard about the ghoul. Everyone has. Honey, you're in over your head, aren't you?"

I laughed, weak with relief. "More than you know."

"Oh dear, oh dear." She stopped abruptly in front of me and craned her chin up, and I was struck by the funny angle; I don't think I'd ever met anyone who had to look *up* at me. She must have only been 5 feet tall. "I'd better make tea, Marlene. There's terrible trouble in your face."

"Trouble with Tribbles."

She brushed past me on her way to the door as though she either didn't hear me, didn't get the Star Trek reference, or didn't think it worthy of a response. "And while it's true that trouble teaches, sometimes the lesson isn't pleasant."

"Yeah, I hate learning," I agreed. "My brain's already full. It hurts to stick more stuff in there."

She stopped, her eyes narrowing behind her lenses. Her face transformed from charming grandmother to scolding teacher.

"Don't do that, dear."

Surprised, I could only wait wordlessly, feeling scolded like a kid.

"Debasing yourself isn't as endearing as you think it is, and your playing dumb frustrates those who know you're more capable than you let on. You're a brilliant young lady with a doctorate to prove it, and friends in high places who respect your opinion and seek out your advice." She waggled a prune-y finger up at me. "Don't dumb yourself down. You're not fooling anyone."

I nodded, embarrassed, as she went to the front door at turtle's speed and flipped the **OPEN** sign to **CLOSED, PLEASE COME AGAIN!** Two steps up into an alcove, there was a reading station with a library table and six chairs. It took her two pulls but she tugged one out and patted it meaningfully, then toddled off behind a curtain on a far wall.

I browsed the book wall for a minute under the watchful gaze of the perching cat, who winked at me in friendly contemplation. I had a feeling if she was a floor cat rather than a gargoyle-on-ledge cat, she'd have been rubbing my legs by now, purring. I pulled out a couple books I'd purchase, knowing I should have come here much sooner. As the warm sun beaming into the center of the store fell heavy on my shoulders, I took a deep breath, smelling sandalwood incense and the crisp mix of familiar herbs in the air: angelica and lemon mint and thyme, and the black licorice scent of fennel.

I let the stress squeeze out of my neck as I clenched and unclenched my shoulders and rolled my head back and forth. For the first time in days I felt safe, optimistic and productive. The mixture of certainties was heady, empowering. I was going to get some solutions, today. No more wondering and head-scratching. No more running. No more crap-shooting random spells that I hoped would help. Ruby Valli would be a powerful ally. Relieved, I went to the alcove and poured myself into a chair.

Calling out the big guns now, bitches, I thought. *Look out, Sherlock.*

The library table was set up with pencils and tiny white squares of paper in oak blocks. The pencils made me think of Batten's soft palate impalement, and made me wonder if he'd ever actually done it. Of course he had, I thought. He's a carnage machine. Then I thought about his inevitable flight out of my life, to blustery Michigan of all places, and the fact that I could do nothing about it. Should do nothing about it. Except maybe one last romp for old time's sake?

Bad idea! my brain scolded.

Best idea we've ever, ever had, my private parts retorted, completing a full-body coup and plotting how I might bring Kill-Notch Batten to again to miraculous surrender, how hot it would be on a scale of one to *oh holy fuck*, while I suffered thigh-trembling, pulse-quickening, breath-stealing, bordering-on-rapture memories of Mark's thickness surging inside me, slippery and eager, his hips pumping furiously, skin slapping mine as he groaned and gasped in my ear. I swallowed hard and shook the memory out of my head; dizzy with lust, I damn near fell out of the chair.

Jeez. Harry was right: I had to get the damn hunter out of my life. The only thing Batten and I had was sexual chemistry, and titillating as it might be, it was still only chemistry.

Mrs. Valli came back with a tray and I realized suddenly that I had one hand squeezed tight between my thighs. I stood abruptly to take the tray from her like a good girl. She relinquished it with an appreciative nod.

"My hands are not what they used to be, I'm afraid."

It occurred to me, as I snuck as sideway glance at her pouring out a spicy-smelling dark tea from a Brown Betty teapot, that she looked every day of her supposed 93 years. DaySitters are always a lot older than they appear, aging in appearance about five years for every ten that actually went by. But Ruby's age had never clued-in for me before seeing her thin, transparent skin in the light streaming like a accusing finger from the overhead dome. Depending on how old she was when she first Bonded to Gregori Nazaire, Ruby could conceivably be into her third or fourth decade after 100. Without looking down at my hands, I scrawled this observation in my mini notebook and then slipped it back in my pocket.

Her knuckles were bent into a crook, but not so much that they seemed swollen with arthritis. Despite her shaking, she insisting on pouring, and on handing me the delicate porcelain cup, which clattered like a terrified hostage against its saucer. Her hair was thinning, coiling in soft white curls around her ears, and I could see her pink scalp through her careful hairdo.

She seemed fragile until you looked into the clear magnitude of her fierce blue eyes. There was strength there that could not be denied, reassuring wisdom and an enviable catalogue of knowledge. It was more than just her precognitive abilities; the subtle unnatural colour of magic was upon her like the sweep of melon-pink blush on a ballerina's high cheekbone. It wasn't something you could put your finger on exactly, but anyone who'd been in the presence of power knew: this woman had it in spades. Whatever influence her elder revenant fed her only added to what she already wielded. Again, I thought, *a potent ally.*

"What fanciful gloves, Marlene." She indicated my frog-embroidered cuffs while gazing at me steadily, like she was waiting for a confession. "A gift from one of your many admirers?"

It was an odd assumption, but sorta true, and I admitted it with a nod while I sipped my tea.

"I've got problems," I started, sipping more tea when she indicated I should. I closed my eyes to savour the strong flavour. It tasted like I'd licked India from the Bay of Bengal clear across to the Arabian Sea. I asked politely: "Chai masala?"

"I mix my own bedtime blend, lots of cloves, very comforting." She set her own cup down on its little chintz saucer. "Tell me everything."

I finished my tea in one gulp and watched as she refilled. "I should start at the beginning. Danika Sherlock—"

Ruby interrupted, "Danielle Smith-Watson is her proper name, isn't it, though? Yes. That stage name of hers is just plain silly."

"Yes!" I agreed. In a rush of relief, I explained what had happened.

"Oh dear, oh dear. Dreadful, what jealousy will do to an unstable mind," she said sadly.

I hurried on, "She put Kristin Davis' eyeballs in my jar of newt bits!"

"How grisly," Ruby agreed, blowing steam carefully across her tea.

"And now you're going to ask why I had newt bits ..."

"Of course not, honey." She sat forward. "You white witches, you don't understand how your 'morals' limit your choices. But does not everything in nature take from everything else? That is the lesson of the Mother. And yet when a witch takes the force of a natural living object, it is considered black magic."

Uh ... "Well, I see your point. But the line is drawn, and it's a clear one."

"Don't argue with me, missy. I had magic mastered when your mother was still shitting her pants. It's a chalk line, meant to be redrawn as circumstances arise."

I blinked at the dark flicker across her face and bit down hard on my tongue. Trying not to imagine my mother shitting her pants, I thought: *Don't argue with the Potent Ally, stupid!*

"Well, thanks." I guess. I sipped my rapidly cooling tea. At the lower temperature, the nutmeg was overpowering and my tongue felt coated. "The spell I used was called the black-watch."

"I see," she said, as though I'd cleared up some mystery. "What else would someone of your mediocre caliber be capable of?"

Mediocre ... So much for "brilliant" Marlene. Biting my tongue was starting to hurt. "I'm not entirely certain how Watson got into my cabin and put the eyes in my jar. Or how she put a head in my mailbox without the cops at my kitchen table noticing. Or how she came in while I was home and stole all my gloves from right under my nose ..."

She interrupted, "If you were more educated in such things, you would know: the gloves should concern you much more than the eyes."

I felt my face go carefully blank. Did Ruby Valli just suggest that stolen gloves trumped punctured human eyeballs from a murdered twelve year old floating in a jar of newt bits?

Ruby was nodding. "A personal object worn so often and so close to the skin can be used in so many ways against you. But of course, she did it all with witch-walking." She pulled one of the books around on the table and licked her fingertip, shifting through the pages until she thudded her forefinger on a spell. Looking at her thick, elderly fingernail drawing across the lines made my skin crawl, though I couldn't have said why.

I scanned it quickly. The spell cheerfully outlined the creation of a grisly object, its upbeat tone not unlike Julia Child outlining the recipe for a delicious honey spice cake. The result was a fetish, and not the kind involving lubed cleavage or toe-suckling.

I read aloud: "The witch will sever the middle finger of her right hand using the knife of her enemy held in her left hand. The witch will scrape clean the bone, and carve the following sigil into the bone with a shard of broken mirror anointed with the scent of her enemy. Throughout the duration between the current moon phase and the first night of the waning moon, the witch will drink only undiluted blood, and consume only skin peeled from her own ..."

I saw stars, shadowy stars against the yellow sunshine-filled backdrop of the gleaming oak table and the off-white paper before me. The table swam up at my face and I jolted, bracing myself. Ruby's soft, old hand landed on my forearm, where she patted me reassuringly. My vision cleared instantly.

"Flesh magic. I though Watson was too crazy for complex magic," I said hopelessly.

"She would have left behind the fetish to cloud your mind, allowing witch-walking, and she'd be wearing your gloves, or other intimate items of clothing. It would only work in the parameters of the spell, the current residence of the one it was attuned to, that is to say you. Once the bitch was inside, the spell would temporarily cloak her from being seen in the house."

Bitch or witch? Freudian slip? One I agreed with, so I didn't correct her.

"Even from my revenant companion?"

"Oh of course," she chuckled, conceit sneaking into her voice. "There are many ways to toy with the mind of an immortal. They aren't the only ones with power."

Ruby used the arms of the chair to slowly inch her way back to her feet in what looked like a painfully stiff progression, then shuffled behind the counter to retrieve a book bound in a strange yellowish leather. I snuck my notebook out again and jotted *glamour*: *witch-walking, middle finger*, *flesh magic* and *bitch* underlined three times.

Ruby's book made an impressive, hefty bang when it hit the library table. Its cover was printed with her personal sigils and signs; a grimoire, her own book of shadows.

"I think the eye in your pocket at the funeral home might have ruined Danielle's plan. Likely, she was prepared to raise the ghoul after the funeral and send it to Shaw's Fist, to your cabin, to retrieve its eyes, to which it would be attuned. You got that eye too close and it prematurely kick-started the whole darn spell."

The look she gave me was almost scathing, and my belly crawled; I suddenly felt like a child who knows she's in trouble but not why. "That's what I thought, too. I guess I screwed up." *Why am I apologizing for ruining a spell aimed at killing me in my sleep?*

"Here. No don't touch." She slapped my fingers away when I reached for the edge of the paper. I withdrew them. "I'll read it to you." Her voice boomed in the airy space, carried up into the glass dome and echoed around us. "*Immunda phasmatis, immunda phasmatis, immunda phasmatis, vindicatum vestri praemium.*"

Okaaaaay. "I don't … erm, speak Latin."

"It's goetic conjuring. "Unclean spirit, claim your prize." The ghoul is then lured with a piece of itself, eats the object, the demon in turn devours the object's soul. The witch releases the demon with thanks and praise."

"Am I the object in that whole mess?" I blinked, my stomach chilling even as my breath whisked away.

"Unfortunately, yes," Ruby said. Under the table, her rubber boots squeaked against each other. "More tea?"

I nodded, letting my eyelids fall shut; they were suddenly quite heavy. "I knew you'd have answers. What can we do?"

"First thing is your safety, honey," she said seriously. "We must put you immediately into psi-stasis so no one can find you, and then you must go, both you and Lord Dreppenstedt, into witness protection."

Now that I had official, expert confirmation of my suspicions, slipping out of town in the dead of night sounded right. I had to send Wes home to Mum and Dad in Canada, at least until we could figure out how to battle a homicidal goetic witch. Then Harry and I would go to his flat in London, or his home in the south of France.

"Psi-stasis," I said softly. "And escape. That's the first step, you're right. It's going to take more than just a cold saltwater bath for this. She's been in my home. Before I go, I have to get her out. I have to break her witch-walking spell so she isn't standing over my shoulder while I'm booking my flight and making arrangements."

"Send it in a circle," Ruby advised calmly. "You're going to need the eyes-of-light spell."

"I'm not familiar with it."

"I am, dear, I am." She made a thoughtful noise. "It requires both wildcrafted goldthread and Mediterranean silphion."

My hopes sank. "Goldthread was harvested to extinction in the 1800s," I groaned. I'd never even heard of the other herb. "Isn't there a more modern version of this spell?"

Ruby smiled gloriously, shaking her head. "You've forgotten where you are, dear?"

I exhaled hard, relieved. "You have some? How could I possibly ...?"

"Marlene, don't be silly," she said, reminding me once again of Grandma Vi's warm, unruffled manner. "You're a rising star, a lovely talented slip of a girl. I couldn't let anything bad happen to you if I could help in any way." Her softly-curled claw of a hand touched my glove, patted it reassuringly. "I have some, but it's in a special humidor in the cellar, and I don't go down the stairs anymore. My Gregori won't be available to help me until dusk, of course. We should start as soon as possible, though."

My brain jotted. *Is his casket down there in the same room as the humidor?* Other than Wesley, who didn't count, I'd actually never met another sane and sociable revenant. My only other revenant sighting was vile Jeremiah Prost. I wondered if Gregori was anything like my Harry.

"I'll fetch it," I offered. "If you trust me near Mr. Nazaire's casket, which you totally can." I couldn't imagine what other treasures she might have stashed away down there, guarded by her ancient companion. Extinct herbs! Maybe she had false unicorn root. My fingers itched inside my gloves; as one form of magic sensed a sympathetic power source, the Blue Sense trembled to life, aching to be released like a cock in a strip joint. I hopped to my feet and went to the door behind the cash desk where she pointed.

"Of course I trust you, dear. I know you're not going to touch him," she assured me. "You get the herbs, I'll look up the spell we need. The humidor is set high in the wall, but there's a step stool there, or there was, last I checked. It's been more than a year since I could manage the stairs." She laughed softly, and behind her thick lenses the laughter in her eyes was jolly and full of something else ... "Getting old is hell."

"Just tell me where the light switch is." My hand slipped along the wall while I tried to see past the third step down. The blackness down there was a solid barrier.

Ruby's chai tea breath was suddenly blowing around my shoulder. She leaned one frail hand against the doorjamb. "Let's get you safely out of the way."

Wait, wha--

Two deceptively strong hands thrust into my lower back. Jerked off balance I plummeted forward, flung headlong down the stairs into the dark.

C42

I tucked around my head as I plunged down the stairs, bracing for impact. The force of elbows hitting the treads jarred my teeth. My knee hit an edge and there was a sickening crunch. I cried out, one yelp, and whapped into the cement floor, my wind knocked out in a silencing huff.

I whirled to a stop as my side hit the corner where the wall took a sudden turn. The not-quite-healed wounds in my belly wailed to attention, their tenderness soaring. Gasping to draw air into lungs that no longer seemed to work, I forced my eyes open to seek out the source of danger.

Ruby jogged agilely down the stairs. *Jogged,* dear God. Her glasses (*a prop,* I saw now) bounced on their cord against her bosom. She snatched my elbow without consideration to injury, claw-like clutch dug into my flesh, finding the joint. Dragging me with no trouble across the coarse floor, her hand an inescapable clamp, enough to pull ragged sound from my throat. Old chipped paint grabbed the fabric of my jeans. My exposed arm raked along cement. My knee throbbed, already swelling. I wriggled to free myself from her pincer-grip. No arthritis there, no sir.

Weakness hit me with a sinking swell, dragging me down even as I fought it.

"Finally," Ruby commented, dropping my arm and planting both hands on her hips, frowning. She consulted her watch. "Eighteen minutes. You drink to much caffeine, your body is accustomed to it."

"Eighteen ...?" I widened my eyes as wide as they could go, but still my vision was slippery and my eyes didn't obey my directions.

I was vaguely aware we were not alone; two blobs of indeterminate construct stood against the wall like silent sentinels, faceless golems, vague muddy shapes waiting with their arms above them in appeal to the sky. In the center of the room, unnaturally-violet candle light bounced off an obsidian mirror. In the circle a woman sat tied to a chair, her long-haired head slumped over chin to chest, a spill of strawberry blonde covering some of her nudity but not enough.

"Dan ..." I slurred with realization. *Danika Sherlock.* I could think it but my mouth wouldn't make the words, my tongue skimmed the words. I tried to bring my eyes up to Ruby's but they only made it as far as the toes of her Wellies. "You ... why ... I don't think so good."

"Never take tea from a stranger, dear," she advised, a tad late.

Fuckanut. "Drug ..."

"I drugged you, yes dear, clearly not enough. You're still running that cunting mouth of yours."

I summoned my strength to spit, "Suck my left—" and promptly got a mouth full of rubber.

Ruby didn't kick like an old lady. My lips crushed against my teeth and pain shot up through my face. I tasted blood instantly.

She pulled me to standing, an amazing feat considering my knees didn't work and I wasn't especially eager to help her. Supporting my whole weight, she moved without effort toward the odd purple light. That was bad, my woozy brain reported. No good can come of purple light, unless you're at a rock concert. I tried to resist and found my sagging limbs useless. Forced into a pile on the floor next to an ominous iron ring, I slid onto my belly as she started humming. Ruby produced lengths of thick rope from a nearby dust-covered bushel barrel, knocking loose several mismatched leather gloves that looked vaguely familiar: pink, tan with fur on the cuff, blood red. Blurrily I stared at them, trying to make a connection through a melty haze. *Mine.*

My head fell to one side and my eyes rolled down to crawl over the floor with growing panic. On the cement beneath me, black chalk was barely visible against the dark grey paint: intricate stars, different than Wiccan pentagrams, curved inward as though stricken with disease, anorexic. Starving, emaciated symbols, each star covered with tiny writing in a foreign tongue and curling sigils, like the ones I'd seen desecrating my office.

If I could keep my head from swimming, I was sure I could figure something out. OK, so I got tricked and beat up by a little old lady. Who hasn't? That's no reason to cry. But I *was* crying. As she tightened rope around my ankle, my shoulders shook and my nose leaked. She jerked my arms behind me and bound them together and I could do nothing to stop her.

Ruby pulled a big wooden stand with a triangular shelf into the center of the circle, where her obsidian mirror tilted to catch the flickering light of two candles, their deviant colour a cross between French lilac and February crocus. They made me think of my brother's new eyes, his revenant eyes, and my thoughts bounced to Harry (*I should have brought Hood after all, Harry*) and then to their babysitter, that hottie with the stakes (*I should know that guy's name, cuz I think I fucked him a couple times*) and finally to Danika. Her right hand was missing the middle finger, the stump red and smooth, cauterized and covered in what might have been melted wax. It must have hurt. How I wished I could enjoy that sight, but I found myself feeling sorry for her.

A heavy, sulfurous odor belched from the wicks of Ruby's candles, and the light that curled out around them turned sickly luminous grape-jelly neon. There was something terribly wrong with it, but my grey cells were too sluggish to put it together until she began her incantation, her voice low and sonorous.

"Come, ethereal incarnate. Come, enigma solved, He who must answer all. Come presently in form daemonic, specific to thy summoning."

The light flared under her command, and Danika stirred, her filthy mud-streaked hair swaying like a strawberry-blonde curtain.

"Come, demon, known as Beroth of Sanchoniaton, Berith of the Sichemites. Come, face the tetragramaton, Great and Terrible Duke Bolfri of the Grave, thy desires to be fed. Come, Seer of the Past, Present and Future. I command thy otherworldly presence."

When Danika let out a billowing, choking cough of desperate refusal, the hairs on my arms stood straight up. Her head whipped from side to side, gagging, trying to deny entrance. Ruby's voice climbed, deep and filling the room.

"Speak without guile, demon, in my mother tongue, of things infernal, and do tremble here before this circle, here visibly, here affably in the manifest that I desire!"

An invisible finger of warmth slithered along my jaw line then, the heat intensifying until it was hot enough to leave a singe-mark on my skin. Queasy with dread, I used my shoulder against the floor to worm backwards, my rubber legs ignoring commands. Blood-tinged fluid appeared near my chest in a round shape that had no obvious source. Another pool of it formed nearby out of nothing, puddled around unseen footsteps, phantom cloven hooves. I braced myself for whatever might be about to pounce from the shadow between this world and the nether, or the depths of the Eversea, as a low vibration began under the floor, shuddering the very cement.

Danika's spine jerked rigidly, the legs of the chair teetering back then falling to right with a clunk. She wriggled upright like a serpent worked her spine, except her head which hung low.

"I will be fed," Danika's mouth rasped within the waterfall of her hair. It was not her voice. It was not *anyone's* voice. It was the scratch of evil in the room, something between a canine's injured howl and the low reverberation of an angry cat, a disembodied voice from the hollow of her throat that raised my hackles in a quilling rush.

"In time," Ruby promised lightly. She turned to face me. I was sure I'd see an unbalanced and disheveled face now, but Ruby was still calm, cool and definitely collected. Somehow that was worse, much worse. She informed me, "Today is your lucky day, Marlene."

I've been called many things. I wasn't going to stand for Marlene. "Name … *Marnie* …you stupid bitch," I managed.

Ruby's foot flew again and I saw it coming but what could I do? Tied to the iron ring at her mercy, I took it square in the face. Pain ribboned across my cheekbones in both directions from my nose and I tasted blood anew.

I snorted outward, trying to clear the blood from my nostrils. "What did we …ever do?"

"Prancing around in the limelight, for one, like fucking whores. Camera whores. Fame whores. Power whores. But you're a flash in the pan, aren't you? You've proven you can't do anything right."

I hocked from deep in my throat and spat blood-tinged phlegm at her.

She looked at it, on the hem of her skirt. "You'll never amount to anything."

"If you believed that … " I said with effort, "You'd let us fail." I wrinkled my face to see if my nose was broken and the pain was so intense I thought I might vomit.

"You waste precious resources and you're too much of a risk. If I can profit from taking those resources and dealing with the risk, why shouldn't I? Everyone wins."

My drug-addled brain stored that away for later, since it made no sense in my present state.

"You drove Danika mad … tried to get her to kill me." I had a light bulb moment. Danika's *That is the promise* comment. "You promised … if she brought Harry, you'd help her Bond to him. She'd get a new companion to fill …hole in her psyche."

Ruby shrugged. "All I had to do was tell her that you and your little boy-toy Mark Batten killed George Cuthbert, and show her how she could have vengeance. She was practically frothing at the mouth to have her vengeance."

"I had nothing to do with–" I cried, but then it struck me so hard my throat clammed tight. Batten knew Ruby, said he had worked with her. In the past, he'd been a vampire hunter, a well-paid, freelance hunter. "You paid Mark Batten and his crew to kill George Cuthbert."

Ruby hissed a laugh; it sounded like a disturbed nest of snakes.

"I will untie you, demon," Ruby said, touching the back of Danika's bent head. Danika's chin rose, though her eyes remained shut. "And Danielle will have her vengeance in the circle. Does she hear me, demon?"

"She hears her mother-mistress," the demon confirmed with Danika's mouth, with his own garbled voice.

Ruby grinned, her eyes flashing. "You will tear Marnie Baranuik limb from limb, Danielle. Now, while you live, or after your death, you shall not rest until your deed is done."

Tear? Limbs? My head cleared in a sobering rush, panic driving adrenalin past the drugs and into my veins for fight-or-flight.

"Her name's not Danielle," I shouted, and Danika blinked her eyes open, surprised, confused. "Her name is Danika Sherlock and she's the gorgeous, famous TV star who replaced your sagging ass!"

"It's no use, fool, her mind has long been my play thing," Ruby laughed at me.

"What are you, a James Bond villain?" I said. "The least-hot Bond girl ever? Pussy NoMore?"

"Bond," Danika said, baffled by the words coming out of her mouth. "James Bond. Shaken, not stirred."

Though delirious, it was Danika's soft purring mid-West accent now, pushing through the influence of the inhuman visitor within her, enough to get me excited.

"Danika, listen to me," I said, forcing my tongue to work properly. Whatever drug Ruby had put in my tea had my limbs lead-heavy and the rest of my body ache with the need to sleep, but my mouth was back to songbird-clarity. "Ruby Valli paid Batten to kill your companion, to kill George. Just like she gave another hunter *my* address to come and smoke Harry out. Didn't you, Ruby? Who was he? Some local hooligan?"

Danika's head came around at me and a thin keening fissured out of her throat. Wrenched free of the demon's control, she wailed: "George! *Geeeoooorge!*"

Ruby folded her arms and smiled at me. Her apple-pink cheeks were round and soft and lifted smile lines into the creases of her eyes. "What makes you think Mark Batten isn't still on my payroll?"

I tried to ignore that, because it didn't help me right now, but my heart couldn't un-hear it. It hammered sick and hard under my ribs, leapt with terror, contracting in a dread-squeeze. *He's with my Harry,* it said. *Notice, he's always with Harry, lately.*

Focusing on Danika, I struggled to keep her attention.

"It was Ruby's plan all along, Danika. She's been using you to keep her own hands clean, just like she used Batten, and who knows how many others? She uses everyone. Now she wants to use you to kill me, and for what? Do you think she's just going to hand over Harry to you?" I raised my voice to be heard over Danika's broken-hearted clamor. "Don't let her win. You're just another sacrifice for her altar. There's no new companion for you, Danika, only death. It's Ruby's fault George is dead."

Danika moaned, "George," as though her motor was grinding down.

"Danika, she'll break the promise. She already has!"

Danika's moaning ended abruptly. Her chin fell even and her eyes bored into mine. For a fierce second, sanity and understanding blazed in her aspect; she poured fully back into herself, mentally filling her psyche with clarity and realization. Though it was an invisible change, I could tell the instant that Danika Sherlock thrust the demon completely from her exhausted body, and summoned her will for vengeance.

So could the demon's conjurer. Ruby lunged forward behind her. For a second, it must have showed in my face, because Danika's eyes flew wide. She screamed: "Mom, don't! *Moooommeeee!*"

The jagged point of a knife tore the front of Danika's delicate throat, sending a foaming jet of blood splattering across my face, lashing the revenants on the wall. It was over in a heartbeat.

Something behind me, barely alive, drew a shuddering groan as it stirred.

C43

I had been abandoned.

The odd purple candle light was fading in the mirror as the wax sank to nubs. Somewhere Harry was likely waking, stretching his sleep-stiffened body languorously like a cat in silk on his big four-poster bed, lighting a cigarette. Maybe Wes would be rousing in Harry's casket. My Cold Company would soon be asking Chapel and Batten where his DaySitter was. He and Batten would waste precious time they didn't know *I* didn't have, trading barbs and hassling each other, while Chapel realized I'd been gone too long and was not answering my cell phone. Probably my phone was ringing right this second in the Buick out front, filling the hot car with the Inspector Gadget theme song. The Buick. Where my gun was. Again, I had not known when to use it or how. And I was going to die in the middle of the day, surrounded by the sour stench of blood, death and bodily fluids.

I considered my options: A) Be a human sacrifice or B) … ok, there wasn't a B. Was there?

What would it feel like to be ripped limb-from-limb, I wondered? Was Danika really going to rise from the dead to complete the deed? I'd already seen one ghoul.

Her own daughter. More than just random jealousy; hating the very girl you created. So much for motherly nurturing. I knew all about being rejected by your mother, but my mom never used me as a demon's sock puppet. I hadn't seen a familial resemblance before, but I hadn't been looking.

As the drugs fully receded from my dulled mind, I was able to taste fear; it did not taste good. I figured it was only a matter of time before Ruby had some other living host body for her demon to enter. Or maybe that was my new purpose, here. What did that feel like? Or maybe she was just going to torture me. *Just*. How long would she hurt me, and with what implements?

I lifted my cheek off the floor and found it sticky. As my eyes adjusted fully to the lightless room I could see shelves of tools, mostly woodworking tools: vices, files, rip saws, carving knives and gouges, chisels. They didn't look dusty or unused, which bothered me, because I wanted to believe they had been there from the last owner of the shop. What I really didn't want to know was what Ruby needed the planes for, but my brain still hates me, and it tripped along several flesh-removing options.

My eyes fell to the circle. Summoning a demon didn't sound all that difficult. You called it by name and title, kissed its ass a bit, and it came. Of course, I'd only just seen my first live ritual. And what demon would wanna help me? I didn't know any demon names, did I?

The spit on my tongue stung with a sudden excruciating sweet heat, that tart cinnamon candy heat. *The Overlord?* He was a demon king. He had better things to attend to than ... well, hell, I was a servant of one of his revenants. He should be on my side, right? I could give it a shot. What did I have to lose, here? Except blood, sanity and lots of flesh, if Ruby grabbed the plane off the shelf.

"Hear me, Asmodeus," I said real low. "Prince of Lust, Father of the Line Immortal, King of the Old Believers. Faithful ... uh, backer-upper of ... yeah, no, that's not going to work. The faithful servant of your creation calls you to—*ow!*"

My left nipple twisted suddenly with such an unbearable intensity that hot pain shot down the nerves deep in my chest to tangle around my heart. An invisible force tweaked it again with joyous, sadistic fingers. I cringed and, with my arms tied behind me, could do nothing to rub away the feeling. "I am the faithful servant of—*ow!* Motherfucker!" Both nipples twisted in unison, pinching hard. "OK, *sorry!* I was going to invite you out to play, but forget it."

So, no Overlord. Asmodeus, the prurient father of the vampire lineage, was playing purple-nurple with my girly parts like a tipsy adolescent and would be no help. My options at this point were limited.

My eyes crept to the revenants chained to the wall. The young dark-haired one was Patrick Laurier Nazaire; I knew this immediately. He had owned the sunglasses before Danika tried to force the Bond on him. Patrick was, at this point, uselessly insane. Starvation-weakened arms bound across his chest as if he was already in a straight jacket, he licked the chains that rested across his shoulder, looking through me. If he were ever freed, he'd leave a swath of slaughtered bodies in his wake, until the day someone like Batten did the nation a rowan wood favor. That thought made me wonder if Ruby was bluffing about Batten being on her payroll, but the idea made my gut churn, and to keep from *yurk*ing-up I had to consider something else and quick.

That left Ruby's immortal companion, Gregori Nazaire: a blond giant of a man, well over six foot seven, probably very distinguished at full health, looking like someone's frightfully realistic but under-stuffed Halloween prop chained to the wall, clothes hanging off his frame. Jeans and a white button-down dress shirt covered in months worth of filth. 1400 year old poets wear Levis? Who knew?

Why had Ruby chained up her own revenant? Had he tried to stop her from doing the rotten crap she'd been up to? If so, that indicated he wasn't completely evil. Maybe he was trustworthy. Maybe he could help me. Maybe we could help each other. Or, maybe Harry was right and I was utterly naïve.

"Mister Nazaire?" I breathed, experimentally. The sound of his name coming out of my own throat made my legs go numb and I suddenly needed to pee real bad. It would serve Ruby right if I whizzed on her chalk circle. That is, after all, the best-known folk cure for beating demons: pee your pants and run like hell.

"Mister Nazaire?"

The revenant did not respond.

I used the grippy toes of my Keds to push myself closer, my feet tingling as though asleep. The rubber soles scraped loudly in the echoing room, smudging chalk writings. I glanced behind me then pushed again, until the rope dug in around my ankle. An inch closer. Again. Closer.

I left the candlelit spot in front of the mirror behind, and *scrape-shuffle-snaked* my way into the cool dark by the back wall. My thighs quivered like Jell-o inside my pants, and sweat greased the skin under my bra's underwire.

I could smell him now, faintly, like a skeleton nearly desiccated, weeks-old carrion cooked to dry bones, ligaments cracking in the summer sun. I wished I didn't know what that smelled like. Other people didn't have to know. Then again, it was a slight improvement on the smell of blood and loose bowels in a clod under Danika's chair.

Up close, Gregori Nazaire hardly looked real. His flesh was a horror of shrunken musculature, paper-thin skin, blue veins roping emptily and visibly beneath. A belt held up his jeans; new holes had been punched in it to tighten it enough to keep his pants up. I wondered how many times Ruby had broke in a new belt hole and adjusted his pants around his dwindling waistline. His chest, sunken within his white button-down dress shirt, didn't rise or fall.

But I knew he was not gone: underneath that light cooked skeleton smell was the sharp familiar tainted sweetness of burnt sugar.

"Gregori?" I whispered. No movement, no hint that he'd heard me. The smell of the chains against his skin was like a sweaty, oiled coin. They'd blistered his skin, not a lot but enough to tell me there was significant silver content in the iron. The only way you'd be able to keep a revenant of his age chained to a wall, even with silver, is if he'd been starved for quite some time before you put him here. She must have locked him in his casket for years, blocked his escape with crosses. Starved him into submission.

Who knows how long he'd been tormented? If I got any closer and he woke up slavering and insane, I'd be within reach. It would be pretty stupid to look for help from a starving revenant you've never met, and end up with your face chewed off. What would Harry say? He'd have "Served her right" carved on my tombstone so generations could see a dumbass mistake cost me my life.

Before I got any closer, I had to know whether or not Gregori Nazaire remembered who he was, if his faculties were intact, if we would be able to help one another, if there was a chance I was only trading death-by-torture for death-by-draining.

"Monsieur Nazaire?" I tried with my clumsy French accent. "Master Nazaire?"

Nothing. I took a deep breath and struggled to my knees to lean up closer, as much as the ropes allowed, prepared to thrust myself back into the safety of my bonds if he lunged at me.

Danika Sherlock's blood had splattered the bridge of his nose but hadn't awoken him like it had the other revenant. Patrick watched everything and nothing with glowing green eyes that showed no sign of sanity whatsoever. Gone deep into lich-form, his tongue worked madly, scenting in the air like a snake on crack cocaine.

Probably better to take my chances with ole G'Naz, here. And I shouldn't try street nicknames for him, either; I'm not cool enough to pull it off, and he probably wouldn't like it. What if I quoted some of his stolen poetry? What was that line I'd read this morning?

"*Taken down and worked dry,*
the fairest maiden left fairer
still by aching heart and straining yard …"

My throat closed over the words, nausea rolling in my belly. Nope, no revenant erotica, no romance for the dying or the dead. *Ick, blerg* and *blech*. I tried a more formal route, cleared my throat and whispered solemnly:

"Death Rejoices, glorious Elder."

The revenant's eyelids fluttered, but did not open.

I said it again, my voice soft with respect. "Death Rejoices, cherished master of the grave, keeper of the gift of immortality."

Nazaire's neck seemed not strong enough to bring his head up, but his eyes did open and they slinked sideways in my direction. The irises were pure airy platinum, shining with calculating intelligence, yet guarded. Wary.

His bloodless, parched lips parted.

"Hail, honoured DaySitter. Centuries untold celebrate your gift of submission," he said formally in return.

His voice, though dry and weak, hinted at rich sumptuousness. I thought at full power it might be sonorous, a voice for singing opera, or belting your point across a courtroom. Not a voice for a skeletal dead guy in jeans. A voice for a three-piece power suit guy. I smiled up at him, reassured by the steadiness in his voice. He knew who he was, and what I was. This was a good start, a promising start.

"Death Rejoices, Master Nazaire," I responded one last time. "Do you know who I am?"

His nearly transparent eyelids fell closed again, lashes casting shadows on pale flesh. Maybe it was an effort to keep the lids up.

"My name is Marnie Baranuik. I worked with Ruby at Gold-Drake & Cross before she retired."

"Fired," he said.

"She was fired." I felt my eyebrows soar. "Because there were younger psychics coming in to take her place."

Nazaire's head shook. "Kidnapping."

My brain scrambled. "They fired her because they found out she was kidnapping other psychics' revenants?" He nodded. "Like who? Patrick Laurier?" Another exhausted nod. "To what end?"

"Power ... must make sure her *dhaugir* is dead. I hear ..." His chin came up again, but he was to worn down and dried out to manage it for long. "Many hearts. Many hearts beating ...the *dhaugir* ..."

My brain scrambled for a definition, but the drugs interfered. The word *dhaugir* was very familiar, and I knew he meant Danika: *dhaugir,* a DaySitter's human mystic whipping boy, taking her pain, doing her dirty work.

"Ruby was feeding captive revenants to forcibly inherit their different psychic powers?" A nod. "And where she couldn't, she had vamp hunters go in and stake them?" He nodded again. "Like George Cuthbert? Danika refused to give him to her mother, at first. So Ruby had George killed." Nodding. I was right: Ruby was never going to give Harry to Danika. "She used her daughter to do the dirty work, as her bondservant. Her *dhaugir*, the one who takes pain."

Nazaire's lips twitched into a sorrowful quarter-smile. "My pain will not affect Ruby as long as the *dhaugir* is alive."

She can't be alive, I thought. *A dagger in the throat? She's gotta be dead.* Still, part of me wondered, with all the black magic in this room, and that small secret terrified part forced me to crane over at the body. "If I get out and find Danika still alive, I have to call an ambulance," I thought aloud. "I can't finish the murder. I will not kill a human being. Not Danika, not even Ruby. It would taint my soul forever, do you understand that?"

Nazaire didn't answer, but I thought he looked disgusted with me.

"How long has she been betraying you with other revenants, master Nazaire?"

His eyes squeezed shut with agony and words would not come. I was sorry I asked. I couldn't imagine how it would hurt Harry to watch me parade before him an endless line of revenants, to try and Bond them to me by force, psychically raping their kind before the watchful gaze of the one immortal I had sworn to obey, and to discard them in trash bags like common stove ash when I failed.

"None of that matters, now," I said. "I'm here. I'm going to get you out of here. We're going to help each other."

A tear escaped his left eye, clear and very human. It trailed down the monstrosity of his face, the weathered caverns of his cheeks. I'd never seen a revenant cry before, hadn't in all honesty thought it was possible. I took it as another good sign, though. Encouraged, I scraped forward another two inches until I was kneeling directly beneath him. At this angle I could have serviced him with a fine blow job. Horrified that my mind had even gone there, I diverted my eyes directly up to his face.

"Honoured elder," I said with soft respect. "If I feed you, will you be strong enough to escape your bonds?"

His eyes flew open with undisguised hope, and he rasped, "Yes."

I clarified: "And you'll get me outta here when you're free, right?"

"I vow to do all I can for you, DaySitter, for all time."

The words hit me in the gut like a fist hitting a drum; I had a feeling that was a bad thing, but pushed worry aside in favour of the fierce hope in his face, stirring my own into action. He licked his lips quickly, and between them I could see the elongated, yellowing fangs of a creature who had been around far too long for Crest White Strips to do him any good. They weren't nasty like stained human teeth can get; they gave the impression of ivory tusks, or the curved natural canines of the big cats, having taken on the dull tone of decades of hunting and feeding. If ever in my life I'd considered a safari in Kenya, the sight of Gregori Nazaire's fangs nixed that plan. I was gonna get the shakes next time I went to the damn zoo.

I considered my newest problem: in his high chains, Nazaire had some leeway but couldn't bend down far enough to reach my neck, and I couldn't stand, nor get closer or higher. The best he could do was lick Danika Sherlock's blood spatter off my face, which he eagerly did with stale breath and trembling tongue while I cringed (*Taken down and worked dry, the fairest maiden left fairer still by aching heart and straining yard ...*) and set my jaw hard so as not to scream. It wasn't going to be nearly enough, like giving Bill Cosby the stir spoon from the pudding but keeping the pot at arm's length, only a lot less funny.

His mouth moved over my cheekbones, seeking, on the hunt with a terrible thirst, his frantic hunger an animalistic huffing in the back of his throat, and again I was struck by the image of a lion in the wild, King of the Jungle. Mammoth fangs, three times bigger than Harry's, brushed my skin but did not pierce without express permission; they sent needle-prickling along raised goose bumps wherever they traced, like the cold wash of fever chills.

"Don't worry, master Nazaire, I'm going to feed you just as soon as I can figure how." *This is as dumb as trying to call Asmodeus but here goes ...*I bit my tongue hard. Hard enough to draw blood. I tilted my face up to him, mouth open, and prayed. "I'm trusting you."

Gregori Nazaire took my offered mouth swiftly, hard and furious, sucking with his dry lips until my hesitant mouth was vacuum-sealed to his. Massive fangs sank in, expertly questing into the soft flesh, first finding purchase in my gums. While those shallow marks bled profusely, dousing his thirsting mouth, he finally pinned me in place by claiming more satisfying, meaty property in the back of my tongue.

I tried to hold still so he wouldn't rip the damn thing out of my head, and rolled my eyes far away, focused on the jet-dark corner of the room; I didn't want to watch the way the fresh infusion of life would change him from shrunken monster to vibrant being, what was swelling and where, and how his eyes flamed with orgasmic victory so close to my own darting orbs. With the exception of sex partners and the eye doctor, no one should get this close to your face. Ever.

In a thudding, tumbling suddenness, there were sounds above us: cracking, breaking, shattering, loud voices and scrambling boots, banging doors. I could no more move than I could say anything other than *urk!* Nazaire, tucked deep into his own personal feast, was oblivious, desperately suckling my tongue. The moment I started getting dizzy, I felt something even more alarming: Nazaire's own tongue playing sensually along my bottom lip, sliding into my mouth. Despite my horror, my body responded with a helpless zing of arousal; he felt it with a myriad of revenant instincts and, encouraged, he moaned into my mouth.

I heard the basement door forced open and a rush of louder noise and thought: *saved by the bang*. Any longer, and the revenant sucking my willing tongue might get the wrong idea about us. I would have tapped his shoulder if I could get a hand free, or belly-nudge his toes if I could reach, but roped like a prized calf I could only squirm, helpless as he moved from tongue to bottom lip, hoping he couldn't drain me completely from my face. I felt his fangs break through my lip to the other side and cried out an objection into his mouth, though it strangely didn't hurt.

"Hold your fire!" Batten ordered behind me. "Hold your fire! Marnie?"

Nazaire's fang-clinch broke; with a disturbed, impatient growl, he let me up for air.

"I'm OK!" I gasped, craning my head. Now my bottom lip gash hurt, as Nazaire's soft, possibly unintentional mind control waned. "Don't shoot!" My tongue felt like a slab of liver, flapping and wounded in my mouth. "Danika's dead. Both revenants need help, get them out of here! Where's Ruby? Find *Ruby!*"

That was when Harry snaked down between Batten and Hood and two cops I didn't recognize. Harry diagnosed the blood on mine and on Gregori's lips, the older revenant's extended fangs and flushed cheeks; Harry's face mottled with fury, his eyes glittering with betrayal.

Harry boomed, "What transpires here?" still coming, fists clenched and shaking.

Uh oh.

Nazaire answered the challenge with a testing, swooping roar of his own; human shoulders all around hunched in unison like synchronized swimmers dunking, their heads sinking as if being dive-bombed by a hungry dragon.

Chains popped open with a *clang*-clatter as a new-fed Nazaire flexed, flinging shattered silvered-iron bits across the cement floor. Filled with power for the first time in who knows how long, he released it around him, inundating the room with radiant supremacy. At 1400 years old, he was the greater power; fed and flushed his potency thrummed through the air as a nearly visible wave, crackled just under the skin and vibrating in the bones like a cranked subwoofer. Something new inside me answered his call, ripped up my body in reply; for a split second, Harry looked like the villain. I crammed my eyes shut and yanked my brain back under control.

Nazaire bellowed, "The bleeder is mine!"

Wonka-wha? My head whipped around. "Wait! Since when?"

Nazaire towered above me, where I fell back on my heels and wrestled with the ropes in futility; he aimed his ice-shard glare full-blast at the competition, ignoring the humans as inconsequential. Taking one lumbering step in Harry's direction he threw back his shoulders, taking up lots of space. There was no question who the dominant creature was, but Harry, undaunted, drew himself up to full height, bristling in response.

"She calls me master and offers the chalice of her blood to my lips," Nazaire declared. "She lays the collar of her Bond at my feet. And I accept."

I yelped, tugging madly at my wrists, cursing whatever schmuck invented rope. "There was no chalice! There was no collar!"

I smelled sulfur and above in the store there was a human scream followed by the pop of three gunshots in rapid succession.

Harry's lips pulled back from full fangs and he launched through the air, snarling. Nazaire's jaw dislocated like a snake and dropped open wide, revealing a second set of fangs below the first. I had to do a double-take, thrust my head forward and blinked to make sure I was seeing right. *Holy hell!* That unearthly monster face was at my mouth? His inhuman roar caused a second bout of quicksilver human flinching and the cocking of useless guns.

Batten hesitated only a second before using the commotion as cover. His big tactical folding knife sawed through the knots binding me to the iron ring, then slashed free my arms. I tried to stand and toppled forward. He caught me easily, propped me up with one of my arms over his shoulder.

"Get out," he ordered the cops behind him. "Out now. *Go, go.*"

Nazaire's head jerked around. He slammed Harry into a wall as though he could sink him into the very stone, then turned on us, hissing.

I clutched at Batten and shrieked, "Stake!"

Batten dropped me, whipping his hand into his ankle sheath. Nazaire was too fast, slamming into Batten and slamming him to the ground. Batten had his knee up, using it as leverage to haul the revenant up and over his body, but Nazaire pulled him along, and during the roll, neatly maneuvered Batten back under him. Nazaire reared to strike, and with cobra-like swiftness, lashed out. There was a shocked cry that I assumed came from Batten, until Nazaire's face came away with a shriek, smoke rising from his lips; Batten's holy water cologne, applied liberally, had done its job.

I whipped around and plunged my hand into Hood's jacket pocket to grab his wooden stake, turned and chucked it at Batten as he vaulted up from the floor. Nazaire recovered and flew at him, arms spreading open in the air. Time decelerated, and I saw with clarity the stake slide into Mark's hand then plunge precisely up between Gregori's ribs and into his heart. A perfect shot. A masterful shot. Kill-Notch's 106th mark made. I waited for the *poof.*

The force of the revenant's impact knocked Batten to the floor, but Mark rolled easily backward to his feet in one practiced move. There shouldn't have been an impact. Nazaire should have exploded instantly in a cloud of dust. The elder revenant pounded cement and instantly rebounded to his feet again, puppet-like, wrenched up by otherworldly strings. His eyes flashed victoriously.

"It is not sorb apple, presumptuous human," he hissed. "You reach too far, hunter. It shall profit you nothing, save it be a speedy demise. Now, remove thyself from my prize!"

Sorb apple. Rowan. "Mark, evacuate now! Harry? Harry, wake up!" I shouted, and swung around to face-off with Nazaire, making fists. Harry was shaking his head to clear it, struggling to his feet. He needed a minute, and I had to give it to him.

"That's it, tough guy. I'm done with your crap. For one, don't hit my Harry. He's prettier than you are, and I don't want his nose out of joint. And another thing, "*aching heart and straining yard*" Really? That's your idea of romantic poetry? Fuckin' gross."

"Marnie!" Batten barked, incredulous.

I ignored him. "See this? This fist might be small, but I can do bad things with it. Bend over, I'll show you."

Nazaire's chin jerked back like I'd slapped him. Maybe it was my impudence that lit within his eyes the need to dominate. I recognized this look: Harry's surprise at my casual cheek. And where it usually caused in Harry a brand of doting exasperation, in Nazaire it illuminated a dread need to squash me.

"Arrogant wretch!" Nazaire spat.

"Bring it, Batface," I encouraged, eyeballing Harry's progress over his shoulder. "Let's see you shake that thang."

I braced for it, starting a slow deep haul on Harry's power, funneling tendrils of it, pulling it in. There was a flurry of activity behind me on the stairs as cops, most of whom had never seen a revenant, never mind a pair at one another's throat, retreated at Batten's command. With any luck, I'd last more than a few minutes fighting at Harry's side, allowing the humans to evacuate.

Harry came at him again from behind, his fist hammering the back of Nazaire's elbow. It snapped unnaturally forward with an appalling crack, the bone shard tearing through his shirt. The older revenant swung, spinning mid-air in a motion that defied gravity.

When Nazaire made his move at me, pushing forward through the air in an audible rush, I was ready for him. I launched into him, throwing my shoulder low.

It was like getting hit by a Mack truck. Something *slam-crunch*ed and I hoped it was just a cookie breaking in my pocket, not a rib. The revenant shed me like I weighed nothing, tossing me into the crevice where floor met wall. When he lifted his face to snarl at the humans, the last cop to remain on the stairs panicked and unloaded a clip at his center of mass. Nazaire blinked down at the painful but harmless blossoms standing pale blue like ink where his heart was limply struggling to push my blood through his awakening veins. A burbling fountain of revenant nectar leaked there, harmlessly.

Harry pointed furiously hard at Batten with an unspoken command. The FBI agent gave an accepting nod, grabbed me out of my sprawling mess of limbs on the floor by the seat of my pants, hauling me to my feet at a run. I stumbled with Batten attached at my hip up the stairs. My feet felt like big sloppy seal flippers, and I nearly fell twice.

"Get off me, you big stupid ogre."

"Get the fuck up those stairs," he hollered, but hesitated. Concern for Harry? That I understood, but not coming from him. "*Go*."

"What's that, smoke?" I said, lifting my face.

One of the cops shouted down at us: "Owner set her furnace room on fire then vanished. Get out, get out!"

I shrieked over my shoulder: "Harry! *CODE 6!"*

Batten had his big shoulder wedged under my armpit before I knew what he was doing. It made for awkward running. Noises behind us. I dug my hand into Batten's bicep and whirled him behind the cash counter where Ruby had stashed her knitting. We went down in a body-pile. *Weapons.* I eyed the knitting needles when my eyes fell on a huge automatic gun with weird, lumpy attachments. I scrambled over Batten's angry, wrestling form and grabbed for it, whirled around and aimed it at the banging boot-steps. Chapel.

"Out, out," Chapel commanded.

Batten grabbed my shirt and it tore in his fist. He hustled me back to my feet and yelled, "What the fuck are you thinking, *gogogo."*

I shouted, "The book! I need her book!" and broke away from him, my knees like rubber but desperation steeling my spine.

Batten cried: "*MJ for fuck's sake!*"

I grabbed the grimoire in one hand, the gun in the other. The book's cover was disgusting to the touch, squirmy almost, seemingly alive under my fingertips, and I nearly dropped it, held it out ahead of me with a grimace.

Someone screamed: "*OIL TA*—" as an explosion rocked the back room. Flames belched into the store and the blast made a gigantic splinter in the dome overhead. A split second of ominous silence filled with our furtive scrambling for the door. Every hair on my head prickled with dreadful understanding. The dome shattered, and deafening shards of broken glass rained down on our heads.

I shoved the book over my head and ran like hell.

C44

The ride home was done in that total wordless silence that followed any major disaster. The local pop station played songs that none of us actually heard. Talk radio would have been more useful, because at least then somebody would be having a conversation. The windshield wipers ticked and patted rhythmically back and forth, making mechanical music while headlights tunneled through a light snow, washing out everything to a jittery black and white picture show.

Ruby had disappeared during the explosion, literally disappeared, in front of several sets of mundane human eyes that would never see the world the same way again. Gregori Nazaire and Harry shared the sudden instinctual need to flee upon my bawling "*Code 6*" followed by the warning stench of smoke. My revenant had followed the elder into a room filled with old caskets to leap up through a cellar window and out into the fresh evening air. The explosion and rushing human activity had scattered them apart, their fight abandoned, at least temporarily. I wondered what would become of Gregori Nazaire, a starving ancient revenant released upon the world.

Harry said tightly, "Did you have a terribly nice visit with Ms. Valli?"

"Ruby isn't a very good hostess," I answered. "She didn't serve cookies with the tea. Also: instead of sugar cubes, she used roofies. At least I got a trophy." I held up the gun. "I think it's an Uzi. You know, for Israeli commandos."

Batten said, "That's a paintball gun."

"A paintball gun for Israeli commandos," I tried.

Batten whipped his sunshield down to glare at me in the mirror; I was not in the mood for his reflected evil eye, so I focused on watching the red rocks whiz by out the window. "It'll come in handy, you'll see," I muttered, plunking my temple with my forefinger. "Method to my madness."

In the driver's seat, Chapel's Blackberry summoned. He let it ring eight times, maybe in too much of a daze to hear it. When he answered, his conversation was brief. He then told Batten, "Firemen recovered Danika Sherlock's body."

Batten nodded. "Good."

"It got up, bit a hunk out of the chief's forearm and ran off, leaving half her face behind."

"Not good," I breathed. A second ghoul. Fuck me. "Harry, you don't happen to have a cookie in your pocket?"

Harry massaged his eyebrow with his fingertips around and around as though his headache could be cured by playing with his piercings. No one spoke while Chapel drove in a grim silence. I used Harry's handkerchief and spit to try cleaning the remainder of Danika Sherlock's blood off my shirt front.

"I'm starving. Where's Wes?" I asked wearily. "How'd you know to come to Ruby's to get me?"

Gary took one hand off the steering wheel to point Batten to a bag in the front seat on the passenger side floor. Batten sorted through a grocery bag and handed me a bag of Cheez Doodles. The salty snack stung the deep fang wounds in my mouth; Gregori Nazaire hadn't been gentle, not like my Harry. Oddly enough, the not-gentle part of it had stirred something primal in me, some lizard-brain part of me that liked being taken by a forceful male. I wondered if that made me a bad feminist.

Silence fell again, filled with my fishing around in the plastic bag. My crunching seemed ridiculously loud. The weight of their unknowable thoughts crowded me, pressed in on me, even as their distance made me feel hollow. It was an irritating blend, and one I needed to fix if I was going to start feeling some relief. My nerves were still jangling almost audibly inside me like the jingling of an old fashioned rotary telephone.

"Well," I said finally. "At least we know whodunit."

Harry's voice was low, and wounded. "Do you have any earthly idea what you have done?"

I had *some* idea, but probably our versions were wildly different. "I escaped a crazy homicidal psychic for the second time in three weeks?"

"As you will recall, your half of our Bond was damaged by your reckless necromimesis spell in the Ten Springs Motor Inn."

"Reckless is such a harsh word," I smiled wanly.

He did not turn to face me, just stared out the window at the night; with his preternatural acuity, he saw everything as well as I would at high noon. "We hadn't nearly repaired the Bond enough to withstand the mystic intrusion of your feeding another."

I swallowed a half-chewed Doodle. "Intrusion?"

"Gregori Nazaire's Bond was also broken. And you offered him the gift of submission: of blood, hope, and life." Harry refused to look at me. "You offered him everything."

Batten didn't turn around, which I appreciated. He left us in the privacy of the gloomy back seat as he asked, "What does that mean, exactly?"

"He has Bonded, for his part, with *my* DaySitter," Harry clipped precisely, his roiling angry passion returning like a cold wave billowing across the bench seat. I pressed down on my thighs to try and stop them from quivering. "The revenant equivalent of infatuation, obsession. And it is entirely likely that a heart-broken, bitter, melancholy 1400 year old Frenchman will haunt our steps evermore."

Batten said, "Do you really think—"

"A Frenchman, for God's sake!" Harry exploded, as though the significance should be apparent to us. One of his hands clutched the bench seat, the other rolled into a ball and pressed into his stomach like he was in visceral pain.

"Now you're being melodramatic," I soothed. "I saved his life, and he appreciated it."

"You gave yourself to him."

"I didn't spread for him, for fuck's sake."

"That is all you think about, isn't it? Your cheap, prurient needs," Harry accused. "He is not simply going to recover from this."

"Sure he will. After a few days of moping, he'll move on. It's just puppy love."

"Love is for the living," Harry snapped. Usually when he said it, he tempered it with a sad smile. This time it was bitten off with his Arctic brand of temper.

"Well, whatever it is, it's entirely one-sided." I pointed a Cheez Doodle at him. "It's not like I promised to go steady with him or anything. Besides, I turned on him, to fight him."

"An imprudent act that did not escape my notice," Harry muttered.

"Probably that means we're broken up."

"More likely, t'will enflame him to impress upon you until *you* are broken. It is with great consternation that I must inquire whether you called him Master."

I rolled my eyes. "Only as a sign of respect."

"And one wonders, where did you get the idea that calling an elder revenant 'Master' was a form of respect?" he asked tersely.

"Back when you made me study sheets and sheets of notes for months on end, about revenant/DaySitter etiquette and lifestyle before we did our Bonding, all that formal speech, proper manner of approach, the wording of respect and honour, submission and devotion. The

"Death Rejoices" and the "honoured elder" and … oh." I stared at the side of Harry's face. "That's only for Bonding."

Harry didn't answer me. Chapel didn't move a muscle that wasn't directly related to driving. Batten was rubbing a hand over his face and staring at the dash.

"You don't really think he's going to come around to see me again?" I asked.

"You heard him. "The bleeder is mine." "I accept." That means but one thing," Harry said. "You have become his world."

Fuuuuuck that. "I already have two dead guys in my friggin' house, only one of whom I invited to live with me." When he didn't reply, I said, "He was just drunk off his first feed in ages. You know, like at college when Jimmy Ghirardelli got blitzed in the bar and swore he fell madly in love with me at first sight. Then after I slept with him, we both realized he was wildly exaggerating, and when he sobered up he didn't even call?"

Harry's mouth tightened with displeasure but I thought I heard Batten softly snort a laugh in the front seat.

Harry said carefully, "Revenants do not exaggerate, wildly or otherwise."

"But they do get drunk, my point there being: Ruby slipped something in my tea. Whatever Ruby gave me flowed into Gregori during his feed."

"His feed," Harry lamented. Then, more possessively and with wide-eyed incredulity: "*His*."

"He was just stoned off his ass and talkin' smack, Harry."

"The drugs which Ruby slipped you were tranquilizers, meant to pacify and sedate." He leveled that ash grey gaze at me and watched as the realization hit me. "Yes, MJ, the creature that very nearly put me through a wall without effort on his part was significantly weakened by the drugs in your system and the fact that he'd only regained strength from a lengthy infirmity. Now imagine when those drugs wear off, and he, at full potency, returns to claim you from my possession."

"He was feeling threatened. Confused." I attempted a smile. "He was bluffing."

"Revenants do not bluff."

"So what are you going to do?" Batten demanded, turning now in the front seat, fingering the volume dial on the radio down a notch. He aimed his question at the immortal. "You can't have him coming around all the time, trying to be with her."

Harry's eyes flicked knowingly at Batten. "A disquieting probability about which, I am sure, no one here would be very keen."

"Uh, least of all me," I reminded them.

"You can't legally stake him," Chapel said quietly. "Technically Nazaire is a victim here. All he did was take an offered feed, and defend himself from an attack. We may be able to get a restraining order if he becomes a problem."

"A piece of paper can't protect you from a human stalker any more than it can keep a lovesick vamp at bay," Batten said. "Harry, do you have any ideas about how to fix it?"

Harry's gaze slid sideways at me and he gave a long drawn-out sigh of disgusted defeat. "In light of its obvious consequences, one must wonder if you have somehow masterminded this whole event to its unfortunate conclusion."

"I don't know what you're getting, at but it sounds like an accusation. Now what are we going to do about Gregori's little undead crush on me?"

Harry settled his weight further into the leather seats, his coat bunching around his shoulders, his collar hiding his jaw.

"You leave me with no other choice. In order to repair and cement our Bond," he said with profound disapproval. "I shall have to make love to you, of course."

C45

I choked on my Cheez Doodle and breathed in Doodle dust.

Harry handed me a new handkerchief with a grand roll of his eyes. By the time we pulled onto the road at Shaw's Fist, I'd hacked up a lung and cleared the powdered cheese from my chest. When I handed him the handkerchief back, he put up a palm to decline, and the movement drew our attention to a flat square of white on the seat, wedged beneath Ruby's paintball gun.

Neither one of us moved to touch the envelope. Ruby Valli's revolting grimoire was tucked under my Keds on the floor of the SUV in front of me. Maybe thc envelope had fallen out of the book of shadows? But no, it hadn't been there a second ago. I was sure of it. Considering the dour contemplation on Harry's face, he was sure too.

He plucked it up between two fine fingers, holding it up to the passing street lights. On the back of the envelope was a single word in thin gold ink. It read: *Asmodeus.*

It's a good thing I'd finished the Cheez Doodles. They really are a choking hazard. I needed a Dr. Pepper something fierce; I could barely swallow. Harry was opening the envelope, the Feds none the wiser to what was going on in the back seat. Until of course the revenant's blasting English bellow rocked the car, and both agents jerked, the SUV swerving in response to Chapel's start.

"MJ!" Harry exploded.

"What now?" I belted back. "Whatever it is, I didn't do it!"

The hand holding the envelope quivered as he read it again. "Do you mind then explaining why I am holding a response to an invitation that I do not recall giving you permission to extend? Explain to me, please, why the Overlord is giving serious consideration to your invitation and will make a resolution at His earliest convenience?"

Oh. That. I scrinched my nose. "Because I thought I was gonna die and I was grasping at straws?" *Infernally crispy straws?* "I didn't think He really heard me. I mean, He heard me, but He didn't do anything to help me. Except tweak my nipples. And not in a good way."

Batten did a full body turn in the front seat, both eyebrows rocketing up. His mouth popped open but made no sound.

Harry's did. Harry's made an angry, warning growl. "You made a plea to the Overlord?"

"Just a teensy tiny experimental one."

"Aloud?" Harry thundered, seeming to loom in the back seat of the SUV, filling it with his unearthly presence, radiating cold heat. "Did you call out to Him aloud, by name?"

"Well that's how you talk to demons. How's He supposed to know you're talking to Him specifically if you don't name names? Like during a spell when I call upon Aradia, I always say Her—"

"Well, He may very well accept," Harry cut me off, dropping the invitation with a tiny paper slap on the bench seat. "I hope you're happy."

"He can't come *here!"* I cried, flapping a hand. "Not to the cabin. I don't need Him now, He's too late, He'll have to go away!"

"You cannot tell the Overlord to 'go away'," Harry sighed, retreating into his coat. We pulled into the driveway and he made a slow stream of soft shell-shocked expressions under his breath, like a man finally returning home from war.

The wheels were turning in my head. "Suppose He did come."

"I would really rather not." Harry closed his eyes.

"Asmodeus could track Ruby Valli and punish her. He could find Dead Kristin and Dead Danika. He could find ole Gregori and talk some sense into him. Maybe a visit from the Overlord isn't the worst thing that could happen."

Three sets of incredulous eyes turned to me. I banged my door open and flung one leg out to the cold night air. "Then again, I've been wrong a coupla times ..."

Wesley was waiting in the doorway for us, his big hair cranked back in a guy-tail under a ball cap facing sideways. He'd draped Harry's black silk robe over his bony frame; if he wasn't wearing something under it, Harry was gonna plow him one. My brother's bright blue eyes were wide with anticipation. I didn't even ask. At this point, whatever his problem was, it was going to have to wait. It didn't even matter. I'd summoned the creator of the revenant lineage to some sort of soiree, and apparently the demon king was considering it. Yippee!

On top of that, I had a crazy-ass old lady in the wind, but presumably still wanting me dead. Check that, an *invisible* crazy-ass old lady. Those were the best kind. I had not one ghoul, now, but two on the loose, with few ideas about how to catch them, or what to do with them once I did. I had a 1400 year old French revenant (according to Harry, the *French*ness was the very worst part of it, though I wasn't sure why) infatuated with me. The hot guy I wanted to screw was moving to Michigan. My brother was undead. And I'm pretty sure I officially ruined my chances of having a steamy first sexual encounter with Harry; the weighty condemnation in his voice and the rolling of his eyes promised it would be brief and perfunctory, a wham-bam-thanks-for-the-Bond thing.

I had to fix at least one of these problems before Asmodeus decided to drop in for milk and cookies.

"Get out of my face, Wes, I swear," I mumbled on my way to the fridge. I popped a Dr. Pepper. "You have no idea how bad I wanna punch someone right now."

"Actually, that's what I want to talk about," Wes whispered, eyeballing the Feds out of the corner of his eye. "In private. Now."

"What, me punching you? We can do that here." I chugged Dr. Pepper and coughed on the carbonation burn. The fang wounds in my tongue stung, making my eyes water. Harry moved past me to the pantry and slipped into the stairwell going down to his chambers, not speaking, not looking back.

Wes made an unhappy noise and I looked back to see his eyes had wilted to pansy purple again. It reminded me of the goetic summoning candles, as though they were dancing inside my brother's skull.

"Have you figured out how to *not* do that, yet?" I asked.

"Do what?"

I wanted to cry with exhaustion. "What do you need Wes?"

"I really need to talk to you in private," he stressed, wringing his hands. I'd never seen a guy do that before. I couldn't think of anywhere outside of golden age cinema flicks that I'd seen anyone do it. "Before it gets too weird in here."

"Gosh, why do you think it's about to get weird in here?" I asked him flatly. "Because your sister is radiating homicidal rage?"

Batten interrupted us. "Hood just called. Dunnachie is missing."

I blinked. "Missing how?"

"As in, he hasn't been seen by his wife or anyone in his precinct."

"Dunnachie has a *wife?*" It occurred to me that this wasn't supposed to be the shocking part. "Missing since when?"

"December eighth, went out to buy bread and never came home."

I threw up my hands. "I have enough to worry about. I don't have time to keep track of Mundanes. I'm tracking ghouls and goetic witches and demon kings. Dunnachie's a big boy. He can take care of his own problems!"

Wesley had gone very quiet and still. I diagnosed this to be the same *don't notice me* stance he had tried when he found my stash of

Playgirl magazines in 1996 and ratted me out to Mom. Now, he also had the stillness of the undead. The guilty silence was the same. I don't know how Batten missed it while he grabbed a soda, mumbled something about my failure to buy beer, and then joined Chapel in the office, where Chapel was talking heatedly on his phone.

Wes said quietly, "Batten thinks I killed that cop."

"He doesn't think that," I assured him.

"Oh yes he fuckin' does," Wesley hissed, and grabbed for my elbow. He'd only touched me for a second, a brush of fingertips, when he pulled back. His whole body shrank away from me.

I studied him, setting my can down. "What the hell is your problem?"

"Your Talent. I don't want you to, y'know," His lip curled. "Know all my stuff."

I stared him down. "I know stuff without my Talent, too. Because I know *you*. Go to my room."

He started to speak and I pointed hard. "Now."

We shut the door behind us and I watched as he went to my bed, crawled into it, pulled a pillow into his lap. There were more problems on his face than I could handle. I let my head fall back until my shoulders screamed that they weren't going to hold its weight like that much longer; my breath left in one long sigh.

"Wesley, in ten minutes, I'm going to bed. Alone. I am going to sleep. All night long. I don't care if ghouls come a'knockin'. I don't care if a lovesick immortal howls at my window. If a demon king descends upon my front porch, He can just fucking wait there until I'm ready to host Him, cuz I have earned some goddamn sleep and I am going to have it."

Wesley nodded as I spoke. I don't think he actually heard any of it; he was rapidly agreeing to whatever I said. I should have told him to go clean out the entire shelf of cookies at Mum's market in Ten Springs and bring them home to me.

I said calmly, "So you have ten minutes, Wes-Wasp, whatever your name is. I am only giving you ten minutes because, even though you are a soulless fiend now, you are still my brother. Speak now, and then get out."

"Harry said time is different for revenants."

"Harry doesn't like other guys' privates getting near his stuff." Clothing, towels, DaySitters. He was sort of territorial that way. "So I hope you're wearing something under that robe."

"He said that I have to be 250 before I'd be strong enough to offer the Bond and get a DaySitter of my own. And he said that I have to be about 600 before I could turn other revenants. He said I probably wouldn't develop my Talent for a year or two. That it takes that long for, uh, UnDeath to really settle in."

I said tiredly: "He's the expert. Are you thinking I have information contrary to that? Information that you wanna hear?"

"He also said that sometimes young revenants go crazy. That UnDeath has mental health complications for some people, if the have a pre … per .. propensity? Predisposition? Like, if they have crazy people in their family tree."

I narrowed my eyes. "If you're talking about me, buster, you better watch your mouth. You're already on thin ice, showing up here all glowy-eyed."

"Marnie, either Harry's wrong about the Talent, or I'm going crazy."

"Eat someone, you'll feel better." I nodded thoughtfully. "Shit, drain *me*. I think that would maybe solve all my current issues."

Wesley was shaking his head slowly, his eyes full of moisture, glossy with welling tears. Shit, another crying immortal. "You don't believe me."

"It's not that I don't believe you," I said, lowering myself to the bed beside him and letting exhaustion pull me right down into a ball. "I love you. You're my blood. But I just can't focus on this right now."

"Why not?" His eyes flickered, like a candle wavering precariously in a drafty room. The Husky-blue intruded through the violet but only briefly, and together they made an inky mess of his pupils.

I hadn't explained all of the problems I was having. I doubted Harry had either. And certainly neither of us had talked about my sex life or lack of it, or my unfortunate not-so-secret not-so-professional attachment to Batten.

"So you *are* sleeping with him," Wesley said quietly. "I thought it was just his fantasies. Not memories, not actual … God, gross. So, you guys actually fucked so hard you nearly broke a motel door? No, don't tell me, I really don't want to know if this shit happened or he just wishes it would."

I sat bolt upright, shedding my tiredness all at once. "Who said so?"

"Other than him? You. Just now." Wesley aimed a forefinger at his temple like a gun and pulled the trigger. "I can't *not* hear you. Right here. Everyone's thoughts. They're scrawling across my brain like stock market quotes."

I let out my breath. "Holy shit. Telepathy?"

"Maybe," Wesley said uncertainly. "If it's not my imagination. Think something at me."

My eyes cut to my nightstand drawer and I thought, *My vibrator is neon green and six inches long.*

"No it's not, it's purple, I peeked," Wes said, his grin lopsided. "And it's more like nine inches. Friggin' horse cock if I ever saw one. Do you gals really need that much? Jesus."

"Oh my God," I whispered, grinning. I don't know why. It should have been bad news. But it wasn't; true telepathy was beyond rare. Excited, I tried again. *How much of this are you hearing?*

""How much of this are you hearing?" All of it. Exactly. And I'm hearing the shit you aren't trying to think at me either. Like, you have nervous gas and you're holding in a fart, wishing I'd go away so you could let it out. Which is kinda stupid, since I'm your brother. I've heard you fart like a million times."

I threw my arms around his neck. "This is so cool, Wes!"

He laughed into my shoulder. "I guess this means I'm not crazy."

I wouldn't go that far, I thought in his direction.

"Hey," he poked me in the ribs, then hugged me back, harder. "If you're happy does that mean I'm going to be okay?"

You don't touch me because you don't want me to know ... what, exactly? I thought at him.

Wesley tensed like he was considering pulling away. "Sort of hypocritical, eh? Since I can hear all your thoughts now."

"My hands form the stronger psi-bridge," I explained, showing him my gloves. "Hugging me probably isn't going to open the lock on your mental diary."

"Good to know."

"You, however, now have an unfair advantage over me," I informed him. "What can I hide from a telepath?"

"I really wish you'd hide something," he said frankly. "Like maybe you could stop having sex thoughts. Altogether. Forever."

I let out a sharp laugh then realized he was serious. "I'll make you a deal. I'll try to stop thinking along those lines, if you tell me every time you overhear Batten thinking along those lines."

"You mean every time he thinks about nailing you?" Wes scrunched his nose up, and his perfectly angelic face crumpled. "Sick."

"Fine, then I'll daydream about every guy I see, in vivid, perverted detail."

"Ugh, okay, okay." Wes mock-shuddered with disgust. "You have a deal. How do you want me to signal it?"

"Scratch your nose?"

Wes's shoulders quaked as he laughed and shook his head at the same time. "Fine. Man, you've got it bad for this dude. Weird, right, cuz he's a vampire hunter, and you're a revenant's midnight snack? I don't see how that would work, with Harry. Good thing Batten's moving away."

My smile died. "Did you hear that in his head?"

"Chapel's. And yours."

I nodded. "Your ten minutes is up."

"I know," Wes said, his grin widening. "You were just thinking how you couldn't wait to get rid of me so you could dive under your pillows and have a nice, long cry." He paused at the bedroom door, cinching Harry's robe tighter. "I'm not going back to Mum and Dad's."

"Oh yes you are," I said tiredly, guessing that I'd been thinking *that* too, in the bowels of my brain where things bounced along without my knowledge. I stripped off my socks, wriggling my toes in the cool air. "As soon as possible. It's gotten nuts around here. I can't see how I can make sure it doesn't get worse. I need you somewhere safe." When he squawked I put a hand up to silence him. "I mean it Wes. I need you to be safe."

He leveled a long look at me. The shade of his pupils had slipped back to blue and softened around the edges; staring into them was like gazing at Portland Bight on the coast of Jamaica on a bright spring morning. "Hey, I wanna be safe, too, Marnie-Jean. Why the hell do you think I came to you?" He pointed at my nightstand, where a familiar bottle of multivitamins rested. "Picked you up a new bottle, your other one felt light."

He closed the door without a sound, and I checked the mirror behind me. The black-watch spell notified me of two intrusions: Ajax and the second debt vulture, assigned to Wesley, both high in the trees, both sleeping with one eye open. No ghouls, no invisible crazy ladies (*I think*), no legions of demons or a fat demon king. The crypt beetles must have found some dead thing to chew on elsewhere, because they weren't on my property. I saw no spitting carrion spiders slinking around in the dark. All was quiet.

Picking up the vitamin bottle and wrangling with the child-proof cap, I guessed Harry was going to have to reign in his temper before he came to fix our Bond. With no one to impress, I could throw on my grandfatherly plaid pajamas and big furry socks, and bundle myself up under extra quilts. My body begged me to do so as soon as possible. The cap finally screwed off and I shook a couple pills into my palm.

And blinked. These were not my vitamins. I frowned at the label. These were friggin' horse pills if I ever saw them, huge orange things that looked nothing like what I'd been taking for years. I set them aside and slipped into my pjs, but something nagged me. I went to the bathroom and opened the cabinet. The same pill bottle sat there beside Harry's boxed oval hairbrush. Popping the lid, I saw the little white pills I was accustomed to taking, twice a day. My last thought before dragging to bed was: if they're not vitamins, what's Harry been giving me all this time? And why?

C47

I only woke up because someone was trying to kill me.

Batten was tapping me with his big knuckles, right in the center of my forehead, as though the place where a migraine was blossoming was a door to the office of my consciousness. I'd never been woken with such casual disrespect before; it made me want to pinch his scrotum until his eyes popped out. He was crouched beside the bed, and his fresh-brushed minty breath hit me in the nose. I swatted like he was a pestering gnat.

"Got news," he said. "Get up."

"Go choke on your own dick," I advised, rolling over and shoving a pillow over my head, then a second, cramming it tight with one bare hand. Batten ran a finger along the back of that hand, rubbed my knuckles softly; I didn't have the mental wherewithal to wonder what that was about.

"Come on. We let you sleep in, it's late afternoon. Get a move-on. Chapel's waiting in your office."

"Tell Chapel to choke on it, too. Alternatively, you could gargle each other's balls. Whatever's easiest."

"We got a call ..."

"Mark, I'm exhausted. There are gross and scary things out to get me. In completely unrelated news: I'm never leaving this bed again for personal reasons."

I heard his knee hit the plank floor, and a shuffle told me he'd given up on the crouching and taken a more permanent stance. My only recourse would be to melt his face off with my morning breath, but then the chances of me sleeping with him again would be remarkably poorer. Still, it was something to consider.

His voice was tentative. "Forensic accountants found Neil Dunnachie's name in Ruby's books."

A brand new level of headache started budding on one side of my face, right below my eyebrow. I knew this feeling. I hadn't fed Harry enough; ms-lipotropin withdrawal was starting to kick in. Usually a good deep feed would fix it, or a handful of Advil, though I'd rather do the first. I burrowed further under my nest of pillows, sliding a hand under my belly wound to poke and prod curiously at the lack of pain there.

I asked hopefully, "Does Dunnachie do landscaping on the side?"

"Lump sum. 4800 dollars about three weeks ago. Standard payment for a vamp staking. Or at least, it used to be when I was freelancing."

I had no doubt that Batten had done work for Ruby Valli. Before they knew each other through Gold-Drake & Cross? After? During? Guess it didn't matter, unless the answer was *still*. Then I was in trouble. "You're thinking Neil Dunnachie fire bombed my kitchen?"

"I'm saying it's possible that he was the one." His voice got more serious. "He's been missing since."

"Did you know he was a hunter?"

"Still don't," he said. "Assumption of innocence."

"What does the Prince of Thieves say?"

A beat. "Who?"

"His partner, former Detective Sergeant current Sheriff Robin Hood."

"Pretty sure Hood said his name is Robert."

"You buy that?" I brought my hand back up to my temple and pressed on the divot. "Go get me some Advil. Medicine cabinet, second shelf next to Harry's extra strength Listerine."

"Hood says he's got no idea about Dunnachie. I believe him." He paused. "What do you think?"

"I think you need your hearing checked, because I told you to get me some Advil. Pretend I said please."

"About Dunnachie."

"My brain isn't going to work so good today. Especially since you make a fuckshit manservant," I sighed.

"You'd best remember that. And I'm gonna excuse the attitude because you're obviously in pain. Give me some insight, here."

"Look, Hood didn't even buy the idea of revenants, never mind hunters, before he met Harry on the seventh. Empathically, I never felt anything from him but constant wariness and surprise. Hood's not accustomed to monsters."

"That's a world of change for Hood. Meet first vamp on the seventh, see your first ghoul on the ninth, find out your missing partner's a vampire hunter on the tenth."

I tried finger-pressure on the bridge of my nose to no avail. "Ruby paid Dunnachie three weeks ago, you say?"

Batten made an affirmative noise, thoughtful. It occurred to me, under the safe dimness of the pillows, that we were—for a moment—working together instead of fighting or fucking. Maybe I should drop the attitude and see where this brand new phenomenon got us.

"If it was for a staking, Dunnachie's not new at it. He waited for you and Chapel to drive away before smoking us out. Not sure why he didn't wait for day light. Maybe he had faith in his abilities despite the time of day. Maybe he didn't see Wes arrive, or didn't know a new revenant when he saw one. Maybe he had to strike when the iron was hot, because you Feds were always around during the day."

"Think Dunnachie's alive?" Batten asked me.

Man, I was glad I was hidden under down and cotton. I couldn't see how Harry could have lost him in the woods, on land, at night … that made no sense to me. I knew him too well. Human on a snowmobile vs. immortal's shadow-stepping and night vision? Chances weren't great for the human unless he was covered head to toe in holy water and silver crosses. Not to say he wasn't.

"You think Harry killed him," I said, muffled under my pillows.

"Not necessarily," Batten said slowly. "I'm saying it's possible Harry tried to stop your brother from killing him. New vamp threatened by fire, defending his sister, things get out of hand, thrill of the hunt triggers him, older vamp trics to step in but he's too late …"

My head exploded from the pillow pile like an erupting volcano.

"You've got some nerve, Mark Batten, to come in here and *oww—*" I hissed, putting one fist to my eyebrow to quell the shooting pain, "And wake me with a rap of your fist and tell me you think my brother, whom you've just met, is a murderer."

His eyes flicked to the front of my plaid pajamas, an undisguised peek, maybe in hopes of sloppy buttoning. "You disagree with my hypothesis?"

"Heartily." Shouting hurt my brain, so I dropped the volume. "With gusto."

"Would you ask them?"

I opened my mouth to let out a torrent of insults then stopped, blinking. "I can't think of a reason why not. Harry will be very insulted, but I'll preface it with "Batten thinks this, not me."."

"Wesley won't be insulted?"

"He already thinks you think he murdered Dunnachie."

"Why would he say that?"

Again my yap snapped firmly. "Could I get some caffeine and Advil before we continue this conversation?" *And a toothbrush? And a comb? And a make-over?* "I feel like I'm vaulting willy-nilly onto a hangman's stage to show off my mad tap dancing skills."

He put both hands on his thighs and used them to thrust himself to standing. "Would you drink coffee if I made it my way?"

I hid a yawn and grimace behind my hand. "Better let me do it. Tell Chapel I'll be there in ten."

There wasn't enough Advil in the world to fix the psi-headache that was brewing now, any more than an umbrella could stave off a tsunami in the South Pacific. I pulled a double shot of espresso and downed it without putting a single thing in it. After I had blinked myself awake, I realized I needed Harry. I couldn't feel his hunger, but it wasn't too early to seek him out for his acronychal feeding. He had to be famished, and I was hurting.

Withdrawal usually didn't hit me so soon; I had gone 6 weeks in Buffalo apart from him, because I'd had oxy-lipotropin, an artificial ms-lipotropin substitute on trial in pill form. I'd suffered a few annoying symptoms, the odd headache and some irritability, but I'd also been adjusting to working with Hard Ass Batten for the first time, so it was hard to tell where the crankiness was coming from. I tried to remember the last time I'd fed Harry and came up empty handed, vaguely recalling some yoga and a black and white movie. It might have been years ago; it certainly felt that way. It wasn't like us to get off schedule like this. I knew he was letting me recover from my injuries, but I felt fine in that respect. Better than fine. The wounds had healed faster than the stitches dissolved. Internally, I was confident that if the surgeon took the staples out now, he'd be startled by the recovery.

I popped my head into the office to catch Batten off-guard, on one knee in front of my gun safe, fiddling with the dial. He made a comical jerky snort-grunt.

"So busted." I grinned. "Get out of my shit."

"Just making sure your gun was locked up."

I was pretty sure the Beretta was still under the front passenger seat of the Buick, which Sheriff Hood had kindly had some uniforms drop off late last night. Looking back, I saw that bringing the gun into the magic shop would have been the better choice, although since I didn't see the attack coming, I might have shot my butt off when I was pushed down the stairs. Maybe Mark was right: some people just shouldn't own guns.

"It's in there," I assured him. *There* meaning the Buick, not exactly a lie. "Where's Chapel? I made a crapload of coffee."

"He must have gone up to grab a late shower. Been working all day in here, unlike some people." Batten moved to my herb cabinet, peeking in the doors with a frown. His gaze skimmed the shelves like he was looking for contraband. "Cream, if you have it. Otherwise double milk."

"Oh yes, welcome to the Starbucks that is my home. Imagine for a moment how pleased I am to serve you." I put two fingers to my temple, felt thudding there in concert with my pulse. "You know where the fridge is, jackass. If you're looking for marijuana to bust me for possession, it's third shelf on the far right. If you're looking for poisons, they're marked with a smiley face. Be back in a few, checking on the dead guys."

I slipped through the pantry into the narrow stairwell that had been, when Harry first bought the cabin after the shooting in Buffalo, a rickety set that seemed more ladder than stairs. We'd had them redone while he redecorated the cold cellar, which had previously been used to store preserves and root vegetables. It was now his "bed chamber" as he called it, a place for a decadent 4 poster bed and a double-wide cherry casket, a video game center complete with high-backed leather gaming chair, and his ever-present space heater.

I didn't even pause in my steps after I saw it, because it didn't register for the shock that it was; in fact, the only part of me that registered what I was seeing was my throat, which made a startled little noise akin to strangled horror. Then my brain bucked, tried to kick the image violently out of my mind before I could fully grasp it, and my hands flew to either side of my face like if I didn't hold them there, my head was going to fall apart. My one foot slipped out from under me as most of my body reeled to a rejecting halt and the other bit didn't get the orders. I banged my shoulder on the door jamb, felt nothing.

The broad, pale stretch of muscular back leaning in a graceful arch was Harry. About that, I had no doubt. The bare lines of him were etched in my mind, the sharp cut of his shoulder blades, the lean cleft of his waist. The hand that braced his shaking arm in a long column, fingers curled against the gleaming cherry lid of the casket, had my name lovingly tattooed in flowery script, the ink a shock of contrast against his alabaster wrist. His shoulders were bunched up like a big cat preparing to pounce, but he already had his prey by the throat.

Gary Chapel's legs lay under him, the cuff of one navy trouser leg sloppily hiked to reveal argyle socks in tan and blue. Chapel was utterly motionless, and my first fear was that he was dead. The second, following only an instant later, was that he wasn't.

The worst thing was the look on my brother's face as he worked at pulling blood from the vein in Chapel's wrist. I wasn't sure there was even a word for it, for surely no human could ever experience such bliss. The flush of a feed was making his arms shake, but Wes held carefully onto Chapel's forearm, tilting it just so, reminding me of all the cautious feeds I'd ever given Harry in the rec room of the Baranuik home, back when we were new to one another.

I couldn't see Chapel's face. I didn't want to. I was pretty sure the reeling nausea in my stomach couldn't handle knowing.

Wes' eyes drifted open like he was rousing from a long night in an opium den. He fixed his heavy-lidded gaze on me, blinking sleepily, and with the sudden realization that he might have his meal taken away, his fingers dug possessively into Chapel's tender inner elbow. More animal than man, a bull dog with a stolen soup bone, he watched with horrible wilted-violet eyes to see what my next move might be. His lips curled back in a twitch and I caught a glimpse of gums above fangs, flushed pink with blood.

Chapel must have sensed the tension on his arm, the deeper pulling at his vein, because his other arm tugged at Harry's in warning.

Harry didn't look up. His voice was firm and half-muffled. "I am not done."

"Marnie …" Chapel gasped.

"She's fine." Harry knew I was there.

I slammed my palm into the casket lid like a teacher with a ruler-strike on a desk, and barked, "Marnie is *not* fine!"

Wesley detached and pushed back to rest on his heels, his head falling back and a great, rattling sigh leaving him.

Harry whipped his head around, his fangs slick with crimson. "I said you're sodding fine."

"And I say, fuck you in the ass, you two-faced ingrate," I shouted.

Harry released his meal. Chapel's knees buckled and he did an awkward, embarrassed shuffling unfold to his feet, propping himself against Harry's gaming chair. A great and terrible shudder ran through him, and from the way he swayed I was surprised he didn't topple.

I watched his stumbling progression with reluctant concern. "Gary, if you're well enough to excuse us, I think my Cold Company and I need to have a chat."

Chapel looked, for once, unsure. His fingers fumbled at the buttons on his pale blue shirt. Business casual for feeding someone else's companion behind their back. "Should I be apologizing right now?"

Harry cut me off mid-inhale, answering for me: "Of course not, Agent Chapel. You've done absolutely nothing wrong."

"Nothing wro—" The insistent glare from Harry's ice-shard eyes took the words out of my mouth. "Just go please. Wait, where do you think *you're* going?" I stabbed a finger at Wesley as he inched to his feet. "My advice to you, little brother, is that you'd better sit the fuck down."

"Think you should be talking to two immortals in that tone of voice?" Wesley said boldly, but when I jammed my hands on my hips he backed down, looked away.

"Oh is that what you think, Wesley? You're a badass revenant now, you can do whatever you want? Read my mind: am I scared of you?" I threw thoughts of rowan wood spikes at him and he flinched, hurt flickering in his sickly violet eyes.

When Chapel was gone, I whirled on Harry. "You snake. How long has this been going on behind my back?"

Harry pulled his legs up onto the casket lid with the rest of his body, folding them into a flexible cross. "It has not been going on behind your back, my love. You were well aware that I would be feeding while you were incapable."

"You said you had o-neg in the freezer. That was barefaced lie."

"I think you'll find that Agent Chapel's blood type is in fact o-negative." Harry made a show of licking it off his lips, slowly, his platinum eyes daring me to argue. I wanted to slap him hard, but slapping a revenant is akin to suicide by cop. "He might not be in my freezer, exactly—"

"Harry!" It came out as a pitiful wail, which wasn't my intention. The sorrow just sort of leaked out.

Harry's face went through a prompt rotation of surprise, concern and distress. "You're heart-broken by this. Why is this so?"

"Look at yourself!" I said hotly. "Did he undress you?"

Harry laughed with surprise. "No, my love. Agent Chapel is not a bender."

I made a stab at translating, for clarity. "Gary's not gay?"

Wes laughed sharply. "The amount of times he's pictured bending *you* over your desk and givin' it to you up the—"

"*Wesley!*" I yelped, shrinking in my clothes with embarrassment. "Need to know basis!"

Harry sucked his fangs in condemnation in Wesley's direction. "You simply must use discretion, young one, as we have discussed at length." He cocked his head at me. "Your brother needed to learn how to feed properly from a willing partner. And Agent Chapel, for personal reasons, needed to know about the process as well."

"Personal reasons?" I repeated.

"As I have said."

"How many times did he need to know?" I snapped. "And why is it his "need to know" extends to the state of your rippling abs?"

Harry's eyebrows crept upward as though he were channeling Agent Batten's. It furthered my irritation in a way I couldn't describe.

"Rippling ..." he said in flattered wonder, running a hand over his midsection. He was pleased and he let it show. Under the flickering light of his mock-candle wall sconces, his gold court ring drew attention to the faint flush of life he'd acquired from the feed, though his hunger roared sudden and fierce in my own veins, the call to feed him strong;

he had taken a bare minimum from Chapel. "Wesley, I would speak to your sister alone now, if you will excuse us."

Wesley frowned at the older revenant, considering. His gaze washed across Harry's face, a violet searchlight. After a moment, Wesley's spare and diminutive shoulders fell. He touched the front of his faded blue-on-grey plaid t-shirt, fingers feeling, maybe for the tell-tale dampness of a bloodstain. Then he nodded once and darted up the stairs.

Harry motioned to a tidy pile of clothing draped on the couch, the white dress shirt hung in such a way on the corner so as not to require ironing. "I merely removed my morning jacket so that it would not get spotted. And the shirt was brand new, love. It soon followed."

"I want to know everything."

"A bold request. I do not, in faith, know everything."

"Don't fuck with me Harry, you know what I mean."

He put a hand up to soothe me, nodding. "Agent Chapel has private, personal reasons, my love, for making such a request of me. I would not betray his confidence." He shrugged, as though this was not his fault. "Understand ducky, he has never had the opportunity to pick the brains of the living dead of a ..." he searched for a word and settled on: "Friendly sort."

"It's not your brains I'm worried about. I'm tempted to take a pickaxe to them myself at the moment."

Harry's eyes widened slightly.

"Jealousy," he whispered, so low I couldn't imagine it was meant for me to hear. He scanned me with an intensity that was downright uncomfortable. "This is new."

Frustrated, I blew my breath out slowly. "You're saying this was all Chapel's idea?"

He wiggled his fingers at me, and I turned to see a pack of menthols on the side table. I handed them to him. "Splendid, thank you."

I watched him pinch a cigarette between his lips and light it. I told him, "I haven't seen any marks on him."

"Nor should you. I'm hardly new-turned," Harry sniffed disdainfully. He drew his legs up and refolded them lotus-style. Putting his elbows on his knees, he steepled his fingers and drew on the cigarette, making the end burn a brighter orange. He hadn't fed enough to kick-start his lungs but inhaled deeply on the drag and exhaled curls of smoke in my direction.

"Batten could have you arrested and staked for this," I hissed, glancing over my shoulder. "He'd say you coerced Chapel, and push for a warrant."

"Don't pitch your knickers, love. He would never do such a thing."

"Oh yes he would."

"And risk Chapel retaliating with news to the authorities of his fraternizing with a well-known forensic psychic consultant from Gold-Drake & Cross? They've both broken rules, love. It is the way of men to break rules when it suits their desires. Besides, do you think me so trusting?" He exhaled slowly through his nose, trailing smoke like a drowsy dragon. "I had Agent Chapel write a full disclaimer before I allowed him the honour, signed and dated, to protect myself legally."

"I want to know Chapel's so-called personal reasons."

"Please do not be cross with me, ducky, you know I am hardly so boorish as to betray a confidence."

Anger and betrayal was still filtering hotly into my gut.

"Seeing its effect on you, perhaps I shouldn't have given in to him this evening." He studied me unhappily. "I was confident you knew."

"But then you also knew it bothered me. I've been stressing for days. Empathically, through our Bond, you felt I was sick with worry and confusion," I said plainly, smacking the back of the chair. It occurred to me at the same time as he looked perplexed at something that was flittering through his head. "You *liked* that I was upset."

"Yes," he said, bemused. "I think that may be a fair statement."

"But why? What did I do to deserv—" I broke off, drawing a deep breath. "This is about Batten."

He cut his eyes to the far side of the room. "I quite hardly think it is."

"Is so," I accused. "You're jealous of him."

Harry's laugh was a sudden delighted eruption that tickled down my spine and prickled my skin. When his face came up, his eyes were sparkling.

"Oh my love. You know I am a thousand times more magnificent than he." He hopped off the casket. "Even if we turned him, and he were in the same preternatural league as myself … darling, he would be centuries behind me in polish and sophistication."

"And lacking your buckets of modesty," I groaned. "Fine, if you're not jealous of Mark then what is it? Why do you want me to feel all squinky? Especially seeing I'm at wits end with everything else that's been going on. I mean, that's borderline crap-weasel of you."

He agreed with a thoughtful nod. "It is a petty streak that I am disappointed to discover in myself. Perhaps ..." He came to offer me one of his hands. "Perhaps I needed to know."

"What do you mean?"

"That you still want me. Your possessiveness was refreshing. Sometimes I feel that you view me with the barest of patience. That I am a nuisance. An inconvenient, sucking parasite. That you regret ever ..."

Stunned, I took a running leap at him and threw my arms around his neck. He fumbled with the cigarette, dropping it.

"You silly, stupid creature." I squeezed him hard, grasping hard muscle under my hands, pulling him as close as possible, wedging my face into the fragrant hollow in his neck. "I don't regret it for a second. The day you came into my life was the day I started living."

"Do not think me so foolish that I cannot perceive that my arrival prevented you from having a normal life."

"Who the hell said I want a "normal" life?"

"You do, every crudding day," he said sadly against my hair. "How you want to be left alone, how you hate the psychic nonsense, how you do not want to work or leave the house or see anybody. This is all my fault, of course, and I encourage it, because at least inside you are safe and out of harm's way."

"My being a bitch has nothing to do with you."

"I am afraid it has everything to do with me, love, and always has. My irritation becomes yours, my unease and displeasure. This is the way of the Empath and his companion. When added to your own unhappiness, it has made you the bundle of raw angst you are today."

"Harry," I drew back to look him in the eye. "I bitch and crab and whine, but I never mean for a second that I don't want you around, or that I'm unhappily stuck here with you. I'm not miserable for escape. I am profoundly honoured to be your DaySitter. I want you for always. Okay?"

He released me so he could bend to pick up the cigarette from the cold stone tiles. He blew it clean and tucked it between his lips. For a moment, he studied me. "So I was wide of the mark?"

I assumed that meant "wrong" and said with a smile: "Brace yourself, your Lordship, it happens."

One corner of his lips twitched up. "It still felt awfully good, after all these years, to have you crazy with possessiveness as though we were some newly bonded couple."

"I wasn't crazy," I gave him a swat. "I was ...mildly perturbed."

"Please, *mon petit chou*, you wanted to rip into Agent Chapel's thinning hair like a seedy vixen in a pay-per-view cat fight," he teased.

"That's because you're mine!" I warned playfully, making a fist and shaking it in his face. Harry grinned in reply. "Mine, all mine. Got that, bloodsucker?"

"You are truly terrifying. I must of course submit to your will," he answered, putting his hands on my hips with familiar affection.

"Damn straight. And if I ever catch you doing that to Gary again—"

"Catch him doing *what* to Gary?"

I craned my neck slowly to see Batten on the cellar stairs, ducking under a low beam.

Harry exhaled cigarette smoke noisily and said under his breath: "Bloody hell, MJ."

C48

My big mouth had very effectively derailed our work session. At least I was good at something. I'd never met a situation yet that I didn't manage to destroy. I was the Godzilla of paranormal law enforcement, guaranteed to tromp all over the Tokyo of your investigation! I wondered how much it would cost to get a bigass trophy made: World's Best Fucker-Upper.

Strained silence followed a brief, explosive fight where Brains admitted to Brawn he had a private "issue" with the revenants he was working through, and that it was personal: every bit as personal, Brains stressed, as Brawn's sexual infatuation with a certain co-worker that would go politely unnamed. I squirmed in my chair and pretended to study the white board, where pictures of Ten Springs Motor Inn's room 4 in all its bloody glory were safer scene look at.

We did a quick review, the men barely speaking and even then, through their teeth. I didn't know which one worried me more. I didn't enjoy seeing Batten flushed and irritated, but when wasn't he? In fact, it was his standard mode when working with me. But Chapel's loss of control was a different animal. His hands shook as he typed. Sweat had dampened the armpits of his shirt; his crisp ocean-scent deodorant smelled nice, even though the rest of him disgusted me. How could he have done this behind my back? I had suspected, but I wish I'd never seen it with my own eyes. I couldn't look at his face; at the same time I couldn't un-see it, him laying prone, legs dangling, feet splayed, either exhausted or completely relaxed. At least I didn't recall a tent in the front of his pants.

His neck tie was missing again. Now I knew why. How many were laying on Harry's plush-carpeted floor, abandoned beside the couch or under the edge of the bed skirt? And why? What were his reasons? I respected that Harry wouldn't tell me but I didn't like it. I deserved an explanation but didn't think it was going to happen any time soon.

The discussion of why Dead Kristin hadn't come to reclaim her eye made me go stiff and squinky; she hadn't come because I hadn't made her eye accessible. It was still locked in my gun safe with the stolen sunglass lens belonging to Patrick Laurier Nazaire, deceased, and the mad psychic's daughter Danika Sherlock, *sorta*-deceased. Revenants and precogs and clairvoyants, oh my! I penciled in my Moleskine: *witch-walking* and *flesh magic* and *Ruby's grimoire*, the last being off-limits for me to even consider touching. Harry would have a fit if he caught me fingering through a black witch's notes.

My gaze fell on the froggy pencil holder that held my number 2s, the one Batten had drawn black fangs on with permanent marker. I turned it around on the desk to face the Feds, said:

"Do we have the Davis family's permission to destroy the ghoul?"

Batten brought his dark blue eyes up from the pencil holder with the tiniest bit of playfulness around his eyes, hiding his mouth from Chapel behind his fist. An admission. Not that I needed one.

"Do we need it?" he asked without a trace of humour.

"Well, she was their daughter," I told them. "Unless Ruby releases the demon who's holding Kristin's spirit hostage, we have only one other option: burn Kristin's body to a crisp. Pretty sure we should get written consent before we try that."

"Is that standard?" Batten asked, looking between Chapel and I.

I shrugged. "My first ghoul slaying, sorry. The law's probably fuzzy on ghoul slaying, if it exists at all." Chapel was typing, but he had no answer after a few minutes and I continued: "We should also get permission from Danika's next of kin, if we can find anyone other than her charming mother. I don't know for sure that Danika would come here. But Ruby's demon is controlling her, too, so there's no telling."

"What about this witch-walking you said Ruby and her daughter could do?" Chapel said. "Is it only in effect while Kristin's blind eye is still here?"

"Unless she's gone and plucked out some more blind eyeballs and planted them around my cabin. Oh," I rubbed my sore head. "I just scared the crap out of myself again."

We discussed Neil Dunnachie next, and while they danced around the subject of where the missing deputy might be, and whether or not he was responsible for fire-bombing my home, I focused on the white board and the pictures some clever cop had snapped on his cell phone of Ruby's basement before the oil tank blew. Pictures of empty caskets, three of them. *Three?* Silver chains. Crosses. My gloves in a basket. Firemen fighting a blank spot in the images that must have been Patrick Laurier; the firemen had tried to get him off the wall and then gave up and evacuated before the whole thing came down.

Without knowing I was going to say it, I heard: "Canon 5."

Their conversation drifted to a questioning quiet and they waited for me to speak again. I had to pause and figure out where my brain was trying to lead me.

"Canon 5 states: the DaySitter shall incur a measure of the revenant's pleasure and pain, for they are inexorably linked through the Bond." Part of me jumped on this: how could we use it against Ruby? She'd still been feeding Gregori, as the strength of her power attested. Her Bond may have been weakened, busted, but was there enough left to hurt her through Gregori Nazaire? Was that even possible? And could I injure an innocent revenant just to draw Ruby out? That didn't sound quite right. Could I pleasure him to draw Ruby out? *Eeeeuuuuww*. But those were my choices, pleasure and pain.

Another part of my mind burbled with confusion: Harry had been shot twice with a .45 at the funeral home. But I didn't feel a thing. My half of our Bond, the psychic bit, was broken but his was intact. Should I not have physically felt his pain? The Feds were waiting for me to explain, but I didn't have answers, only more questions. That was pretty much the last thing we needed. And then my brain skittered elsewhere, somewhere ugly.

Harry had said something as he crumpled to the floor. He had pointed, and said something about "her" but pointed directly at Chapel. Memories flickered, coyly danced away, stripped one shoulder and winked at me, then sunk back into shadow. Whatever it was, my brain wasn't getting the whole picture. The fan dancer had covered up and gone home.

A soft knock interrupted my brain-wracking, and Wesley poked his head in. "Marnie. Harry's asking for you. Downstairs. Code 9?"

"Gents, if you'll excuse me."

Wesley scratched his nose meaningfully at me. I cleared my throat, wondering exactly what sort of libidinous thoughts Batten was having about me that Wesley was trying to relay. I tossed my Visa on the desk.

"Order up some pizza for us, pineapple for me. I'll be back. Don't let Wes eat any." I avoided Chapel's face, but caught the slight unconscious folding on his wrist where Wes had fed.

Batten stood and followed me out of the office, grabbing me by the elbow.

"Don't suppose you'd like to explain code 9?"

Code 9 meant I had a very hungry revenant who couldn't, and wouldn't, wait patiently a minute longer. "Not especially."

For a minute his cop-face went up; I couldn't penetrate it, and I sure as hell couldn't sense him. "Marnie, I need to know something."

"Oh dude, there's so many, many things you need to know. How'd you narrow it down?"

"Are you in love with Harry?"

I blinked at him and burst into laughter. “Are you on crack?”

“That’s neither a yes or a no.”

I chose my words carefully. “Love is for the living. The dead aren’t capable of it, any more than sociopaths are capable of mercy or remorse. There’s just a certain part of their brain that no longer works that way.”

“What part of the brain?”

I floundered. “Hell, I don’t know.”

“Don’t you have a doctorate in preternatural biology?”

“No one knows, that’s my point. It’s as of yet undiscovered. Happy?”

“Are you?” His face was dead serious. “Happy, I mean?”

“I have the odd moment of contentment,” I said, feeling defensive. “I’m not always this crabby. It’s you. You bring out the worst in me.”

“And what does Harry bring out in you?” He chewed inside his mouth. “What does Harry offer?”

“He’s devoted and loyal,” I replied. “But no, he doesn’t love me. Couldn’t. Even if he wanted to. And that’s why I can’t love him back.”

Batten was shaking his head. “I don’t believe that. And deep down, Marnie, neither do you.”

I looked past him to the pantry. “Do me a favour?” I asked.

This seemed to take Batten off-guard; he waited for the *fuck off* that didn’t come, then nodded.

“In my bathroom linen closet, beside a red box, is a bottle of multivitamins. Little white ones. Got a lab nearby that can test them?”

Batten was quiet for a moment. “Why would you—“

“Yes or no,” I cut him off. “If no, fine. If yes, take a handful but not the bottle, and please, don’t ask me any questions. Just want a chemical breakdown. Can you do that for me?”

“Of course.” He gave me a look that said I should know better. “I’d do whatever you needed me to do, Marnie. You only have to ask.”

C49

The lights in the chamber were extinguished. Beside Harry's ostentatious four poster bed, taking up a grand amount of space in the very middle of the room, quivering candles had been set strategically on ornate floor stands. The casual observer might not have noticed the double-wide casket in the back of the shadow-curtained room but I didn't miss it; I'd been there on many a cold winter morning, warming Harry with my body heat, curled up with my face pressed to his chest. Both glossy halves of the cherry wood lid were flung up, and against the perfect white satin interior the bumper stickers were dark and unreadable. I knew them off by heart: all the places he'd been, little phrases that pleased him. "*Heaven or bust*", "*Devil's Playground, Mojave, California*", and my favorite: "*What happens in the casket stays in the casket*". I had always wondered: would the same apply to Harry's bed?

My companion stood just out of my line of sight behind the bed's white sheers, playing coy with eyes that had known four centuries of seduction, knowing his distance now would drive me bonkers. I caught a glimpse, the filmy impression of him shirtless in the well-warmed room, showing off the hard-won rewards of all that yoga in cut abs and hard angles. His preternatural power boiled in the air, a controlled simmer that vibrated under my skin, and nervous energy slithered down my spine. Was he nervous, or was I? I couldn't tell. Maybe both. My head was still thrumming with the need to feed him, the withdrawal heavy and urgent.

The chamber door shut behind me with an audible click, though Harry hadn't come past me to touch it. I narrowed my eyes at the revenant as he came into full view with a smile, the perfect picture of courtly innocence.

"Okay, spill. How'd you do that?" I demanded, felt my gloved hand go to the hollow of my throat almost protectively.

His answer was a shallow bow, a slight graceful sweep of pale arm. "I can do a great many wondrous things, my love, as I am sure you are aware."

"I didn't know you could do *that.*"

His pale grey eyes, by far his best feature, were backlit with a new dark light tonight, as though he were thinking wicked thoughts of honey, silk and a shameless loss of willpower. *Oh boy*. Inside my bra, my nipples tightened almost painfully.

"Tonight I will show you countless tricks sure to ... " His lips spread with promise and he licked them, a quick pink flash. "Amaze and delight."

Yikes! It occurred to me he had used Code 9 to mean a whole different kind of emergency, which kick-started a sexual stirring in my gut so frighteningly strong that I fought it down, shoved it away. A rare blush burned into my cheeks.

Harry's forehead displayed a moment of confusion as the rush of my arousal hit him and just as quickly dissipated. He took a step back, tilting his head in question.

"Too much?" he asked carefully.

"Wouldn't say that, no."

If he'd been doing Mark Batten's frantic speed-of-light lovemaking, I wouldn't have time to feel edgy. No, this reminded me of the first time I'd fed Harry, not knowing what to expect, hesitant of imagined pain, honestly more than a little grossed-out at the prospect of a dead man touching me. The latter was no longer a problem, except a tiny mischievous part of my brain wanted to know if his dick would be cold like a cherry popsicle inside me.

His platinum eyebrow piercings twitched up in a playful arch as though he'd read my mind.

"Sorry." I swallowed hard. "I'm ... nervous. Oddly enough."

"It is my place to remedy such an affliction, and remedy it I shall," he soothed, letting one pale hand drift in my direction. An invitation. "Come now, ducky. It's only me."

"Only?" I choked. He made the room small with his presence, though he was not a large man and never had been. Ever before, his companionship had been the best I could have hoped for: comfortable, familiar. Now something else was up for grabs so to speak and I felt unworthy. His upright carriage and effortless poise made him seem too perfect, unreal, and even when I finally put my hand into his, he seemed to shift in and out of a lurid daydream.

"You've been in my arms a thousand times or more," he reminded me. He brushed my cheek with the back of his other hand, drawing me a step closer. My feet had forgotten how to work. It amused him, and he smiled knowingly, very aware of the effect he was having on me.

"We should maybe talk about this, before we go any further," I whispered. "A full-fledged official meeting. A pro-con list. I'll take notes ..."

One fine finger tilted my chin up and he captured my lips, quieting me with the tender press of his cool mouth. Not the invading

Kill-Notch force I was accustomed to, Harry's lips were soft, hesitant, tasting mine as a bee to nectar as he moved in closer. His hand took the small of my back, cupped me as though we were dancing. I tried and failed to suppress a tremor of intense fascination that brought a deep chuckle from my revenant.

"We certainly must talk," he agreed. His unearthly-quick fingers slowed to unbutton my jeans with teasing, methodical care. "A serious talk is warranted."

My heart was crawling wild and untamed up the back of my throat, crowding me, making it hard to breathe past its crazy-wired thrumming.

"A talk, yes, I can talk, assuming I can still breathe," I managed, nodding like I was in a trance. "Talking I can do."

"For you need to understand ..." The slow hand moved to crawl up the back of my t-shirt, inching up my spine. Taking a full handful of the fabric, he rushed it up over my head, pulling my arms up with it. "Exactly what you're getting into."

A bed? A casket? A gimp mask? My hazy brain tripped along dark and somewhat alarming possibilities while he considered me with a calculating gaze. I realized I had no idea what aroused Harry, none whatsoever, and maybe I should have given that some thought before now.

"I have been intimate with all my prior DaySitters, you understand," he confirmed, giving me a jealous jolt that wound me even tighter. The back of his hand brushed up my bare shoulder, raising all the little hairs with a tickling sweep of pleasure. "Each one promised they would not take the gift lightly. And yet ..."

I had to clear my throat to speak again around the heart slamming just below my voice box. "Gift?"

"Making the Bond's most intimate aspect active opens the door to the Overlord, as he is the Prince of Lust. All that He has to offer would be yours," Harry admitted reluctantly. "And they took it. They all take it, eventually. I cannot allow this to happen with you, my only love. You must understand the temptation, the ruin that could befall us both. The door will open, and once open, it shall never close. Even so, you must forevermore refuse His constant offers of power. We have taken such pains to remain ... pure. Risking that now, here, tonight, could cost us so very much indeed."

There was regret there, carefully set aside so it wouldn't show on his face. But I felt it on the undercurrent of our healing Bond and my brain squirreled away this walnut of truth, because surely it meant something. I couldn't fathom what at the moment. I was too busy looking down at Harry, wondering when he'd dropped to one knee to finish removing my jeans, which now lay in a denim pool at my ankles. His too-quick movement was unnerving at the best of times; when he was stripping me it was downright disquieting. I stepped out of the jeans, my skin so alive it sang in the chamber's always-warm air.

"So that's why you haven't ... we couldn't ..." I stammered. "But now?"

"We must," he warned, his voice leaving no room for argument. "I will not allow Monsieur Nazaire an inch of room to maneuver in this matter. The Frenchman has already taken too much."

There was uncertainty in Harry's battleship grey eyes, but it fled quickly. There was no doubt, however, about his own allure; graceful as a cat and fully aware of it, moving as always with that indefinable elegance, he tossed aside his black and chestnut paisley bedspread. His was a lordly sway rather than a swagger, hips lean and cocky under deep black silk sleep trousers I'd never seen him wear before. Maybe he'd never worn them because he knew he'd be irresistible in them. A small smile returned to play on his lips as he let me watch him, enjoying the way my hungry gaze ate him up. He had given himself over to the inevitable and was determined to do this his way.

Harry went to his knees beside his bed while I stood uncertainly alone in the center of the room, hugging my trembling middle, waiting, wondering what I should do next. In no-nonsense cotton bra and panties with the cartoon frog print, I wished I'd had the foresight to dress for the just-in-case. This was an occasion that called for sexy lace. I was so glad Harry refused to have mirrors in his chambers; I didn't want to see Plain Jane right now.

Harry worked at a noisy lock.

"Are you sure you're ready for this surge forward in our Bond, pussycat?" he challenged, his elegant British voice ending in a very male growl.

I swallowed hard, nodded boldly. "Been ready for years." *Or I thought I was.* "You're the one who always said no."

Harry removed a heavy set of iron shackles from a chest under his bed; they rattled and clinked as he attached one end to the bedpost.

Will I never learn to shut up?

"Such uncertainty." He suddenly appeared inches above my mouth, radiating that demure sensuality that drove me nuts. I started, trilling a little yip of surprise. He whisked it off my breath with another soft kiss. I sank helplessly into it, an addict to her hit, my head spinning. This time his tongue made a darting, too-brief exploration before he withdrew.

He looked over his shoulder to the shackles then back at me. The smile that spread over his lips finally reached his eyes and they danced. "Shall I quiet your mind?"

My heart drummed urgently, reminding me of its crisis. “Are you hiding a patchwork monster under the bed who might need electroshock later?”

“Do be serious, love,” he admonished.

“I am! Those chains aren’t for me, are they Dr. Frankenstein?”

“Just a precaution.” His full grin flashed glistening fang this time. “I would hate for you to get out of hand, my pet.”

Gulp. He didn’t wait for a reply. His forceful arms were roped with rigid muscle but he them used with surprising gentleness to lift me. It took him a mere heartbeat to lay me down on a wide expanse of silk sheets the deep golden brown-red of good cognac, sliding to prop himself on one elbow in one smooth, dynamic motion.

When his cool hand lighted at the curve of my breast, I was surprised my bra hadn’t magically disappeared like my shirt and pants. His thumb grazed over the thin cloth, lightly at first, then with a far more purposeful sweep. He fingered down the smooth fabric and exposed me, that masterful thumb lingering midair atop my stiffening nipple. When it finally landed, a brush of ice, I was struck plain stupid by a cold tingling shot from chest to groin, making my breath catch hard in my throat. I reached out for him, fingers itching to pull his face to my throat. *Feed, feed,* my strung-out brain thrummed.

Harry was all smooth skin and hard muscle as I played my hands along his taut stomach and over the broad expanse of his shoulders to the back of his neck. He didn't resist as I urged his face to my chin. A delicate sweep of lashes cast shadows across his cheeks and then brushed the delicate, sensitive skin of my neck.

Harry linked his powerful fingers into mine and I felt small and fragile. I wondered where my gloves had gone. The commanding press of his palms on mine swept me under the tidal wave of his Talent, and a psi-bridge snapped into place with an audible whip crack. My arms pulled upward, but just as I wondered why, Harry’s fangs sank into my jugular. His deep thrust penetrated, pinning me in place, surprising a small cry out of me. I only vaguely heard the shackles jostle, and the cold push of iron on my wrists only made me notice how incredibly hot the rest of me had become.

Harry’s hunger tugged at my vein, and when his heart first hammered into action, his hips writhed and ground against my side and he let out a low moan. He shifted, his hasty one-handed undressing shaking the bed. The sound of silk coming off his skin made my core slick.

He covered me with his naked weight. God, he was hard, hot from his feed, *so hot*, I marveled, so beautifully thick, throbbing against my hip bone. My body eagerly arched under him, my skin finally, *finally* delighting in the feel of his. Had anyone ever been this thrilled in the history of womankind? I tried to reach for him and found my arms trapped above my head, dragging from me a whimper of need.

"Try again," Harry demanded, his reply ragged, gruff . He tongued my throat as I struggled; apparently my lovesick brain is too dense to get that my little arms can't break iron clasps.

"More," he compelled, rasping hungrily. I obliged, wrestling in the irons to get free so I could touch him, wanting so badly to clutch the smooth, stiff erection teasing me. He sank fang again, this time at the side of my right breast.

I gasped, "Please? *Please* Harry."

His hand slid between my thighs and eased them apart as a growl trapped deep in the back of his throat escaped. He pressed just the tip against my moist lips, rendering me speechless with anticipation. I wriggled while my heart jack-hammered insanely. Lust gnawed low in my belly. Yet he hovered, teasing me with it, his mind licking through the psi-bridge to feel the need bucking through my body, suffocating my sanity.

His thickness surged into me all at once, a powerful thrust that rocked the bed. My hips curled up to meet each long thrust that followed. I thought he'd lose complete control but he stroked with agonizing slowness as though he had all night to do so, gaining momentum with aching delicacy.

"My own." His voice was a tremulous gasp as he struggled to hold back. "Not yet, my soft, sweet love. Not yet."

He paused then and did something I didn't expect: he brought his hand up and pressed it to my ribcage, just above my diaphragm, and said softly:

"This my gateway, this guarded by the unseen and trod upon by the unclean, this immortal causeway I do forever share with you, in accordance with our everlasting Bond."

My back rocked up off the mattress, filled with an inescapable shower of heat, like a castle's portcullis thrust open but instead of pouring out an army of horsemen it blasted me with infernal heat. I filled with a fat tongue of lava. I wasn't breathing; I could swear my heart stopped in my chest. Then just as suddenly as it began, it ended, and I fell back into the sweat-dampened sheets, mussed and dizzy, shackles clanking.

And something had changed, had *definitely* changed. Every nerve in my body jitterbugged with potential. A doorway that could never be closed had flung open wide, offering Hell's tempting promise, the snake's apple for Eve. The weight of the Great Adversary briefly noticed us and moved away, lumbering into the void and leaving us both affected by full-body quakes. My belly knotted with sickness.

"Here is your test, my angel," Harry said, barely a whisper. "I need to hear you say it."

I had heard the heavy footsteps of the devil. Not just the Overlord, though the demon king Asmodeus was bad enough. No, the awareness of the Great Adversary Himself had swept my paltry mind, I a momentary blip on His radar. I had felt Him, could feel Him still. I could sense, just below the average every-day psi I usually pulled forth, a hotter, more powerful version offered up; Groper 2.0. Drunk with the possibilities, I had to mentally back-peddle fast, back from the precipice of temptation.

"Harry?" I felt blind with terror, needing the comfortable familiarity of his voice more than ever.

"Say it, my love. You must."

All of the revenant's DaySitters must have given him exactly the same promise, so how could my words, no different than theirs, offer him any sort of reassurance? Maybe it was the price he'd put on it. Maybe that's how he knew I was serious. Or maybe our Groping, each to each, allowed him to see the sincerity and determination I really did feel.

"I'll never call on Him, Harry." I turned my temple to his chest and let out a long sigh. "I swear on Mark Batten's life."

My appetite flared anew, and he knew it. He laid an indulgent hand between my thighs again and stroked softly while my body went helplessly weak under his touch and I felt that sweet pressure humming down low, an onslaught of delicious tension. Strung out, I heard myself begging, and when I called him by name, he drove faster, so I said it over and over. He brought me to the brink, held me there until my cries overwhelmed him. I rocked forward in my restraints with a frustrated plea.

And that was when his iron-clad control snapped, disintegrated in one spectacular shiver. I knew this feeling; his whole body was shaking with the need to take me and I was more than ready for it. He rode me hard, hips driving me into the sweaty sheets until I gasped and cried out, hands balled in fists, railing against the chains. Twisting and arching, wishing I could sink my fingernails into his gorgeous ass, I felt him shudder with his release. He threw his head back, exposing his fair throat.

I couldn't help myself; I lunged up and bit him.

C50

By the time I'd caught my breath and settled the thunderous applause of my pulse, I realized I may have hurt him. I snuck a peek sideways.

Harry lay on his side, his body a mountain between me and the door. His lids were heavy with contentment. The hollow of his neck was a familiar, fragrant shelter marked by an ugly welt in the shape of my teeth. I pressed my open mouth there, kissing his skin, running my tongue along the new-filled vein pumping there.

"Harry?" I said drowsily. "What if I'm addicted to you now?"

He laughed happily, one hand's fine fingers playing through the sad, shorn remnants of my hair. I would have done the same, but I was stuck in the revenant's restraints, my sweaty skin smelling faintly of iron.

"The scent of your arousal is intoxicating." His voice, purring against the side of my neck, sent a hot wet jolt between my legs, awakening me again, making me want more.

"Jeez, you're gonna make me blow my cork again if ya keep talking like that."

"Such a fuss you make," he observed, slightly smug, one of his hands trailing lazily down my belly. "If this room weren't soundproofed, your agents might think I were killing you down here."

"Are you bragging?" I murmured, smiling into the curve of his shoulder. "Cuz it sure sounds like you're bragging."

"I have of course been complimented before on my performance, but never with such raucous enthusiasm. It was quite encouraging."

"Well, I encourage you to please cum again," I invited, to which he playfully *tsk-tsk*ed. Far from shocked, his eyes gleamed with answering heat. "Can I get out of these now?" I rattled the chains on the headboard. His answer was a wicked little smirk. "Guess that's a no."

"Sleep now, my naughty little muffin."

With our sex hot and vivid in my memory, I was sure I'd never sleep. But Harry turned my body away from him so that he could spoon behind me, and the minute his heart fell in audible rhythm with mine, surging like a pump in his chest, my eyelids dropped closed. One last waking breath from the deepest recesses of my lungs and I was gone.

I stirred sometime later with the feeling that something was different. Naked, pressed up against someone else's flesh, I came to with a start, and my wrists jerk-stopped with a loud metallic clatter, forcing me to remain pretty much where I lay. I craned around to find Harry smiling down at me in the near-dark around full fangs.

Most of the candles had burned down low. I let my head fall back into the silk pillows, rocked it to the side to stare up at him.

"I dreamt about you," I confessed. "We had smoking-hot sex and then you gloated about how awesome you were."

"That does not sound chivalrous, and you should know I am always a gentleman," he said with a knowing smile.

"Ha!" was my brilliant reply. Words couldn't express how *not* like a gentleman I saw him, now; when I tried to think how to say it, my brain scrambled like eggs on a hot, buttered pan.

For some reason, he felt it necessary to point out, "I am not your ham-handed FBI agent."

"No. You're not," I agreed, but let it drop. I wasn't about to bad mouth one lover to make another feel good. Harry knew exactly how fantastic he was; he didn't need to hear it. He brushed a stray hair away from my forehead.

I felt woozy, like I'd gorged myself on pleasure, an orgasm OD. Could a girl die from that? Deadly delirium? Was this the doing of Harry's infernal Overlord, the Prince of Lust? Were his demon fingerprints all over this bedroom? I was willing to risk it. I wondered if this was a one-time thing with Harry, an enjoy-it-while-you-got-it deal. Just in case, I allowed my tongue permission to roam, stroking the soft trail of hair along the hard flat plain of his chest, pushed my cheek there, felt the thud of his well-fed heart pumping like magic where it was normally still.

"I need to hear it one more time," Harry said softly, with a vulnerability I'd never heard from him before.

"I promise, Harry. I will not call on him."

Harry produced a big ornate key and without another word, unlocked my shackles.

C51

I'd tucked Wes away; after enduring my brother's miserable, flashing-angry glares, I'd shoved him in Harry's casket and told him to shut up and go to sleep. I understood the problem: Wes was hearing every thought in the house, and this had been a rotten night for it: Chapel and Batten fighting, both of them thinking their obscene thoughts, both Feds wondering where Harry and I had disappeared to, while Wes was painfully aware of the answer. The last thing Wes said to me before he closed the casket lid was:

"Batten's gonna ask where you went. He knows, or he thinks he knows." His fingers curled under the lid as he lowered it over himself slowly were pale against the ebony wood, which made me cringe. "He's falling to pieces, but he has to hear it."

Falling to pieces? That didn't sound like the minor territorial jealous reaction of an ex-lover. Maybe Wes was being overdramatic in interpreting; he was a new telepath after all, he couldn't begin to grasp the fine-tuning of psi. On my long walk up the stairs with my head hung low, I had images of walking the plank, or striding up to the guillotine. That can't be a good sign. I needed to distract Batten from the fact that I'd spent all evening in Harry's room. It was going to be hard to avoid the subject, since I smelled like sex and sweaty iron, not to mention Harry's cologne had rubbed off all over me. I pulled the front of my t-shirt out and stuck my nose down to sniff. My Cold Company smelled yummy, and the scent made me want to turn right back around and go back for seconds. I shouldn't have to feel guilty about that, but I did.

I was about to hit the top step when I had a light bulb moment. Ok, it wasn't a bright light bulb, maybe a 40 watt, but compared to my other ideas, it was fucking brilliant. Instead of joining Chapel and Batten's heated resumption of their argument in the living room, I spun on my heel and went down into the cellar again.

Rummaging through the basement storage closet for possible supplies yielded Carrie's small octagon fish tank with coils of old aquarium hose, a circular BBQ grill, an empty gas tank, some chicken wire (why the hell did Carrie have chicken wire next to crumbling mildewed boxes of dried tulip and hyacinth bulbs?) bags of peat and manure and black earth to amend the tricky soil in the Denver area, and a rusty shovel. I gathered some choice goods and started piling them near the stairs.

Next step: get Batten and Harry out of the cabin. They'd never approve. Wes wasn't awake to care; he hadn't adjusted to nocturnal living and was still wanting to sleep after dark. Chapel wouldn't approve either, but now that I had him by the short n'curlies (feeding a revenant, mister Supervisory Special Agent? *Tsk tsk*) I was pretty sure I could handle his objections.

Getting Batten, however, to go anywhere with a revenant was going to take some finesse: not my strong suit. I found Harry's keys in his top drawer with two dozen pairs of argyle and angora socks and no underwear; my immortal Commando. I slipped Harry's car key off a giant key ring that looked like it should belong to a dungeon master, and put it in my back pocket.

When I found my Cold Company, he was with Batten in the living room, in his wingback chair, one long leg slung over the arm in his usual reading position, holding a big floppy trade paperback. The cover said: Fire Fighter Prep.

I yanked it from his hands with a, "Nope," opened the door to the woodstove and tossed it in.

Harry stared at me, unblinking. "They have a night shift. I'd be in fire resistant apparel, my pet."

I ignored that; it was beyond ridiculous. Instead, I addressed a very grumpy FBI agent on the couch who looked like he was about to snap.

"Good evening, Mark. I need you to do me a favour."

"I've been known to do favours."

"Great. Drive into Ten Springs to the all-night grocer to get me some female stuff." I smiled winningly, complete with fluttering lashes. "Harry knows which ones, he can go with."

Batten's eyebrows pinched together. "Why can't you go?"

"PMS makes me a danger to the general public."

"That's not the only thing," he pointed out. "Let Harry go get your stuff."

"Harry makes the night cashiers nervous. They end up ringing the silent alarm and trouble ensues. Just go."

Batten asked Harry, "Why do I get the feeling she's trying to us out of here?"

"Fine." I have an exasperated sigh. "Want the truth?" I dug deep. "I'm in love with Gary Chapel and want to be alone with him. That's right, I said it."

Batten's stunned blink was followed by a disbelieving smirk that he fought unsuccessfully. "Since when?"

"Well, lately I've noticed that ..." I planted my hands on my waist, cocked my hips to the side. "Nerds are sexy." I mentally scrounged for more believable justification. "The way he stares at me over the rim of his glasses really turns me on."

Harry groaned, swinging his leg down from the arm of the chair. "I do not think I shall take pleasure in watching this farce much longer."

"She's gotta be the worst liar ever," Batten agreed, pained. "What do you figure she's up to?"

"Quite certainly it will be something neither one of us will enjoy," Harry replied. "Do be honest, my pet. If it is privacy you need—"

"Yes, that's it," I said, surprised I didn't think of it right off that bat. "It's Masturbation Monday and you guys are throwing off my routine."

Mark rubbed his forehead creases as though they caused him pain. "Don't think that bird's gonna fly either."

"My darling," Harry admonished. "If this is the case, should we not take Agent Chapel away from the house?"

"I might need him!" I blurted.

Harry nearly coughed up a mouthful of o-neg from his goblet.

I hurried on, "For protection. If the ghoul comes. While I'm ... y'know. Would you just *go*, please!"

Batten shrugged. "I could use some fresh air. You got the tires replaced on the Kawasaki, right? Mind if I drive?"

The revenant looked horrified by the idea of another man piloting his bike, glancing at me with dismay. "Is there something in this for me?"

Batten shrugged. "I'll tell the cashiers you're a wealthy bachelor looking for a new wife."

"Not entirely a falsehood." Harry's eyes lit with the humour. "The helmets are in the mudroom."

I waited for them to put their boots on and trudge out the front door before collecting my materials and hustling them up the stairs. Chapel was upstairs, recovering from his steamed fight with Batten and his draining feed of two immortals. But for my shifting things around, the house was mausoleum-quiet. The back yard was as Leviathan's abyss, without the faintest scrap of starlight above, bringing to mind Hell's yawning black maw. Another winter storm rolled in slow on dead air, pushing heavily at the tops of the trees. I left the light on over the kitchen sink, and remembered my mother when I did so: she always said to leave a cheery circle of light to come back home to. Just doing so made me feel a touch warmer, and in a rush I missed the times before Harry, when my mother still wanted me around.

Keeping one eye out for Chapel, I passed the office mirror and checked to make sure the reflection was just me. The black-watch spell had not encountered any new intrusions; the mirror showed only my own freshly-screwed but careworn self. I had to admit, sex had put a fetching glow in my cheeks. Sadly, I also had a nice set of pimples blooming on my chin, probably from me resting my chin in my bare hands too much out of exhaustion.

I shrugged into my parka and hauled my materials out the back door, slogged through the snow, scanning for any other footprints. Ajax was sleeping with his new friend in the closest Aspen; they had reached some sort of tentative peace, the way two housecats will after fighting for dominance. Ajax didn't stir when I strolled past, and neither did Wesley's unnamed debt vulture. Under cold, crisp white stars, Shaw's Fist was dark and mysterious like Batten's deep blue eyes, with the same unknowable depths.

Digging a hole in the dirt floor of the boathouse had sounded like a good idea in my head, but then a lot of things do: driving to rescue my mortal enemy, sleeping with a heartless jerk, scarfing a whole box of Oreos in less than ten minutes. Reality is usually far less feasible, full of unconsidered problems. The boathouse, for one, was unheated; it was no more than 33 degrees in there. The ground on the far side of Harry's covered sports car was hard as a rock, frozen stiff. I had to put my Keds on the shovel and jump my full weight onto it with each dig. I got about two foot deep before I ran out of space to put the excess dirt, and had to haul it down to the end of the boathouse where an old canoe with faded paint lay on its side.

The smell of fresh-turned dirt blended with unused life jackets gone musty over time. A cockshut melody of pre-storm wind pressing bodily against the old building harmonized with the constant clunk-*chink* of my digging and the low electric hum of the chest freezer. My breath fogged in front of my face, and before long I was sweating under my clothes and aching everywhere. Under my gloves I felt blisters forming on the heels of my palms. Pretty soon I was on my knees, scraping and struggling to make the hole deep enough.

Finally, shivering with the now bone-deep cold, I tossed the shovel aside and slid the BBQ grill and long butane lighter under the car in the darkest shadow behind the back driver's side wheel. I found a long-handled fishing net and a Timberline fishing knife in Carrie's tackle box, on the back bench.

I turned off the car alarm, unlocked the gas cap and tucked the aquarium tubing into Harry's gas tank, tentatively putting my lips to the clean end, prepared to suck, hoping I was right that Harry's obsessive need to keep things "as they should be" would extend to keeping his precious toy topped-full of fuel. I gave an inhale through my pursed lips to start the gasoline flowing up toward my mouth.

"What the hell are you doing?"

My heart kicked. Choking on gas, I spat on the ground then tucked the running end of the hose in the cold pit. It sounded like someone piddling in the corner.

Batten's shadow in the doorway was waiting for an answer, so I said, "Taking a whiz?"

"Try again."

"Huffing gas fumes?"

His faceless shadow crossed its arms.

"You won't like the real answer, so why ask?" I stood, crossing my arms too. As he moved forward and the work light washed his face, something hard in his eyes made me cringe. I could tell by his all-brought-up-to-speed tone that he knew I'd gotten laid. Did he know it all? The shackles? The devil's footsteps? How could he? "Why are you still here? I thought you were leaving."

He came deeper into the yellow glow, his eyes tracing the car's shape under the tarp. He lifted one corner of the stretchy fabric cover and then, as though not believing what he was seeing, peeling the tarp back further and further, his excitement demanded that he strip the car, had to throw the whole thing back. The tarp rustled against itself as it fell aside. Batten's breath whistled out.

"Holy fuck," he whispered, adding white clouds next to mine. "Do you know what this is? This is a Bugatti Veyron EB 16.4 Sang Noir."

"Whatever. It's a car." I discretely wiped my tongue clear of gas taste on the sleeve of my puffy pink parka.

"Is this yours?"

A sharp laugh shot out of my gut. "Yeah right. Like I need something like that."

"Something like … don't you know what this is?"

"Yeah, it's Harry's baby. Whatever you do, don't—holy hell!" I yelped. "You're *touching* it!"

I didn't think he could help himself, though. One muscular hand drifted in mid-air as though daring himself, landing softly. Mark stroked the car's super high-gloss piano black finish with reverence, a slow, almost affectionate caress, like he was applying oil to the length of a swimsuit model's taut belly. This went on for some time, while the trickling sound filled his stunned silence and the smell of gasoline swam in the boathouse's close quarters. Finally, he got to the Bugatti's windows, pressed his nose up against the glass, cupping his hands. A nervous, excited laugh escaped him. He sounded like a little boy in front of a candy store, except for the swearing.

"Look at that fuckin' interior. Fuck me, Jesus. He doesn't drive this?"

"Not in the winter. Never in the winter."

"Why the hell are you driving that shit Buick if he can afford this?"

"Hey, what's wrong with the Buick?" I demanded. "I like the tank, don't disparage the tank!"

I knelt on the clumps of churned frozen dirt and put gas cap back on, wiped up spill down side with the rag. Batten was still heavy-breathing on Harry's Bugatti like a sex addict at a strip joint. "Do you have any idea how much this thing costs?"

"Nope, nor do I care. You were going now?" I reminded.

"Marnie, the tires alone for this car cost twenty-five grand."

"Oh, come on. What kind of maniac would pay twenty-five thousand dollars for ..." The rest of that sentence was pointless: Harry would. Only the best for Harry. It was almost as much as he paid for the cabin.

I studied Batten, wondering if he had wood. He certainly looked near-orgasmic. His bottom lip was quivering, caught under the straight white clutch of a hard bite. I had never considered Harry's fondness for expensive sports cars to be much more than a shiny hobby. Certainly I'd never become aroused by the sight of one. Batten's reaction was fascinating; I wondered what he'd say if I suggested ...

"You know, if you promised to feed Harry every day," I breathed in my most devilish voice, "He'd buy you one of your very own."

Batten hand clutched his middle like he'd been shot in the stomach with the Surprise Cannon. He cut his eyes at me over the Bugatti's roof, noted my Cheshire smile, and visibly wilted. "Very funny."

"Sorry. He's not even gonna let you ride in it. Don't ask him. Pretend you didn't see it."

"Why have it if you won't share?" he said, and again he reminded me of a young boy raging about the unfairness of life. I frowned, wondering if he just meant the car, my nose getting slightly out of joint.

"It's not mine. I don't make the rules."

"You could make him share," he wheedled.

I laughed, amazed. One of his big hands went up to massage his temple, like the sight of the car was causing his brain to go on the fritz.

"Zero to sixty in two point four seconds," he told me, as though it mattered. "Top speed two hundred and fifty-three miles per hour."

"Kinda silly, since the speed limit around here's 55. You wanna get a speeding ticket for eighteen thousand dollars?"

"That's not the point," he informed me so seriously I had to laugh a second time. He squinted into the interior again, and I tossed my rag at him.

"Wipe off the saliva or he'll know you were out here. I don't drool on cars."

"Any possible bribe you can think of to get him to let me sit in it?"

"Maybe if you lube up, bend over and grab your ankles?" I suggested, grinning from ear to ear. A confused grimace tore down his eyebrows only for a moment, then he wilted some more.

"I'm serious, Marnie," he said.

"I'm not. He ain't interested in your orifices. Hot blood and insane speeds are Harry's only weaknesses, and he doesn't trust you enough to let you get close to him or the car."

"What about …" I could see him racking his brain for anything he could possibly offer. When I shook my head mock-sadly, still grinning, he swore and buffed the breath-fog off the windows, shining the glass with the reverence usually reserved for altar boys preparing the Eucharist. "I don't think I can handle being this jealous of Harry. I'm not going to be able to sleep tonight knowing this monster is out here, just sitting here, waiting to roar."

I chortled. "It's a *car*."

"It's not a …" He reigned himself in, resigned to a life without Bugatti. "Fine. We're on our way out. What are the chances that you're going to accidentally blow yourself up in here?"

"That's pretty insulting." I thought about it. "Less than fifty percent."

"That good, hunh?" His eyes strayed back to the car's cloaked shape.

"I'm not using magic, just my brains," I assured him.

He lowered his face and shook his head, refraining from the obvious comment. "You should move Harry's car outside."

"Gee, your concern for my welfare has me all choked up." I flipped him a gloved bird.

"It's a two million dollar car, for fuck's sake. They only made fifteen of these," Batten stressed.

"Yeah? Well there's only one Marnie Baranuik."

"Thank God," Batten muttered. "Seriously, move the goddamned car if you're going to do anything stupid."

"Moving Harry's car *would* be doing something stupid. He'd rip me a new one."

I heard Harry's motorcycle rumble to life, and Mark's head turned. He hesitated. *No no, don't ask, don't bring it up*, I thought frantically, Wes' words rattling through my brain: *he has to hear it from you*. His eyes snuck sideways at the car again.

"Need anything else at the store? Chocolate pudding? Pepsi? A flamethrower?"

I turned away to put the tubing aside. "Don't make me like you."

"Can't help it," he replied, and his boots crunched the snow as he retreated to join the revenant. I smiled with my back turned, smiled in relief, smiled privately in the dark, away from him. I placed the little kitchen fire extinguisher beside Harry's insanely expensive car.

I considered the Bugatti, shrugged, and went to fetch Kristin's eyeball.

C52

The shriveled scrap of eye looked ridiculously small in the fish net and as I walked around the back yard with it swinging before me, queasy and faint, positive the grand scheme I'd hatched wasn't going to work in the limited free time I had wheedled. With the handle clutched in my oven-mitted hands, I flounced about in the growing breeze, making sure to flutter the eye in the gusts, hoping this would summon the ghoul from thin air. The eye was barely a scrap of filament now, and there was a heavy dose of doubt thrumming through my veins; what if she didn't sense it? How would I lure her, if not with this? What else could possibly draw her out of hiding? Maybe she wasn't even nearby. The black-watch spell showed me only Ajax and Wes' unnamed vulture in the yard.

But the stench blowing across the lake left little doubt; somewhere, the remains of Kristin Davis were shambling, or swimming, or lurching around. I had maybe 45 minutes before Harry and Batten cruised back to the cabin with a bag full of very unnecessary feminine hygiene products. The wind dropped, and a sound pulled my eyes to the dock.

That's when I saw her, barely visible beneath the planks. How long had she been festering under there in the lake with her head half-caved in, poisoning my water and lurking until it was time to come at me again? It wasn't often a dream came true, especially not a drippy oozing undead nightmare like Kristin Davis' stubborn ghoul. The thing that was once a pleasant, friendly twelve year old blind girl discovering a love for Beethoven was now a horror of epic proportions, a horror that had apparently made a new home under my dock.

Corpse beetles had devoured most of her fleshy parts, gorged themselves, and would come back to finish the rest soon no doubt. She didn't seem to mind. Her bare ligaments creaked and stretched. Her mouth gaped stupidly, but there was an infernal intellect behind her empty sockets that made the space between my shoulder blades crawl. When she craned her head in the direction of the fish net, where her soggy, stringy eye was swinging, my stomach hit the floor.

I pelted for the boathouse door, the ghoul a foul shade clambering at my back as I whipped around the back of the car and grabbed for the rear end of the Bugatti to slow my speed to make the turn. My Keds pounded frozen dirt as I jumped the open hole. The goopy fish net fell from my grip. I heard the ghoul scrambling close behind. For a second I thought she'd jumped the trap too, or saw it in time to shrink back, because her footsteps stopped.

Then Dead Kristin made a bone-clattering thud into the pit, raining hard earth in an icy shower around her. I skid to my knees, my brain screaming *hurry hurry hurry*, swiping the BBQ grill from under the car and slamming it down atop the hole.

My breath left in an explosive rejoice, half-whoop half-coarse gasp.

The ghoul's questing, claw-like finger bones scrambled at the rusty iron grate like hard little worms wriggling to find purchase. On one knee, I pounded one dusty Ked on the grill to hold it down, kicking more dirt down in her rotten face.

"Sorry, babe," I said, not really sorry for the ghoul at all, but wishing I could spare Kristin Davis this end.

I threw off the oven mitts, fished under the car for the butane lighter, didn't find it. My mouth went dry as Dead Kristin's bony hands thumped and the metal bars clanged my death knell. Her old raisin of a face came up suddenly, all gnashing teeth and pale pink gums, rocking the grill, oblivious to pain now. I gave a little shriek and flung my hands away from her, keeping pressure on my foot as hard as I could. Craning, my bare hands fanned under the car, fingers questing desperately. Her mouth opened and her slimy black prune of a tongue lolled out along the sole of my shoe. *Blerg!*

I brushed against the butane lighter's frost-covered plastic end. Finger-tipping it closer so I could grab it, leaving my foot on the grill, I backed my body away as far as my arm would go, aimed the lighter at the side of the pit, and flick-flick- *kafoompf.*

The gasoline caught in a searing blast of flames.

I jerked my sneaker away, but the grill clattered as she shoved it up, so I stomped it down again, wary of the licking fire consuming its target.

Cooking ghoul smells a lot like burnt cheese. I'm adding that to my list of things I wish I didn't know. With an inhuman shriek, the ghoul curled into a ball, acrid green smoke rising from its eye sockets, crumbled nose and mouth. I forced myself not to think about Kristin; I could hear her little preteen voice caught behind the ghoul's agony. When the monster she had become shrieked, I slammed my eyes shut and told myself this was for her own good. Something inside me went cold, hard and still, something that had always before been soft and warm. Part of me died, and I wondered if this was how murderers felt.

When the blackened hands fell away, I removed my Ked and inspected the gooey melted bottom. The rubber was like singed cheese, smoking and hanging in strings. Probably I should shove it in the snow.

I dusted my hands off on the oven mitts and thought, *What do you know? I didn't fuck it up.* I looked around to see if anyone was here to witness my triumph.

Dead Danika Sherlock stood drooling in the boathouse doorway.

C53

I heard Chapel slam out the back door with a shout as I threw myself backward, wind-milling rapidly behind the Bugatti, mindful of the BBQ grill to make sure Dead Kristin didn't fly out like the monster's second coming in a bad horror flick. The second ghoul smelled worse than the first, *fresher*, more like old cheese and dirty socks; she hadn't served as a smorgasbord for corpse beetles and she had both her eyes, which trained in on me, tracking my every move. What had brought her here? My intuition squealed something unfathomable, and I'm sure if I wasn't soggy-brained with terror, I might have made sense of it.

Chapel was calling my name; behind Danika's ghoul I could see him running while doing that two-handed gun-aiming pros do, which I'd always thought was a pretty cool trick. I'd never seen it done outside of an episode of Cops. He sighted on the back of the ghoul's head. Pointless, I thought, and he should know it. Instinct, I was guessing.

"Marnie, get out of there!" He called over the snow, closing the distance between us. I whipped out the kitchen fire extinguisher and ran forward, feeling like a badass. The ghoul snarled, dropping a wet hunk of flesh off her decaying lip. I aimed for that spot with the butt of the fire extinguisher; the solid can made a resounding clang as it rocked her head back.

"That's for stabbing me," I shouted, and hit her again as she lurched forward. "And that's for lying about Mark. And this is for trying to steal Harry."

Chapel was there then, grappling with her, hauling her by the armpits. I backed away, kicked the BBQ grill off the already-blackened pit and turned to instruct him. It wasn't necessary; he shoved her forward at the dark gap, thrusting her so hard that her left arm flew out of its socket with a wet crack and skid under the front tire. The rest of her tumbled in a pile, scrambling as she collapsed, one remaining arm flailing. I hit the flicker on the butane lighter again and the residual gas lit like magic, trapping Danika's ghoul in a fiery embrace.

"Arm!" I barked, and Gary kicked it to me. "Grill!" Gary booted that to me too. I shoved the oven mitts back on and muscled the grill down over Danika's still-muscular arms, as she fought to toss it off. The pit wasn't deep enough to keep her in, if she was determined enough to explode out of it. Her jaws chattered and I removed the hot grill to kick her in the mouth.

"Knock it off," I roared, frantic to be done with this. "Don't be a little bitch and *die already*."

I kicked her again. Her head snapped back, leaving a big smear of rotting flesh on the toe of my Keds. Her teeth fractured, splitting her tongue in half. Horrified, I forced the grill back down and stood on it with the opposite foot, giving the left one a dose of burning love.

Dead Danika flew into a wildly flailing, pitching hysteria, sickly wet noises popping in her throat. I turned my eyes away so I wouldn't have to watch her face melt off in a big waxy slab.

As soon as the hands stopped clawing, I pulled my foot back and gave it and the pit a few blasts with the fire extinguisher. Then I foamed the Bugatti so Harry's two million dollar car wouldn't go *kablooey*. Charred ghoul bits mixed with foam spit up and floated out of the pit into the air.

But it wasn't over. After the foam and charred ash settled, a warmth remained, a sickly heat that did nothing to warm my spirit or put me at ease. I felt my lips moving even before I could imagine the problem.

"Beroth of Sanchoniaton, Berith of the Sichemites, known as Duke Bolfri of the Grave, here and below, Seer of the Past, Present and Future. I witness thy Great and Terrible otherworldly presence, and hereby free thee of thine unnatural chains to mortal flesh."

A shriek to rattle the boathouse window ripped through the air and blew past us, shoving out the door and into the night. When our hair settled and our shoulders un-pinched, I craned my neck and snuck a peek at Chapel.

He looked like a man in a trance; his mouth opened, but he didn't seem to be able to make any sort of sense, so he closed it again. When he did speak, he said:

"What the hairy fuck?"

I'd never seen him baffled, and I sure as hell never heard him swear, *ever*; a laugh, sudden and straight from my quivering knot of a gut, exploded into the night air behind the vanished demon. I was victorious. Exhilarated.

"Burnt the heck out of my Keds, but I think the ghoul problem's solved." I tossed the fire extinguisher on the ground with a clang. When I was sure my knees weren't going to embarrass me by buckling, I took a few shuffling footsteps toward him. "Thanks for, uh … Danika."

"I've got your back," he said dazedly.

"I'm sorry you got ghoul scum on your hands."

"Not your fault." He dropped his too-wide eyes down and examined the smears on his palms and in between his fingers. "I'm going to throw up."

I nodded in complete understanding. "I might do that too. We'll take turns."

"OK." He backed out of the boathouse. "I'm sorry about before. About overstepping the boundaries. I owe you an explanation."

"Maybe later," I suggested. "Right now, I'd love a shower. And then what do you say you and me celebrate by getting rip roaring drunk, Gary Chapel?"

Gary bent to pick up his gun, looked at it like he didn't understand why he even carried one any more. "Where is everyone else?"

"Buying me tampons and chocolate." I motioned to the stinking ghoul pit. "I have PMS."

He surveyed the damage. "Obviously."

"Batten drank all my gin, but Harry always has absinth," I said, putting a hand out to grab his elbow. "How about it, SSA Chapel? Are you on duty tonight?"

"I don't see why the hell I should be. Hey Marnie?"

"Yes, Gary?"

"I meant what I just said: I've always got your back. Why didn't you …" His face appeared pained. "I hope you know you can always call on me. You never have to face any of this alone: the Motor Inn, Ruby, any of it. I wish you hadn't gone alone."

I bit my tongue, casting a glance at the reeking boathouse, where Danika had finally come to rest. "Look, I'm no angel. I don't pretend to be. I had to go to the Motor Inn. She had something on me, threatened to expose it to the media if I didn't help her. It was self-interest on my part."

"Don't protect him," Chapel advised with a shrewd look. "Mark's a big boy, he can take care of himself. And when he can't, it's my problem, not yours. If he knew that's why you went, he'd say the same thing."

I kept my face blank. "I have absolutely no idea what you mean, Gary."

"All right," he conceded.

"It's all water under the bridge," I sighed, trying to change the subject. "The Green Fairy awaits. I'll get the bottle, you get the sugar cubes."

A furious squawk made both of us flinch. In the distance, Ajax and Wesley's debt vulture had taken flight to defend their turf against a third bird, a creature of generous proportions and enormous swooping wing span. I cast my chin around nervously at the yard, looking for movement. Looking for Gregori Nazaire.

"Too bad Ruby Valli didn't follow her bitches in," he mused, then caught himself. "Monsters. I don't say the b-word. Officially, I didn't say any of that."

"Officially, I didn't hug you for sayin' it," I said, and planted a big wet one on his cheek, squeezing him hard. Taken off guard, he was stiff in my arms, and didn't relax until I said: "It's fine, Chapel. Harry isn't going to rip your head off for a hug."

He let his breath out, patting my back. "But Gregori Nazaire might. We should get back inside."

By the time the familiar growl of the Kawasaki rumbled out front, Chapel and I were showered, re-dressed, smashed on a very old bottle of Pernod Fils and acting silly. Slightly more sober than he, I was able to register the fact that Gary Chapel was an amusing drunk. His smile was every bit as warm and professional as ever, but when something tickled him he let loose a high, bubbling giggle that set me off over and over. Half way into the bottle, I'd realized that having Chapel feed my Harry suddenly wasn't the worst thing in the world. Especially now that I'd seen a ghoul's face slop off.

Wes joined us in the front yard to greet them, complaining about a craving for cheeseburgers. I didn't have the heart to tell him he couldn't eat real food anymore, not now, not yet; there's only so much you can tell a new dead guy in one day.

We let Harry and Batten know about the ghouls. The expressions of shock on their faces were priceless, if a little insulting. I couldn't blame them for being surprised, but did they have to go on and on about how unlikely it was that I had succeeded? Harry offered me the bag of female stuff he knew I didn't need; I hoped there were cookies inside. Our fingers brushed as he passed it, mine warm and sticky with slopped booze, his cool and firm.

An ill spark lit between us and his hand shook. Without warning, Harry's gimlet gaze bleed past silver to pure white, and the voice that purled on the back of his throat was unrecognizable, inhuman. "MJ ..."

Shot through with panic, I put my hand on Chapel's forearm to steady myself. "Gary ..." I choked on my warning. "Oh God, Gary. Back. Get back!"

And Harry whispered: "Run, my love."

C54

Wesley whipped around and lunged at me, hissing, fangs bared. I slugged his open mouth, feeling the press of mouth-hot enamel against my bare knuckles. Psi flung open a link, a blood-red wash of wild hunger, uncontrolled. Ducking, I fell under Wes' reaching arms, scooted through his legs, heaving the Buick's door open and plunging inside.

"Get in the car, get in the car!" I hollered over my shoulder.

The minute the doors slammed behind us, the Buick was rocking over on its side. I fished under the passenger side seat for my Beretta while Batten was distracted. With a window-shaking slam, the car rolled onto its roof. I folded into an awkward flailing ball upside down, my neck bent unnaturally. Flipping over, feeling as dexterous as a walrus on a bicycle, I watched through the windshield as Harry grabbed the side of the car and gave it another heave.

"Hold on!" I warned as the old Buick came off the ground. This time, glass broke somewhere, and the inner workings made horrible crunching metal noises as one revenant rolled it and the other slammed bodily into it from the driver's side. Batten poured out the bent passenger side door and Chapel and I followed; we beat-feet across the frozen ground, not near enough to the house to make it. The SUV's black shadow was the closest shelter.

Behind us, the Buick tumbled end over end landing with a teeth-jarring smash, crumpling into itself when it came to rest.

Batten exploded: "Fuck!"

I slugged him in the arm and shouted: "Don't look back, just go *go!*"

"What's going o—"

"Don't stop!" I screamed. "SUV! SUV!" We dove in, making room for one another in a desperate pile of arms and legs.

We'd barely shut the door when Wes slammed into the passenger side. The safety glass held, but wouldn't for long. Dropping in front from the sky, Harry's fist pulverized the hood. Metal crumpled with a screech. Harry bared his teeth, saliva flying from behind his fangs as he hissed in frustration. My hackles went up and stayed there. I'd never seen him feral and out of control, but I knew it was as bad as it could get.

"Don't make eye contact!" I reminded over the sound of the pummeling. "They'll try to snag you with their mind control. Keep your eyes averted!"

Chapel's shirt had been torn down one arm and his skin shredded by the Buick's splintered metal grabbing at him. Blood plumed down from Batten's nose, and he ran the back of his hand to swipe it clear.

"Kit's in Harry's room."

"You'll never make it," I panted. "I'll go."

"Fat fucking chance," Batten snarled.

"I'm faster than you could ever be," I assured him. "And I'm the only one who can—"

Chapel pointed past our faces. "Brace yourself, *they're going to flip it!"*

The windshield burst in a glittering hail of glass and a back tire blew with a bang. My face dropped into the gear shift hard. A solid welt sprang instantly on my forehead like a black knuckle.

I crawled over the seat into the back, yanked down the back seat pad, accessed the spare tire well, wrestled the tire out, shoved it in Batten's lap. "Chapel, get in," I barked. "And stay down."

He blinked at me. "I can't do that?"

"If anyone should be hiding in there it's you," Batten told me sternly, "But we gotta get out of here before they crumple us into a big metal Rubik's cube."

"We're going to climb out, so they can shred our throats?" I challenged. "And you call me a dunce?"

Chapel's hand quickly went through his pockets for a spare clip. He didn't have one. He looked hesitant to drop the gun, though it was useless in his hand. "Why are they doing this?"

"Someone got them by the feeding instinct, throwing them a big fat dose of feral aggression. And I bet I know who."

Chapel said, "Ruby Valli."

"Could she do this with black magic?" Batten asked.

I was pretty sure Ruby Valli, left to her own sick devices, could do anything. With her shop burnt down and all her supplies gone, I didn't know how she'd come up with something so complex so quickly, but I didn't have time to worry about it. "Has to be her. The only other person who hates us this much ..." *Is dead, Dunnachie is dead*, but I was careful not to finish that thought aloud. "Is a vampire hunter. He wouldn't have the skills to do this."

Batten studied the look on my face, sniffing freely-running blood back up into his nose, then nodded; I thought maybe he agreed with my thought, and not what came out of my mouth, and wondered if my eyes had told all.

Batten put the seats back and cranked them into a half-sleep to create cavity. Wes was crouching in the corner by the rear window, making an ungodly noise in the back of his throat, pounding holes in the SUV's body like it was paper.

"Marnie, get in." Batten motioned to the cavity, voice raised. "Don't fuckin' argue with me, just do it."

I pulled the Beretta out from my back and shoved it unceremoniously in his face.

"You get the fuck in, asshole, before they make me accidentally pull this trigger." Batten dove like he'd been kicked in the temple. The SUV rocked again. "Now, I'm sure I told you: I'm faster than you. The reason for that is, right now, wearing his dinner fangs and trying to work out how to crack this shell to eat the tender morsels inside. *I'm* going. You're staying, both of you."

That being said, I really didn't know what the hell I was going to do, once I got inside the cabin, but it was a safer place to think over my options. I hoped it wouldn't come down to getting Batten his kit.

I tumbled over the seat back and kicked at the weakened car window, spider-veins of fractures making it unclear. I had to do it three times, but finally squares of safety glass showered my ankle. Wrangling out of the shattered car window took what felt like forever, considering two slavering revenants in a blood rage were on the other side of the car whipping jagged-edged chunks of the SUV's metal around. I felt like I was fishing for sharks with my legs as bait.

The second my head was clear I threw myself in a clumsy roll and got to my feet. I booked-it for the front door, afraid to look where the vamps were. Breath streamed from my nostrils in furious puffs.

Wesley's alert, a high keening wail of hungry triumph, roiled over the yard behind me. An answering bellow from deep in Harry's throat told me I had two seconds, tops, to get in the house. I was wrong. 190 pounds of angry monster impacted my back and catapulted me forward into snow. I flung one arm out to stop my spin. Coming to rest, I shook my head clear.

Fangs ripped and shredded into that hand; I felt little bones bend like twigs under the pressure of Harry's jaws, threatening to snap. The high-pitched sound that tore from my chest was an entreaty that went unheard, but there was no pain.

The hand wasn't appealing enough. Harry snarled his dissatisfaction and threw it away from his blood-smeared lips, and moved closer to eye my neck. My hand felt like a slab of throbbing, useless meat.

"Harry! Harry, it's me, please come back to me," I begged, nearly weeping as my un-chewed hand pushed the front of his shirt. If he got on top of me, I was done for. But he didn't.

He reared to strike from the side, honed-in on my throat. I shoved two fingers up fast at his eyes and his head darted aside, the curve of his neck reminding me of a cobra.

"Mind your manners, revenant!" I attempted, my voice sonorous, surprising me. "Death Rejoices, for your DaySitter calls you forth from wild pursuits, and you *will* listen. I command it."

He bayed, caught in the throws of ecstasy at the scent of blood spilling from my palm.

"Or not," I answered. I flicked my injured hand, watched bright red spray lash the snow, drawing his eye for a split second, which gave me an instant to make a break for it; sheer luck allowed me to slip from his sudden grab. Launching away, I sprinted through the air to the porch.

My knees wobbled, threatening to pitch me back down, and my brain taunted, *He's coming, he's faster, you'll never make it.* I threw one glance back at the decimated SUV over my shoulder, saw a swirling blur of black coat around pale flesh, kept pounding the ground, fists clenched and pumping. Three steps away, two, one, my quivering lips moved non-stop:

"Lord Guy Harrick Dreppenstedt, I revoke your welcome to my home! Wesley Alexander Wasp Baranuik Strickland I revoke your welcome to my—" I felt the brush of fingers on my neck and dove, "Home!"

I tucked and rolled. The rag rug skid with me, and I hit the hallway wall in a human ball. My Beretta went skittering out of my pocket down the hall until it hit something and jumped to a stop.

Both revenants hit the open doorway at a full run, the preternatural rush sheering the very air. They struck the spectral barrier with an audible crack, like a shot. It shuddered the door jamb, rocked the cabin like it was made of popsicle sticks. But it held.

Unwelcome, Harry staggered onto his heels, face contorting furiously. He threw back his shoulders in one quick move, shedding his long black coat in an irate jerk. His ghostly pallid chin jut forward and he roared at me, demanding my surrender. I huddled around my bleeding hand, cupped it against my middle and waited to witness the outcome: Un-Invitation in the real world? I'd done a second year paper on the theory of Un-Invitation, but like most preternatural biology, theories went untested for decades.

Harry's lip curled back, revealing the fangs that normally worked gently at my skin. Now they were weapons, cutting blades, killing canines. A sad brand of terror tore a hole in my heart. His eyes, beaming arctic white now with widening pupils eating up the expanse, rattled me more than anything else, more than my inability to catch my breath or the sickening drumming in my head or the sight of the ruined cars in the drive. His eyes were empty of recognition, empty of his fine English dignity and grace, empty of his affection or sex; they had fled to pure primal heat, wanting only to rip me open like a bag of blood. They dehumanized me utterly, and for a moment I hated him for it.

Fingers of his mind control wriggling in the front of my brain shook me out of my self-pity then; they sought any hold they could master, a subtle pull at my willpower. Quickly, I broke eye contact, dropping my gaze to the threshold, where on hands and knees Wesley waited, slavering for his meal. My brother's lolling head came up and through the pale rainforest of his long knotted hair, his piercing eyes also tried to catch mine.

I crammed my lids down and my lips tightened too, squelching a sob I hadn't known was building. *Monster.* I heard my mother's voice, and in that instant I agreed with her. *Monster*, she had pronounced, and this was why Harry was never to come back to her home. And now her only son, her baby, was wavering between trying to rip me open, or returning to the SUV for another hunt. Wes focused-in on my rapidly-jumping jugular and another high wail leaked from his throat.

On shaking arms, I peddled backward, making distance, thinking as long as the revenants could see me right in front of them, Batten and Chapel were safe in the demolished SUV. Maybe they could even slip out, slip away, down the road to safety. I held onto that hope until my wrist encountered a foreign rubber obstacle. The obstacle moved, tapped up and down, jiggling my hand with it.

I tilted my head back to look.

"Hello, Marlene." Ruby Valli beamed down at me, a toothy smile, eyes glistening with victory. She had my gun.

C55

I'm not sure I even thought about it. Must have been my lizard-brain at work. My lizard-brain is miles from ladylike. As I flipped to hands and knees, one arm shot up and I punched the old lady in the box.

Ruby's air went out in a whoosh and she squeaked as her knees clamped together around her injured crotch. I scuttled past her on hands and skidding knees like a kid playing horsie as she popped her invisibility spell again, vanishing. The office door was awash with weird colours, flickering light, sickly green; I couldn't look, didn't have time. My skin crawled along one shoulder and I launched to my feet in a full-out run, arms akimbo, dripping blood from my palm, aiming head-long for the mudroom. A bullet popped in the kitchen, another, and lead zinged past me to hit the fridge with a metallic report. I scrambled behind the shadowy corner of the washing machine, using its bulk for a shield, pausing to think frantically, what to do, where to go, and also: *damn shit fuck!*

Inside or outside? Inside, with the invisible lady, who might be training my own Beretta around the edge of the washing machine at my skull right this second? (My forehead skin crawled with the knowledge that it was highly likely.) Outside, to be ripped open by the sweet, loving revenant I trusted implicitly until tonight, the last thing I see being the mats in my baby brother's unfortunate Viking dreadlocks as he waited for his turn to lap at my vein juice? Lord and Lady, are those my only two choices?

I heard the kitchen floor's tell-tale squeak and knew Ruby had crossed in front of the oven, skulking in this direction. Dread spilled cold acid into my churning belly. Ears perked for another sound, I worried I might be too late to make any choices. There were no shadows falling in the open doorway. Shouldn't she still cast a shadow? I waited, pulse rocketing through my veins, my brain screaming *go, go now, just go* but my body unable to so much as flinch. I was stuck, glued by indecision, trapped by doubt and unadulterated terror.

A crash out front and an echoing snarl told me one of the Feds was visible to the revenants, distracting one or both of them. We were out of time. I was out of time.

My eyes fell on Ruby's paintball gun. I'd taken it from her shop; its new home was my laundry room. Could you beat someone to death with a paintball gun, while she was shooting real bullets at you? I inched a hand toward it, but before I could commit a paint-splattered suicide, the back steps resounded with thudding boots.

Batten burst in the back door, and I bellowed, *"GUN!"*

His instincts were damn good; he dove to the floor, rolled fluidly as Ruby fired. As his face came to mine, I pointed back out the mudroom door. One big hand hooked for me, but I was already in motion to tear after him into the back yard.

We hurtled break-neck through the dark toward the boxy shadow of the boathouse. Trees loomed, inky branches swiping to stall our flight. Ruby's fourth shot went wide, breaking the old window to the left of the boathouse door. Mark's hand didn't falter on the door; he wrenched it open, grabbed me by the shoulder, and hauled me around into the cover of his body as he raked us both inside. The door shook as he heaved his broad shoulder to it.

"Window's breached." His hard breath fogged my forehead. "Revs are going to smell blood and be in here in two seconds. Any ideas?"

Absurdly, my brain focused on, *He finally called them revenants. Why now?*

Motion outside. We both froze, going utterly still and stone-silent. A second noise, something *crunch-squeak*ing. Rubber boots on ice; it was the worst sound I had ever heard. I looked up, past Mark's whisker-stubbles. Blood was caked in the corner of his nose, and I had the insane urge to press pause on life so I could fix his boo-boo. Tears welled in my eyes and my vision blurred. Probably just residual gas fumes and roasted ghoul stink, right? In the near dark, his eyes were flung wide, darting, alive with urgency. *Alive. Still alive,* I thought. *Dark Lady Above, if you keep him this way, I promise I'll give up cookies forever.*

I asked, "Chapel?"

"In the spare tire well of the SUV, with both my guns, but the revs know it. Wes is trying to split the SUV open." His breath huffed out, streaming hot jets down on my forehead. "It's only a matter of time before he makes a big enough gap. Bullets only slow them so much."

"Chapel shot them?" I cried, but instantly regretted even asking. "I need you to get to my office." A plan drawn aloud before I could really scramble my mental reinforcements into formation, it was shaky at best. "Ruby desecrated my pentagram and my herb supplies, but we're going to use that."

"I don't know what to do when I get there." He inched his neck up to the broken window to take a fleeting glancing outside, then ducked. "I'll get *you* to the office."

"Unarmed? Good luck with that," I pointed out. "Once I'm clear of the back door, you go." I touched his face to make him look down at me. "Can you listen to me?"

"I'll distract Ruby," he insisted.

"No." My voice came from between clenched teeth. "You'll go to my office, get out the pouch labeled lavender from the cabinet. Don't touch what's inside. What did I just say?"

"Lavender. Don't touch." He shook his head. "But you'll know what to do—"

"You're mundane, so you can touch the pouch. Just don't touch the herb inside. Also, take out the big jar of salt. Now there are two *ifs*. Ready?"

"I can't let you go out there."

"Mark: if there are red candles around the outside of the pentagram, kick them over, and dump the salt on them until the flames go out. If there are red candles floating in a bowl in the center of the pentagram surrounded by green votives, you need to dump the lavender pouch into the bowl, then extinguish each green candle in the liquid in the bowl before putting out the red candles." I reached up to brush away the dried blood from his upper lip. "Say it again so I know you have it right."

He repeated what I'd told him word for word, not looking at all convinced. I nodded. "Ok, after you do this, go to Harry's room and throw his hatboxes out of his closet."

He had other plans. "I'll hook right along the edge of the water and draw her fire, while you go left along the property line to the neighbour's."

I let out a frustrated *grrr*. "You're not listening again," I snarled. "I'm on deck. Right?"

He shook his head no. I made a fist out of my bleeding hand, winced as several not-so-impressed bones didn't respond.

"Fuck you. If you trust me, I'll owe you one."

"One what?" Something flickered in his dark, unreadable eyes, but as usual it was lost to me.

"After you fuck the spell, go downstairs. There's an antique revolver in one of the hatboxes. Get it, then hurry to the SUV and help Chapel out."

"The revs—"

"Will come-to, after you fuck up the pentagram." *I think. I hope.*

His eyes pitched from the window back to me, plunged into mine deeply like he was trying to divine the future, the outcome. If the answer was in my face, I sure as hell didn't put it there. He nodded once. "Lavender," he breathed. "Salt. Hatbox. Revolver. Is it loaded?"

"Should a revolver always be kept loaded?" At his nod, I said, "Then it will be."

He nodded again. "Get Chapel. Then?"

"Get that hard ass of yours to safety." At his doubtful grimace, I assured him: "I'll be fine." *Oh, what a lie*, but I must have sounded confident, because he didn't argue.

"Where are you leading her?"

"Hell if I know," I admitted. I hiked the paintball gun to my hip and half-stood, keeping low. "Ready?"

Clearly there wasn't a sane answer to that and he didn't insult me by attempting one. The sound of rubber on ice again spiked my heart and I relinquished control on the part of my brain that was thrumming with the warning not to do any more stupid things.

I lunged up, putting my shoulder to the door with a bang. Sprinting from the boathouse, making lots of noise, I like to think I looked dangerous, like a guerilla fighter storming up a Columbian coffee field, minus the camo and gear. Probably guerilla fighters don't whinny and gallop aimlessly like a badly-beaten donkey when they hear gunshots like I do, though. Falling wasn't an option if I wanted to keep the paintball gun. I clutched it with both hands and loped into the Stygian shelter of the woods nearby.

I'd lost count of her shots, but there was no reason she couldn't have a spare clip from my room. zigzagging through barely discernable tree shapes, I picked out a clump of even darker cover, a bush of some kind. I vaulted into it like a long-jumper, feet first, landing hard enough on my ass to jar my jaws together with a clack.

I opened my mouth wide to gulp one deep breath then struggled to slow my breathing, quiet my panting, still my motion. My ears perked for sounds: rubber boots, ice or snow compression, the snuffling of ravenous revenants gone over to monster. I picked up labored breathing and decided on instinct to press deeper into the woods.

I sprang out of my hiding place, turning to fire off a few paintballs into the night to keep her attention, hitting only tree trunks. Muzzle flare lit up the forest to the left as the Beretta went off twice in quick succession. Bark erupted from the tree beside me as the second bullet grazed my collarbone. I slipped back in surprise, too shocked to scream, flailing into a prickly bush, its naked winter branches clawing me. No time for pain. I shoved to my feet, wrestling my clothes from the bush's grip, and took off again, praying Mark remembered what to do, praying he didn't touch the monkshood in the lavender pouch, praying the revenants hadn't eaten Chapel and decided that the chase through the woods was interesting, appetizing enough to be next on their menu.

I heard the lake before I saw its moonlit plane. Too exposed, I bled back into the undergrowth, getting down, dropping the paintball gun to explore my shoulder wound. I had to pinch my lips hard together not to cry out. Heart clobbering in my chest, I closed my eyes. *This is how I die*, I thought, *but that's ok*. Cut down by a villain is okay. Cut down by a villain makes sense. But tossed to my end by Harry's hands? *Please, heavens, not by Harry's hands.* I could bear anything but that.

I knew I hadn't lost her. Even if she ran out of bullets, she had too much of an advantage over me to give up tonight. As far as she knew, the revenants would take care of the Feds, leaving her free to exact her final revenge. She'd keep coming. I knew I would, if I were in her rubber boots.

I searched for an escape route. A boat would be great. Visible, under the high light of the moon on the empty lake, though if I got far enough before she started firing, Lord knows she seemed a crap shot, maybe I'd be okay. But there was no boat. No canoe. The water was giving off a warning waft of frigidity I could feel from where I lay. Harry had said it was about 35 degrees; I'd be dead in minutes if I tried to swim for it.

There were plenty of thick, bushy arches along the water's edge. My eyes adjusted to the darkness as I tried to hear past the thready thrashing of my pulse. I needed to hear her. I had to hear it coming. Abruptly, my toes tingled with the notion that I would die without warning, one unceremonious slug to the back of the head. My shoulders hunched down and my head darted from one side to the other, and that's when I saw it.

One of the black forms along the edge of the water had a distinctly mechanical shape. A snowmobile, overturned, nearly toppled into the water. I gathered my courage, daring to belly-crawl with the paintball gun towards it like a soldier through No Man's Land, hesitating at every sound in the wintery night. What I wouldn't give for the cover of crickets and wild animals in full brush, or a nice noisy thunderstorm. Even gathering wind would be better than this too-silent calm. I crept another two elbow-lengths forward, wondering if the wetness down my front was melting snow or if I'd finally pissed myself. Too close to the snowmobile's cover for any more subtlety, I rushed the last ten feet on my knees. And nearly fell into the body of Neil Dunnachie.

The chief deputy had been dead for a while; the cold had preserved the bloodless shock on his face, so he appeared to stare over at me as though demanding an explanation: why had I shuffled into the solitude of his open-air grave? Probably my expression didn't match his; I wasn't the least bit surprised to see the unnatural turn of his neck.

I was glad he was dead. This sentiment didn't surprise me either, though it did shame me. Despite the fact that Harry was right now trying to gain access to Gary Chapel's jugular, Neil Dunnachie had tried to kill us. For that, he got what he got. I knew immediately, I was never going to report it. If I lived through the night, my first duty would be hiding this broken body where no one would ever find it.

Forgetting Ruby for merely a minute, I pulled my right glove off, touched the exposed spine above the bulging vertebrae at the spot where his head didn't look quite attached any more. There was no blood, no gore, just shining white bone. The Blue Sense lurched into my mind, sending me off balance. I rocked against the snowmobile with my wounded shoulder, but only the vision held any importance: my brother's unnaturally strong hands, fleet and straining rage, depressing the bones, knuckles white, jostling Dunnachie's head in precisely the way it was never intended by nature to go. The instinctual feed that followed, Harry's urgent protests. I broke contact so I wouldn't have to see any more.

I jerked my glove back on and scanned behind me, forgetting Ruby would be undetectable. Could I rock the snowmobile back to right, and would it drive? Was it FUBARed? Would Ruby shoot me while I was up on it in the star's spotlight, trying to start it? Hell yes, my instincts reported. Stay low, and in the dark.

Then two things happened at once. Rubber boots made a hasty retreat back in the direction of the cabin, startling me into a paintball-ready pose. And my cell phone trilled the Inspector Gadget theme song loud and jarring in the too-silent night, jolting my heart with panic. I whipped it out of my pocket to turn it off but saw my home phone number on the call display.

I answered, "Fuck me!"

"Spell's broken, revs down. But I think she's on her way back. I see her in the mirror—"

The black-watch spell. If Ruby made it back to the office she'd shoot Batten and restart the spell and we'd be back where we started. "Harry's down how?"

"Don't know. Ruby's fuckin' fast…back yard…porch!"

"Harry's gun," I instructed, pelting back in the direction of my probable death. I held the paintball gun close to my chest as I ran, weaving in and out of the trees.

Harry's shadow-stepping form leaped from nowhere, with Wesley on his heels. Harry's stern grabbing hand sent me out of my momentum and I spun to look at him. His eyes pleaded, horrified but in control again. For how long?

"MJ, it is not over—"

"I know. Get as far away from us as you can."

"No time," he said hoarsely. With that took three running steps toward the lake. The surface of Shaw's Fist was like a gleaming mirror under starlight, so dark it was almost sable. Harry launched in a graceful arch and plunged into the icy water.

A shriek tore out of my throat before I could catch it. I vaguely registered Gary Chapel's boots beating the ground beside me as we moved in tandem like a flock of gazelles to the dock. Gloomy water swallowed Harry's boots.

Wesley surged ahead of us, slicing past me in pursuit of Harry's wake, curling up through the cold night air and plummeting also into the unknowable depths of Shaw's Fist.

Pain ripped through me but only for a second. Chapel doubled with an anguished cry, gun dropped. The Springfield XD Tactical skittered across hard-pack snow, spinning away. I felt the hypothermic waters rush to surround my own head, though my feet remained planted on the dock. Gary lunged up to grab me hard from behind, encircled me in his arms; I guess he thought I was heading into the water after my companion, but I knew better. Two minutes in that water and I'd be a goner. Harry would be ... well, not fine. But not dead.

Harry settled in for a cold, hard rest, sliding down through the depths as the frigid waters slowed his brain waves. I could feel the cold silken water spilling across his skin, surrounding him so completely and inescapably as he languidly stroked down toward the deepest bowl-shaped cleft in Shaw's Fist, taking to his rest mournfully, regretfully, but with acceptance. Lower now, as the water became heavier, the lake's gurgling music louder in his ears. Black. Icy. Sleepy. I heard a moan and it was coming from me. As I wrapped around Chapel like he was the last dry land in a drowning world, the living-dead version of a diver's Rapture of the Deep overtook Harry, pulled his thoughts into the tremulously giddy zone, a panic attack on psychedelic mushrooms. Then Harry broke our connection.

A cramp of loss tore through my guts; Harry wasn't resting. Harry was laying under the bitter water, alert, in wait. I felt him, and felt *through* him, and heard through him—all the glugging, sloshing sounds of his sanctuary—and heard his thoughts. I'd never heard someone's thoughts before, because that wasn't my Talent. Was Wes somehow transmitting, telepathically, in his own desperation? The loss of Harry was an unbearable emptiness in my belly. Chapel fell to his knees, dragging me down within his clawing arms. His knees made a hollow *thunk* upon the dock. The instant hypothermic pain that should have transferred from Harry to his proper DaySitter did not. The cold was spilling through our mended Bond, but quickly whisked away, constant but ephemeral. Like having one arm in a glacier-fed stream, the cold, aching pain was moving across me.

"God, oh God," Chapel panted, curled in a ball around me.

"Get in the house," I breathed, my eyes filling with hot tears. "Harry can't block me from this. I'm going to be forced to share it." But it was *us*, not me, and I didn't have time to wonder why.

I forced my eyes away from the hateful spot at the end of the dock where Harry had slipped out of my life; I had no time to grieve. Things had to happen quickly now. If I didn't keep my head, Harry's efforts would be wasted and three of us would pay dearly. Harry trusted me to figure this out fast.

At the same time as Chapel went into convulsions, the back door slammed open, but no one came out. Shots fired; again, muzzle flare spot-lit the cold air. I palmed Chapel's head, thrusting it down to cover him as he seized under me, then came up on my knees, lips peeled back in a snarl. Propping the paintball gun under my armpit, aiming the gun at the muzzle flash, I fired off repeatedly at the empty night, spraying paintballs randomly into dead space.

Wrinkled old lady forehead appeared under a splotch of brilliant yellow paint. I aimed lower, covering her face with splat after splat. Rubber boots struck snow and ice quicker now, full tilt. My Beretta, abandoned from her hand, appeared as it left her spell area and skimmed across the snow. Out of bullets? So, why was she still coming? I fired more, furiously, to uncover what was approaching. Yellow paint hit hand, knuckles, and the grip of a long, narrow cook's knife I recognized: Harry's favourite 8 inch carbon steel Sabatier. *Lord and Lady, don't let me fall to Harry's own knife.*

I straddled Chapel protectively, firing until the paintballs were gone. With a desperate shout, I threw the paintball gun at the charging woman. She batted it out of the way, closing the distance between us too fast, her hate-filled face streaming yellow rivulets. I went through Chapel's pockets for a weapon, but all he had was a short stake in an ankle sheath. Struggling to my feet, I braced myself, facing her with my useless stick, eyes glued to that knife in the air, flexing my left forearm up to defend my head. Her strike would go right to the bone, knowing how Harry kept his kitchen utensils sharpened. Closer. I braced for it.

The water beside me plumed; something shot up and out. Long white arms slid out of the water in terrible slow motion. Electricity zinged across my skin, tickled in the crevices as Gregori Nazaire's ancient power heaved across frothing water. The jet of energy from the elder hit me like a surge from a wall socket, and I hit the ground belly-first. Icy currents purled through the yard, invading my lungs, filling the air like a bucket to the brim, the smell of burnt licorice and the rich crumbling earth of the grave.

He rushed over my head, driving me forward to protect Chapel's twitching form. Impacting Ruby, he took her in a rolling flip over the other side of the dock and into the shallow water. Ruby's hand grasped wildly into the night. The water churned. I crawled over Chapel's shoulder to the side of the dock.

Gregori Nazaire's gaunt, hollow-cheeked jaws clamped around his misbehaving DaySitter's neck while Ruby's figure kicked and thrashed, pumping blood from her jugular into the frigid waters of Shaw's Fist.

"Stop!" I shouted, wrapping my fingers tighter around the stake. "Just hold her, revenant! *Batten!*"

Gregori's shoulders bunched as he sank enamel deeper into Ruby's carotid.

"*Batten!* I mean it, Gregori, back off, let her—"

Flesh tearing, wet smacking noises, and Gregori's face came up over his right shoulder with a giant flap of pink meat caught between a double row of teeth. A crimson jet struck the underside of his chin. My gorge rose while his eyes lit with victory. Without thought, I drove forward, bringing the stake up in a high arc and slamming it down on the broad target of his back, just under his left shoulder blade.

Good thing I blinked; a cloud of ash hit me in the face and I choked, whipping the stake back in towards my chest. Hauling breath, I coughed hard to expel 1400 years of dead revenant out of my lungs. No air, I couldn't get air. Pounding on my chest with my fist didn't help as wet ash clung inside me, in my nostrils and coating the roof of my mouth and the back of my tongue; he tasted like moldy felt, tart charcoal and overcooked beef. When I opened my eyes, all I could see was Ruby gurgling around her torn throat, flayed open to the tonsils, floundering knee-deep in grey, dust-powdered water.

I dropped the stake with a little splash and hauled her by the armpits onto the dock. With two hands I covered the wound in her throat, rasping around ash, "Don't move, I've got you. You're under arrest for the murder of Kristin Davis and Danika Sherlock, and conspiracy to murder me. Keep still, I'll call for an ambulance. *Batten!*"

Gregori's last thought flashed into my awareness with a push of forced psi, though I couldn't tell you why or how, dulling my awareness of Ruby and the pressure to get her help; a vision of warm summer nights in Paris, (*why are my hands warm and wet*) all the glories of the City of Lights offered up to him as swelling bosoms and swan-like necks bent to his will, cherries on a plate of gold (*something thrumming, barely fluttering now, under my palms*) the heavy fragrance of absinth, all the passions of the blood lulling him in his final second. He was not afraid.

I needed Mark. I glanced over my shoulder at Chapel's still-twitching form. Correction: *we* needed Mark. I pressed down harder on Ruby's wound, trying to stem the flow of blood, palms slippery with the heat of ebbing life as it pumped out under my hands. Horrible sucking noises slopped from her collapsing trachea.

As though I'd summoned him by thought, Batten finally broke out of the back door with a huge revolver in his hands, trained at the ground. I'd never been happier to see Jerkface. His approach to the dock reminded me of a movie, old shots of soldiers picking their path cautiously through the tangled jungles of a Hollywood Vietnam set.

Eyes everywhere, he set one foot on the dock and barked, "Where's the vamps?"

"Over," I got out, before my throat clamped shut.

"Who got dusted?" he demanded. "Did you dust one?"

"Get your cuffs," I ground out. "I've got her."

"Marnie—"

"Call for an ambulance."

"Let go," Batten said, his voice dropping as he went to one knee. He tried to peel my hands away.

The gears in my brain wouldn't click forward. "No, I've got her, *I've got her*."

"Look at her, Marnie. She's gone. Let go."

I looked down at Ruby through eyelashes gluey with wet ash.

"I had her." My fingers had pressed so hard in my fervor to stop the bleeding that the wound had torn, but that wasn't what killed her. Her own companion had done that. She was dead. It was all over. The thought didn't make sense. *Shock*, I thought. *I can't focus. I can't think.* I nodded wordlessly, as though somewhere in my brain, the skeleton of language was dangling high in a rafter, unreachable. While Batten ran a hand over my face to clear the damp ash, I coaxed words enough to choke:

"I tried to do the right thing. I swear I tried, Mark."

"I know you did." He started to pull me towards him when he looked down at the dock. "Gary?"

I gazed down at Chapel's shuddering and finally gears clicked. Chapel's lips were blue. His too-wide eyes tried to focus up at my face and failed.

"Oh shit," I breathed, head spinning. "Get Gary inside."

C58

Chapel's sympathetic hypothermia wasn't the worst of his problems, but it was the only thing we could fix without Harry. I suspected Gary had committed to something much more serious; I should have known a lot sooner, and would have if not for all the distractions. While Batten ditched Ruby's spell junk out onto the front lawn and made his horrible interpretation of coffee, I gathered warmer clothing for Gary, tossed firewood and crumpled paper in the woodstove and lit it, then ran to fill a hot water bottle and grab Harry's electric blanket from his casket. As we fussed over Chapel on the couch, I could tell Batten wanted to ask but was afraid of the answer. I wasn't in a place yet where I could supply any comfort so I didn't broach the subject.

"There's a bucket under the bathroom sink," I said. "You better grab it."

"Do I want to know why?"

I clipped, "I don't want your boss blowing chunks on my couch, that's why." Bad enough the faint stench of ghoul slime still hung in the air. Harry had done a thorough cleaning, but some things clung, the smell of putrefaction being one of them. I grabbed my pink Moleskine mini and jotted down anything I had noticed that might help me put my finger on whether or not Gary Chapel had made a commitment, something a fair bit more serious than just covertly feeding someone else's revenant. I wrote: last time I felt pain? *Healing stitches? Harry's shooting? The hypothermia? My hand …* I looked down at my right hand, the flesh punctured, weeping, something inside possibly broken. I felt nothing.

Batten hesitated, looking lost.

I sighed. "Look, do you want to explain to assistant director Johnston how and why SSA Gary Chapel died of sympathetic hypothermia while working this case?" I appealed. "Imagine the paperwork."

"Why is this affecting Gary?"

"Do you remember I told you about dry hypothermia, regular non-feeding wraith state, a form of temporary death in which the revenant thinks and feels nothing? Harry and Wes have plunged into *gelid* hypothermia. It's more like cryostasis. They'll not reach the same deep resting state. They'll be alert through every freezing minute of it.

God." I rubbed my arms, horrified. "Harry hates being cold. Why did he …"

But there was no sense asking that, and the answers were too upsetting. He was being used as a weapon against me, and he wasn't going to allow anyone to fuck with our Bond any more than they already had.

"Oh, Harry," I breathed. I tried to fight the tears away, not entirely sure how Batten would respond. I didn't think I wanted him to comfort me. Still, my tear ducts wouldn't obey. They spilled over. I didn't bother to wipe them. I made notes instead, putting my emotions into clean columns to parcel them out: *missing him already. Need to warm him. Need to be near him.*

"Chapel's fed Harry more than just that once," Batten guessed. "He's created some kind of sympathetic link between them?"

"It's more serious than that, unfortunately. He's taken on a rather regrettable role, but before you freak out, it's not something Harry did without Chapel's permission. Chapel would have had to ask for this. He'd have to volunteer. Knowing Harry, Chapel must have done some fast talking to convince him."

Chapel darted off the couch for the restroom.

"I'll go," I told Batten, putting my Moleskine down. "Could you build the fire up a bit more?" I wrapped my afghan around my shoulders. His arm outstretched across the doorway stopped me.

"Marnie, what happened out there?" Batten asked.

I paused, wondering how much of Gregori Nazaire was still smeared across my face. I'd never killed anyone before this week, living or undead, and so far I was blessedly numb about the whole thing, but the fact that his remains were strewn on the surface of the lake and dusting my snow-and-ice-speckled dock made me feel squinky. I opened my mouth to explain, but after a moment of pained silence in the face of a man who had 105 kills under his belt, I shuffled off after Gary without a word.

When I found Chapel, he was clutching the toilet seat, retching like he'd eaten a whole pail of bad oysters. I ran the warm water in the sink, wet a monogrammed wash cloth, (my petal pink, not Harry's forest green) and laid it on the back of his neck. I lowered my voice because I knew my psi-headache was only half of what his would be; his would be mental fireworks and grey-cell implosions.

"If you weren't my boss, I might tell you that you're a moron."

He groaned, then vomited hard.

"You've been taking my pain away," I said, not a question but a statement. "After the hospital, my healing pain should have been worse than it was. When Harry was shot at the funeral home, I didn't feel a bit of his pain. I should have. Now this ...care to explain?"

"We needed to keep you focused."

"We," I repeated, and guessed: "This was decided after the Ten Springs Motor Inn?"

"I need an ambulance." His voice echoed in the toilet bowl. "I need a doctor. I need ..."

"The hospital can't help you, Gary. If they give you something to stop the vomiting, it'll just delay this. If they change your body temperature too fast, the excess ms-lipotropin in your system will cause calcium to cross the membranes of your brain cells too quickly, flooding them and probably popping a whole bunch. The PCU needs its Special-est Agent to stay brainy. Not to mention, when ms-lipo pops on the tox screen, the hospital staff would have to report it; your superiors would know about your feeding a revenant."

Gary's back arched as he heaved again. I closed my eyes, breathing out slowly to ignore the smell, and drew him a glass of cool water from the sink. "Drink this. You're going to get dry heaves if you don't."

"There's no Special-est Agent," he muttered, his fingers scrambling on the water glass as he took it. I took his glasses off the bridge of his nose and set them on the counter, then used the damp wash cloth to clean his chin for him. He looked up at me bleary-eyed and sallow-cheeked.

"Yes there is," I told him, trying to smile. "I really hope you brought a tooth brush."

His shoulders fell. "I'm sorry."

"Don't be." I handed him the cloth. "Just tell me the truth."

He hurried to hug the bowl again, but nothing happened. He just sat there panting into the toilet. A shudder rocked him. He drank some more water.

"I found mention of the *dhaugir*," he said finally, gulping air. "When I read your report on the history of slaves and revenants in France in the early 14th century. I asked Harry how it worked."

I sat back on my haunches. "The *dhaugir* isn't enslaved to a revenant, he's a human slave who belongs to a DaySitter, who channels any negative effects of the Bond. A sort of mystical whipping-boy." I watched the side of his face for a change in his expression; it was clear I wasn't telling him anything new. "I'd have been a lot more careful if I'd known I was sharing my pain with you."

Chapel waved it away, and closed his eyes. "Harry didn't want you to know."

"Betcha didn't think I was this much of a walking disaster," I leaned against the counter. "Harry gave you some pretty bad advice. You do know it's not up to him how this ends?" He floundered. I let the other shoe drop. "Harry can't release you from this type of Bond. Neither can you. That's up to me, and I'm not exactly sure how it's done."

"Swell," he mumbled, and I could have sworn his spitting in the toilet had less to do with the taste of bile and more to do with regret.

"You must have fed Harry a whole bunch of times," I surmised. "He said it was your idea, that you had personal reasons to approach him. He said that was none of my business but I beg to differ."

"You deserve an explanation. In the past," he rasped, sitting back on his heels. "A fairly old revenant offered me the Bond. I turned it down, but always wondered if I'd made a mistake. Maybe the biggest mistake of my life. For decades, I've hunted the lawless ones, the monsters, as if to prove to myself I'd made the right choice. But seeing you so happy with Harry ..."

"This is happiness?" I smiled weakly.

"It made me wonder again if I screwed up, out of fear. I had to know what it was like, to feed one."

"I should have warned you both: you can't offer Harry a warm vein. It isn't something he has the willpower to refuse. He won't hunt someone, but if it's laid at his feet ..."

"I had to know. And I'm sorry. It wasn't what I thought it'd be like, at all. I'm sorry. It's so much better. So much better. Like a drug. I'm sorry." He whimpered before emptying his guts again, panting and sweating. "I know I did wrong by you, Marnie. I knew even before I did it, I won't pretend I didn't. It was selfish. I tried to make up for it, by offering the *dhaugir* ..."

"Made yourself a little pact with the devil, hunh?" I said, not without sympathy. "So, boss: I killed our victim, her killer, and her killer's killer. Am I fired yet?"

Chapel said weakly into the bowl, "I was hoping you'd consider working for me directly, full-time."

Was I really considering a job opportunity after I'd killed two ghouls, dusted a 1400 year old poet and let an old seer bleed to death? Could my life get any weirder?

"In what capacity?" I asked. "Official screw up?"

"Preternatural biology consultant."

I laughed out loud; it was harsh in the little bathroom, even to my ears. My robe was hanging on the back of the bathroom door. While Chapel's head was hung, I slipped out of my snow-and-ash-crusted clothing and belted the dry robe tightly, taking a little comfort from the warm terrycloth against my cold damp skin. Then I washed my face, ignoring the feather-grit drippings in the sink that swirled around the drain but didn't go down, lacing the white marble with streaks of grey-black.

"You better stick with Gold-Drake & Cross," I advised. "My brand of help is not good times for anyone."

Chapel stared up at me seriously. "I want you." Then, maybe in case I misunderstood, he added: "I want your brand of help."

I looked from one of his eyes to the other, wondering how much of that had to do with his infatuation with Harry, and how much he actually wanted *my* help.

Batten called out from deep in the cabin, his voice an exhausted re-revving like a tired mule getting to its feet again. I wasn't sure I wanted to know what he was yelling about this time but rushed into the mudroom anyway while he unbelted his well-worn kit.

"Stake," Batten barked. I heard wood cylinders hit the linoleum, the hollow clattering of multiple lengths of hand-whittled rowan. Handmade stakes had far more power if the one who made them believed they would work. Batten was old hat, he showed no doubt. He stood in show-down mode, a stake in both hands, some sort of pointy silver contraption I'd never seen before in a belt sheath; this was what he lived for. For a moment, I accepted that he was pretty damn awesome in his own right, and if I ever needed a monster killed, I knew who I'd ask first. I touched Batten's quivering bicep, dug my fingers in until I was sure he felt it.

"Back off, hunter," I cautioned. "Down, boy."

"Look."

Wesley was laying out on the dock, face down in the stirred wet slush, his long blond tangles wrapped with what looked like frosted lake weeds. He wasn't moving. His drenched clothing hung across his narrow shoulders and skinny legs like a shroud.

Seconds later the surface of the lake exploded and Harry's dark figure rose straight up like he'd been jerked by a bungee cord; a burbling otherworldly menace, a sopping, black-clad creature, skin pale and drawn, he looked nothing like the Harry I knew. He landed hard on the dock, boots striking sure and solid in a wide-legged stance. Gregori's remnants were still powdering the snow curves and ice clumps on the wintry dock like icing sugar on a half-eaten donut, and I winced, physically flinching, as Harry's dripping boots ground into the ash-laced slush. A scolding frantically galloped through my brain: *Don't trample your elders!* And on its heels: *Mind the dead guy!* and if I hadn't pinched my lips together and swallowed hard, I might have erupted into an hysterical giggle.

Disoriented and still showing the after-effects of Ruby's spell, Harry bared his fangs at the yard, and found us with his gaze. I touched open the screen door, put one sock foot on the back step, and waited to judge his reaction. He watched me steadily with eyes so piercing-silver they faintly glowed in the dark like a cat's catching headlights. But Wes didn't move, Harry didn't rush me, and nothing else moved in the night.

I heard Batten shift into motion behind me and warned him back with a soft noise. He made a protesting grunt and told him, "Stow the ego, vampire hunter. Watch and learn."

I stepped all of the way out of the house, flicking my gaze down to make sure Wes wasn't moving yet. The cold wood of the back steps bled through my socks, but I was Ked-less, having scorched my only pair. I had high heels close by, but heels and pajamas? In the snow? Please.

Wes' pale hand lay in the scrambled snow at the end of the dock, fingertips half-buried like he was clawing his way under. *Did they just move?* A young revenant turned feral would not be as easily cured; an older, Bonded revenant had blood memories of connection to his human to draw upon, whereas the new dead did not. Another inch closer to them. *Is Wes moving?* My toes curled in anticipation inside my socks, which now had snow stuck to their fluffy soles. *I should have peed before coming out here.* One more step. I pulled up short, needing to get closer to my Cold Company, not daring to push it too fast.

There was no recognition in Harry's blank, hungry stare, but neither was there aggression. I started again slowly toward the revenant—*no,* I thought, *this creature is Batten's vampire*—holding out my injured hand, feeling no pain. Logic told me that no matter what happened, I'd only feel the pain for a second before it was whisked away to my *dhaugir*, but that didn't make my hand stop shaking midair. Harry caught the scent of blood in the air and his lips parted. His eyes locked on the wound on my palm.

I didn't see him move; in a rushing blur he was on me, my back crushed into the trampled snow, the impact hard enough that my molars clacked together. Jagged compacted ice-shards heaved under my shoulder blades. I wriggled, my robe gaping as I tried to avoid getting a face-full of mad, aimless fang. I heard Batten inhale sharply.

The back door slapped open but I shouted: "Back in the house, Kill-Notch!"

Harry's hand tore my robe aside at the shoulder. He struck suddenly, savagely, for my jugular. Fangs sank in hard and deep. I didn't mean to cry out; when I heard it, I choked it off. Blood pulled forcefully from my carotid, tugging, making my neck tense and ache. I made a whimper of complaint and put one hand on each of his shoulders to push him back slightly; it was like trying to shove a mountain out of the way. I'd never had to ask Harry to be tender, before; ever the gentleman, he'd always been soft and hesitant with his feeds. I whimpered, and started saying his name quietly over and over, hoping he was hearing it, praying that our Bond would defrost his addled mind.

"Come back to me, my Harry," I whispered, shoving my hands into his hair and contracting my grip. "Harry, you're hurting me." His arms were trembling bad, the flesh I could see where his collar gaped was so pale it looked blue. The sound of my voice made him pause before continuing his drawing, so I continued saying his name, dizzy, wondering if this is how I'd meet my end, in the cold snow under the one person I trusted more than anything, drained to empty.

The feed became tentative. His cool, inquisitive tongue flickered out to lick and explore the wound. His grip on me loosened, and when it did, my stomach unclenched; relief roared through me, filling my eyes with the hot sting of tears. System overload. I shuddered and wrapped myself around him tightly. There was a snap of smoking-hot molasses, and a curious moan, like a man coming awake from an erotic dream.

Harry pulled his face up out of the crevice of my neck, licking the corner of his mouth with a bewildered expression. His cashmere grey gaze scanned my tousled robe, my naked shoulder, my pale thighs bared to the night wind; he shook his head with familiar exasperation.

"Oh, my only love ..." he said with a cluck of his tongue. "So inappropriate to the weather."

C59

Before I could crawl into bed, there was one last thing I had to do.

On my knees, the crusted ice on the dock felt like shards of broken glass through my jeans. Dust pan in one hand, brush in the other, I scanned the peaks and valleys of ash-covered snow, gazing at a long life now lost. I tried to imagine all the things that Gregori Nazaire had seen the beginnings of, all the inventions, the revolutions, political upheavals, social changes; I was so taken with my train of thought that I barely noticed Batten's heavy boots trudging through the snow, though the sound of the snow crunching ran out across the lake. The night was as still as I'd ever seen it; I could hear Batten's hot exhale behind me. He didn't tell me how late it was, or how cold; he just waited for me to talk.

"Didn't seem right to leave him out here," I said quietly, my glance daring him to argue.

I didn't think Batten would get that, but it had to be said. It was the same way I'd felt about turning from the cemetery after Grandma Vi's funeral. How could I walk away? She had to stay. The ash along the ground was all that remained of 1400 years of life, damned now to Hell, gone to the air, as easy as a single swing of my arm. My first staking; hopefully my last.

Kill-Notch crouched beside me, his broad shoulder close to mine. He took the lid off my Kermit the Frog cookie jar and peeked into its empty interior. "I'm not going to pretend to understand what you're doing out here." He stared out at the lake past me. "Come inside, get warm."

"I will ... soon as I'm done."

After a moment of speculative silence, Batten got down on his knees and held the dustpan for me.

C60

Squinting into my bathroom mirror didn't help make the reflection any prettier. Neither had a layer of mascara, a swipe of lip gloss and a handful of mousse run through my spiky locks. Now I just looked like a fem-version of Billy Idol. Maybe it didn't look as bad as I thought? I made big kissy lips and did rock-on finger motions in the mirror. Nope, not cool enough to pull it off. Needed some black leather and a studded collar.

I went to grab my blush and noticed with dismay a small square envelope on the marble countertop. The gold ink said: *Asmodeus*. The sight of the Overlord's name made my innards sink.

Hot damn, I'd done it, though: I'd gotten rid of both ghouls, the 1400 yr old poet and the crazy ass old lady. I'd kept Kill-Notch from staking my companion, brought Harry back to his senses, and together we'd all helped ease Wes back into normalcy. It had taken three pints of B positive and a couple of earth-rocking backhands from Harry that would have KO-ed a human, but it had worked.

I opened the envelope. In flowing script, the demon king reported: *Due to the construction of Our new casino in Las Vegas Nevada We have postponed Our appointment until a time better suited to Our schedule.*

Postponed? Not cancelled ... postponed. The Banker at the Baccarat Tables of Hell was busy in Sin City, so he had—my brain settled into an unhappy pool of goo at the base of my skull and I let my head fall back to study the bathroom ceiling, hoping for a Get Out of Demon Meeting card taped above.

I abandoned my morning preening and stomped out to find the Feds still occupying my kitchen. They looked far more well-rested than I felt. I went to the pantry for ... no, I'd made a vow. A hasty vow, but a vow nonetheless. I had promised the Lady that if she got Batten's hot ass safely out of this mess, I'd give up cookies. For good. Boy, I promise some dumb things.

"What happened here?" Batten indicated my hair. "Wind storm?"

I patted my wild, tangled mop. He didn't need to know about my misadventures with mousse, so I distracted him by taking the mug of coffee out of his hands and sipping it. And was immediately sorry.

"This is probably the worst coffee ever made."

Batten accepted his limitations with a shrug. "Gonna be okay?"

"Of course, it's just coffee," I said.

"I mean, once we're gone?"

"Are you kidding? With you two nosey cop-types out of my house, I can be alone for a while. Hunker down like a hermit."

"Should I run to Mum's Market and grab you a stockpile of cookies?"

"I don't think I could eat em," I sorta-confessed.

Batten crooked his finger at me. The motion both irritated and aroused me in a mingling goulash of emotions, but I accepted this with defeat: Mark Batten was probably going to annoy me until the day my consuming lust for his hot bod finally killed me. I followed him into the hall, and while he put his boots on and shrugged into his coat, I watched his butt. Frankly, if I had to give up cookies to save his ass, I should be able to look at it whenever I want.

"Hood's giving me a lift to the airport." He lowered his voice. "Do something for me?"

Hell, yes. "I doubt it, but there's no law against you asking."

He sucked his teeth and his eyes narrowed. "Just check on Gary for me, once in a while?"

"Oh sure, stick me with nerd-sitting duty while you go play hockey up north." I smiled. He answered with one of his own rare smiles, complete with deep laugh lines and a glimmer of straight white perfection. My heart lifted like someone had pumped it full of helium. Those teeth had once teased along my jaw line to toe-curling results. I couldn't believe I wasn't going to have the pleasure again. Life was so unfair.

Batten grabbed his duffle bag and his grandfather's tan belted hunting kit and hovered with one boot on the bottom porch step, looking like he had something final to say, some last goodbye, like the hero at the end of a black and white drama before he heads out of the heroine's life forever. Maybe he'd put some thought into it. Maybe it was going to blow my socks off. Or, maybe it would make us both incredibly uncomfortable. Or downright miserable. I head him off.

"If you take much longer, I'm gonna have you arrested for trespassing," I warned.

"Ran those pills to the lab while you were sleeping in," he said. "They came back as ..." He checked his hand, where he'd scribbled it in pen, and sounded the word out a syllable at a time. "Bremelanotide. Treatment for hemorrhagic shock. Considering the stab wounds, that's not odd."

It wouldn't be, I thought, if Harry had just started giving them to me, but I'd been taking these same little white "vitamins" for a decade. "What else are they used for?"

He smirked, as though he knew a secret. "Erectile dysfunction and sexual arousal disorder, nothing that applies to your injuries."

Why the hell would Harry want to make me *more* horny, and then refuse to sleep with me until absolutely necessary?

"Good working with you, Snickerdoodle. It's been … interesting."

"I kicked ass," I said flatly. "Don't you forget it."

Batten took a long, shrewd look behind me into the cabin, then flashed a second smile that nearly brought me to my jelly-filled knees. "Whatever you say. See you in a few weeks."

I watched his ass until it was stowed in the passenger side of Hood's truck. Then I heard it: *weeks?*

Cutting my eyes back at the threshold, I watched Chapel come to give a two-fingered salute goodbye to Batten. "What the hell did he mean by weeks?" I asked.

"He's going to Costa Rica for three weeks. He needed a break."

"And then Michigan …" I let it hang so he could fill me in or correct me.

"No, Boulder. He's turned down the promotion. He's staying with me at the new head office."

Lost in my boggling, I tried to ignore the soaring ridiculous hopes of my idiot heart.

When I didn't reply, Chapel continued: "He said the winters in Michigan would, quote, 'kick his ass.' Funny, I thought he grew up there. It's what he's used to."

We stood watching Sheriff Hood back out of the drive, and long after the Ford F150 was out of sight, we stood listening to the sound of it bounce back from the gravel road. Then even the sound was gone, and all we had left to keep us company out there was the cold wind that the trees were sheltering us from. *He can't do this.* Batten living in Colorado? My Colorado? What the hell for?

"Is he touched in the head or something?" I finally said.

"Touched," Wesley snickered, joining us from the kitchen, dressed in his usual plaid button down flapping open over a white t-shirt, and threadbare jeans. The lake's depths had tangled his dreads with dull, winter greenery and I'd been forced to chop a few of his long dreads off. He had a strange gap on the left side of his head, and didn't seem bothered by it one bit. "Touched is one word for it."

I said, "When did he decide this?"

"Last night, after a long talk with Harry, oddly enough." Chapel offered, looking away. "I should get my things packed."

"When you're up to it," I said. "Don't push yourself. If you're still weak, just crash here."

He cleared his throat, considering Wes and me over the tortoiseshell rim of his glasses: the new revenant, and the klutzy DaySitter whose physical pain he channeled. "I think I'll get out of your hair. Will I be seeing you Monday?"

I hadn't officially accepted his offer. Working for the PCU (especially now that I knew Batten would be at the Boulder office) sounded like *work*. Yuck. Part of me would really rather lounge around with Harry and do whatever it was the idle rich did all day.

"I'll be in touch," I promised him, and watched him go upstairs to pack.

Wesley said, "That Batten dude's teeth look like they belong in a damn Colgate commercial."

"Wes, please."

"It's *Wasp.*" And then, "Big ole Tom Cruise mouth when he grins. Should have seen him last night; after they smoked some cigars and Harry gave him the Bugatti, I thought he was gonna do the jumping-on-couch thing."

My mouth went dry, and while I struggled not to show it, I knew damn well my brother the fledgling telepath was hearing all the questions skittering in my brain. I turned to search his Nordic sled dog eyes as he wolfed down a second Oreo. He seemed to be enjoying watching me squirm.

"Harry did what?"

Wes shrugged. "Just before the sun came up. Harry told Batten he'd store the car until he got back from vacation, but after that it was all his."

My brain did some painful gymnastics. A 435 year old man does not just *give away* a two million dollar sports car to a vampire hunter. What kind of deal had they hashed-out, exactly? Wes scarfed down another Oreo. I wasn't allowed to eat Oreos anymore. My eyes narrowed to slits.

"Do me a favor, Bumblefang," I snipped. "Before you eat any more real food, Google: 800 pound Fat Dracula."

Wes gave me an alarmed look; *Point: Marnie*. He read from the archives of my brain everything I knew about adipose tissue and revenant physiology in a split second then tromped muttering towards the pantry.

I heard the phone, and hoped Harry would pick up on his line in the basement; I didn't want to talk to anyone who would call my home line. After seven rings, Harry hadn't picked up, so I went to the office, trying not to see the burn marks, the stains from ghoul scum on the rug, the desecrated pentagram and the black ink fangs on my frogs.

My sister Carrie. I slid into my office chair and started spinning it in circles, laying my head back against the rest.

"I found Wes," I told her. "He's gonna hang with me for a bit."

"Is he broke?"

"Broke?" I smiled in spite of myself. "Understatement of the year." Gulping cold coffee I winced at the bitterness of Mark Batten's awful brew. I gave Carrie a quick update of my love life, such that it was, because that's all Carrie's ever interested in. I left out the bondage with Harry, and how my struggling turned him on; I didn't wanna give her nightmares.

"So what should I do about work?" I asked her.

"Concentrate and ask again."

I thought I heard someone in the kitchen. My voice dropped to conspiratorial, pulling a light blue Moleskine around and scribbling on the inside cover little doodles and hearts and then starting a Pro and Con list about my future *sans* cookies. "What should I do about working with Mark?"

"It is decidedly so."

Decidedly so? "Do you think Harry bribed him to go, or to stay? I mean, why the hell would Harry want Mark Batten to stay?"

"Most likely."

"Carrie, are you just reading from the Magic 8 ball? I told you not to do that."

"Works on Dad," I could hear her smile through the phone. I rubbed off my glove and pressed it to the phone. Carrie was happy. I was happy. A minor miracle for those two things to occur simultaneously. My cheeks pinch up into a silly grin.

"Oh, really?" I replied. "Our booze-addled father doesn't realize you're acting like a plastic novelty prognosticator? Shocking."

"Look, why would your little 'partner' Harry ask a hottie like Batten to stay with you? Oh ... is the vampire impotent?"

"Revenant," I reminded her.

When I didn't disillusion her about Harry's manhood, she took it as a yes and continued her path of reasoning: "Harry's paying a man-whore to do you. Suddenly, Buffalo makes much more sense."

Harry made no noise as he entered the office, but the cool push of air preceding him bristled the hairs at the nape of my neck, and without turning around I whispered, "Hi, Harry."

"Good day, ducky," he greeted. His garnet cufflinks and wrist tattoo crossed my view as Harry set a cup of espresso on the scorched desk blotter in front of me. Then he took the phone from my ear and said with grand town crier-like pageantry: "Good morning, Carole-Anne!"

No one called Carrie "Carole-Anne" except Harry, who didn't care that my sister hated it, and was not afraid of her retribution. "Yes, I am quite sure that you do," he replied to something my sister said. "Could one inquire as to the nature of your call? I see. Only, I regret to inform you that MJ simply cannot abide your manner of counsel right now, for I am given to understand she is in the market for, how did she put it ... *uncritical affection*."

Without waiting for my sister's response, he hung up. I mentally scored him another million points on the scoreboard of my mind as he moved into the middle of my office. In a rush of black wool, he removed his tuxedo jacket and dropped it in a puddle on the floor. His top hat he casually tipped forward off his head into a waiting hand, then tossed on my desk, barely missing my pencil holder. I smiled around the lip of my espresso cup; though amused by his sudden carefree attitude, I watched in silence with the upward curve of my eyebrows expressing astonishment.

My Cold Company aimed the stereo remote out the office door to the kitchen, and my little cabin filled with the slow early strains of Tom Wait's "Little Drop of Poison." The immortal extended to me one pale hand of invitation and my forearms quilled with goose bumps in reply.

Sliding around the desk I went to him, wanting to ask him about the Bugatti, and the "vitamins" of bremelanotide, sensing I should let both questions lie. For now.

As though he'd read my mind, Harry asked, "Do you trust me, my pet?"

"Of course, my companion," I said immediately, forcing doubts from my mind.

"It has been ages since we danced the Tango." He cupped the small of my back. "Do you remember the steps?"

"Please, Lord Dreppenstedt." I looked up at him through my lashes, bluffing. "I could Tango your argyle socks off."

"I think you will find me most pleased to discover this," he said huskily, drawing my body in a tight jerk against his.

As his agile hips rocked one leg forward in a sensual advance, I retreated one of my own, lead by his powerful stride. His slinking, sinuous sway was impossible to duplicate with my human body, but I held my own. The platinum rings in his brow twitched with approval. Casting me out in a whipping spin, he tucked me back forcefully before I could recover, pressing me back with his brazen stride once again.

When he drew one hand down the length of my arm I shivered, and his pupils bled rapidly to lambent silver in response. The abrupt dip was unexpected; I went soft and limp, letting him arch me. His chin brushed mine, smooth-shaved at this time of the morning, smelling of his fresh 4711 cologne. A hint of cool soft lips drew along my skin. I heard the metallic clink in his back pocket as he drew us upright, knew the sound immediately: the keys of his big iron shackles. When my heart kicked into a hard rhythm of anticipation, it pulled a happy little murmur from his throat, and the sound of it made me laugh with delight. With victory.

When he brought his eyes up to mine, they were lit with a dark and wicked light.

"Oh, my only love." Harry grinned around full fang. "Such a fuss you make ..."

The End

AJ Aalto is a proud native of the Niagara Region. Born in St. Catharines, she currently resides in Thorold, Ontario with her wonderfully peculiar husband Jason and two quirky kids, a puppy that drives her bonkers and two cats who are undoubtedly plotting her downfall. When not writing horror or dark urban fantasy, you can find AJ researching inappropriate subjects, braying her unladylike guffaw at inappropriate humour, mentally undressing strangers or sitting cross-legged on her front porch eating peanut butter M&Ms by the fistful.

www.ajaalto.com